DEAD LAST

Also by James W. Hall

Silencer (2010)
Hell's Bay (2008)
Magic City (2007)
Forests of the Night (2005)
Off the Chart (2003)
Blackwater Sound (2001)
Rough Draft (2000)
Body Language (1998)
Red Sky at Night (1997)
Buzz Cut (1996)
Gone Wild (1995)
Mean High Tide (1994)
Hard Aground (1993)
Bones of Coral (1992)
Tropical Freeze (1990)
Under Cover of Daylight (1987)

Essays

Hot Damn! (2001)

DEAD LAST

James W. Hall

 Minotaur Books New York

This is a work of fiction. All of the characters, organizations, and events portrayed in this novel are either products of the author's imagination or are used fictitiously.

www.minotaurbooks.com

Library of Congress Cataloging-in-Publication Data

Hall, James W. (James Wilson), 1947–
    Dead last / James W. Hall. — 1st ed.
        p. cm.
    ISBN 978-0-312-60732-6
    1. Thorn (Fictitious character)—Fiction.   2. Serial murder investigation—Fiction.   3. Miami (Fla.)—Fiction.   I. Title.
    PS3558.A369D43 2011
    813'.54—dc23
                                              2011026758

First Edition: December 2011

10 9 8 7 6 5 4 3 2 1

For Evelyn, always

ACKNOWLEDGMENTS

First and foremost, I want to thank Matt Schudel, whose masterful obituaries for *The Washington Post* inspired me to write this novel, and who answered my questions with the same grace and insight that characterizes all his writing. And I'd like to thank Terry Miller for giving me access to the set and actors and crew members of one of the best shows on TV. Terry, a friend for many years, has risen to the top in a challenging business without ever losing his good humor and charm and creative vision, skills that help him command the respect of his talented and motley crew. And to Al Hallonquist for his professional and no-nonsense assistance with the police procedures he knows so well.

I know that nothing good lives in me, that is, in my sinful nature. For I have the desire to do what is good, but I cannot carry it out. For what I do is not the good I want to do; no, the evil I do not want to do—this I keep on doing.

—Romans 7:18–19

TEASER

THE INTRUDER IS WEARING A blue stretchy catsuit that covers every inch of flesh as if he'd been dipped in indigo wax. He's tall, slender, with wide shoulders and narrow hips—an elfin creature slipping down the murky hallway.

The bodysuit's slippery sheen plays tricks with the frail light, making the prowler appear and disappear like a bashful spirit as he steals through the shadows, moving down the corridor past one shut door after another.

This could be a shabby hotel, or some other failed institution—a VA hospital, a public housing project gone to seed. The ceilings are high, the plaster walls pitted and peeling. Mounted high on the walls, brass sconces cast gloomy light toward the ceiling.

When the intruder reaches a large mirror hanging on the wall, he halts and seems captivated by his own shadowy reflection. He reaches toward the mirror, a finger extended. He touches the glass, tip meeting tip.

A breeze, salt-heavy and breathless, moans through the building.

The blue man breaks away from his reflection and moves on. Somewhere down the hall a television is playing—a cop show with gunfire and sirens. Overheated dialogue punctuated with the yelps and cries of an actress simulating mortal danger.

In his left hand the blue man carries a slip of paper the size of a dinner check. His other hand is empty.

Halfway down the corridor the blue man stops before a shut door and leans close to examine the card fixed to it—the name of the occupant.

William Slattery

The blue man gathers himself, then opens the door and slides into the room. Several night-lights illuminate the room. Their yellow light glints off the guardrails of the bed and gives the room a sickly cast.

The blue man, sleek and lithe, draws close to the bed and looks down at the codger lying there. The sheets are drawn to his throat. Spun white hair halos his head. His face is wan. Dark splotches on his cheeks and forehead. His eyes are shut.

Blue Man places the paper on the bedside table, then takes a cautious grip of the pillow beneath Slattery's head. He tightens his Lycra fingers and snatches the pillow free.

Slattery blinks and stares up at the faceless man.

The intruder holds the pillow to his chest and is silent while the old man blinks again to clear his vision. Is he still asleep? Is this a dream? Then he cracks a toothless smile.

"Hey, buddy, why so blue?"

Maybe Slattery's old and frail, but he's still a joker.

When the blue man does not reply, the old guy's eyes tighten, the humor drains away. He turns to his bedside table and sees the clipping. The blue man holds still.

"Aw, cripes, you're the obituary guy. Fuck me if you aren't."

Blue Man is silent, unmoving.

"You gotta be joking. Old fart like me? Come on, kid, why bother? Cancer's taking me down soon enough."

Is that a noise in the hallway? The blue man looks at the door. But after a moment he seems satisfied it's nothing and turns back to Slattery.

"Listen, sonny, you won't believe this, but just today I was talking about you. I was saying to my buddies what you need is a first-rate PR guy. And hey, guess what? Just so happens I was in that racket for fifty years. Here in Miami. Promoted some big names out on the beach. Godfrey, Sullivan, hell, I got the Beatles their first stateside gig. You heard of them, right? The Beatles?"

Now the blue man seems to be listening, which emboldens Slattery.

"Like I say, you got the goods, this act, you could parlay this into something big. It's creepy shtick, leaving an obit at each scene, taunting the cops. Got the FBI and the TV talking heads lathered up over what the hell the obits mean.

"That's flair, buddy, but hell, you're not reaching your full potential. Keeping it in South Florida, hey, that's penny ante, if you'll pardon my candor. What you need, you need to make a splash. Put yourself on the big stage, go national, make your mark in Chicago, Dallas, L.A. You're a hustler, right? You want money, notoriety, whatever. We're all hustlers, right?"

The blue man is finished listening and he raises the pillow.

Slattery stiffens, saying, "Come on, let's work this through. I'm being frank. You got something going, a gift for the ghoulish. No offense, Mr. Blue, you aren't getting the audience you deserve."

When he sees what's coming, Slattery starts to yell for help, but the pillow crushes against his face, cutting him off, and the blue man leans his weight into it.

The sheets bulge and ripple. The old man's hands break free and he flails his skinny arms, clawing wildly. He's a fighter, but no match for the blue man, who bears down until Slattery's arms slow, and finally drift back to the sheets.

Still the blue man applies pressure. Seconds pass and Slattery's body relaxes against the mattress.

The blue man raises the pillow and drops it at the foot of the bed. He stands still for a moment surveying his work, then picks up the paper from the bedside table and tacks it to the corkboard on the wall beside Slattery's bed. It's a newspaper clipping with jagged edges like the blade of a circular saw.

He turns to leave, but something in the bed catches his attention. A noise? Movement? The blue man returns to his victim's side and bends low, presses a Lycra finger to Slattery's throat. Could he be alive? Was he faking?

He tips his head down to peer into the dead man's face.

Slattery erupts. He's upright, huffing, lashing his right hand, then his left, a catfighter with his claws out. He snatches at the blue man's face. Stuns him momentarily, then the blue man punches Slattery flat in the nose, but the blow only revs the old man's thrashing hands.

The blue man draws back his fist for another strike, Slattery slapping and slashing, when one of the old man's fingers snags the seam at the blue man's throat—where hood meets bodysuit.

Slattery freezes. Weighing the consequences.

It's a standoff, neither moving. Then, slowly, the blue man raises a hand and takes hold of Slattery's frail wrist, and begins to pry the man's hand away.

But no. With a wild grunt, Slattery strips off the hood.

Revealing a woman with short platinum hair.

Slattery slumps back. Breathing hard, nothing left.

The woman has winter-gray eyes, skin as pale as sun-bleached bone. She has a high forehead, arched eyebrows, severe cheekbones, and swollen lips. She's exotic, a stunner with the dramatic bone structure and imperious bearing of a runway goddess who has grown immune to cameras, harsh lights, and prying stares.

She lets Slattery drink her in. He's shocked, too exhausted to speak.

She moves her blue hands to his throat and closes her fingers.

"It's all right," she says in a soothing voice. "I'll be gentle."

Her hands tighten and the old guy makes a feeble swat at her arms, but he's got nothing left. As the seconds count away, his eyes close. The vigor drains from his features.

When the woman is done, she settles Slattery's head on the pillow. Just so. Arranging him to look as serene as a strangled man can appear.

She straightens his hair with a gentle blue hand. There's a postcoital poignancy to her gestures, as if the intimacy they shared has touched her.

Finished, she pulls the hood back on and tugs it into place.

She turns to the corkboard and straightens the page, admires it.

It's an obituary from the newspaper, a three-paragraph summary of the life of some girl named Annie Woodburne. The headline reads

Molecular Biology Student, Planned to Teach

The woman in blue turns from the obituary and walks from the room. The door closes. Slattery is motionless. His expression flat.

A beat, another beat.

"And cut!"

Gus Dollimore rose from his canvas chair, pulled off his earphones, draped them around his neck, and looked around at the assembled cast and crew, then raised his fist and pumped it twice.

"Terrific stuff. A real nut-grabber. You guys killed it."

Sawyer Moss held back a smile. Gus was hamming it up for their visitor—the guy sitting next to Sawyer with this week's script open in his lap.

The usual turmoil resumed. Two dozen crew members hustling and bustling, making ready for the next scene. The unit production manager was on his handheld radio barking orders, first assistant director on the cell with some off-site problem. Grips, gaffer, camera guys, the cable draggers and equipment haulers, the makeup and hair assistants, the stand-ins, assorted construction men and prop people. Guys taking down the lights, carrying off the bounce boards.

The DP, Bernie Bernard, consulted with Mills, who was still strapped in the leather harness carrying the weight of the Steadicam. It was Mills, head cameraman, who'd trailed the killer down the hallway, staying tight on the blue suit, playing with the shadows.

Bernie and Mills huddled at the monitor, studying the playback of the last few seconds. The hand-fighting, hood ripped off, the actors' expressions.

"Tell me we got it, Bernie," Dollimore said. "Tell me it's perfect."

"Could've opened the lens half a crack more. A few shadows I don't like. But it's decent. Good enough for cable TV."

Mills chuckled; the best boy and one of the electricians hid their smiles in deference to the outsider.

Sawyer unfolded his call sheet to check the next setup. A dozen more scenes to shoot before they punched out tonight. Next up was an exterior in the courtyard—murder aftermath, patrol cars and EMTs arriving, Miami patrol officers, then the homicide guys shuffling in, rumpled, with their thimbles of Cuban coffee. Some dialogue with the owner of the nursing home—she's horrified at Slattery's death. Nothing dramatic, but a necessary bridge.

Sawyer Moss rose from the canvas chair where he'd watched the scene play out. To his left their visitor stayed put.

Everybody else on the set, men and women, were dressed in cargo shorts or ratty jeans, T-shirts, running shoes, lots of baseball hats, as scruffy as a bunch of carneys at the county fair.

But not their visitor, who was decked out in beige slacks, shiny loafers, a teal guayabera embroidered with palm trees, and Louis Vuitton shades cocked up into his curly black hair. A California dork's notion of Miami chic.

Murray Danson had flown in last night from L.A. to watch them shoot the tenth episode. The studio's rep, Danson was there to go over the books, but mainly to deliver a face-to-face update. Where the ratings stood, what the sponsors were saying, how much longer Gus Dollimore and his merry band had left before cancellation.

Not long, is what Sawyer Moss guessed, seeing Danson's grim look.

Sawyer was head writer for *Miami Ops*. His break into the film biz was less than a year old and already it was in serious danger. A nasty black mark about to be entered on his permanent record. The writer of a flop.

The season's main storyline was Sawyer's invention: A killer has a fanatical obsession with *The Miami Herald*'s female obituary writer, whom he considers his personal oracle. Apparently he's found secret codes hidden in her obits, codes he uses as blueprints for his killings.

The Miami homicide detectives investigating the killings are stumped, and the geniuses at the FBI put only one guy on the obit case, some old schlub who's counting the days till retirement.

Meanwhile, the killer is wicked smart, leaving behind at each scene the very obit that guided him to this particular victim. No one's managed to find the link between the obits and the victims. Even the two crack Miami Ops agents can't figure out what's steering the killer. Every trap they set has failed, every lead dead-ended. In the four episodes aired so far, the Ops team has wrapped up a dozen flamboyant criminal enterprises, the usual whacked-out Miami bullshit, but their ongoing investigation of the obit killer has them stymied.

They always seem to be two steps behind. The guy's onto their every move. Naturally they suspect a leak. But where?

This week's big reveal was that hood coming off. The killer's identity exposed. Badda-bing. First of all it's a she. And second, this particular she is Valerie, the blond twin of Madeline Braun, one of the two Ops agents. Identical twin. Two gorgeous Brauns, one dark haired, one blond, one good, one evil. There's your leak. And a juicy twist.

A year ago when Sawyer pitched the obit plot, the studio bright boys were unmoved, and Gus was only lukewarm, saying, "Serial killers are boring, an exhausted vein, clichéd, done to death." But pigheaded Sawyer believed he'd found a new angle and fought for the concept and kept tweaking, adding the bodysuit and some kinky sex, until finally Gus came around and convinced the faint-hearts at the Expo Channel.

To pinch pennies, they made Gus show runner, executive producer, and full-time director. Gus Dollimore, man for all seasons. If the show's a hit, Gus is superman. If it fails, good luck finding work in the TV biz anytime soon.

Season starts, they're cruising. Gus is all in, the actors are digging their parts, crew's onboard, then pow! Day after the premiere, the critics let loose. Reviews ranged from brutal to bloodthirsty, and the ratings flatlined. Last week in its Thursday time slot the show was running dead last. And against the other three TV series shot in Miami, same thing. Dead last.

Today, July 1, with the fifth episode airing tonight and four more already shot, edited, and in the can, there was no turning back on the storyline. Episode ten, the one they were shooting this week, would air in five weeks. If it sucked, it sucked. But they were locked in to the obit plot.

Oh, sure, Sawyer could fine-tune the four season-ending scripts, amp up the sex, flash some bare ass, blow some shit up, but with the breakneck pace of production, shooting an episode a week while prepping for the coming week's shoot, there wasn't time for major course corrections.

And now, after having a long look at Murray Danson, the guy's humorless L.A. face, Sawyer thought, Shit, this was what doom looked like. Sawyer's film career was about to crash and burn.

Danson stood up, yawned like he was bored silly, then flicked his hand at Dollimore. Outside. They needed to talk.

The big moment coming.

Sawyer waited for Gus to wave him over to join in, but he didn't. The two left the room, disappeared down the hallway.

Dee Dee walked up, still in the blue Lycra, hood off, blond wig gone, finger-combing her short black hair. Scrubbed of makeup and without the lighting effects, Dee Dee was no longer a brutally gorgeous goddess. She was back to being simply a svelte hottie with an edgy vibe.

"That was cute," she said. "Slattery's line about the killer not getting the audience he deserved. A nod to our shitty ratings."

"Glad somebody noticed. Gus didn't say a word."

"Gus has more on his mind than navel gazing."

Smiling at him while she gave him shit. She could get away with it, being one of the show's stars and because, okay, Dee Dee was also Sawyer's erotically gifted girl. Not to mention Gus Dollimore's precious daughter. Yeah, yeah, Sawyer knew that all added up to a risky incestuous stew. But hell, in the last few years complicated relationships had become his specialty.

"Slattery's speech," Dee Dee said, "it runs long. Felt padded."

"I thought it had a nice rhythm. Guy's trying to talk his way out of getting iced, using the only skill he has. But the huckster's lost his magic."

"I was tapping my foot. It took forever."

"You could've said something on one of the early takes."

"In front of Danson? Come on."

"Well, we can't reshoot." Sawyer glanced at the empty door. "We're two thousand over budget for the week, with all that overtime last night."

"Who's the star of this show, sweetie? Me or Slattery?"

"You got major minutes, Dee Dee. Your face was the payoff."

"But he got the kickass speech. That scene was about him."

"All right. I'll bring it up with Gus."

"All those horny males in our demographic, who do they want to see? Me in a catsuit with my perky tits, or a sad old guy in a hospital bed?"

"You're right, Dee Dee."

She leaned close.

"What's your gut saying?"

She nodded toward the hallway where Danson and Gus were talking.

"Danson is not a happy cowboy."

She smoothed a blue hand over her ripped abs. Dee, the fitness freak.

"Maybe his chaps are chafing."

"Yeah, maybe they are."

"I could take him back to his hotel, loosen them a notch."

"The hell you will."

She gave him her don't-get-possessive glare. Half serious, half not.

Flynn Moss drifted over, still in his street clothes, no scenes for him till the afternoon shoot. Khaki shorts, white T-shirt, flip-flops. Dee Dee's costar, Flynn played Janus, the ruthless rogue cop, master of disguise.

Flynn was Sawyer's twin. Maybe a smidge shorter but otherwise they were duplicates. In every nonphysical way, however, they were galaxies apart. Sawyer, the brainy one, calm and measured, a loner by instinct. Flynn, the action figure, ballsy, down and dirty, the last one to leave the party. The guy with a hundred hangover remedies.

And Flynn Moss was most definitely not a fan of Dee Dee Dollimore's. Zero respect for her acting skills, and totally unmoved by her sexual allure. Feelings that were bitterly mutual.

Dee Dee gave Flynn a mock smile, then turned and flounced away.

"Nice creep factor, Sawyer." Then he slipped into a perfect impression of Dee Dee's voice. " 'It's all right, I'll be gentle.' "

"Glad you liked it."

"Then boom, she strangles the geezer. Good work, bro. Finally embracing your dark side."

"Dee Dee thought Slattery's part was padded. She wanted more lines."

"Fuck her, she always wants more lines. If she had her way the show would be one long soliloquy by Princess Dee Dee. The rest of us standing around worshiping her twitchy butt."

"You're too hard on her, man. She wants what's good for the show. Like the rest of us."

"And you're majorly pussy whipped. Sure, she's yummy and all that, but the girl is killing our box office all by her lonesome. Less she talks, the better. Keep her in that suit, hood on, flaunt that bod, give her six words per episode max—or better yet, gag her with a jockstrap—and watch our ratings climb."

"Cool it, Flynn."

"Kidding, man. Just kidding."

"Sure you are."

Gus walked back into the room alone and everyone lowered the volume. The verdict was in. The crew sneaking looks to get a clue.

He stood there a minute, organizing his thoughts.

Gus Dollimore had the emaciated hardness of a man grimly determined to purge every ounce of flab. Around his eyes the skin was pinched, and his cheeks were as taut as boiled meat. He wore his jet black hair in a military crew cut. In a forgiving light, Gus might be mistaken for a hard-living forty-five instead of a man at war with sixty. He wore a black jersey and white silky trousers that swished around his long legs like luminous smoke as he walked over to Sawyer.

"Give us a minute," he told Flynn as he took Sawyer's arm and steered him to the far corner of the room.

Flynn made a sloppy salute, did an about-face, and marched off. A little pissed, though Flynn damn well knew the chain of command. Until he was a bigger star, he was below the line, down with the rest of the hired help.

Gus's grip on Sawyer's biceps was rigid.

Not good, Sawyer was thinking. Definitely not good.

"So here's the deal." Gus shot a look at a set dresser talking on her cell nearby. He jerked his chin at her and she backed away out of earshot. Gus released Sawyer's arm just as his hand was going numb.

"We're cancelled," Sawyer said.

"No," Gus said. "Danson gave me a number. A target."

"Viewers?"

"A million more."

"No way."

"A million new customers," Gus said, "or we're on the street."

"By when?"

"Episode ten, five weeks from today."

"Bastards want that many eyeballs, they need to run some freaking ads."

"We know that isn't going to happen," Gus said. "This economy."

"So we're dead."

Gus looked at the bed where Dee Dee had strangled Slattery. Eyes taking on a hard glitter. Sawyer could feel the radiation coming off the guy.

"You got an idea?"

"Fuckers want a million," Gus said. "We give 'em a million."

"Like it's that simple."

"Everything good is simple."

"So talk to me."

"Look, kid, I been kissing ass so long, I put myself to sleep every night counting butt cracks. This show tanks, no way I'll claw my way back."

"What's on your mind?"

Dollimore watched two prop guys roll the deathbed from the room. The nursing home where they were shooting would have it back in service in time for afternoon naps.

When Gus spoke again, his voice was barely a whisper.

"Question is, what're you willing to do to survive?"

"I'll write my ass off."

"Cut the Boy Scout shit."

"What do you want me to say?"

"I'm not talking about scribbling, hotshot. I'm asking, are you willing to get your hands dirty to keep us working? Me, your brother, this crew. That shit you had Slattery say, is that just garbage, or do you believe it?"

"Huh?"

"Making a splash, all that."

"I'm not following you."

Gus grimaced and waved a dismissive hand.

"Tell me what you want, Gus, I'm there."

11

Dollimore leaned close, breath to breath, appraising him, Gus's harsh brown eyes roaming Sawyer's face. Whatever he saw made him grit his jaw and huff out a disgusted breath. Without a backward glance, Gus stalked offstage.

ACT ONE

SLIPPING INTO
SECOND PERSON

ONE

IT WAS SATURDAY, MID-JULY, AND Thorn and Rusty Stabler were drifting through Trout Creek, a half hour west of Key Largo by boat. On the fringes of the Everglades, this northern corner of the Florida Bay was dotted with tiny islands and flats that rose into view at low tide to become vast sandbars where egrets and herons feasted on mollusks and stranded pinfish and shrimp.

Narrow unmarked channels snaked across the grassy bottom and cut close to the mangrove islands, making it a tricky place to navigate even in a shallow draft skiff like theirs. All across this region the turtle grass was scarred with prop trails from novice boaters who'd strayed into the shallows and plowed deep grooves at high speed, leaving their idiotic signatures in the sea floor for decades to come.

The Bogies, Stump Pass, Nest Key, Alligator Bay, Trout Cove, Little Madeira, Long Sound, Joe Bay, Tern, and Eagle keys. The islands and sandbars, bays and coves of this remote area were as familiar to the two of them as the slopes, curves, and soft undulations of a lover's body.

Unanchored, they rode the tide, their live shrimp jigging past the mangrove roots where the groupers and big snappers lurked. For this mindless sport, none of Rusty's casting skills or dexterity was required. It was the kind of half-assed fishing that day-tripping tourists indulged in.

Though it was beneath her abilities, Rusty was beyond caring about such things. Today it was the air they were after, the pure, hard summer light, the wayward scent of wilderness. One by one, they were going to hit all her favorite fishing holes, a stations-of-the-cross pilgrimage around the bays and flats and creeks of the upper Keys. Spots both of them had fished since they were kids.

Rusty Stabler, his lover for the last two years. The longest connection Thorn had ever managed with a woman. Longest and most solid, and now it had become by far the most painful.

He watched Rusty twitch her line, putting action in her bait. Hip cocked against the center console, eyes fixed on the water's surface, waiting for any riffle, holding the rod with a loose readiness, reflexes alert. Like Rusty of old.

Twenty yards up the creek a trio of dolphins appeared and took their sweet, silky time rolling past. With a quiet smile, Rusty monitored their journey.

To the east, the ruddy flush of dawn crept above the horizon, and its glow seeped upward into the pearl-gray sky. A breeze passing through Joe Bay sent ripples fanning across the creek, keeping the mosquitoes off. Somewhere inside the dense web of mangroves an osprey hit its high strong notes, twelve in a row, a pause, then twelve more haunting cries as if it were making its morning devotions.

He watched as the dolphins moved into the bay, taking their magic elsewhere.

Rusty motioned at the water off the stern. "Heads up."

Thorn turned as a fish nudged his bait. He popped the line, set the hook, and knew in half a second it was another runt. His third in five minutes.

"You're on a tear, Thorn."

He brought it alongside, released the small gray snapper, then fixed another shrimp to the hook. He glanced at Rusty, returned her smile, and pitched the bait close to the mangroves.

"Tide's picking up; we should do a little better now."

"When was fishing ever about catching fish?" she said.

Thorn was silent, watching their trailing baits.

"Oh, shit. Listen to me getting all Zen."

"Nothing wrong with that," he said.

As he watched, something hard and ugly shifted inside Rusty's gut. She winced, closed her eyes, and slumped forward.

He peeled the rod from her hands and set it in a holder.

"All right, that's enough. We're going in."

"And do what? Lie on my back, stare at the ceiling, and wait?"

"Rusty, you're hurting."

"I'm okay." Her face was pale and she swayed as if the boat were wallowing. "I'll sit down, take a breather. But I'm not ready to go in."

She turned from him, edged around the console, and settled onto the casting platform. There was a dry rasp in her breathing.

He slid his rod into the holder alongside hers and came over. It was a minute before she had her breath back and looked up. Her hazel eyes were muddied by the drugs and pain but they remained unflinching.

"This was a mistake."

"Stop it, Thorn. This is exactly right. I can't imagine a better ending." She drew a breath and wiped away the shine of sweat on her neck.

"Ending?"

"You know what I mean. Right here, right now. This is perfect, exactly where I should be today, at this stage."

She looked away, taking a moment to regain the rhythm of her breath. When she turned to him again, her eyes had cleared.

"Ease off, would you. Even if you have to fake it. Okay? It makes things tougher with you tensed up, fighting so hard."

Thorn was silent. In the last few weeks he'd tried every upbeat phrase he knew, anything to encourage her, brighten the gloom. Then yesterday, with a fierceness she'd never directed at him before, she ordered him to stop. They were past all that bullshit. Three rounds of chemo had done nothing; the morphine wasn't touching her pain. It was no longer a matter of if.

After her outburst, her voice had steadied and her face had assumed the calm bemusement of one who no longer dreads anything.

Now Rusty reset her Heat cap on her hairless scalp and turned her eyes toward the empty bay.

"Trout Creek," she said. "I caught my first fish over there. I ever tell you about that?"

He nodded.

"I did?"

"A big-ass grouper. You were nine, came out alone in a plastic boat with a ten-horse Merc. The damn fish towed you for about half an hour before you wore it out. Like Santiago and his marlin. That grouper got you addicted."

"When did I tell you that?"

"It doesn't matter, Rusty."

"When, damn it?"

"I don't know, ten minutes ago. Maybe fifteen."

"Shit." She shook her head, frowning.

"It's nothing. It's okay. Everything's fine. It's the drugs."

Gradually her frustration passed, and she sighed and her lips softened again, coming as close to a smile as Thorn had seen from her in weeks.

She rose and opened her arms and Thorn stepped into the embrace. She held him firmly, then eased her head back. The fit of her lips was as flawless as ever, though he could taste the acrid bite of the chemicals lacing her blood.

He pressed deeper and lost himself in the kiss, until finally Rusty drew away. She touched a finger to the stubble on his cheek, drew a slow line down his jaw, and gave him another peck before stepping back and retrieving her rod.

They returned to fishing, watched their baits, and were quiet. The air was radiant and thick with the sweet labors of summer, the swollen moon-driven tide, the scent of hidden orchids and reptiles sunning themselves on the high limbs of the mangroves. On the water's surface, the lacy shadows of branches and leaves trembled with every breath of breeze.

For the last week the Keys had been under the spell of a confluence of celestial events that caused the bays and ocean currents to swell several feet higher than normal. Around the island, seawater was washing over the rocky beaches and heaving high against seawalls. Thorn's own dock was three inches below the waterline. Because the moon was in perfect alignment with the earth, at perigee, its closest approach to the southern hemisphere in decades, the increased gravitational pull was tugging at anything with even the slightest water content. A reminder of the bewitching forces calling from deep space, many of them still unnamed, unmeasured, their effects not yet known.

For Thorn the link between the swollen tides and Rusty's illness was unmistakable. Of course, the idea that earthbound matters could be controlled by invisible powers beyond our realm fueled the religious faithful, stirring them to spiritual awe and devotion to a higher power.

But not Thorn. It only jacked up his rage.

Surrendering was not in his nature, especially to forces that were nameless and intangible. For weeks as Rusty battled her illness, he'd been yearning to take something by the throat and throttle it. To go tooth and claw with Rusty's tormentor. But there was nothing there.

He was reeling in his line, about to take a break, when something big crashed his bait. The rod jerked from his fingers, clattered across the deck, and was heading overboard when he stabbed at it and found a grip. Twenty feet of line burned off the reel. Out in the creek the buckle of water was closing on the mangrove roots when Thorn yanked it to a halt.

"I think we got your grouper," he said. "Or one of its grandkids."

He tightened the drag, won back some line before the fish turned again and bulled back toward its lair. Those roots were coated in barnacles with razory edges, and the slightest brush would slice the lightweight monofilament.

Thorn leaned back and horsed the fish to the right, dipping the rod tip and cranking the slack until he had the fish alongside. As he grabbed the light line and kneeled to unhook it, he caught a flash to his right and looked out in time to see a shark heading toward the helpless grouper.

Ten feet away, it would tear into the fish in seconds.

Thorn jerked the line to his mouth, bit it in two, freeing the fish. Through the clear water he watched the old warrior scoot back to the safety of the mangroves. The shark, a six-foot brown, sailed past, missing it by inches.

But then, as if the natural laws of physics didn't apply to it, the bulky predator veered right and was on the grouper in half a second. Blood blossomed at the edge of the mangrove roots; the water boiled for a moment and was still.

"Goddamn it."

He watched the shark thrash, inhaling the last of the grouper, then it departed. A moment later a school of glassy minnows swarmed in to mop up the final floating chunks. Seconds after that the creek was still, a freshening breeze sweeping in from the east, the incoming tide flushing away the last signs of carnage. When he turned around, she'd vanished.

"Rusty?"

He stepped around the center console and found her sprawled face-down. Her head twisted to the side, cheek mashed against the deck. Her eyes were open, milky and unseeing.

Across the creek the osprey screamed and screamed again.

THE MIAMI HERALD

Monday, July 19

Rachel Anne "Rusty" Stabler, At Peace on the Water

By April Moss

Rachel Anne Stabler, who was born in America's landlocked heartland but came to cherish the watery paradise of her adopted home in the Florida Keys, died at her residence in Key Largo after a short illness. She was 46 years old.

For decades, Rusty explored the waters of the Florida Bay, the Everglades and the Gulf of Mexico, first as a youngster in her own skiff, and later as a charter fishing guide, taking anglers onto the saltwater flats or into secluded creeks and bays in search of tarpon, bonefish and other elusive prey.

Born in Starkville, Oklahoma, Rusty Stabler arrived in the Keys at the age of 6 with her single mother, June Ellen Stabler, who had come to those remote islands in search of a fresh start. Rusty completed high school at Coral Shores High in Tavernier, where she struggled with her studies. "As a sophomore she fell in with a tough crew," said former principal Matthew Shane. "She was flunking most of her classes, then one day she walked into my office and threw down the gauntlet. She said if the high school didn't start teaching something useful, we were going to lose her and a lot of others like her. She was lit up."

Frustrated with the lack of response from Shane and other administrators in the school system, Rusty organized students and parents to pressure the Monroe County school board into offering an accredited course in outboard engine repair. Though on repeated occasions the board dismissed her appeals, Rusty persevered, gathering petitions and organizing her fellow students and their parents. Because boating plays such a central role in the Keys economy and its history, Rusty felt the school system was failing to prepare students for island living by neglecting a marine studies curriculum.

Her resolve paid off. In the fall of Rusty's junior year, an outboard engine repair course was offered to students at Coral Shores for the first time. "Nobody had any idea how popular that course would be," said retired principal Shane. "Nobody but Rusty."

After graduation, Stabler devoted herself to building her charter fishing business into a thriving enterprise. According to Ron Marden, president of the Upper Keys Chamber of Commerce, Stabler became one of the top fishing guides in the Florida Keys. "You always got your money's worth when you went out with Rusty. Her rig, *Sunny Daze,* wasn't the slickest skiff out there, but by god, her anglers always caught fish, even when things was dead, and nobody else was getting a bite. That girl just had the gift."

"When she started out, Rusty was the first girl guide in Islamorada, and the guys on the dock weren't pleased," said Captain Harry Sanders, a guide with sixty years' experience in the Keys. "They hazed her, made her life hell. If it bothered her, she never let on. She had a quiet, modest way about her. She wasn't some pushy women's libber, which helped, but what finally won over the guys was the way she put her clients into fish. Day after day Rusty kicked the other guides' butts. That gal could outfish anybody I ever run across."

Through Rusty Stabler's continued efforts and financial contributions, today that single course at her former high school has grown into a complete program consisting of more than two dozen classes in electronics, navigation and marine science. Attracting master mechanics and nautical engineers and university professors from around the globe, many of them Rusty Stabler's fishing clients, Coral Shores High School has developed one of the premier marine vocational studies programs in the nation.

Rusty was spearheading a fundraising campaign that brought in $600,000, all of it designated for a new wing at her alma mater, space which will be used exclusively for the program her efforts brought to life over three decades ago.

For the last few years, Rusty had put her charter fishing business on hold while she accepted a new challenge as chairman of the board of Bates International. Based in Sarasota, Bates International, the largest family-owned agribusiness in the U.S., is the second-largest landowner in Florida, where its holdings include phosphate mines and sprawling cattle ranches in the central regions of the state. "In a very short time Rusty accomplished some amazing things," said Jill Montrose, a longtime Bates board member. "Ms. Stabler was turning BI into one of the worldwide leaders in ecologically responsible food production. She had to fight for every inch of gain she made, but she had amazing grit and dedication."

"Rusty was as strong-willed as anybody I've ever met," said her friend Laurence Sugarman, a Key Largo security professional. "Even towards the end, when things were darkest for her, Rusty was still upbeat. She believed she'd had a magical life. Far richer than anything she ever expected. Her only regret was that in the last couple of years her work with Bates kept her off the water. That was where she was most at peace. Out in her boat."

In accordance with her wishes, Rusty Stabler's remains were cremated and her ashes spread at sea after a sunset celebration at the home of her husband of less than a month, Daniel Oliver Thorn.

TWO

ON YOUR WAY TO THE kill, you slip into second person. This happened naturally at the start and felt comfortable, so you stayed with it.

At these moments it becomes the way you think. There's you and the other you. You speak calmly to yourself, and you listen calmly to yourself speaking. The you in the mirror conversing with the other who stands before it. The two of you doing this together. Both halves of an echo.

After this many times, the process should be easier. But no, you must rehearse, talk your way through each step. Remind yourself to watch the ball, concentrate, stay loose. You are the coach, you are the player.

In most ways each new one is more challenging than those before. As if you've used up something you had at the outset, the commitment, the inspiration, and now you must work harder to manage each step. To conjure the act. To keep from fucking up.

These are not thrill kills. Committing the act, watching them die, there is no dark ecstasy. This is, in fact, a challenge beyond anything you've ever attempted. But it must be done. When the obituary appears, you wait the proper interval, then go. It is your calling. Your way forward.

This journey is the longest you've undertaken for this purpose. You'd rather keep your murders local, but that's not your choice. The targets are selected for you. There is no free will.

In Dallas you retrieve your checked bag. You find an alcove, unzip it, check to see that the weapon has not been tampered with by security. It hasn't. The paper sack is still stapled shut, the cash receipt undisturbed.

You take the airport shuttle downtown. Go inside, buy a paper, find a seat, pretend to read. You could be a guest, or waiting for a guest to arrive. It is unlikely that anyone will recall you, but it's possible that a video cam will capture your image and one day the detective pursuing you will attempt to read your purpose in that lobby.

Your goal is to confuse someone you have never met. Of course you know that one day soon they will uncover your crimes, find links between the murders. And they will be on your trail, using computer searches and TSA security videos and all the high-tech procedures that track killers. You know all that, but it neither frightens nor deters you. You prepare for that day. You welcome it.

You're like a film actor who understands full well that his every action and gesture will be viewed and dissected in a dark room in some not-so-distant future. This is your art. You are the director, you are the star. You disappear into your part, and watch yourself disappearing.

After a while you exit the hotel, hail a cab, tell the driver to take you to the airport. At the rental car counter you use the second ID you've obtained to rent a vehicle. You pay by credit card, using the one you bought on the streets of Miami. These are simple measures, what any smart killer would do. Zigging and zagging, appearing to do one thing but doing something else.

The Lyrca suit is folded up among the clothes in your bag. It compresses to the size of a hardback book. The weapon is still inside the manufacturer's box, and that box is inside the paper sack from the sporting goods store in Miami where you purchased it. All perfectly legal.

Across the desolate countryside you drive the rental car. Eventually there are signs for Broken Bow, Antlers, Heavener, Blanco. Pioneer names for redneck towns. Farmland, rolling hills, few trees. A scrubby landscape, more browns than greens. You buy gas with cash. You stop for a late lunch at a fast-food place along the highway. You studied the maps, memorized the route.

You arrive at the small town in Oklahoma, drive through the decaying business district, swing by the white frame house where your target lives. A woman in her sixties. She should present no serious physical problems.

You've studied the street names from an Internet map. Now you note the streetlights, their locations along the route you've chosen. You observe the trees, how densely leaved they are, picturing how much light will be cast along the path you will take. It will be brighter than you'd like, but not as bright as an open city street. The moon is new, so its glow is not a factor.

Because it is hours before dark, you circle back to the interstate and cruise north, then pull into a Wal-Mart parking lot, slump in your seat as if napping, and watch to see if anyone pays attention to your car. If they do, you will leave. They don't.

When the sun sets, you drive back to the area where your victim lives. Because it is a small town, you park your rental in a location where you are least likely to be noticed, where strangers congregate. Tonight your staging spot is a country music bar called Blue Heaven. Five blocks from the target's house.

In the parking lot, a half-dozen pickup trucks and several family cars, a tow truck and two panel vans. It's a popular place on this Saturday night. There was no way to know that in advance, but you're glad it's busy. You park beside a dark pickup truck. On the other side of your car is a Dumpster.

From your suitcase you take out the Lycra suit.

Wearing it on these occasions makes you strangely beautiful and free. But there is obvious danger. On only your second outing, you were stopped by a cop in an Atlanta neighborhood. It was dark, but his headlamps caught you in their flare and he pulled over and hailed you, keeping you in the blinding lights. You were wearing the suit, and you carried a butcher knife inside a paper sack.

Your heart was seizing, but you didn't run. You kept your voice under control and told the officer you were simply experimenting by walking around in the suit to see how it felt. A harmless prank. A dare. You pretended to be embarrassed. You were submissive. I didn't know it was illegal, you said.

The officer was a country boy, a know-it-all eager to show off his mastery of law. Drawling as he explained the suit itself was not the problem, it was the hood. You were in violation of Title 16, Chapter 11, Section 38 of the Georgia statutes—the anti-mask law. It was unlawful to wear a mask, hood, or device that concealed the identity of the wearer. Exemptions were made for traditional holiday costumes and persons lawfully engaged in trade and employment or sporting activity for the purpose of ensuring the physical safety of the wearer, or because of the nature of the occupation or trade. A person could wear a mask intended for a theatrical production or masquerade balls.

Are you, he asked, on the way to a masquerade ball or a holiday party or a sporting event? No, sir, you confessed, you were not.

Didn't think so, he said. Hellfire, boy, what were you thinking?

You don't know what to say, so you say nothing.

It's not just Georgia, he explained. Other states had similar statutes, growing out of anti-KKK laws.

You told him you understood. You didn't realize it was a crime.

He ordered you to remove the hood and without hesitation you pulled it off, showing him the face you prepared for just such an event. You held your hand in front of your eyes to shield the glare of the headlights. You tilted your head just so, and shifted your feet to angle yourself sideways. In that moment you realized how this situation could work to your advantage. This could be the break you need.

You apologized. You intended no harm. You were doing it as a lark. You keep that open hand in front of your eyes.

He could have detained you for prowling. He could have demanded to see your ID. Asked to examine the contents of your shopping bag. But his radio was squawking and he was distracted by it. Bigger fish elsewhere.

After a silence, he accepted your explanation, and you were allowed to walk away in your black suit.

Two weeks later, here in the parking lot of the cowboy bar, you strip out of your clothes. It requires limberness and patience. You've learned to bend and stretch around the steering wheel. Shoes first, pants, then underclothes, and last your shirt. You arrange them on the seat beside you, stack them in a tidy pile. When you return in a while you will be jangled and it's important the clothes are organized. Seeing them will calm you.

When you're naked you wriggle into the suit. Some people refer to it as a unitard or a catsuit, but the proper name is Zentai. A Japanese word that simply means "bodysuit."

The stretchy material is skintight, nonreflective black. The hood assumes the shape of your face and skull. There are no eyeholes or mouth slits. The material is sufficiently thin at those places so your vision is only slightly impaired and breathing is easy. When the suit is in place, you fit on the special shoes. And you are ready.

Your hand is on the door latch when you hear voices, and look into the rearview mirror. A couple is crossing the parking lot. In the outside mirror you watch them stagger, heading toward the pickup beside you. The man wears a string tie and a cowboy hat and the girl a low-cut top and a miniskirt. They are clinging to each other, kissing and groping.

You could duck down and try to hide, but you don't because this encounter might also prove useful. You're running out of time. Such risks are becoming more necessary at this stage, so you remain motionless in the seat behind the wheel and wait as they approach. They stop at the tailgate of the cowboy's pickup and share a sloppy kiss. Then they separate and the girl in the silver skirt and dark top comes down the aisle between the pickup truck and your car.

You take your eyes off the mirror and wait for her approach. You hear the truck's door open and the cowboy saying something drawly. "Get your sweet ass in my truck right now, woman." The woman answers: "I don't know if I like the way you're speaking to me, sir."

You turn and look out your window. Her butt is an arm's length away.

She climbs into the truck and reaches back to close the door, but stops.

She leans toward you. She's seen something but doesn't know what it is. It's dark. She's drunk, she's sexed up.

She stares at you for three seconds, four. The cowboy says something you can't hear. Then she slams the door. The look on her face has changed. She's not sexy anymore. She's not drunk. Her mouth is open, eyes large.

The truck starts. It has loud exhausts, a throaty rumble. He backs out of the space, and you turn your head to see her again, staring at you, at the black shape in the front seat of a car, her eyes squinting through the dark.

The two lovers head off into the night. She doesn't know what she saw. But whatever it was, it scared her.

You have infected her evening. She won't be able to get you out of her mind. If she tells the cowboy what she thinks she saw, he'll have a good laugh. He'll call her loony, a drunk. He'll screw her anyway, but it won't be as pleasurable as it might have been. You've invaded her imagination and she won't be able to get rid of you.

You take the weapon out of the suitcase, strip away the packaging. Some minor assembly is required, no tools necessary. You tear the cash receipt into pieces and ball up the brown paper sack. You get out and throw the trash in the Dumpster. You know, of course, this act is sloppy and could lead to your undoing, but you do it anyway.

The parking lot is quiet. No one around, just the thump of the jukebox inside the cowboy bar. As a precaution you decide to relocate your car. You don't think a cop would take the woman's story seriously and send a prowl car to the bar. She's drunk. But you play it safe.

It is one thing to be discovered, quite another to be caught.

You get back in, drive a mile east, and park near a school you noted earlier. The white rental car is a common make. It has Texas plates. It blends into the neighborhood.

You open the car door, step out. You absorb the darkness, and the darkness absorbs you. You can feel the warm night air brush across the suit. You are naked but you are not naked.

You listen to the crickets and the call of a distant owl. You reach into the car and take out your weapon. You carry it like a warrior marching into battle. Through the darkness you walk the short distance to your victim's house. No traffic passes. Most houses along the way are dark. A few have a single light burning inside in this early-to-bed town.

When you reach the house, you find it dark as well. You are energized. Naked in the night. But also concealed. An unseen spirit gliding through the summer air, hearing only distant cars, the yowl of a tomcat jousting with a rival, the hum of the power lines, crickets answering crickets. Bats flicker through a streetlight.

You are alive with the fever of the moment.

You circle the house. You are looking for signs of other occupants. Potential trouble. There is only one car in the driveway, an old Volvo. The yard is unkept, grass long, bushes overgrown. No yard furniture. A light glows in a single window. You hear no noise from inside. You return to the front.

You mount the steps, slip inside the small screened porch.

You were planning on ringing the doorbell or knocking. To wake the woman, draw her to the door groggy from sleep, then barge through and do your quick work. But as astonishing as it seems, the door is unlocked. A lazy backwater way of life is still flourishing—at least for one last night. Tomorrow this town will know fear. Locksmiths will be busy.

You step into the stuffy darkness of the foyer. The scent of fried food is in the air. Cigarette smoke, booze. You have formed no image of the woman you've come to kill, but these odors make you picture her as fat, wearing curlers. You see her feasting on Doritos and rum and Coke while chain-smoking and watching a late-night talk show.

You dissolve that image. It interferes with your clarity of purpose. It confuses the issue. You do not care about these people. You don't build a case for them or against them. You don't interact or engage. Keep contact to a minimum. Kill and leave. These people are pawns. They are nothing.

You locate her bedroom from the slit of light beneath the door and the density of cigarette smoke. You open her door slowly and step inside. By her bed a radio plays classic rock tunes quietly. A brass ashtray is overflowing. Her bedspread is littered with file folders and yellow notepads. She's propped up on pillows. She looks at you from behind a sheaf of papers that she's been reading. Gripped between her lips is a ballpoint pen. Purple ink, purple scribbles in the margins of the papers. Her hair is loose, streaked with gray, and it hangs down her back. She wears reading glasses. For someone her age she is attractive. Slim body, alert eyes. With those glasses and the pen in her mouth, she looks scholarly, not the kind of woman you'd expect in this hick town.

You raise the weapon, show it to her. Your purpose should be obvious.

Joni Mitchell sings sweetly. The expression on her lips doesn't change. Eyes on you, calm, maybe a flicker of interest, but nothing else.

She removes the ballpoint pen and sets it on the bedside table.

"That's some kinky suit. What's it called?"

You say nothing.

"Okay, so what's your beef?"

You're quiet. You're not there.

"Well, someone obviously has a problem. The person who sent you."

You move closer to the foot of the bed.

If she's frightened, she doesn't show it. She watches you with her papers propped on her stomach as if waiting for you to leave so she can resume reading. As if strangers wandered into her room all the time, then wandered out again.

"I had my kinky phase," she says. "Back in the day. Ménage à trois once. Some light bondage with a young fella. Whips, leather restraints. It was interesting for a while. But I got too old for games."

You move along the edge of her bed, coming closer to her left side. She's wearing a loose white T-shirt. The bedspread is folded back, exposing the waistband of her pink pajama bottoms. A narrow strip of flesh is showing around her navel.

If this woman was heroic or impetuous, she might try to toss the papers at you and use the distraction to bolt for the door. That appears to be her only hope. Unless there's a pistol you don't see, or a knife, or some other weapon hiding beneath the sheets. Which of course is highly doubtful.

In the arm holding the weapon you feel a spring-loaded tension growing. You begin to raise it, choosing your entry spot. Somewhere around her navel.

"I'd love to know who hired you," the woman says. "It was those abortion nuts in Tulsa, God's Children. Am I right? No, no. It was that FBI dick in Dallas. It was him, wasn't it? Jerry Jeff Peters. Go on, tell me. Was it Jerry Jeff? That jerkwad would love to piss on my grave."

You hesitate. The mention of law enforcement flusters you.

"Now listen," the woman says. "Let's talk this out. Give it a minute, I bet we can mediate this. Shit, you can mediate anything."

You stand silently, gathering yourself, regaining composure.

As the seconds pass, you watch the amusement in her face drain away, replaced by a more solemn look, even a hint of dread.

"No dice, huh?"

You say nothing.

"You know, it's funny. I've always counted on words—my story winning out over the other guy's. But words don't cut it for you, do they? Am I right? You're way out there beyond the universe of language."

You wait no longer. You raise the weapon quickly and bring it down. At the last second she makes a wild swat at your hand. But she is too late.

The blade penetrates flannel and flesh. She grunts, emits a single squeal, a high-pitched burst like a schoolgirl with exciting news. Her papers scatter to the floor. She squirms. Her eyes widen, then shut. She writhes. You complete two more strikes. Plunging the final one deep into her body as though you are planting your flag in the soil of a conquered land.

When she is quiet, you turn from the bed. You peel back the suit at your hip and extract the newspaper clipping with the edges cut into a jagged pattern. You lay the obituary on the woman's bedside table.

Rachel Michelle "Rusty" Stabler, at Peace on the Water

You leave the weapon behind, buried in her flesh. Another gift to the authorities. Let them work with that, see where it leads. You leave the room. Walk from the house. The darkness absorbs you. And you are gone.

THREE

MONDAY MORNING RUSH HOUR. DEE Dee was hogging a space at curbside check-in at Miami International. Warning signs everywhere. This area for arriving passengers only. Park, take out luggage, kiss your loved one, and go. No waiting. Towing enforced. But rules didn't apply to Dee Dee Dollimore. Rules were for losers.

For the second time the same cop came over to move her along. With her ragtop down, Dee Dee cocked her smile up at him. Cuban guy, forties, with slicked-back hair and a clunky gold wristwatch, hairy arms. He took out his ticket book this time, his patience exhausted.

"One more minute. Pretty please. Two shakes of a lamb's tail."

"You can't park here."

"Forty-five seconds, I promise. Forty, thirty-nine."

"You have to move. Now."

She looked into his eyes, warmed up a smile. Took off her Prada black-framed glasses. Narrow rectangles, the studious look. She was wearing a starched white shirt with a boy's navy blue tie. Her pleated miniskirt was red plaid with black and green. Like she was heading off to Immaculate Heart for a day with the nuns.

She stared into the cop's eyes and touched a fingertip to her lean thigh, inched the plaid skirt up to expose more sleek skin, a glimpse of her white panties. The cop blinked, lips parting. He stood for a moment, ticket book in hand, then warned her again it was a no-parking zone before he took a last look at her crotch, and went off down the line of cars to harass somebody else.

Dee Dee's ride was a Bugatti Veyron W16.4. Red and black, inside and out, as molded and sleek and deadly cool as a superstar's basketball shoe. Ten radiators and four turbochargers and a computerized rear wing system that kept it from flying off into the next galaxy. Gus leased the car to maintain a flashy profile around town, but with the show in the toilet, he was dumping the lease. Dee Dee could jet around till Friday, then the car went back.

Five minutes passed, still no Sawyer, and the same cop returned with his stern look, leaning down, getting his face close to hers, wanting the full show this time. She walked her scarlet fingernails down the lap of her skirt, watching his stern face soften. The tip of his tongue showed at the corner of his mouth. All but drooling.

Then Sawyer Moss was at the passenger door with his overnight bag.

"Hey, kids. What's up?"

The cop straightened, took a moment to get his strict face back.

"You with this lady?"

Sawyer lifted his luggage into the jump seat.

"Guilty as charged. She giving you a hard time?"

"What I'm giving him," Dee Dee said, "is a hard dick."

Dee Dee cranked the engine, waited till Sawyer snapped into his safety harness. Cop standing there, riveted by the after-image of Dee Dee panties.

She slipped the shifter, revved the horses, and shot into traffic.

Sawyer settled back into the sculptured leather.

"So how'd it go?"

"Not even a kiss hello?"

Through the dense traffic, Dee Dee swerved the Bugatti to the far right lane and idled. With horns honking around them, they tongue-kissed until Sawyer's eyes were blurry.

Back in traffic, she said, "Okay, so how'd it go?"

"The Dallas airport sucks big time."

She headed south on Le Jeune Road, clogged with morning rush, Dee Dee whipping into openings, making decent time. Sawyer feeling sick.

"You saw the Nielsens."

Sawyer said yes, he'd seen them.

"Dropped a full point with the eighteen to forty-nines. We're in a death dive. Two weeks to break a million, that sure as shit isn't happening."

"Not without divine intervention."

"If Daddy bombs, he'll never work again. You going to let that happen, Saw?"

"I'm doing what I can."

She took Flagler east, jumping onto backstreets when things looked sluggish. Hitting seventy in twenty-mile-an-hour zones, blasting through four-way stops. The Bugatti with multiple G-force pickup, deep throaty engine.

Her eyes were fixed on the red light.

"How was your weekend?"

"Lazed around the pool. Nothing much."

"I called your cell, left messages."

"I shut it off."

"I got worried, you didn't answer."

"You don't trust me, cutie?"

"Of course I trust—"

Light went green and Dee Dee slingshot away, zero to sixty, a blink. Sawyer's back G-forced against the seat.

She screamed down Flagler. This morning they were shooting inserts at the Floridian nursing home where William Slattery was killed, a splinter crew doing five seconds of this, three seconds of that. Close-ups of the funky deco architecture, pans of all the old folks in their bathrobes and wheelchairs. Quickies of Janus and Madeline. The nursing home made for a colorful background and it was a freebie, because the owner of the Floridian was friends with Garvey, his grandmom. Which was why Gus decided to milk the place for the rest of the week.

Making a TV show, Sawyer had learned, was all about nickels and dimes.

"So, sugar, what's going on with your mommy dearest?"

"Like how?"

"I called her to say hi, do some girl talk. She was pissy as shit."

"She's just stressed with job issues. Paper's laying off a lot of her pals. That's wearing on her."

"She was harsh. Rushed me off the phone like I was selling time-shares in Afghanistan."

"Don't take it personally."

"How else should I take it?"

"It's not you, Dee. This is her MO. She sees me getting serious, the hackles go up. She was just a kid when she had Flynn and me. She's supersensitive about us not making that mistake."

"You're a long way past being a kid."

"Not in her mind."

"She give you a date when it's safe to get serious?"

"Ignore her, Dee. She likes you fine. She's just got issues."

Sawyer gripped the door handle as Dee Dee slammed through traffic. Overtaking cars, trucks, motorcycles, dodging fenders by inches, tromping on the gas, pinning Sawyer's head to the seat.

"On a scale of one to ten, how smart are you, Sawyer?"

"Where's this coming from?"

"Like test score smart. You kick ass on the SAT?"

"I forget. It was like a century ago."

"Nobody forgets their SAT."

"All right. Yeah, they were fine, ninety-something percentile."

"Well, see, there's your problem."

She swung into the parking lot of the Floridian. The Honey Wagon was there, a big white RV where the cast members peed and catnapped. Crew members queued at the catering truck for their scrambled eggs and burritos. Union contract mandated three squares a day.

She shut down the engine.

"Maybe you're too smart. Brainiacs like you overcook everything."

"Where we going here?"

"I read the scripts for the last episodes. Too much talk, not enough action. All that flowery shit doesn't sound real. Like boring people talking to other boring people."

Sawyer was quiet, his feelings hurt.

Dee Dee said, "You want to make it in this world, you gotta dumb down. Dial back the brain power."

"I'll take a look, Dee Dee."

"Am I being too hard on you?"

"I can take it."

She turned her head and gave him that dirty-girl sleepy look.

"I like a man who can absorb punishment."

This woman had only known Sawyer for a few months and she had him totally pegged. Truth was, he knew he was too smart for his own good. At sixteen Sawyer graduated prep school. With his test scores early-admission offers flooded in. He picked Harvard, prelaw, not that he gave a shit about the legal world. It was all about the perks, picturing the Mercedes, mansion on the bay, a yacht, all that. He flew through under-grad, finished his BA in two years, was out of law school by twenty-two.

Top Miami firm snapped him up. A month after he passed the bar he was stuck in a windowless office doing rote work, reviewing docu-ments, proofing bullshit letters. He walked into a partner's meeting, said he wanted to start litigating; get his feet wet and his dick hard is how he put it. They laughed, not at his joke but at him.

He left them chuckling, packed his briefcase, and bailed. No expla-nation. Didn't tell them he'd been hanging out on a movie set, watching Flynn playing a bit part in a prime-time series shot on Miami Beach, and he'd fallen over his fucking heels in love with the film scene.

The day after he left the firm, Sawyer began work on a spec script. Finished it, tore it up. Finished another, tore it up. Learning the form was tougher than he'd thought. Left brain staying with the formula, right brain coming up with people, dialogue, the emotional core. What he discovered was, he loved making shit up. Something out of nothing. Start with an empty page, fill it up, like magic: poof. First time in his life he'd been challenged. Like a god with his private universe, every-thing his own, every action, every word, everything down to the smallest detail.

A year later, he was selling scripts to three different TV series. When he heard Flynn was doing tryouts for *Miami Ops,* Sawyer wrangled a sit-down with Gus Dollimore. They hit it off, and here he was.

Dee Dee reached over and scratched a fingernail across his thigh.

"Did I hammer you too hard? You pouting?"

"I'm fine. I don't mind criticism."

"I speak the truth," she said. "No matter how painful. Always."

"The truth is our friend."

"Give me more people to kill. I like killing people. It gets me wet."

Smiling like it was a joke.

Dee Dee's hair was black and lustrous, a Hepburn pixie cut. Today she was dressed in her usual campy outfit: plaid miniskirt, white short-sleeve blouse, a man's tie, Buster Brown shoes, and kneesocks. She did it as an attention grab. A fuck-you to political correctness. Not everyone got the joke.

Maybe she was a little old to be playing dress-up, but he was cool with it. Over the years Sawyer had dated Goths in their corpse paint and black lipstick, dressed for perpetual mourning. He'd had a fling with a labor lawyer who rotated through seven identical Armani suits, all blue pin-stripe, and he went out with a sound technician for a while who wore nothing but khaki trousers, penny loafers, and white polos. People found a style, got stuck. Goth or raver or schoolgirl, hell, it was just another flavor. And good god, Dee Dee had that body and those *Kama Sutra* moves. She'd introduced him to some freaky shit. Kept him off-balance, hungry. Maybe it was love, maybe just animal heat. He was still sorting that out.

She had winter-gray eyes, hard cheekbones, a juicy mouth. Best abs he'd ever seen. You could roll marbles down the grooves. Ripped arms. Skinny frame with those tight one-scoop breasts. She didn't bother with a bra. Her feisty nipples always poking the thin material of her white schoolgirl shirts.

She was right about April sending negative vibes. Sawyer's mother hadn't warmed to Dee Dee. Even had trouble speaking her name. Some visceral girl-girl thing going on. Maybe it was her schoolgirl outfits, maybe something else entirely. Who could tell with mothers? Especially his.

Dee Dee climbed out. Sawyer stayed put, taking out his phone.

"Look at you. Now you're pissed."

"I need to answer some e-mail."

"You're sulking."

"I'm fine. You're right about the scripts."

"Story should move as fast as this freaking car."

"Got it."

"And hey, while you're rewriting, give me some better lines, would you?"

"I'm trying."

"Try harder. Some reviewer in Chicago said I was dumber than a blond rock. Make me smart, Sawyer. Rescue me quick, baby."

Dee Dee twiddled her fingers, blew a kiss. She sidled over to the catering truck, high-fiving a couple of grips, all the guys and a couple of the girls sneaking looks at her supple backside.

She saw Gus, went over, started talking to him. Gus nodded, nodded again, listening to her while his eyes homed in on Sawyer.

Sawyer totally dug this woman. Since the moment she walked up to him in the Gansevoort Hotel bar, where he was having a martini during the *Miami Ops* get-acquainted bash. He and one of the stunt girls were cozied up, working through the preliminaries.

Dee Dee stood between them silently, and when the bartender came, she said, "Whatever this young man's having. And keep them coming. I'm taking this one home tonight."

After a while, the stunt girl drifted off. Sawyer and Dee Dee kept drinking. Back at her condo in the Grove, the next twenty-four hours was a red flashing strobe. They clawed, sucked, chewed, and wrestled. All that hot Friday night and all day Saturday and into Sunday afternoon, no rest. Half a year later, it was still hot. Sawyer's libido cranking. Always some new kink pushing Sawyer way beyond his comfort zone. The woman was a sexual mastermind.

Which was the exact opposite of her role on the show. Playing against type, Sawyer wrote Madeline Braun as an all-work, no-play professional. A lady with major sex appeal, but when guys hit on her, they got total frostbite. Sawyer's idea was to play up the sexual tension between Madeline and Janus, building toward a season-ending romp between the two.

Miami Ops was *Dirty Harry* redux. With two vigilante cops working in secret—their boss, chief of Miami PD. Sick of coddling evildoers, contemptuous of the laws that hamstrung his department, Chief Levine gave the two supercops free rein. He funded their work, covered their tracks. Left them free to kick down doors, take out thugs or whoever got in the way, extort confessions—no court orders, no Miranda, no apologies. Just get it done even if the occasional innocent citizen was sacrificed. It being Miami, the crimes were outlandish, collateral damage high.

Both agents had nasty skill sets. Madeline Braun was a former officer in Shabak, Israeli intelligence, gorgeous in a brittle fashionista way. She could bewitch the baddest baddie, slip past the burly guys with a flutter of her eyes, and if some bozo didn't fall for her charms, she dispatched him with razor blade implanted in her fingernail or used an old-school scrotum kick.

Janus was part magician, part cutthroat who could transform himself into any character the script called for, male, female, dangerous, wimpy. He had a hair-trigger temper, zero respect for the law, and a black belt in every martial art known to man. Week after week he crushed the bad guys' bones, and with reluctant witnesses, he used his sandpaper and power drill with abandon.

So far the duo had brought down Nicaraguan white slavers, a group of cyberscammers from Ukraine, Iranian counterfeiters, a ruthless gang of Koreans smuggling endangered parrots, Haitian loan sharks, Columbian child-smut peddlers, and other exotic barbarians. Without the vigilance of the Ops team, it seemed Miami would be drowned in a tsunami of evil.

Gus sold the Exposure Channel on that broad outline and on the show's tricky tone. One minute it was tropical noir with gritty violence, demonic bad guys, and back-alley crime, then it swung to flashy beaches and bikinis, tongue-in-cheek one-liners. That was the test for Sawyer, tight-roping that line between dark thrills and goofs.

Gus was strolling over, phone to his ear, watching Sawyer.

Sawyer got out and waited for him in the shade of a banyan tree.

Gus came close, still listening to the voice on the phone.

Face empty, eyes locked on Sawyer.

No good-bye, just snapped the phone shut, slid it into his jeans pocket. Gus doing black today. The jeans, a silky T-shirt, black loafers, glossy black wraparounds cocked up on his forehead.

"Understand you were in Dallas."

"I was."

"Dee Dee says you went to see Danson."

"He was going to be there on business, invited me for a sit-down."

"There on business. That's your story?"

"It's not my story, it's what happened."

"He invited you, what, like called you on the phone, said, Hey, Sawyer, come out to Dallas, I'd like to play footsie?"

"His secretary called. Didn't say what it was about."

"So behind my back you decide to go see the studio's top money guy."

"Come on, Gus. It wasn't like that. He called me. I thought I could work the generation thing. Shoot the shit, get Danson on our wavelength. I went on my own nickel. It didn't work out."

"And for some reason you didn't tell me about this meeting?"

"Secretary suggested I should keep it hush-hush."

"And you took that to mean you should keep me in the dark."

"I'm sorry, Gus. That was wrong. I should've alerted you. My bad."

"Funny," Gus said. "On the phone just now Danson said none of this happened, there was no meeting."

"That was him you were talking to?"

"Him, yeah. Dee told me your story. So I rang him, asked him what the fuck was going on, he said I'm mistaken, there was no appointment with you or anyone else on Saturday. Not on his schedule; he hasn't been in Dallas in years. Has no reason to call you."

"Then something's fucked up," Sawyer said. "His secretary, Millie, she said two P.M. in the Ritz-Carlton lobby, Danson wanted to discuss the show. I waited two hours, no Danson. Called his office, nobody there on Saturday afternoon. I've called half a dozen times, they put me on hold, don't come back. I've e-mailed, left messages. The guy stood me up."

"Somebody's played a trick on you, son. Somebody conned your ass. People like Danson don't call writers. I'm the show runner here. Danson talks to me, then I talk to you, the cast, and the rest of the crew. That's how the food chain works, babe. You don't go having clandestine meetings with a studio guy. It doesn't happen."

"Who would con me into something like that?"

"Unless, of course," Gus said, "you got some whole other thing working in Dallas you don't want anybody to know about. Is that it, Sawyer? You got a piece of ass stashed out west?"

"Danson stood me up. We had a meeting at the Ritz for two, he didn't show. That's the truth."

Gus rubbed his chin and glanced off.

"If you say so, kid. You keep telling that story. See where it gets you."

FOUR

THURSDAY AFTERNOON, WHEN SUGARMAN PULLED his Honda into the crushed seashell drive, Thorn was down by his boat basin prying loose a small boulder from the seawall. He carried the limestone chunk to a patch of lawn twenty yards from his house, dropped it at his feet, glanced toward Sugar, then turned and walked back to the seawall.

It was coming up on two weeks since Rusty's death. Everywhere he looked he still heard traces of her voice or caught hints of her sun-baked scent.

Sugar shut his car door and came over and stood waiting by the rock.

Same age as Thorn. Swedish mother, Jamaican father. Former sheriff's deputy, now a private investigator. As tall and fine-looking as an A-list Hollywood charmer. His chiseled bone structure had been polished smooth by the years. Steadfast as anyone Thorn had ever known, Sugarman was first in line when the hard chores were assigned. Thorn's trusty wingman. But always ready to get in Thorn's face when required. Faithful Sugar. Loving, strong, bull-headed Sugarman. A rock.

Exactly the last person Thorn wanted to see just then.

"You need help?"

Thorn grunted and marched back to the seawall. Sugar tagged along to the water's edge.

"Nice to see you're finally out of the hammock, up and doing."

As Thorn squatted and jimmied loose another boulder from the muddy embankment, Sugarman crouched and started prying free the one adjacent to it. Pitching in, uncomplaining. He followed Thorn back to the open lawn, lugging his own jagged stone. He dropped it a few feet away from where Thorn stood.

"Not there," Thorn said.

"Okay, where?"

"It's going to be a circle."

"All right, good. A circle. How big?"

"Big," Thorn said.

"We gonna make a campfire? Get drunk, sing manly songs of yore. 'Give me some men who are stouthearted men who will march . . .'"

Thorn turned away and headed back to the rocky seawall.

They toted rocks in silence for half an hour, Sugarman respecting Thorn's black mood. They made a few dozen trips, carrying forty or fifty stones. By the time they were done, the southern end of the seawall was dismantled, and the circle in the grass had a ten-foot radius.

"Next high tide, your yard's going to flood. But I guess you knew that."

Thorn didn't reply.

"Am I invading your privacy? Wink your right eye for yes."

Thorn stared at him and said nothing.

He and Sugar had been buddies since the schoolyard days. Thorn, a loner by choice; Sugar, an outsider by blood. The oddball kid who was half black, half white with a face too pretty for his own good. A bully attractor. At six years old Sugar learned to fight, a necessary skill for a cute kid with his racial mix. Too many times to count, when the tough boys ganged up on him, Thorn jumped in. Their friendship was forged in those kunckle-busting brawls.

Lifelong friends, Sugar and Thorn had survived the usual traumas and tragedies. They'd also endured some traumas not so usual, episodes of bloodshed and savagery that teetered on the edge of illegal. They had, more than once, been forced to extreme and messy forms of justice. Those were episodes they never rehashed, the side of their bond that stayed in shadow.

Once the circle of rocks was done, Thorn stepped back and eyed it.

"Now what?" Sugar said.

Thorn shrugged, so dazed by the thrum of his racing blood that at that moment he couldn't recall why he'd wanted to construct the circle.

"Well, okay then," Sugar said. "On another matter entirely, just in case you're interested, I took care of that business in Sarasota. You're now totally cashed out of your controlling interest in Bates International, which, I have to admit, involved some dollar figures so big I can't bring myself to say them out loud. So many zeroes, my throat constricts. Suffice it to say, you're no longer a corporate mogul. Bates is broken up, pieces sold off; all profits owed to you have been transferred to seventeen different charities. Mainly greenies, but a few others, early education, homeless shelters, battered women, abused kids. I followed Rusty's outline. You guys made a lot of good souls very happy. I got the list right here."

Sugarman dug a folded paper from his jeans pocket and held it out.

Thorn took the sheet, balled it up, and tossed it into the circle of stones.

Sugarman looked at the paper and said, "I thought cutting you loose from Bates was going to be complicated, but it wasn't. Turns out Rusty began the process before she got sick, did the paperwork to divest you of all the titles, rewriting charters, scrubbing your name from the minutes of board meetings. So you're out of the picture entirely. It's like all that never happened. And best of all, Thorn, you're penniless again."

"Good."

"I mean, dirt poor, destitute. Insolvent. Don't have a pot to piss in."

Sugarman was devoted to his thesaurus.

"You're also safely back below the sweep of radar. Records expunged, history obliterated. You're nobody. Less than nobody. Far as the world of capitalistic free enterprise is concerned, Thorn never existed."

"It's a happy day," Thorn said.

"I don't know if you saw the obituary in the *Herald*."

Thorn was staring out at the lagoon.

"That woman, April Moss, did some excellent research. There's stuff in there I didn't know about Rusty. About the marine studies program getting started. How rough it was for Rusty as a guide. April went above and beyond. It was very generous of her."

Thorn stood his ground, weathering the moment.

"I called her after it came out and thanked her. She said to tell you hello. Tell you how sorry she was for your loss. We talked for a while. She's a good lady. Smart, sensitive. I didn't realize you two knew each other. How come I never heard of her before?"

"It was a long time ago. Very brief."

"Back in your one-night-stand days?"

Thorn didn't reply.

"Well, she's nice. And she's single."

Thorn turned and squinted at him.

"Rusty's not gone two weeks, and you're trying to set me up?"

"Hell, no. I liked her. I was thinking of asking her out myself."

Thorn was silent, looking at the circle of stones.

"I brought you a copy of the obit in case you didn't see it."

Sugar drew the clipping from his shirt pocket and held it out to Thorn.

"I saw it." Thorn turned and walked back to his house.

He went inside and returned several minutes later with an armload of framed photographs and a table lamp. He heaved the junk into the center of the circle and went back inside.

When Rusty died, some crucial atom inside him had cracked apart and all the wild-eyed craziness that was stabilized by her presence went into a state of fission. Attractive and repulsive forces, knocked out of equilibrium, were releasing some mind-melting pulses. He'd tried to contain the meltdown but apparently it was too late. The chain reaction was under way.

Thorn knew this would be finished only when it had run its course, when all the electrostatic forces had neutralized their equal and opposite valences. Until then he could only stand apart and observe the mad electrons radiating around his body, and listen to the delirious hum in his head like some turbine spinning ten times past its tolerances, and observe himself committing acts he only dimly comprehended.

For the next two hours, while Sugarman watched from a lawn chair, Thorn made trip after trip into the house, returning to the circle of stones and pitching more of his accumulated possessions onto the heap.

Things he'd purchased himself, gifts from friends, items he'd inherited, objects he'd made by hand like his collections of carved wood plugs and bonefish flies, which for many years had been his sole source of income. He tossed a hinged maple box containing a hundred hand-tied flies he'd set aside for his own use some day, a day that had never come, and never would.

He carried out rods and reels, three mounted fish he'd caught as a kid, his first clumsy attempts at taxidermy, a half-deflated basketball, a pair of old prom shoes still glossy under decades of dust, scuzzy flip-flops and ragged sneakers he'd outgrown years ago that were forgotten on a back shelf in a closet down the hall, and the dresses and flowery skirts of women who'd shared his bed for a time and left them behind in the haste and confusion of their final getaways. Sarah, Monica, Darcy, Alexandra, Rusty, and the others. A string of hard-nosed, beautiful ladies.

He hauled out an assortment of straw sun-hats his adoptive mother, Kate Truman, used to wear when she was fishing with her husband, Dr. Bill. The woman had died twenty years ago, but the hats were still haloed with the lilac scent of Kate's favorite perfume.

He threw her hats on the pile, along with cardboard boxes containing documents Kate had accumulated: tax statements, paid receipts, and income ledgers from her fishing guide business decades past; a vast hoard of paper where dozens of palmetto bugs scurried for safety, stacks of papers that were irrelevant when they were filed away, and were a hundred times more irrelevant every year thereafter, yet Thorn had never had the heart to toss any of them out until that day.

When the mound grew to the edge of the rock circle, Thorn walked to the boat house north of the basin and took down a can of kerosene from a high shelf. He brought it back and walked around the edge of the circle, splashing it over the pile.

"Your flies, Thorn? You've got thousands of hours invested in that."

"You want them, take them. Now's your chance."

Sugarman made no move.

"I wouldn't want to hamper your fun. But buddy, you might want to wet a line again someday."

"Then I'll tie some new flies."

Thorn dug a wooden match from the pocket of his shorts and scratched it against a stone. He held it out, studied the flame for a moment, then bent down and touched it to a framed photo taken aboard the ancient thirty-foot Chris-Craft, the *Heart Pounder,* Thorn at sixteen, shirtless, his hair longer and blonder than it ever was again. Thorn was grinning at Sugarman, who with Kate Truman's help was holding up a sailfish he'd just hauled from the blue-green waters at the edge of the stream.

Thorn watched the fire take hold and when he was sure it was fully caught, he plodded back to the house to resume his cleansing.

FIVE

FOR THE NEXT FEW HOURS while the bonfire raged, Thorn hauled out more junk. At midnight gusts of sparks were still swirling skyward. Sugarman dozed in the Adirondack chair, waking up now and then when Thorn crashed a table or bookcase into the flames.

Around two in the morning, Thorn carried out two suitcases, set them on the grass near Sugarman's chair, and nudged his friend's leg. Sugar woke, his hand swatting reflexively at a mist of mosquitoes.

"Something for you."

Sugar stretched and rubbed his face. Most of the smoke was riding out to sea on the off-shore wind, but a thick haze had collected around the sheltered dock lights and hung like melancholy fog.

Thumbing open the latch of one suitcase, he took a look.

"Well, at least you haven't completely lost your mind."

The case was packed with books, some Thorn had reread many times over the years. A collection of paperback sea stories, mysteries, and adventure yarns, and some bird guides and books on weather and Florida history. His Travis McGee paperbacks, some Rudyard Kipling, Patrick O'Brian, and the complete Marjorie Kinnan Rawlings.

"There's more inside. In boxes. Take them with you. Give them to your girls, donate them to the library, or keep them, I don't care."

"Listen, Thorn."

"Don't try to talk sense to me, Sugar."

"Oh, I know better than that."

"I'm starting fresh," he said.

"That's what this is about? Starting fresh?"

"Call it simplifying. All this shit was weighing me down."

"Thorn, you got fewer possessions than anybody I know."

"Now I have less."

They stood watching the swirl of the bonfire.

"In the past, when the bad shit came raining down," Sugar said, "there was always a path to justice. Some righteous action to take. A person to track, clues to unravel. But this is different. Rusty got sick, she fought it and lost. It was a natural chain of events. There's nothing to fix, no way to make it right. You can't track down God and punch him out."

"What God?"

"Okay, okay. You're going to do what you're going to do. I can't stop you, and I'm not about to try. But before I leave I got two things to say."

Thorn stayed put. He was weary beyond endurance. The scream in his head had died to a vicious hum. Nothing he couldn't manage. He'd had tequila hangovers that were worse.

"You won't remember this, but I been planning it for a year. Tomorrow I'm taking Jackie and Janey to the Grand Canyon. We'll fly to Phoenix, rent a car, be gone ten days, seven hiking, plus the out-and-back travel time."

His twin girls were teenagers, living with their mom in Lauderdale. A nincompoop judge had found her more competent than Sugarman.

"So?"

"So I'll change my plans, call off the trip if you need me."

"Why would I?"

"Thorn, you're halfway around the bend. You're having a last-straw crack-up. One thing too many, one thing more than even Job had to handle. Because Rusty was healthy one minute, gone the next. Because she was the first woman in years that could take your bullshit and keep smiling while she gave it back with a double scoop. And because you just spent the day burning everything you own."

"I'm not half done."

Thorn heard the rage in his own voice, but was powerless to stop it. He was skidding down an oil slick highway with no brakes, the steering wheel useless in his hands. Sugarman in his headlights.

"Okay, so I'll be gone till a week from Sunday. I'll have my cell. You need me to come back, call me. You understand what I'm saying?"

"That's one thing. What's the other?"

"You need to promise me you're not about to take your own life."

Thorn said nothing.

"I'm not leaving until I get your word. I won't have that on my conscience. You understand me? If I have to, I'll chain you to a palm tree till this thing blows over."

"You couldn't manage that."

"Don't try me, Thorn."

Thorn stared into Sugarman's eyes and said nothing.

"Okay, if that's how it is, then I'm staying."

Thorn turned to watch the haze moving past the dock lights, teased into action by a draft off the Atlantic.

"Go on your trip, Sugar. Make your girls happy, hike the canyon, take some snapshots, buy them all the pizza they can eat. Tell them Uncle Thorn sends his love."

"Is that your promise? You'll not harm yourself?"

"Go on, Sugar. Be with your family. I just need to get rid of a few things. Simplify, start fresh. Really. I'll be fine. Go."

Sugarman studied Thorn's eyes for a minute.

"Okay," he said finally. "But you know this will pass. It doesn't feel like it now, but it will."

"I know it will," Thorn said. "It's already started."

In tense silence they carted boxes of books from the house to Sugar's dinged-up Honda. When the car was packed, Sugarman got in, started it, and gave his headlights a farewell flash.

Thorn raised a hand and waved at the lights. It took all his strength.

After Sugar was gone, Thorn decided he was too exhausted to toss more furniture into the fire. He had just enough energy left for his clothes.

That shouldn't take long. Thorn's wardrobe consisted of a collection of threadbare cowboy shirts and flowered Hawaiians and T-shirts from local bars and tackle shops. Some shorts and jeans he'd had for thirty years, Jockey shorts so droopy they wouldn't make decent cleaning rags.

He gathered up the shirts and pants and an armload of socks and gym clothes he'd worn in high school and a black pea jacket Kate had given him when he went away to college in Baltimore. He'd dropped out after only two months, long before it got cold enough to wear the thing. It was heavy and reeked of mildew.

He threw the clothes in the fire. Threw the bedsheets in. Threw in his towels and baseball caps and running shoes and boat shoes and an old Timex Dr. Bill had awarded him at his high school graduation. It was still counting off the seconds when it disappeared into the flames.

Stashed at the bottom of Rusty's lingerie drawer, he found her father's Colt .45. When Rusty was five, the tortured man had pressed that pistol to his temple. Somehow he'd only wounded himself with the first shot and managed to pull the trigger a second time before his skull blew apart. A drunk and compulsive womanizer who couldn't keep a job, he'd beaten Rusty's mother for as long as Rusty could remember. The two gunshots woke Rusty from a nap and she stumbled outside to find the old man's body slumped against her swing-set. Her mother kept the pistol and passed it along to Rusty before she died. A ghastly reminder of the man's final hateful act.

Thorn filled a liquor box with Rusty's underthings and set the pistol on top and carried it out to the fire. He took out the pistol, checked the magazine to make sure it was loaded, and set it on the ground at his feet, then tossed her silkies into the flames.

He watched them crinkle and turn to smoke, then peeled off his shorts and the gray T-shirt he was wearing and slung them into the fire on top of Rusty's stuff. Then he stripped off his undershorts and tossed them too. Let their smoke mingle and rise to the sky, and blow away.

Standing naked and barefoot on the soft grass, Thorn stared into the blaze where something in the pile was releasing streamers of blue and green and yellow, like bright ribbons intertwined in the yellow flames. Birthday bows and frilly Christmas decorations coiling into the dark.

A breeze carried the smoke away and his lungs filled with cleaner air.

He picked up the pistol, lifted it, took aim at the fire.

He fired and fired twice more and then a fourth time and was about to empty the weapon when a car's headlights swept across the yard and settled on him. Whoever it was flicked on their brights and cut the engine.

Thorn, naked, holding a half-empty pistol, had an audience.

Through the smoke and dazzle of the headlights he made out the car door opening and a shadow stepping out.

"Excuse me, sir. Is everything okay?" A woman's voice. A stranger.

Thorn said nothing. She reached back into the car and turned off the headlights and walked slowly across the lawn toward the flames. She appeared to be a blocky woman with short hair, wearing trousers and a loose-fitting shirt.

Thorn stepped around the fire.

"I was driving past and heard the gunfire. Everything all right?"

"Everything's fine. No problem. You can go about your business."

The woman held her ground, head tipped forward, squinting through the smoky darkness.

"Well, you see, that's the thing. I think you may be my business."

"You're wrong. I'm nobody's business."

"Are you Daniel Oliver Thorn?"

He didn't reply.

"Though I believe people just call you Thorn. Am I in the right place?"

"That's my name."

"Whew, I wasn't sure. It's so dark out here, no house numbers."

"It's the middle of the night. What do you want?"

"Valid question, yes, sir, it certainly is. Actually, I hadn't meant to stop. My plane got into Miami late, I picked up my rental, drove down to find a motel, then I thought maybe I'd try to find your place to mark the spot for tomorrow. 'Cause that was my intention, to drop by at a decent hour. But I saw the fire, heard gunshots. No way I could drive on."

"What is this?"

"You're the husband of the late Rachel Anne Stabler, known as Rusty?"

Thorn was silent. His body had hardened, lips too stiff to speak.

"I've caught you at an awkward moment. Buck naked, firing a pistol into a bonfire. Maybe it's normal around here. What you folks do in the Keys, a ritual or whatever. I heard things down here get a little strange. But sir, wouldn't you feel more comfortable putting on a pair of pants? Setting that pistol on the ground. I know I'd be more easy."

There was something wrong with her face. He couldn't make it out in the flickering firelight, bad acne scars or burns.

"What's your name?"

"Well, okay, since I'm here, I guess we could do this now if you want."

"I asked your name."

"All right. My name's Buddha. Buddha Hilton."

"Don't fuck with me."

"No, sir, I'm not doing that. That's my given name. It's strange, yeah. My old man was a New Age lunatic. Buddha was a big deal to him."

"Stand over here where I can see you."

He motioned with Rusty's .45, and the young woman complied, stepping to her left. She had her hands clasped behind her back like a monk in prayerful contemplation.

"Mr. Thorn, you're going to have to put that weapon down. I'm a police officer, and having a gun pointed at me, well, that's something I can't abide."

"You're no police officer."

"Well, yes, sir, actually I am. But I assure you, you're not in any trouble. Certainly nothing that would warrant a shootout."

She smiled at him, but when he didn't return it, hers melted away.

He couldn't place her drawl. Ozarks, perhaps, or maybe rural West.

"You're not old enough to be a cop."

"I'm nineteen."

"Like I said. You're no cop. Now get out of here."

"Yes, sir, it's true, I'm a bit young. Still, where I'm from it's legal age, and nobody wanted the job. Small town, low pay, not much action. But my fellow citizens knew I had an interest in law enforcement, so hell, they got together and elected me."

"Where is that? The place you're from?"

She was silent. She drifted a couple of steps to the right, taking a soft angle in his direction. Arms still behind her back like she was cuffed.

"Most people never heard of my dinky town. Just two stoplights, a cowboy bar, a Dairy Queen, and a Dollar General. But maybe you know it, because your wife, Ms. Stabler, was born there. Starkville, Oklahoma."

SIX

THORN WAS DIGESTING THAT, WATCHING her take another step his way.

"Look, Mr. Thorn, before we get any farther along, you're going to need to set that weapon down."

"If I don't?"

"I don't believe we want to explore that alternative."

"You're here on official business?"

"Call it half and half. Official, and personal."

"Forget it," Thorn said. "You got a problem, I don't give a rat's ass. Take it somewhere else. Get out of here. I don't want any part of this. I've had two lifetimes of problems already."

"I understand. You lost your wife, you're mourning."

"You hear me? Get out of here now. Go haul your ass back to Oklahoma. I don't want anything you're selling."

She stepped closer to Thorn by a few more inches. Her face rippled in the firelight. Pale skin etched with black squiggles.

"That's it," Thorn said. "Cop or no cop."

He raised the pistol. Only to turn her around and get her headed to her car. To show her how serious he was. This was his land; she was trespassing.

He saw the first muzzle flash then heard a roar, and another blast and one more after that. His right hand bucked, and on its own, his arm flew straight up in the air like some eager schoolkid waving for attention.

A whanging pain erupted in his hand as if he'd been hammered with a sledge. Thorn stumbled to his right, his shoulder numb. Rusty's pistol, her dad's suicide gun, was tumbling through the grass.

"Okay, now," she said. "Are we cool?"

"You shot that out of my goddamn hand."

"Didn't give me much choice."

"In the dark."

"Firelight helped. It wasn't that tough a shot."

"You missed twice and kept shooting."

"Missed three times actually."

"Christ, you could've blown my hand off."

"I factored that in."

"That's from some half-assed cowboy movie."

Stepping closer, wary, her pistol raised, a .38.

"Movie gunslingers get it on the first try. This was a little messier than I would've liked."

Thorn's chest was hammering. The ash from the fire stung his eyes and his throat burned with its bitter taste.

"Isn't much crime around Starkville, so I spend a good bit of time out at the shooting range. I got a good eye and a steady aim."

Thorn tried to work his fingers.

"Not steady enough."

"Probably should ice that hand," she said. "Gonna get puffy and sore. Could've broken something. Can you move your fingers?"

"You've done that a lot, have you?"

"No, sir. You're my first. Pictured it a few times, but never had sufficient provocation."

She smiled and the firelight lit up her cheeks. They were covered by strange black hieroglyphics.

Thorn tried to make a fist but couldn't close the hand. No fractures but an ache rooted deep in the tissues.

"There's ice," he said. "Inside."

In the laundry room off the kitchen, Thorn found a bath towel and wrapped it around his waist. He ran cold water over his hand while Buddha scooped ice cubes from the freezer and dumped them into a mixing bowl. She stayed at arm's length, pistol at the ready.

When the bowl was full, Thorn slid his throbbing hand among the cubes and examined the woman in the kitchen lights. Her bangs were ragged across her forehead, the hair butchered on top in no discernible style, and on both sides of her head she was shaved to the scalp. It was as bad a haircut as he'd ever seen, as if she'd barbered herself during a seizure. She had a soft oval face and wide-set dark eyes, a small chin, pretty mouth. Though all of that was hard to make out clearly through the hundreds of tiny markings that were lined up in parallel rows across the pale flesh of her cheeks and forehead like a battalion of insects marching into battle.

"Tattoos," she said. "In case you were wondering."

Thorn hadn't been a fan of tats until Rusty converted him. She had an elegant pink butterfly tribal design inked at the base of her spine, just above her rump, a drawing that Thorn never tired of tracing with his fingertips. It was their own erogenous zone. An elaborate and artful G-spot.

Folks like Rusty with two or three tattoos were simply marking themselves with the sacred symbols of their beliefs. Exercising their individuality. But serious tattoo junkies, the ones who covered themselves from head to toe, were a different breed. To them the hot scratch of the needle became a chemical addiction, and their swirly, colorful designs covering every inch of arms and legs and backs and torsos were topographic maps of their pain.

Rusty believed their secret goal was to disappear behind the murals of embedded ink, to divert the eyes of onlookers to the artwork and away from the sad disclosures of their faces.

But even in the world of tattoo freaks, this young woman was an extreme case. The outlandish tats that disfigured her cheeks and forehead and chin were like a veil drawn across her features, all but hiding her from view.

"Okay, you have my attention," he said. "Ask your questions, then go."

"Thank you."

She took her time. Ambled around the kitchen, appraising the ancient appliances, the tile countertops, the pickled wood cabinetry. Still with the pistol in her hand, she touched a fingertip to a line of grout and traced its straight edge down the length of the counter.

"I'm investigating the homicide of Michaela Stabler."

"Never heard of her."

"Rusty never mentioned the name?"

"Why would she?"

At the side window she halted her tour of the kitchen and stared outside at the bonfire's dying flames.

While she was distracted, Thorn quietly slipped his hand from the bowl of ice and stepped around the counter. He eased behind her, eyes on the pistol held loosely in her hand. He didn't know if she was a cop or not. He didn't know who the hell she was. But she was a stranger, and she was inside his house with a revolver in her hand, and in Thorn's view, that was unacceptable.

He set his feet, timed his move, then snapped his left hand for the gun. But the young woman was wound tighter than she appeared. She slid to her right, chopped the edge of her free hand against his wrist, and danced out of range. She brought the pistol up again to sight on Thorn's face.

"Dude, you're getting old and slow."

Thorn held his ground.

"And so predictable," she said. "Rash and brash just like she said."

"Who said?"

"Rusty Stabler, your wife."

"What the hell do you know about Rusty?"

"I know a good bit about her, and way too much about you."

She was studying him intently as if trying to match his face to some image in her head.

"You don't know shit."

"Okay, for one thing," she said, "I know you've been living off the grid since before there even was a grid."

Thorn tightened the towel around his waist.

"I know you punched the ticket for at least half a dozen people over the years. Always for some righteous cause, of course, or in self-defense.

Maybe the people you took down were bad guys, maybe they weren't, but any way you look at it, you've got serious blood on your hands."

Thorn stepped back to the counter and looked around at the bare room.

"I also know that for the last twenty years, you've been a party to one disaster after another. People around you die on a regular basis.

"I know you had a steady stream of women in and out of your bedroom. And hardly any of those ladies came to a good end. All in all, you've put together an impressive list of fuck-ups."

She stared coolly into his eyes the way Sugarman did when speaking some hard truth. It was a cop thing, that disengagement, a necessary discipline in police work—the way they insulated themselves from all the crazed morons they had to deal with, ones who'd lost contact with reason and moral clarity. Cops tended to go far off in the other direction, becoming coldly rational, neutral, rulebook bound. At least on the outside.

"I also know you tie some kind of fishing lures that you sell to a bunch of fussy fishermen. The cash that brings in just gets you by. And I know you don't have a social security card or a driver's license or any kind of legal ID. You graduated from high school but dropped out of college like you dropped out of pretty much everything. Don't socialize, keep to yourself, a hermit, push everybody away except your private eye buddy Sugarman and an occasional lucky lady. Or at least they think they're lucky at first. Until they're dead because of you."

"That's enough," Thorn said.

"I also know the only reason you legally married Rusty Stabler was 'cause she was dying of stage-four pancreatic cancer and you thought it would make her happy to be married. And it did. It made her damn happy. So mark up one success. You made Rusty Stabler happy for a month. Thank god for that."

Thorn was silent. Peering at her, trying to see past that mask of tats.

"I've heard a lot about you, Mr. Thorn, but now that I have a first-hand look, I believe I'm beginning to get the real picture. Here you are, all tragic and tender and starry-eyed, with your sandy hair and your square jaw and blue Romeo eyes. Which helps explain all those good-hearted, innocent women falling onto your mattress.

"But we both know there's another guy inside, a wild-eyed screwup with a taste for risk and ruination. Just so happens, I spent years studying your type. Mind you, it wasn't because I particularly wanted to.

"My own daddy played your game. A charmer who came across as decent and moral, as upright as any man you ever met. Everything dark and twisted he did always started out with noble intentions.

"A lot of upstanding ladies fell for his act. But it was all a fraud. 'Cause inside that man, in his heart of hearts, he wasn't looking for a woman to love and nurture, he was scouting the next calamity. Women thought he was courting them, but what he was really courting was disaster. Any of that sound familiar?"

"I'm honored," Thorn said. "You came all this way to deliver that rousing speech."

"No, sir. I came all this way because a woman got murdered. A good, honest woman who was more mother to me than my flesh-and-blood mom. She happened to be Rusty's aunt. She and Rusty exchanged e-mail, lots of messages back and forth over the years. Rusty described her life with you, what was going on in her heart. And Michaela Stabler shared some of that with me. So that's why I'm here. A woman was cruelly murdered in my peaceful, law-abiding town. And you, Mr. Thorn, are smack in the middle of it."

Thorn held her eye for several moments, then broke away from her biting gaze and padded into the living room. Only two couches were left. All the small stuff, the chairs, end tables, and bookshelves he'd tossed into the fire. The room seemed bigger, cold and strange.

He sat on the long white couch, tucked the towel close between his legs.

"Don't worry about flashing me," Buddha said. "I already had a good look at that ding-dong. It's nothing special."

Thorn glanced out the French doors into the side yard where the fire was burning low. Dawn coming. A pale russet glow out on the water.

"Rusty had an aunt?"

"Michaela Stabler. She was murdered last Saturday night, July twenty-fourth."

"And you think I had something to do with it."

"I don't think it, I know it to be true."

61

"Because of my blemished past."

"That's one thing. But by itself that wouldn't bring me this far."

"Why did you do that to your face? All those marks."

"I didn't."

"Bullshit."

"What do you say we keep this moving in the right direction?"

Thorn's eyelids were heavy, weariness overtaking him. The all-night purge, the frantic cleansing, the roar in his blood had left him empty. The last fumes of his destructive outburst had burned off. He felt as if he might be slipping into a trance. A long, dreamless vacation from earthly cycles.

Maybe if he chose not to fight it, didn't pinch himself, just drifted off into the beckoning shadows, everything would be over. Everything would go away and he could rest for a month. That's how it felt. Drift away and be done. When he woke and returned to his body and his house, it would all be simple again. As easy as letting his head rest against the soft cushion of the couch. Leave this woman, this room, this new crisis, just drop away and go.

"What do you know about Zentai?"

Thorn straightened, cleared his eyes, looked at this small strange woman.

"Never heard of it."

"How about *Iklwa*? Ever come across that word? Know what it is?"

She was studying his reaction with distrusting eyes.

"Sorry to disappoint you."

"*Iklwa*," she said. "It happens to be an onomatopoeia. Know that?"

"A word that sounds like what it is."

"Good. You're one for three."

"And you're way past pissing me off."

Thorn watched while Buddha craned her head left and right, stretching the tightness from her neck.

"Shaka Zulu. Ever come across that name?"

"African warrior," he said.

"Good, good. Early 1800s, Shaka Zulu invented the *Iklwa*. A thrusting spear. Short, good for working in close. In battle, after Shaka's enemies threw their long spears, his soldiers charged and used their *Iklwas* for close-in killing."

"I have a scholar in my house."

"Not really. All that is, it's about ten minutes of Web surfing."

"Where's your onomatopoeia?"

"*Iklwa*. The slicing sound the spear makes entering the enemy's flesh and the sucking sound when it's pulled out."

"Cheery."

Thorn used his good hand to rub the exhaustion from his face.

"Michaela Stabler was stabbed three times in the belly with a replica of an *Iklwa*. High carbon tempered steel with a brass wire reinforced socket and wood shaft. About four feet long. This particular spear was manufactured in Plainfield, Indiana. And it was purchased in Miami."

"It's always Miami."

"The killer did a half-assed job covering his tracks. The torn-up pieces of the sales receipt for the spear were in a Dumpster outside a local bar. That spear was bought with cash in a Miami sporting goods store two days before Michaela Stabler was stabbed to death."

Thorn was quiet, waiting for the punch line.

"Zentai is a head-to-toe bodysuit usually made out of stretchy material. Sometimes they have zippers that join the head to the body. On the tips of the zipper pulls are eyelets where small steel locks secure one zippered section to another. When the locks are on, the wearer can't escape. Those are the ones sex fetishists wear. S and M. It gets them off, I understand. Covers the whole body, eyes, mouth, everything. They have orgies, like a bunch of mummies rubbing against each other."

"What fun."

"On the night Michaela was murdered, a local woman in Starkville, Susan Hooks, had been drinking in the Blue Heaven, our local tavern. When she exited the bar with a gentleman friend, she observed a person sitting in a vehicle in the parking lot. This person was wearing a body suit, black in color. Ms. Hooks was inebriated, but she was dead certain of what she saw, and she came to the station the next day and told me all about it, thinking it might have something to do with Michaela's murder, which by then was all over town. So I went to the parking lot, performed a search, and found the sales receipt for the spear torn up in little pieces inside the bar's Dumpster."

"And somehow this implicates me?"

"I'm getting to that," she said. "First, there's all the overlapping connections. The spear coming from South Florida, and Rusty's death directly linked to Michaela's."

"Directly?"

With her lips clamped tight, she looked up at the ceiling.

Thorn asked her what the problem was. She looked at him and heaved out an aggravated sigh.

"This is unprofessional, sharing the details of a police matter, but I don't see any way around it."

"I wouldn't want you to be unprofessional. Stop right where you are, get up, march back to your car, and fly away home to lovely Starkville. We'll forget any of this happened."

Buddha rose and began to walk the room. She circled it twice, then started to pace behind the couch. She'd tucked the revolver back into the holster under the tail of her bulky white shirt. Like her gray, baggy trousers, her shirt was a size too large, as if she meant to conceal the shape of her body.

She halted directly in front of him, standing in the darkened rectangle on the ancient blue rug where for decades the coffee table had blocked sunlight from a nearby window. That cherry table had been holding that same position until about an hour ago. Now it was smoke riding out to sea.

Buddha rubbed a fingertip along one of the lines of tiny black characters that marked her forehead. In the brighter light of the living room Thorn decided the tattoos resembled letters, some language he didn't recognize, Sanskrit or Icelandic.

"It's nuts, confiding in you," she said. "You with your fucked-up history. One disaster after another all your adult life."

"You being the latest."

A hint of a smile came to her lips but faded quickly.

"All right, go on. Make your pitch. You're going to anyway."

She muttered to herself, some pet curse, then gave him a quick probing look as if taking one last assessment of Thorn's character before she dove in.

Her eyes toured his face. There was worry in them, worry and an ancient hurt, but he also saw the bright flicker of intelligence, the kind that was neither crafty nor clever, but was more sturdy and solidly rooted. For all her strangeness and backwoods demeanor, this was a very smart lady.

She looked down at the floor between them and sighed, deeply dismayed she had to rely on the likes of Thorn.

"Okay, it's like this," she said. "The morning after Michaela's murder, the FBI sent a forensics team from Dallas, and they spent the day at her house doing their usual thing. Examined the scene, dusted for prints, took DNA samples, bagged a piece of physical evidence the killer left behind. They removed the *Iklwa* spear and sent it for tests. They appeared to be acting professionally, in good faith."

Thorn stayed quiet.

"But I'm not buying their act."

"You don't trust the FBI?"

"Not on this one. Not even a little bit."

Buddha came over, settled on the couch beside him. Her scent was flowery with a smoky edge, as though she'd been burning sticks of patchouli incense in her car. While Thorn massaged his aching hand, she drew a piece of paper from her hip pocket and unfolded it, pressing out the creases against her thigh.

She lay the newsprint on the table before him.

"If you don't mind, I'd like to use your facilities. Freshen up a little. I thought Julys were hot in Starkville, but you folks got yourselves some prizewinning humidity down here."

"Down the hall on the left."

Thorn sat for several moments looking at the news clipping. He could see from the headline that it was an obituary for Rusty's aunt.

He understood full well that once he picked it up and read the story, he was a goner. That's why she'd left it. A temptation she must have known he would be unable to resist.

THE OKLAHOMAN

Tuesday, July 27

Michaela Miranda Stabler, Notorious Defense Attorney

By Randolph Whitlock

Michaela Miranda Stabler, who spent over thirty years vigorously defending some of the most infamous scoundrels, rapists and killers in Oklahoma, Texas and Arkansas, died last week of wounds suffered in a violent attack that took place in her own home.

Sheriff B. Hilton of Starkville reported that Michaela (known as Mickey to her friends) had never been concerned about her own security. "Even though she'd gotten death threats for years, like everybody in Starkville, she kept her doors unlocked and was welcoming to friend or foe alike."

Because of her extraordinary record in successfully defending high-profile clients, she'd made a great many enemies, although there were those, like Circuit Court Judge Edwin J. White, who had great respect for her legal talent. "Lots of people despised Mickey because she was so damn good at her job, which was finding the weak points in prosecution cases. She had a way with juries too. Down-home delivery, very wry lady, look you in the eye, speak intelligently. She never talked down to jurors, didn't fake anything. And the woman was brave. She didn't shy away from taking on the most disagreeable cases. She liked to say she wasn't trying to get elected to office, so she could damn well be as unpopular as she wanted. I've seen a lot of lawyers in my time, but Michaela's A-game was as good as the best I ever witnessed."

Michaela Stabler was educated at the University of Oklahoma and completed her law degree at UCLA in 1971. As a young attorney, she worked for a while in the public defender's office in Oklahoma City, then moved back home to Starkville and opened her own practice.

"She was idealistic and positive," Sheriff Hilton said. "But she was a realist too. She knew all about evil and depravity, but she believed great defense lawyers made America stronger. That's what she wanted, to set a high standard and do her part to improve the entire justice system."

It wasn't long after she opened her own practice that she started winning cases. She defended abortion doctors and drunk drivers and alleged child abusers and bank robbers, all with equal dedication. Before long criminal defendants were coming from all over the tri-state area to enlist Michaela's help.

Bobby Boggs was one of those. In 1988 Boggs, 66, was arrested by the FBI in Dallas and charged in the rape and murder of nine high school girls ranging in age from 13 to 18. He was reviled in the press, tried, convicted and hung out to dry in editorials all around the state. The government's case included DNA evidence, eyewitness testimony and a signed confession by Bobby Boggs as well as a video surveillance tape of what appeared to be an abduction of Cindy Mellon, one of the nine girls whose body was found buried in a field close to Boggs' home. It seemed that the state attorney had an overwhelming case against Bobby Boggs.

But Boggs' trial, which lasted six months, ended in a hung jury. The retrial was also unsuccessful. "Mickey picked apart the FBI's case, nit by nit," said Judge White. "The video was murky. It might've been Boggs or it might've been a hundred other men. There were serious problems in the FBI's lab where the DNA was evaluated. Samples contaminated, bad labeling practices. Not just technicalities but full-scale incompetence. And the two eyewitnesses turned out to be about as reliable as drunks on a monthlong bender. Bobby walked. And Mickey had some choice words for the nincompoop prosecutors. Didn't make a lot of friends on that one."

In recent years, Michaela Stabler earned great enmity from law enforcement personnel throughout the region when she successfully defended a series of "cop killers." Police unions and federal prosecutors were uniformly outraged at Ms. Stabler's aggressive defense of several defendants charged with violent crimes, including premeditated murder and rape against officers of the law. "She specialized in scum," said Jerry Jeff Peters, special agent in charge of the Dallas field office. "Now she's got to face her Lord and Maker, and I think she's going to have a hard time talking her way out of that one."

But there was another side to Michaela Stabler that few ever saw.

"Mickey had an enormous heart," Sheriff Hilton said. "She took care of people, the elderly, the sick and the helpless. She donated most of her weekends to hospice work for people around southeastern Oklahoma. She never made a big deal out of it, but in her private time, she was a generous, loving lady. Sitting by sickbeds, running errands for the families of sick folks and drawing up wills pro bono for the dying. Mickey gave great consolation to the people of the Starkville area."

Sheriff Hilton had firsthand experience of Mickey's altruism. A dozen years ago Michaela Miranda Stabler took 7-year-old Buddha Hilton into her home and became her legal guardian after Hilton's own father was jailed for vicious acts of child abuse. She defended the abuser, then adopted the abused. "Mickey lost that case," White stated, "but in the end she won a beautiful girl child."

Friends gathered in Stabler's home for a farewell party last Thursday. "A couple of hundred people showed up, including about fifty protestors," said Judge Edwin White. "But even with all those ugly signs marching on the sidewalk outside, the ceremony that went on within those walls was beautiful. I wish all those folks who so despised Mickey could have heard the testimony about her good works, and seen her home overflowing with love."

SEVEN

THE DOOR WAS OPEN TO the guest bathroom, and Buddha Hilton was standing at the sink staring at her reflection. Her eyes were muddy and there was a faint shiver in her chin. Thorn stayed in the doorway.

"You okay?"

"I'm fine," she said. "Fine and dandy."

"You don't look so dandy."

She nodded at her reflection.

"Talk to me, Buddha. Go ahead."

"It just this minute hit me. I've never been this distance from home. Never had occasion to. Never flew on a jet plane, never rented a car, never did much of anything people my age do. And this damn face. Back home people don't give a second glance, so I kind of stop thinking about it, how messed up it is. But today folks were sneaking looks. Some outright gawkers too; a couple followed me down the concourse, taking pictures with their phones. I kept my head down, kept moving. But just now, when I walked in here, turned on the light, it busted me in the gut. How damn strange it all is."

"Your father did that to your face?"

Staring at her image, it took a moment for her to muster the words.

"From the age of three till I was six. He put it on little by little. All I remember is wailing, looking up at his face and wailing. Not much else."

"Where was your mother when this was happening?"

"Ran off with some crackhead even crazier than my old man."

"Then someone discovered what he was doing and he was arrested."

"Social worker saw me playing out in the front yard one afternoon."

"Rusty's aunt defended him."

"That's right."

"Why?"

"That was Mickey. That's what she did, took on the cases no one else wanted. From what I heard Mickey did a damn fine job. But the jury wasn't buying it."

"Guy still in jail?"

"Paroled, living in California last I knew. I haven't wasted my time tracking the sad old man."

She ran a finger across a red line that had been hidden by her bangs. The skin was puckered and inflamed like a bad rash.

"Had some of it lasered off last month," she said. "All I could afford. It costs a hell of a lot more to get rid of the shit than it cost to put it there."

"Seems to work that way with a lot of things."

On the morning Thorn and Rusty headed out for their last fishing trip, she'd stood before that same mirror and had taken a long look at her shrunken face and groaned at the image. Thorn had tried to reassure Rusty that she was still a beautiful woman. A very beautiful woman. It was true, but his saying it gave her no consolation.

Since she'd died, Thorn had been avoiding that guest bathroom. But no matter how hard he tried, he kept butting into fresh memories of her tucked in every corner of the house. Echoes of her voice, wisps of her scent.

It dawned on him right then that all his fire building today might be a gradual buildup toward burning down this house. Obliterating the ghosts once and for all, Rusty's and all the others.

"You see what it is? My tats."

Buddha brought her face close to the mirror and Thorn leaned in beside her and squinted at her reflection.

"Jesus. Is that English?"

"It's backward. Mirror image."

"What is it? Why?"

"The old man wanted to be sure every time I looked in the mirror I'd have to deal with it. He thought females were vain and he was determined I wouldn't be. That part worked. No mirrors in my house. Not a one."

Thorn leaned closer to her reflection.

"I can't make it out."

"When I was a kid it was clearer. But as the years pass the skin stretches and it goes more and more out of focus."

Thorn waited in silence.

"Ever heard of Buddha's Four Noble Truths?"

"Not really."

"First sermon Buddha gave, he did it at Benares right after he attained enlightenment. It's all about suffering. The foundation of that entire religion."

She pointed at her forehead, then moved her finger as she spoke.

"Karma and reincarnation. How deeds, good or bad, shape your next life. Right cheek is how desire causes all suffering. Wanting stuff, hungering for things, how yearning makes for problems. Left cheek is how we should abandon desire, and the chin, that's about following the Noble Eightfold Path.

"The old man was all set to ink the whole damn Eightfold Path on the rest of my body but they caught him before he got that far, so I guess I'm lucky."

She held his gaze in the mirror. Her eyes had cleared and the sadness had receded. In a moment of weakness, she'd wandered off into the past, into a morass of emotion that had almost swallowed her, and now she was climbing out of that dark pool, shrugging off its aftereffects. He could see her cop face resurfacing, the stubborn mouth, the jut of chin and lower lip.

"It pains me to admit it, but I need your help, Thorn."

"I'm listening."

"But right up front we got to get one thing clear between us."

"Okay."

"I'm not interested in crawling into your bed. Not now, not ever."

Thorn willed away a smile.

"Understood."

"Good."

"You must've tried makeup. That didn't cover it?"

"Oh, sure I can cover it over," she said. "But it's all still there."

Thorn was silent.

"Just like I used to go by my initial, 'B.' People would call me that, but that didn't feel right either. Same as the makeup. No matter how strange it is, my name is my name. My face is what it is. I can't run from it."

At that moment when she smiled, she struck him as utterly indomitable. A woman less than half his age who had fathomed depths of hurt that Thorn could not imagine.

"What can I do for you?"

"Wait here. I need to get something."

She brushed past him and walked down the hall and out the front door. By the time she returned, Thorn had located a pair of blue jeans and a yellow T-shirt on a high shelf in his boyhood bedroom. The jeans were snug and the Caribbean Club shirt was musty and torn, but still an improvement over the towel.

He was making a pot of coffee when she came in the kitchen door with a brown paper sack.

She set it on the floor by the white-tiled island and brought out a Ziploc plastic bag and lay it on the countertop. An evidence bag that contained what looked like a piece of newsprint.

"Take a look. Tell me what you see. Take it out of the bag if you want. Handle it. It's already been through forensics. Nothing helpful on it."

He opened the plastic seal and took out the obituary that April Moss had written about Rusty Stabler. Someone had scissored the edges into a sawtooth pattern.

"I've already seen this. It was in the *Herald* a week and a half ago."

"I found it lying on the bedside table next to Mickey Stabler's body."

Thorn read a few sentences and set the newsprint on the counter.

"So Michaela had an obituary of her niece. Doesn't seem strange. Though the ragged edges, that's a little odd."

"We'll get to the ragged edges," Buddha said.

She dug in the paper sack again and came out with an electronic tablet.

Sugarman had the same kind. He read books on it, sent e-mail, surfed the Web. He'd tried to interest Thorn in its marvels but the gizmo seemed silly. Why would you trust hundreds of books to the memory of some flimsy gadget that could be destroyed with a hard knock? Real books were solid. Part of their beauty was the way they endured the rough-and-tumble years, how their smell evolved, the changing texture of their pages as they aged. Like every organic thing, books matured and decayed, on roughly the same journey as the people who read them.

She brought the tablet to life and did some one-finger typing on its glass surface until she had the screen she wanted.

She handed it to Thorn.

A video was running, a movie or TV show, Thorn couldn't tell. A person dressed in an iridescent blue bodysuit was sneaking up behind a man seated at an office desk. There was ominous music playing, violins, a cello, and scratchy percussions. It was nighttime. The guy was working late. He was hunched over paperwork, scribbling in the margins with a pen. The picture window across from the man showed a panoramic view of a city skyline twinkling against a black sky. The lights were gaudy, the blue, pink, and aquamarine skyscrapers of downtown Miami. But the office guy wasn't looking at the view or he might've noticed the reflection of the intruder sneaking up behind him.

The man's cell phone rang. As he reached to answer it, the blue man moved swiftly, looping a wire over the businessman's head and clenching it tight around his throat. A garrote. The man thrashed, waved his arms, but it was over quick. When his head slumped to one side and blood began to darken his white collar, the blue killer released the wire. He left it around the man's throat and stepped away.

He drew out a piece of paper from somewhere in his blue suit, then leaned around the dead man and lay the newsprint on the desk next to the man's documents.

The camera moved in close to the news clipping.

Its edges were cut in the same sawtooth pattern as Rusty's obituary.

Filling the screen, its headline came into focus for a second or two. A woman named Ethel Rosen from Homestead, Florida, had died and left a large and surprising sum of money to some charity.

The screen went dark.

Thorn set the electronic tablet down on the counter.

"Season one, episode two. A cable show on the Expo Channel. It's called *Miami Ops*. I don't suppose you've seen it."

"Don't own a TV," he said. "Stuck in the Dark Ages."

"Well, I've watched a couple of episodes. The female lead is an airhead. Whole thing's silly and not all that suspenseful either."

"Everybody's a critic."

She picked up the electronic tablet and slipped it back in her sack.

"So that's Zentai? That suit?"

She said yes, that was Zentai.

"How'd you find out about this show?"

"Tracked it down on the Internet. Used a bunch of search terms. 'Obituary.' 'Jagged edge.' 'Saw blade.' Didn't take but two minutes before *Miami Ops* popped up. I read the webpage, the reviews, and bingo."

"Somebody's copycatting a TV show."

"That's how it looks."

"Why?"

"There have to be a why? Crazy people do crazy things."

Thorn shook his head.

"In my long, sordid history, I've had the misfortune of running into a few psychos. Several qualified as full-blown crazy. Insane in the membrane. But they always have a why. What they do makes perfect sense to them."

She nodded, not buying it entirely but taking it under consideration.

"Because Mickey defended cop killers, you don't trust law enforcement, not even the FBI."

"Oh, parts of the FBI I trust just fine. On the national level, they don't give a hoot if Mickey Stabler defended cop killers. That's a local issue. The Oklahoma state police weren't fond of her. Agent in charge in the Dallas field office, Jerry Jeff Peters, he loathed Mickey. He was cheering when he found out she died, I'm sure of that. But national level, no. Quantico, no."

Thorn watched her arrange herself on one of the kitchen stools as if she was settling in for a long stay.

"Familiar with ViCAP?"

Thorn shook his head.

"All your brushes with the law, I thought you might've run across it. Well, what it is, the FBI has a nationwide program to help small-town sheriffs like me. The Critical Incident Response Group at Quantico. They run ViCAP, which is short for Violent Criminal Apprehension Program.

"After Michaela's murder, I got permission to use their database. It's where local crime reports across the country are filed and collated and analyzed. A cop like me out in the boonies, if I want to check if there've been similar cases anywhere in the U.S., I punch in a description of the crime I'm dealing with, I can even use specific search words, 'obituary,' 'ragged edge,' 'spear,' 'Zentai,' *'Iklwa,'* any term you can think of, and the computer spits out comparable crimes in other jurisdictions.

"Of course, for it to spit out something, that something had to be entered in the first place, meaning the local law enforcement agency, the cops in New Orleans or Miami or wherever, number one they had to notice an obituary left behind at a murder scene; and number two, if they noticed it, they had to put it into their report as worthy of attention; then number three, somebody had to scan that report and enter it into the ViCAP database.

"So that's where things break down. Understaffed, underfunded local law enforcement, cops getting lazy, cops overworked, cops not paying attention. The computer is fine. It doesn't care if Michaela defended cop killers, the computer plays fair."

Thorn said, "So this ViCAP database, it didn't have anything."

"Not a damn thing. Not Zentai, not ragged edge, not obituary."

"Then maybe it's not what you think. Maybe Mickey got her niece's obituary off a newsstand."

Buddha shook her head.

"No, sir, the nearest place Mickey could've found a copy of the Miami paper was Dallas or Oklahoma City, hours away. From Monday when the obituary appeared till Saturday when Mickey was murdered, Mickey was at home preparing for a case. I visited with her every single day. She read that Miami obituary same place I did. Online. And she didn't leave her house except for groceries just once. No, sir, the killer left that behind. It's his signature. A taunt. Right out of a crummy TV show."

"You're sure of that."

"Damn sure."

Thorn looked down at the place at the kitchen counter where he'd gravitated out of habit.

Over the years at that very spot, he'd prepared a thousand meals. Cut up hundreds of avocados and must've made a few tons of guacamole, as well as countless burritos and fish tacos, and lots of margaritas. For a second he flashed on all that wonderful food and drink, and the nights he and Rusty had wolfed down tortillas smothered in cheese and enchilada sauce, top-shelf tequila and Cointreau and lime juice. The giddy evenings dancing in the kitchen to music that one of them started humming. This room, this countertop, these walls had borne witness to some of Thorn's best moments, some of his happiest hours with Rusty and Sugarman and others. And now this. This young woman with her tortured past, her spoiled face, and her bulldog resolve. The scorched smell of the bonfire pervading the room.

"I'm going up to Miami tomorrow, talk to the obituary writer."

"Why?"

"She's the logical next step."

"What kind of logic is that?"

"April Moss has two boys," Buddha said. "Both work on *Miami Ops*. One writes the show, the other's an actor in it."

Thorn touched the edge of Rusty's obituary.

"Well, that's too coincidental to be a coincidence."

"Had the same thought. It's that nexus again. The killer's home-based in Miami. The murder weapon was bought there, the TV show is shot there, the newspaper is from there."

"And you want me to be your tour guide, show you the big city?"

"You willing?"

"You strike me as a lone wolf, Sheriff Hilton."

"I am."

"Then why gum up the works with me?"

"Well, for one thing, I thought you might make excellent bait."

"Bait?"

"Somebody's got a strong interest in you, Thorn. I don't know who or why. But I'd like to dangle you in front of as many people as I can, see whose eyes light up. Maybe somebody'll even try to take a bite."

"What're you talking about?"

"It's there on your wife's obituary. Turn it over."

Thorn sighed and did as instructed.

On the flip side of the obituary was a portion of the society page. In the margin beside the pictures of men and women in tuxedos, pearls, stiff poses, and manufactured smiles, his name was printed in all caps. **THORN.**

In bold black ink, someone had traced and retraced the letters four or five times—the way a kid with a crush will spell out the name of his true love, bearing down again and again in the same grooves.

"I don't get it."

"Looks to me like somebody's got the hots for you."

"You did this," Thorn said.

"No, sir. I promise you I did not."

"Then Mickey did it. She knew about me through Rusty."

"That was my first thought. But we can rule that out."

"Why?"

"I know this is weird, but Mickey had a thing about the color purple. Don't know why. I questioned her about it several times, but she never said. Started in her childhood, is all I know. She had pens galore. Fountain pens, razor points, felt-tips, ballpoints. Always jotting down notes, marking up the margins of her books. All her pens had purple ink. Every single pen in her house. Not a red or a blue or a black to be found. And believe me, I looked. Searched top to bottom. Purple ink, every single one."

"I don't believe this."

"Believe it, Thorn. It was on her bedside table, just like that. Mickey lying there dead, and your name on the back of your wife's obituary. The way it's printed, going over and over the same lines, well, it doesn't take a genius to figure out whoever the killer is, he's got a powerful interest in you."

ACT TWO

PURPLE
BASEBALL BAT

EIGHT

OUT IN THE GRASSY CENTER of the Floridian courtyard Gus Dollimore and the director of photography were staring up at the clouds. Not long ago April Moss wouldn't have known why. But she did now.

For the last week she'd been getting an education in the finer points of TV production while several scenes from *Miami Ops* were being shot at the nursing home where her mother was rehabbing from knee surgery. Gus and the cameramen were looking up at the sky because they were waiting for the sun to move past a sucker hole in the clouds and give them a few minutes of precious sunlight, enough to go ahead and shoot their next scene. Natural light, as Gus liked to say, was a fickle bitch.

Set back twenty yards from where the scene would take place, and a few feet behind the canvas directors chairs and the cameras and the lights, were about twenty of the elderly residents of the Floridian nursing home, most of them in wheelchairs. For them this was the day's recreation. Instead of falling asleep in front of their favorite game shows, they could drift off watching a real TV show being made.

As April crossed the yard, she spotted her mother sitting stiffly in her wheelchair parked in the back row of the audience. She picked her way through the crowd, settled into a folding chair beside her mom, and said hello, but Garvey Moss was in a sour mood and didn't reply.

Since coming to the Floridian after a double knee replacement, Garvey had been in a major funk. Not doing her leg lifts, or riding the stationary bike. Refusing to walk. The pain was intolerable and the pain pills made her stupid. The stubborn woman wouldn't budge from her wheelchair.

A full minute ticked away before she acknowledged April.

"TV people stand around more than road crews," Garvey said. "Twenty idiots watching one guy shovel dirt. No wonder everything's falling apart. All those people getting paid, nobody working. Just twiddling their peckers."

Garvey Moss. Seventy-five years old, but with the zest and looks of a woman twenty years younger. Her black hair hung long and straight halfway down her back—not a trace of gray. The same genetic good fortune kept her skin clear and unwrinkled and her brown eyes laser guided. April could only hope Garvey had passed on a coil or two of that DNA. The next few years would tell.

"If I had a say," Garvey said, "my grandbabies wouldn't be mixed up in such a silly business. Those boys would have real jobs where they got dirt under their fingernails and grease on their faces. End of the day, they'd have something to show for what they did. Something solid."

"The boys are happy with their work, so you should be happy, Mom."

April looked around at the rest of the audience. Most were a decade older than Garvey. Well into their dotage, parked at the nursing home for the duration. To her left a woman in a green bathrobe was clutching a stuffed dog to her chest and whispering in its tattered ear. Two chairs down a gentleman was hunched over, playing with the zipper of his tartan plaid pants.

Most seemed to be lost to one degree or another in the same demolished confusion, as if they'd been dropped into their chairs from some bewildering height. All the glowing particulars of their life histories had turned to smoke within them. In the last few days, April had met two or three who were capable of bright gurgles of memory, a smile, a coherent sentence. But most had moved into a postverbal state and seemed to be waiting patiently in this strange outpost for some major organ to fail.

It had been Garvey's choice to rehab at the Floridian. The complex was near the home they shared along the Miami River, but more important, that venerable institution had occupied the same thick-walled stucco building for over eighty years. Garvey Moss had a deep affection for all things connected to Old Miami, and she'd made it one of her crusades to support any enterprise in the city that had lasted half a century.

To April, the Floridian resembled one of those tacky mom-and-pop roadside motels her parents frequented when she was a kid. The place hadn't been updated since cars had fins. Ancient air conditioners chugged in the windows, dripping rusty water steadily onto the terrazzo floors while overhead squeaking ceiling fans idled. On the grounds were a couple of coral fountains full of green slime and a broad lawn, and in a wing at the back was a gym with some unused weights and treadmills, as if the room existed only to pass some state regs. All in all, the Floridian was more funky than charming, with gummy stains on the carpets and ammonia wafting from the shadows.

Even after a scouting visit had turned up the sad state of the place, Garvey was adamant. If she had to suffer through weeks of physio, then by god, the least she could do was support that rare occurrence in Miami, historic preservation.

"Have you been walking today, Mother?"

"I walked ten miles, then ten more. I ran two marathons after that."

"What'd you have for lunch?"

"Cream of vomit soup," she said.

"Oh, come on. I've tasted the food. It's not that bad."

"Everything's from a can. You like it so much, you stay, roll around in this chair. We'll pull a switcheroo."

"Just a few days more. Suck it up, Mom."

"Food's so salty, I'm puffed up like a water buffalo in rainy season."

She thumped a finger on April's wrist and pointed at a man leaning against a column in the breezeway across the courtyard.

"Now there's my type. Gary Cooper meets Rambo. I've been winking at him, but he's a little shy, pretending not to notice."

April glanced at the blond man, then did a double take. A face immediately familiar. There was a sudden hitch in her pulse, dampness on her palms. Sawyer walked past the blond man, coming out of the main complex, script in hand, chatting with one of his assistants, looked over, saw April, and waved. April waved back.

"This place is a geriatric tar pit," Garvey said. "I must have been out of my mind. I should've left my knees alone. Just hobbled off into the sunset like every other gimpy dowager. Why'd you let me do this to myself?"

"You couldn't make it up the stairs to your room, Mother."

"I should've installed an elevator. Or moved to the maid's room on the first floor. Slept on that old purple couch. It's perfectly comfortable."

"It's done now. You'll just have to deal with it."

"I'm going home. I'm sick of this place."

"You need therapy, Mother. Your muscles are going to atrophy."

"You can't hold me prisoner. I'll call a cab, come home on my own."

"Tell the truth. Are you really that unhappy?"

"Unhappy? I hate this place. Look around, it's full of dead people."

Garvey was silent for a minute, rubbing at the ache in her thighs. April watched a young woman in jeans kneel down beside an elderly lady in a nearby wheelchair. Both with the same distinctive jawline—another mother/daughter team. The girl spoke into her mother's ear, but the ancient lady stared helplessly ahead at the buildings across the street.

That scene was April's future, Garvey's future, everyone's damn future.

"His name is Thorn. He's available. His wife just died."

April's pulse threw an extra beat, then another.

Inside her purse her phone vibrated, but April ignored it.

She snuck a look at the man still lounging in the breezeway. Apparently he hadn't spotted her. He was speaking to a person standing beside him. Male or female, hard to tell. Short and blocky, loose-fitting clothes. Bad haircut and a dirty face. Relax, she told herself. Take a breath, no reason to freak.

Thorn was watching the TV crew block the next scene, Dee Dee Dollimore and a male actor standing in the shade while their personal assistants directed handheld fans at their faces and dabbed white washcloths at the sweat sheening their skin. Out in the sun, two stand-ins were holding the actors' positions, giving the cameramen and light guys a chance to adjust their settings.

Thorn.

April was the reason he was here. The obituary she'd written about

Rusty Stabler had lured him back into her orbit. He'd come to thank her, reconnect, ask her out, or something else.

This was entirely April's fault. Of all the people who'd died last week, she'd chosen to fill her limited space with Thorn's wife. Not that Rusty hadn't deserved coverage. She was a notable woman. From humble roots she'd ended up wielding major political and economic power. Outsider becomes insider. Disenfranchised daughter of single mom turns into a major benefactor for the very school that almost ground her to dust.

But April easily could have skipped her. She called the shots on what went in. Naturally Thorn was in her mind when she wrote the piece. On some level she must have been trying to draw him back into her life. God, how absolutely crazy. Look what she'd done. She'd thought about it often, Thorn showing up again, but now that it was happening, she was totally unprepared.

She considered bolting. Race home, lock herself in, take no calls. Forget her mother and go into hiding. But no, of course she couldn't do that. She was an adult. There was some way to manage this. There had to be.

"And how do you know the man's name, Garvey?"

"He's from Key Largo. A girl who used to live down there is a nurse in this shit hole. She told us about Thorn when he walked in the rec room after lunch. He's famous in the Keys. Everybody knows him. He's a roughneck and a lady killer. I said he sounded like just your type."

"You said that in public?"

"I say everything in public."

"What's he doing here?"

"Wants to talk to you. Called your office at the paper, they couldn't locate you, someone suggested you might be here, visiting your poor suffering mother. He's here to interrogate you, dear. It's all very mysterious. There's a woman with him with tattoos all over her face. She's a cop. They're investigating something you did a long time ago in your checkered past."

"Stop it, Mother."

April's phone vibrated again. She pulled it from her purse, checked the ID. Isaac, her assignment editor.

"Don't answer it."

"It's work."

"And I'm your mother. What's more important?"

April slid the phone back into her purse.

"Somebody famous must have died."

"They don't have to be famous, Mother. You know that."

"Have you started writing mine? Before you do, I need to fill you in on the early years. A lot of raunchy stuff happened before you barged onto the scene. I was a party girl, you know. I could shake that thing."

Garvey deemed April's job at *The Miami Herald* shamefully beneath her abilities. April had an undergrad degree from Duke in American lit, did two years at Columbia's School of Journalism, followed by a decade with the *Herald* exposing the frauds and bamboozlers who gorged at the public trough. No journalistic challenge there. In Miami, muckraking was fish-in-the-barrel stuff. The town had been so saturated in corruption for so many years, you couldn't take a step without the mire oozing between your toes.

After a decade and dozens of scandals, April came to the uneasy conclusion that she'd been writing the same story over and over, only changing the names and making adjustments in the cash amounts. When the obit job opened, she nabbed it. She wanted off the street, out of the courtroom, away from the primping TV gaggle.

It didn't take long to realize she'd stumbled into writers' heaven. Obits were gold. A major challenge to her writing skills—trying to capture the human dignity of common people in a few hundred words, the long arc of hard work, family trials, and the triumphs along the way. Short prose poems of lives well spent and those tragically frittered away. The writing was elliptical, like Japanese painting, just the essential bones to suggest the full-bodied existence of a complex person.

"You don't think he's handsome? Now, that's exactly the reason you're still single. Those snooty standards. I don't know where you got that bad trait. Certainly not from me. When it came to men, I could lower my standards at the drop of a pair of trousers."

"Look, I have to go. I'll be back after dinner, Mom. Do your exercises, okay? Stop giving the therapists a hard time."

"Well, if you're not interested in the bad boy," Garvey said, "then I'm staking claim."

As she lifted her purse and started to rise, April saw him coming. The man from Key Largo named Thorn.

She settled back into her chair. This was manageable. It had to be.

He was taller than she remembered, blonder and more wide shouldered. While he was on his way through the maze of wheelchairs, the white-haired gentleman in plaid pants reached up to pluck Thorn's sleeve. Thorn stopped and the two shared a quick conversation that ended in a mutual laugh, then he came on, his eyes on April, a guileless look of familiarity as though the two of them had a long and chummy history.

When he was standing before the Moss women, he looked at Garvey.

"Excuse me, ma'am. I'm sorry if I've misread anything, but were you winking at me?"

"Oh, goody," Garvey said. "Stand back, April, I saw him first."

"So you *were* winking?"

"Is that a problem?" April's tone surprised her, sounding more hostile than she intended.

Thorn shifted his gaze to her.

"No problem at all." His voice was neutral but his eyes were not.

"My daughter is a newspaper reporter," Garvey said. "It's her job to be a hardass. Me, I'm used to it by now, but it puts normal people off."

Thorn smiled at Garvey, then his eyes drifted back to April. Very blue, and in that dazzle of sunlight, turning even bluer.

Thorn turned to the odd-looking woman beside him and was about to introduce her when Gus Dollimore's assistant, the first AD, clapped his hands and made a piercing two-finger whistle.

"Thank you, everyone. We need quiet please. Picture up. Get to your places. Very quiet on the set, please."

The director of photography bent forward, slipped his head under a dark cloak shrouding the monitor's screen from the sunlight.

"This time stay wide," the DP called to the cameraman. "Open up a half stop. Okay, now open up another crack. And would you please get that young lady out of Billy's sight line."

The DP waved at one of the Floridian nurses who had positioned herself in the line of vision of an actor in the upcoming scene. A potential distraction once the scene got started, her eyes attracting his.

Dollimore called out, "Okay, we're rolling. Let's get this on the first try, what do you say? Very quiet please. Let's hear a pin drop. Thank you, people. Cell phones off, iPhones, iPads, BlackBerries, Cranberries, and switch off those vibrators, boys and girls. Whatever you got, turn it off."

The scene required eight takes. By then Thorn had memorized the lines of both actors. The gentleman who was playing the manager of the old-age home rendered his part flawlessly. But the young slender woman with short black hair managed to mangle her brief speech or botch the pronunciation of a word seven times in a row.

She was decked out in a painfully tight sleeveless dress that showed off her ballet dancer's legs and a pair of biceps that she hadn't gotten from lifting china teacups to her lips.

During one break, Buddha leaned close and whispered, "Dee Dee Dollimore, the airhead I mentioned."

Finally, when the actress managed to speak her three lines without a hitch, something was wrong with the light. A cloud passed across the sun in the middle of the scene and the whole thing had to be reshot.

Thorn and Buddha stood together a couple of yards behind April and her mother. Twice April glanced back at him, and she kept shifting in her seat, as if she was considering a dash for the exit.

The director was a lean man in his fifties, with dark hair cut short. Between takes the guy bounced up from his chair, totally wired, talking nonstop to the actors, the cameramen, the guys holding the lights, the sound technicians, anybody and everybody, until the cameras were rolling again.

In the chair beside the director was a sandy-haired kid who sat placidly through all the screwups, rarely looking up from a script that lay open in his lap.

During one of the breaks, Buddha nodded at the relaxed young man and whispered in Thorn's ear, "One of April's twins. Sawyer."

She'd brought along her electronic tablet and she tipped it so Thorn could view the screen. It showed a webpage for the TV show, *Miami Ops*, publicity shots of the cast and the director, whose name was Gus. She slid her finger along the screen and advanced the pages until she came to Sawyer, the show's head writer. A handsome kid with stylishly scruffy hair, dark blue eyes, strong jaw, and a twinkle of mirth on his lips. Looked like a young Viking who hadn't experienced battle yet.

"And his brother," Buddha said. "Flynn. One of the leads."

Again she slid her finger across the screen until another face appeared.

Clearly Sawyer's twin. Almost perfectly identical. His hair was trimmed precisely and was a shade blonder than Sawyer's. His face fuller by a fraction, but the real divergence was in the eyes. Flynn could pass for a fair-haired Viking too, but this kid was clearly a veteran of some battlefield or another. Whatever nasty shit he'd witnessed was lingering in the stern set of his brow, and in his jaw, which was clamped like a man bracing for some jolt he saw coming from a long way off.

When the shooting was finally done, the Floridian's pink-coated staff emerged from the shadows of the building and began to wheel the old folks back inside. The film crew started buzzing around, breaking down the set.

Off to Thorn's right, the old gentleman in plaid pants who had tugged on Thorn's sleeve to mumble something about how damn hot it was rose up from his wheelchair, hopped forward, tilted his face to the sky, and began to howl like a deranged wolf.

The action in the courtyard ceased.

The old guy stumbled into the open grassy area and raised his palms to the sky as if to address the Almighty.

"All right, horndogs, turn your vibrators back on," the old man called out in a croaky voice. "Whatever you got, turn it on, baby. Turn it on."

He basked in the stunned silence for a moment, then he brought his hands to his face and began to peel away a rubbery film—the mask of wrinkles he'd been wearing.

Most of the crew laughed as Flynn Moss revealed his youthful face and swiveled around for the entire assembly to admire his prank.

Some of the Floridian staff applauded enthusiastically—oh those Hollywood cutups. Thorn watched as Sawyer shook his head at his brother's stunt with a smile of grudging admiration, as though the young man had spent a lifetime being upstaged by his crowd-pleasing twin.

April was in a hurry to leave. She kissed her mother and came over to Thorn. Before she could say a word, Buddha stepped between them, taking charge.

"I need to speak to you, Ms. Moss, on an urgent police matter."

April was almost Thorn's height, with fair skin and thick chestnut hair. She wore a light blue sleeveless dress with faint yellow striping, a simple silver bracelet, and a necklace made of polished stones the size and color of olives. Her mind seemed to wander for a moment as her dark brown eyes remained fixed on her two boys, who were sharing a laugh out in the courtyard.

"You know Poblanos?" she said, sliding her gaze to Thorn.

"What is it?"

"Bar downtown. I can be there at five."

"We'll find it," Thorn said.

April took a quick look at Buddha, gave her a sisterly smile, then left.

NINE

THORN DROVE BUDDHA'S RENTAL, A flame-red Ford, east through Little Havana. The car's dashboard clock said 3:20. An hour and a half to kill before Poblanos.

Buddha took out her electronic tablet and busied herself with it while Thorn struggled with the steering wheel. His right hand was so swollen and sore he had to use his left to steer.

"Where we going?" she said, without looking up.

"Key Biscayne."

"Why?"

More finger tapping on the glass screen.

"Guy I know used to live out there. Want to see if he's still around."

"A social call?"

"He might be of help with our project."

"Okay."

"Last I knew he was the agent in charge of the Miami FBI field office."

Buddha looked up and stared at him for a moment.

"Is there something going on between you and April Moss?"

Thorn hesitated a moment.

"Why do you ask?"

"Yeah, I thought there was."

"What'd you see?"

"Something going on," she said.

"I wouldn't call it 'going on.' A long time ago we met briefly. Nothing serious. I don't know if she even remembers."

"She remembers," Buddha said. "Oh, yes."

"You're one of those sharp-eyed cops."

"I'm a woman."

Thorn was silent.

"And you remembered *her* all right."

"It's a curse," he said. "I remember all of them."

"You keep a little black book?"

"I don't need to."

"Well, now," Buddha said. "Is there anything else you haven't told me?"

"I'm sure there's plenty."

"You had carnal knowledge of her?"

Thorn looked over.

"That a joke?"

"Screw, then. Did you screw April Moss?"

"Why is that relevant?"

"I thought so." Buddha shook her head. "One time or multiple?"

"Hey," Thorn said. "We had a brief encounter. It meant nothing to her and it meant nothing to me. A recreational roll in the hay. That's all. Never spoke to her again till today."

"How long ago was it?"

"I don't know. A long time."

"How'd it happen?"

"You want all the dirt, huh? Some kind of voyeuristic thing going on?"

"What were the circumstances?"

Thorn sighed. It was useless to push her away. She kept coming.

"I was having a drink with some friends at a bayside bar in Islamorada. She came up, said hello, started flirting. I think her girlfriends put her up to it. A birthday dare, ladies' night out. Miami girls slumming in the Keys."

"*Her* birthday?"

"Jesus, what difference does it make?"

"You were her birthday present to herself. That's how it sounds."

"Maybe so. I never thought about it."

"Which birthday, like twelve, thirteen?"

"Not funny."

"I don't know what the hell Rusty saw in you, Mr. Lothario."

"I ask myself the same question."

She looked at him for a few moments, then went back to her gadget, typing and waiting and typing some more. She stayed focused on it for ten minutes and only looked up when Thorn stopped to pay the toll at the Rickenbacker Causeway.

Going across the high bridge, he stayed in the slow lane, his usual survival tactic with the crazed Miami traffic. At the summit of the long span Buddha looked out at the blue sweep of Biscayne Bay, the yachts and fishing skiffs crisscrossing the still waters, then leaned forward to gaze north across the upper end of the bay toward downtown Miami, where dozens of office buildings and banks and grand hotels lined the shoreline like headstones in a graveyard for giants.

"You're not in Starkville anymore."

"It's pretty," she said.

"People seem to think so."

"But I can't imagine living here."

"That's two of us."

"It's too big, too fast. Too bright, too many things at once."

"You'd fit right in, Buddha. Everybody's from somewhere else. There's only a few hundred people in this town who were born here. The rest just got off the plane from New Jersey last month. Or swam ashore."

"Key Largo is so different?"

"Different, yeah. But it's changing. We have our share of New Jersey."

Her electronic tablet dinged and she broke away from the view and went back to the screen in her lap.

After a moment, she reached out and slapped the dashboard.

"All right!"

She pumped a celebratory fist.

"ViCAP," she said. "A fresh hit."

Thorn waited while Buddha typed on the pad for a minute.

"See, on the drive up from the Keys I expanded my list of search terms. It dawned on me the average cop wouldn't know what the hell Zentai was. Word's too exotic. He's not going to use that in his report, so it wouldn't wind up in ViCAP. I inputted more generic words, 'Spider-Man suit,' 'bodysuit,' 'unitard,' 'catsuit.'"

"And one of those came up."

"'Bodysuit.'"

"In a homicide investigation?"

"A pedestrian stop in an Atlanta neighborhood three weeks ago on a Saturday night. No arrest made. Some person walking down the sidewalk in a black suit."

"A pedestrian stop? What good is that?"

"It's a step."

"The cop get an ID?"

"No ID, not even a warning citation, just logged it into ViCAP. Whoever this cop was, he must have had a suspicion of something more serious, or he's a major overachiever. I just sent back a query to the Atlanta PD about any unsolved homicides that occurred within a twenty-four-hour period of the stop. And I asked them to have the reporting officer contact me about the bodysuit incident."

"One guy walking around in a bodysuit? That's not much."

"You always so negative?"

"It's not much, Buddha."

She stared down at her tablet.

"What were you burning last night in that bonfire?"

"Stuff I didn't want anymore."

"Like furniture and clothes, that kind of thing?"

"What's your problem?"

"I'm trying to figure you out."

"Keep me posted."

"Why were you burning your things?"

"I don't know."

"Sure you do. Go on, say it. How were you feeling?"

"I don't know. Maybe a little lost."

"And angry," she said.

"That too."

"Angry about losing Rusty."

"Yeah."

"I'm familiar with that sensation. Exactly how I felt with Mickey. Angry, sad, confused. But I didn't set anything on fire."

"I don't know why I did it. When I figure it out, I'll get back to you."

"Seems childish, like a hissy fit. Something terrible happens, you're like, hey, I think I'll go burn up a bunch of my furniture and shit."

"Talking with you is a contact sport."

"Your friends must coddle you, Thorn. We're just having an honest back-and-forth. So that's what the fire was about. Self-flagellation. One hurt to distract from another hurt."

He slowed for the thickening traffic in the commercial district of Key Biscayne, saw the side street he was looking for and made the left turn, heading out to the small oceanside motel along the Atlantic side of the island, the place Frank Sheffield had lived for years. Sheffield was Sugarman's buddy. They'd worked together a few years back on a couple of cases, then on one special operation to help rescue one of Sugar's little girls. Though his contact with Sheffield had been minimal, Thorn's recollection was positive. Sheffield was cut from the same cloth as Sugar. Solid, no bullshit, not one to play games. He wasn't wound as tight as other FBI guys Thorn had met. But even with his light and loose approach, the man got things done.

The two-story motel was still there, shaded by coconut palms and some renegade pines. Those Australian pines had been banned from the county after the last hurricane. The big trees were nonnatives and could grow a hundred feet tall, their trunks five feet thick and heavy with sap, but they had practically no root system. An ordinary squall with forty-mile-an-hour winds could push them over. Somehow the ones around the Silver Sands Motel had survived the ban and the last few tropical storms. Maybe it was because they were sheltered by massive condos built on either side of the motel.

Thorn parked, got out, waited for Buddha to finish up with her gadget.

The sea breeze moaning through the pines had a spooky, harmonic undertone. Thorn had always liked that noise and been partial to those trees for producing it, but still, he wouldn't live in the shadow of one, no matter how appealing their sound effects.

Things looked desperate at the Silver Sands. Out in the sandy parking lot to the north of the pink and turquoise concrete building five bulldozers were stationed alongside a dump truck and some industrial-size trash containers.

With Buddha trailing, Thorn circled the building, peeking in the windows. The place was deserted, every room empty, except for one where a tidy occupant kept his shoes lined up and the queen-size bed was made with hospital corners.

In a tiny block building behind the motel he found Frank Sheffield bent over a lawnmower, tightening down the carburetor. The workshop was full of landscaping equipment and smelled like gasoline and rotten fish.

Frank looked up, saw Thorn, then saw Buddha behind him. His gaze lingered on Buddha for a second or two, then he looked at Thorn and smiled.

"Oh, boy," Frank said. "And I thought it was going to be just another dull day at the office."

Thorn introduced Buddha, using her title.

"Little young to be a sheriff."

"Thought so too, but she is."

Frank got up, wiping his oily hands on a rag. He had on a ragged Miami Dolphins T-shirt and cutoff jeans. No shoes. His hair had gotten scruffy and he had a two-day beard.

Buddha dug her wallet from her purse and flipped it open, and Frank leaned in for a close inspection.

"Oklahoma, where the wind comes sweepin' down the plain."

"And the waving wheat can sure smell sweet," Buddha said.

"Long way from the plains." Frank led them out of the shop into the breezy shade of coconut palms. Down on the beach, the tourists were walking to and fro. Thorn doubted they were speaking of Michelangelo.

Thorn explained the situation. Rusty's death, the subsequent murder of her aunt, the obituary on the bedside table, the TV show with the same storyline.

"You think you got an active serial?"

"Maybe just getting started," Buddha said. "Maybe a one-timer. Too early to tell. But it's a copycat of that TV show. I'm sure of that."

"Life imitating shit," Frank said. "Happens more than you think."

"You've seen that before? Bad guys getting their ideas from TV?" Buddha sounded deferential, a side of her Thorn hadn't heard. In the presence of one of her own, she was picking up on Frank's true-blue vibe.

Frank shrugged.

"Majority of the turdballs I run into never had what you'd call a bright idea. That would require they first have a functioning brain. Mainly they're monkey see, monkey do. Steal a gimmick from a cop show or comic book, then reenact it step for step. You ask them later how they thought of something so amazing, they think they came up with it on their own because they were too stoned to remember where they ripped it off from."

"You're not with the Bureau anymore?" Thorn said.

"Technically yes. Last official day is coming September one. But I've cleared out my desk, briefed my replacement. I'm done. Just coasting a couple of months on stored-up sick leave. I'm not going into the office, which is fine by my colleagues."

"What's going on with this place?"

"The Silver Sands is my Alamo. Sheffield's last stand. Instead of Mexican troops climbing the walls, I got fucking bulldozers trying to knock them down."

Frank led them over to a concrete picnic table with matching benches, all of it inlaid with broken bits of terrazzo.

"Got some Red Stripe. Care for a cold beverage, Ms. Hilton?"

She declined. Thorn surrendered to temptation.

Frank pulled two bottles of the Jamaican beer from the cooler full of slushy ice and handed one to Thorn. He twisted off the cap, had a long pull, and set it on the table.

"Sorry to hear about Rusty. That's tough. Not even fifty."

Thorn nodded.

"You ask what's going on here," Frank said. "Well, I own this old motor lodge and the three acres we're standing on. I been trying to pull permits to restore the old girl to her former idyllic charm. Problem is, the city fathers don't think my humble plans for this prime beachfront will produce sufficient tax revenues, so they're trying to steal it in a court of law. Been harassing me with red-tag code violations and ticky-tack bullshit. Now they say it's in the public's interest it be demolished and replaced by a condo tower. We'll know in a month if the judge agrees. Meanwhile, I whack the weeds, relax in my hammock. Crash in room 104."

"You're living here?"

"Got to make sure those bulldozers don't fire up some night and accidentally knock the old place down."

"Somebody would do that?" Buddha asked.

"It's Miami," Sheffield said. "Whatever you want done, there's somebody happy to oblige."

Thorn sipped his beer and watched the beach people soaking up the late afternoon rays.

"Who's the new SAC?"

"Name's Lisa Mankowski."

Sheffield looked out at the afternoon blaze on the white sands.

"Way you say her name, I take it you two aren't warm and fuzzy."

"Mankowski is about as fuzzy as a steel ball bearing."

Buddha smiled and Frank smiled at her. He didn't seem to notice her tats. There was no curiosity in his eyes. A live-and-let-live guy to the core.

"It's the end of an era at the Bureau. New generation taking over. New rules, new objectives; they call it *retasking*. Centralized management structure, intel-driven investigations. Number-one priority is homeland security, prevention of attacks. Counterintelligence, counterespionage. Everybody wants to play spy. It's not your father's FBI. These days some kid with a view of the Potomac calls the shots. So if you happen to have a crazy-ass killer who may or may not be imitating a TV show running around murdering your citizens, shit, let me see, is that an urgent national security threat? Not really, unless he's using a dirty bomb or a suitcase nuke. Like I say, end of an era."

Thorn finished his beer and rode the buzz a while, listening to the pines hum their ghostly melody.

"Sheriff Hilton here, she's got some issues with the FBI in her area too."

"Is it the end of an era out in Oklahoma?"

"There's some good agents," she said. "So I hear."

"Oh, sure, there's still crime solvers around. Old-school flatfoots. The last of the shoe leather boys." Sheffield had a pull on his beer, then pressed the bottle to his temple. "Just none I met lately."

They sat in silence for a few moments, then Frank set down his empty and dug two more beers from the ice and passed one to Thorn.

"Sheriff Hilton," Frank said. "Did you know your associate here is famous for going off the rails at warp speed?"

"I'm aware of Mr. Thorn's reputation, yes, sir."

They listened to the pines and sipped their beer. Buddha looked at Thorn and made a we-should-go shrug.

"So, Frank," Thorn said. "The thing is, Sheriff Hilton is a wee bit beyond her jurisdiction. And you know me, I'm always outside mine. But despite that, it looks like the two of us, for various personal reasons, are going ahead with this quest for truth. So I was wondering, maybe along the way if something came up where we needed local assistance, you know, access to case files, official muscle—"

Frank raised his hand and cut Thorn off.

"It's a felony to attempt to defile a federal official."

"Defile?"

"Corrupt, bribe. You know what I mean."

He gave Thorn a hard stare, then shifted it to Buddha. In a few seconds his face relaxed into a smile, and he looked at the bulldozers aimed at his quaint motel.

"You got a cell phone?" Frank kept his eyes on the earth movers.

Buddha pulled her phone from her bag.

"My private number, emergencies only. Dire emergencies."

"Understood," Buddha said.

He gave her his number, and she put it into her phone. She dug a business card from her purse and slid it over to Frank. It had a gold official seal on it from the metropolis of Starkville.

"You know Poblanos?" Thorn said. "Somewhere downtown."

"Classy joint," Frank said. "Where cops and their snitches liquor up. Down the block from Tobacco Road. You know where that is, right?"

Thorn said he knew.

"In your travels you ever run into April Moss?"

Sheffield looked out at the soothing roll of the Atlantic.

"I have indeed. I see she's slinging obits now, but she used to be one of their hotshot investigative types. Tore new assholes for more than one dirtbag in her day. She's solid, got good street cred. I'd trust what she gave me."

He and Buddha rose while Frank guzzled the last swallow.

"I've caught that show a couple of times, *Miami Ops*," Frank said.

"Pretty crappy," said Buddha.

"Crappy, yeah. But that girl, one of the actors, Dee Dee Dollimore, she might be worth some face time. Her and her old man, Gus."

"Why's that?"

"They're dirty."

"How so?"

"Probably not related to the situation you're looking at, but I heard some unsavory shit about that pair. Goes way back, never made it in front of a jury. Somebody's lawyer was better than somebody else's lawyer."

"What version of unsavory?"

"Short films. Daddy, daughter, and a lollipop. That kind of thing."

Buddha gave Thorn a questioning look.

"I'll tell you in the car," Thorn said.

"Probably unrelated," said Frank.

TEN

"CHILD PORN?"

"That's what he was saying."

"Father and daughter together?"

"Apparently."

"That's the guy from this afternoon, bossy guy running the show."

"The director," Thorn said. "Couldn't sit still. That was him."

Thorn pulled out onto Crandon Boulevard.

"She's still working with her father. How's that happen?"

"Abused wives stay with their husbands. It happens."

"I couldn't work alongside my dad even if he was on one side of the bars and I was on the other."

"Maybe they both had therapy and got cured," Thorn said.

"Is that another joke?"

"It's a new thing they're calling irony."

"There's things people do I'll never understand," Buddha said. "Things I don't really care to understand."

In silence she looked out her window. They passed the Seaquarium, the Maritime Science and Technology high school.

"So how does that fit in?" Buddha said. "Incest porn."

"Like Sheffield said, it probably doesn't. Make a note of it, set it aside, when we know more we'll see if it fits or not."

"Hard to set aside something like that."

"Yeah, it is."

"Hell, even my father wasn't that twisted. Well, as far as I know. I mean, I think I'd remember something like that."

"You remembered him putting on the tats, you'd remember the other."

Buddha was silent, looking out at the windsurfers and the sailboats and the charter boats coming in from the far reaches of the bay.

"This TV show," he said. "Does the guy in the bodysuit use the same weapon every time?"

"Each show it's different. He picks it after reading the obit."

"So if the real killer is doing that, switching weapons, searching for that Zulu spear on ViCAP, that won't work."

"I put it in just in case. It's all I had."

They crossed the causeway in the opposite direction and Buddha surveyed the view again, but this time she didn't seem as awed. Miami had that effect. Teased you for a while with its gorgeous panoramas, its exotic scents, its sensual drumbeat, then left you hungry for something you couldn't name.

She pulled the Ziploc evidence bag from her purse, took Rusty's obituary out, and spent a few minutes musing on it. When he looked over again she was touching her fingertip lightly to the pointy edges, holding the paper up to the light.

He saw his name shine through the flimsy page. Rusty on one side, him on the other. Rusty with the angels, Thorn with the society fucks.

He took Brickell Avenue north, passing the wall of condos where the young professionals who worked downtown spent their nights, living among the snowbirds from Germany and Canada and Brazil.

Going against rush hour, making decent time, Thorn tried his right hand on the steering wheel but the fingers wouldn't close. It was going to be a while before he was using chopsticks.

"Do you sew, Thorn?"

"Sew?"

"Needle and thread."

"The occasional button on a shirt."

"Did Rusty?"

"What's this about?"

"You know what pinking shears are?"

"Some kind of scissors."

"Scissors with a sawtooth blade. They cut a zigzag pattern. Seamstresses use them to trim the edges of woven fabric so it won't unravel."

She held up the obituary.

"Zigzag like this."

"I wondered about that. It's so regular."

"This shirt I'm wearing," she said, "I made this, and these pants too."

Thorn fetched for a compliment about her clothes, but couldn't think of anything that sounded halfway honest. So he was quiet.

"I make all my own apparel, but I never use pinking shears. What I use is what most everybody uses, a rotary cutter. It looks like the roller they slice pizzas with. That's how you make these zigzag edges nowadays."

Thorn asked her why any of this mattered.

"There's a difference between the zigzags a rotary cutter makes and the one pinking shears do. The Vs on a rotary blade design aren't as deep, the tips of the zigzags are sharper with shears. This obituary was cut with pinking shears, not a rotary blade."

In his rearview mirror Thorn saw the sky darkening out over the Everglades. July late afternoon thunderstorm flaring up right on schedule.

"Pinking shears, they're old-fashioned. You don't see them around anymore. My grandmother used them."

"So we're looking for an elderly seamstress."

She looked over, not smiling, and shook her head in resignation.

"Everything's a joke with you."

"When I can, I like to embrace the light side."

"We're looking for someone who owns a pair of pinking shears. And the pair we're looking for has a nick on the blade."

"What nick?"

"The shears that cut this paper are dinged in one spot. It's very small, but it's there. You can see it, how the blade left a series of tiny indentations."

They were stopped for a red light on the edge of downtown where the condos ceased and the banks and insurance buildings began.

Buddha held up the newsprint and pointed out several imperfections in the jags that edged the paper.

"Probably what happened, somebody was using their shears to cut material and didn't see a straight pin hidden in the fabric, and wound up chomping down on it and dinging the blade. Appears to be about midway up. So from that point on, whatever they cut, they leave that same little notch here and here and here."

She pointed out the places on the newspaper's edge where the scissors had left its signature. Thorn could've studied that clipping for a year and not noticed those nicks. But they were there.

The light went to green and a teenage kid in a black pickup behind them waited a hundredth of a second before he held down his horn. Not just a light tap to wake Thorn up, but a full-throttled fuck-you-get-moving-asshole honk.

Thorn got moving. Going slower than he might have otherwise.

"Too bad there's not a pinking shear database," he said.

"Make a note of it, set it aside." Buddha allowed herself a brief smile.

"Incest porn and pinking shears," he said. "We've had a good day."

"And it's not even suppertime."

Thorn found a parking space on South Miami Avenue a block from the bar. They were ten minutes early. The first few spatters of rain hit the windshield. Thunder grumbled in the west. For some reason he was reminded of an old Labrador retriever he'd once had, the way it moaned in its sleep.

"I'm betting she won't show."

"Oh, she'll show." Buddha was studying Rusty's obituary again.

Thorn watched the rain smear the windshield. He saw a homeless man in a camouflage jacket walking slowly down the sidewalk. He had shoulder-length gray hair and a bad limp. He didn't seem to mind the rain. Maybe it reminded him of the monsoons in southeast Asia back when he was fighting in that hopeless war. Thorn watched him cross the street a half block down, a black plastic garbage bag slung over his shoulder. A man who had trimmed his possessions to only what he could lug. By those austere standards, Thorn had a long way left to go.

"I'm an idiot," Buddha said.

"What now?"

"I've been in a daze since I found Mickey's body. Getting on a jet plane, flying to Miami, shooting a gun out of your hand, watching a big-time TV show being made. I kept looking at this obituary, but my eyes must've been glazed over, and I didn't see the one simple, obvious thing."

"Which is?"

"On the show the Miami Ops agents are always trying to interpret the obituaries. But they never get anywhere. That's because they're looking for connections between the deceased person in the obit and the murder victim. They're not looking at the words of the obituary itself."

"What do you see?"

"Think about it, Thorn. A guy reads an obit in the Miami paper. He's going to use it as a roadmap to kill his next victim. What's he need to know?"

"The name of the victim."

"That's one thing, yeah. And there's at least two more I can think of."

"Where the victim is located."

"Right."

"I don't know, what else?"

"The weapon," Buddha said. "Name, location, weapon. He finds all that hidden in some random obituary. It's like the *I Ching*. You know the *I Ching*?"

"Vaguely."

"It's a book of hexagrams. The Chinese use it for fortune-telling. Hippies used to play around with it. My old man had a copy, he'd get stoned, flip open to a random page, read the hexagram, and his deepest questions were answered. Should he get pepperoni or anchovies on his pizza?"

Thorn licked his fingertip and made a check mark in the air.

"One for the sheriff."

She nodded, pleased to be on the board.

"With good dope," Thorn said, "any book would probably do."

"Probably," she said. "But for the Chinese, the *I Ching* is the universe in miniature. It embodies all the major principles; ease, simplicity, change, transformation, and permanence. Everything in the universe is changing, but underlying all existence are a few simple, permanent principles. Obituaries are the same. People are dying, that's the serious change, but permanent principles underlie all deaths. Constants. Who, what, where."

Thorn considered that. A weighty thought. Way too weighty at the moment. No sleep, no food, two beers.

"So the killer's an elderly Buddhist seamstress."

He smiled at her but she shook her head, not having it.

"The obituaries are the killer's *I Ching*. He's finding his answers there. Name of victim, location, weapon. That's what he's looking for, so that's what he finds. Rusty's obituary led him to Michaela in Starkville."

"How?"

"It's sitting there on the surface," she said. "Listen to this, it's in the ninth paragraph of Rusty's obit, first sentence of the paragraph. " 'Rusty was spearheading a fundraising campaign that brought in six hundred thousand dollars . . .' "

"Spear," Thorn said.

"There's the weapon. Then in the first sentence of the third paragraph 'Starkville, Oklahoma,' appears. Rusty's birthplace. It turns into the location of the victim."

"So the psycho goes and buys a spear and heads off to Oklahoma. But how's he home in on Michaela Stabler? There's no mention of her."

"I haven't got that yet."

The rain shower had passed and steam was rising from the street.

"Which means all that Shaka Zulu, *Iklwa* stuff is irrelevant. It could've been any spear. A generic spear would have been fine."

"Seems that way," Buddha said. "Wrong turn down the wrong street."

She watched a Cuban street vendor walking past her window with a crate of limes. He offered them mutely and she declined with a shrug.

"The guy's stuck on threes."

"What?"

Thorn said, "Read the first sentence of the sixth paragraph."

Buddha looked over at him.

"Go on. Read it to me."

She counted down the paragraphs till she found it.

"After graduation, Stabler devoted herself to building her charter fishing business into a thriving enterprise."

"Third word, sixth paragraph. 'Stabler.' "

"Third word, 'spearheading.' Third word, 'Starkville.' "

"Any other Stablers living in Starkville?"

She considered it a moment, then said, "Used to be several, but they either died or moved off. Mickey was the last surviving Stabler in town."

"Well, there you go. Where, who, how. Three paragraphs down, three words in. Take a spear to Starkville and kill the only Stabler in town. This character has a thing for three."

She held her fist up for a knuckle-bump. Thorn had never bumped fists with anyone before. He didn't travel those circles. But Buddha was smiling, her fist waiting, and Thorn clenched his sore right hand and tapped her fist, knuckle to knuckle. Goofy but good.

"Incest porn, pinking shears, and three paragraphs down, three words in. We're on a serious roll."

"There's something else," Buddha said. Smile gone, mood swinging to somber. "The Atlanta situation. That cop stopping a guy in a black bodysuit. That happened on a Saturday. Michaela was killed on a Saturday."

"People are home on Saturdays. They're off work."

"Maybe Saturday's his killing day. He's got a routine."

"That's a stretch," Thorn said. "Some guy stopped in Atlanta wearing a Zentai suit on the same day of the week that Mickey was killed—sorry, before you can say the guy's got a timetable you need a bigger sample."

She rolled her eyes upward as if she was adding a column of figures.

"What day was Rusty's obit in the paper? Tuesday?"

"Monday," Thorn said.

"The killer reads it Monday, three days later he's bought a spear, two days after that he's used it."

"Okay, he's on a tight schedule. That's about all you can say for sure."

"Who else is on a tight schedule?"

"What do you mean?"

"People we've met in our investigation so far. Who meets that description?"

"You mean the TV people?"

She lifted an eyebrow at him.

"Lots of people are on a tight schedule. Especially in this town."

"Just saying."

She sat in silence, staring out at the rain-slick street. Cars hissed past in both directions. Drivers tailgating, honking, looking for an edge, everyone angry, in a hurry and on a mission a lot more important than anyone else's.

"What's the closest major airport to Starkville?"

She touched a fingertip to the shark-tooth edges of the obituary.

"Dallas/Fort Worth. Three hours south."

"Might want to contact your new FBI friend. Ask Sheffield to pull the passenger manifests for every airline flying Miami to Dallas on Friday or Saturday the weekend Mickey was killed. It'd be a big list, but it's a place to start. Sounds like some fun police work for you."

Buddha was staring out the windshield, shaking her head.

"What's wrong?"

"This doesn't seem too easy to you?"

"Which part?"

"Decoding the obituary. Three paragraphs down, three words in. We're not talking serious encryption, that's some kind of kindergarten code."

"The guy's a halfwit. You heard Frank, we're having a national shortage of criminal masterminds."

"No. This feels weird, like we're being punked. Like it's just lying there out in the open, too obvious."

"It's interrogation time." Thorn nodded at the dashboard clock.

Buddha frowned at the obituary as she slid it back into the evidence bag.

"Time to dangle me in front of April, see if her eyes light up."

"Oh, they will," Buddha said. "They already did."

ELEVEN

AT QUARTER AFTER FIVE, WITH Buddha in the john, April Moss entered Poblanos. She'd changed into gray skinny jeans and a drapy black top that showed her figure but didn't flaunt it. A trim woman with a healthy shape. She'd pulled her dark brown hair back into a loose bun, a few long wisps escaping down her neck.

Thorn stood up from behind the round table and watched her walk across the room. Her lips were clamped, a what-the-hell-am-I-doing look on her face.

He pulled out a chair and waited for her.

She sat. Thorn sat across from her and they looked at each other.

"Where's your friend?"

"The loo."

They waited in silence. Looking at each other, then looking away.

"So now what?" April said.

"It's a bar," Thorn said. "We order a drink, we talk, see what's what."

"It still works like that? I haven't been in a bar in so long, I thought maybe things had changed."

"Order, talk, see what's what. Same as always."

"Like a date."

Buddha appeared and took the seat between them.

"Not like a date," Buddha said. "More like a homicide investigation."

The barmaid came, knew April from way back, fussed over her, long-time-no-see, took her order, Chardonnay, then got Thorn's and Buddha's. Another Red Stripe for Thorn, water with lemon for the sheriff.

"You guys have food?" Thorn wanted to know.

"Fried cheese sticks," the waitress said. "Chicken nuggets."

"Double order of both," Thorn said. "An angioplasty on the side." Nobody smiled.

"Buddha?"

"I'll wait till there's real food," she said.

The waitress gave April a consoling look—the morons we endure.

"This is almost as awkward as our date," April said.

"You remember it clearly, do you?"

"Sure," she said. "It was an unforgettable evening. The moon, the water, all those tequila shots, vomiting in your bathroom."

"Did you take advantage of this woman, Thorn?"

"No, he didn't," April said. "It was fifty-fifty. If anything I forced myself on him."

"But you were drunk," Buddha said.

"We knew what we were doing."

"Whoa," Thorn said. He waved a hand, but neither looked his way.

"You use protection?" Buddha asked April.

"Jesus," said Thorn. "Boundaries."

"Did you?" She was looking hard at April.

One of April's eyebrows cocked as if she might be choosing a zinger from her arsenal. Put this meddlesome teenager in her place.

After a second more of staring into Buddha's eyes, April's face relaxed.

"I didn't think so," Buddha said. "Went flying without seatbelts."

"My colorful young friend," Thorn said. "Still learning her manners."

"It was a different era," April said to Buddha. "We were innocent. We were young and nothing could hurt us."

Buddha nodded. The two women were still glaring at each other as if preparing for mortal combat.

"Hey," Thorn said. He felt like snapping a finger between the two women to wake them from this stare-down. But he controlled himself. One of them might bite his finger off. "How'd we go down this road?"

"I'm happy to drop it," April said.

Still looking at Buddha, April raised her fist, then opened her fingers as if releasing a bird into the air.

"Poof," she said. "Next subject."

April glanced around the bar, nodded to a guy who looked like an undercover narc. Shaved head, ratty jeans, a long-sleeved T-shirt smudged with grime. The woman had connections.

"One of your sources?" Thorn said.

"That's Jeff, our pest control guy. This is his hangout."

Their drinks arrived and April had a quick sip. Keeping her eyes down.

Thorn dredged his memory for images from that night with April. He couldn't remember the sex, the vomiting. All he could recall was what he'd told Buddha. A flirty girl hitting on a local Keys guy, egged on by her posse. He didn't remember a thing about that young April. This older version seemed urbane and droll, quick with acid one-liners. Spend time around April Moss, you'd always be working on the next comeback.

She had an indoor pallor. Skin so pale it had a mother-of-pearl sheen, long fingers, delicate hands. Not the hearty, sun-weathered kind Thorn favored. But there was something about her thin lips and her half smile, and a genuine flicker in her eyes that was intriguing. And that mother of hers, signaling the way April would be some day—that brassy attitude, he liked that.

Two red plastic baskets of food arrived. Thorn offered it around. No takers. He arranged the baskets in front of him and tried not to wolf it. The two Red Stripes on an empty stomach and zero sleep had made him loopy.

"You ever get fan mail?" Buddha asked her. "For what you write."

"Occasionally."

"Anything weird?"

"You'd have to tell me, Sheriff, what exactly you mean by weird."

"Well, give us some examples of your strange fan mail."

"What's this about? What area of law enforcement are you in?"

"I'm a sheriff from Oklahoma. I'm looking into the murder of one of the citizens of my town."

Buddha drew out her wallet and showed April the badge and ID card.

"And that brings you to Miami?"

"You're a professional journalist," Buddha said. "You're in the habit of asking questions, I understand. But Ms. Moss, right now I'd appreciate it if you answered a few."

April looked at Thorn.

"What're you doing here, Thorn? How are you involved in a murder investigation from Oklahoma?"

"That's what we're trying to find out."

Thorn finished the chicken nuggets and moved on to the fried cheese.

"We were talking about any fan mail you've gotten recently, any red flags. The person tried to get too personal, invasive, that kind of thing."

"My mail is usually about factual errors I've made in someone's obituary, or they demand to know why I wrote about one person instead of another."

"And the weird ones?"

"Just weepy, written when they were drunk or depressed. Incoherent."

Buddha nodded.

"You watch *Miami Ops*?"

April said of course she did. Both her boys worked on the show.

"It must be strange to have your work life portrayed on TV. The obituary lady with an obsessed fan."

"I'm pleased Sawyer found my profession worthy of writing about."

"Your character is in the story, but we never actually see you."

"That's as it should be."

"And they don't show much of the obits beyond the headlines."

"No way to do it," April said. "TV is visual. People don't enjoy reading a lot of words on the screen."

April was pulling back, her face taut, her answers turning formal. As if she'd gotten a whiff of where this was headed and didn't like it.

"Does he consult with you? Pick your brain about your job?"

"I don't see the point of these questions."

"Does Sawyer involve you in his writing process?"

"He asks me a question now and then. Just technical things. How I do my research, how I choose my subjects, things of that sort."

"How *do* you choose your subjects?"

April sighed. Resigning herself to this imposition.

112

"Mostly there's not much latitude who I write about. A prominent politician, a famous opera singer, a Hollywood big shot—I do those automatically. But for the local people, South Florida residents, something has to catch my eye, some detail in the person's life that sets them apart. That makes them noteworthy."

"And your research, how does that work?"

"Phone, Internet. Usually that's sufficient."

"You don't go out and interview people, the relatives face-to-face?"

"I've done it a few times, but it's rare. Most of what I need I can get sitting at my desk. I always talk to family members, and look through back files of the paper to see if anything's been written on the person. I talk to four or five people who knew the subject. After four or five, the information almost always gets redundant. Most people aren't that complicated."

"Easy to sum up."

"I don't mean to be flip. That's just how it is. One day to write an obit is normal, two days is a rare exception. Start at ten, get it done by six o'clock."

"Does Sawyer share his process with you? Discuss his scripts? How he writes them, what's going on in his mind?"

"Rarely."

"Do the TV people work weekends?"

"You mean do they shoot on Saturday and Sunday?"

"Do they?"

"No, not usually. Union rules."

Buddha glanced at Thorn. *See, I told you.*

"Do you know what motivates the killer Sawyer is writing about? Why he's murdering these people? What's driving him?"

April measured a breath and considered the question. She smoothed her palm across her forehead as if calming a headache.

"I've wondered that," she said. "But I don't know."

"You think the killer's just flat-out crazy?"

"I hope not."

"Why?"

"Psychopaths in stories, it's lazy writing. A wacko can do anything, it doesn't have to make sense. Sawyer hasn't told me what the killer's trying to accomplish. But I'm hoping it's not a crazy person. If the bad guy has no purpose, the story's meaningless. I believe Sawyer's a better writer than that."

"We were having the same conversation a while ago," Thorn said.

Buddha said, "If the killer's not a psycho, what could his motive be?"

"What possible use are these questions to a homicide investigation?"

"To be honest, Ms. Moss, I'm not sure. I thought maybe I was missing something in the show. Some clue about the killer's motivation that could shed light on our case."

"This homicide you're investigating from Oklahoma, you're saying it bears some similarity to *Miami Ops*?"

Buddha frowned and looked at Thorn.

"That's it, isn't it? Some idiot is copying the show."

Buddha looked off at a far wall with a frustrated grimace. Then she brought her gaze back to April and leaned forward, bearing in.

"I'm cautioning you, Ms. Moss, you can't speak to anyone about this conversation. But I'm not going to lie to you. Yes, the homicide I'm looking into resembles the show your son writes, resembles it in some very specific ways."

"But you're interviewing me, not Sawyer. Why is that?"

"I really can't discuss that with you."

"What are you suggesting?" April stared into Buddha's eyes.

"I'm not suggesting anything. I'm asking questions, that's all."

"Something I wrote in one of my obituaries caused an actual murder? Is that why we're having this chat?"

Buddha sighed.

"That's one of several possibilities we're considering. But at this point we don't know anything for sure, Ms. Moss."

Thorn bit a cheese stick in half and chewed it attentively. How good could fried cheese be? But in the range of fried cheese he'd had, this was definitely on the lower end. Dry, hard, low goo factor.

Buddha had done her best to keep April in the dark. But it hadn't worked. Or maybe she had her own reasons for tipping April to the real situation. He'd have to ask her later.

More likely it was because she was new to the interrogation business and this was a slipup. She was revealing as much information as she was taking in. Cautioning April Moss not to discuss these matters was silly.

Something April had written, and something her son had written and her other son had participated in, had possibly resulted in a murder. Not likely Buddha could convince her to keep quiet about something that serious.

"We were talking about the killer's possible motivation. Has your son mentioned anything about that?"

April stared at her wineglass. She touched a fingertip to the rim.

"Okay," she said. "I don't know if this is relevant."

"Try it."

"Yesterday Sawyer was describing the episode that airs next week. The killer's identity is exposed. It's Madeline's twin sister, Valerie."

"Her identical twin?" Buddha said.

April nodded yes.

"Like Sawyer and Flynn."

"You write about what you know, that's the adage, I believe."

"This twin just showed up? I don't remember seeing a twin in the shows I watched."

"She had a couple of quick walk-ons in some early episodes."

"So Dee Dee is playing two parts. The killer and the cop chasing her."

"Which should certainly challenge her skills."

April took a quick taste of her wine.

"You don't think much of her as an actress?"

"I'm no drama critic." April's tone softened, backing away from it.

"But you're suggesting something about Ms. Dollimore's ability."

"Let's just say, Dee Dee seems to have a limited range."

"And is that how she comes across in real life? Superficial?"

April hesitated, looking toward the bar. Not one to badmouth another woman, but after a moment she shook her head. Too tempting to resist.

"I don't think anyone would ever mistake Dee Dee for a deep thinker."

"How'd she get the part if she's so untalented?"

"Her father, Gus, might've had a say in the matter," April said.

Before Thorn could respond, Buddha cut in.

"Do you know why the killer on the show cuts the edges of the obituaries like that? That saw blade look?"

"To make them stand out, I suppose. But you'd have to ask Sawyer."

"Oh, I plan to." Buddha picked up one of the fried cheese sticks, gave it a sniff, and dropped it back in the basket. It made a pleasant thump.

"On another issue," Thorn said. "There used to be a bed and breakfast on the Miami River around here. It still in business? The Waterway Lodge."

"It's still operating, yes."

"Thought we'd crash there tonight, get back to work tomorrow interviewing subjects. Give us time to dust off our thumbscrews and waterboards."

April looked at Buddha, then Thorn. Strange cop, loony cop.

"Ms. Moss," Buddha said. "Where can we find your son tomorrow? Sawyer, I mean. Do you know where they're shooting?"

"They won't be shooting anymore."

Buddha asked why.

"They've been shut down."

"The show is cancelled?"

" 'Temporary hiatus' is the terminology. Studio doesn't want to sink any more money until they see a ratings improvement."

"So what we saw today, what was that?"

"Some cut-ins, a few seconds of film here and there, just to finish off an episode they already made."

"If we wanted to speak with Sawyer?" Buddha said.

April considered it, then sighed and reached into a side pocket in her purse, took out a business card and a pen, and scribbled an address on the back of it. She pushed it across the table to Buddha.

"They'll probably be on the soundstage. They're leasing a vacant Winn-Dixie grocery store, north of downtown. The production offices are there. Sets, props, costumes. As of now no one's getting paid, but I know Sawyer and some of the others still have things to finish up."

"I don't get it," Thorn said.

"It's the way television works. They're always five shows ahead, five already shot and edited. At this point they could get to the end of the season with what they've completed. But the network is holding back those shows. If the ratings were to bump up, they'll go ahead, put those last five episodes on."

Buddha said, "The show never grabbed me. Didn't really care for the characters. Madeline's too spacey, Janus is so twisted he's a turnoff. And come on, nobody could disguise themselves as well as he does."

"At the nursing home, he fooled me," Thorn said. "I was talking to him, and he seemed like just another old guy in a wheelchair. How's he do that?"

April sighed, summoning patience.

"It's called prosthetic makeup," she said. "He's been practicing it since he was young, like a magic act. He makes a mold of his face, uses latex or gelatin to make the bottom layer mask, then sculpts clay to form the face he wants, makes a second mask from the clay, then overlays that on the first mask. It's very delicate work, but he's better at it than most trained makeup artists."

"Could we get back to the show?" Buddha shot Thorn an enough-already look. "What's the deal? Are they working or not working?"

"It's not that simple," April said. "If Gus or the others want to do any more polishing, or inserts, or anything additional, they work for free. The union people won't do that, but apparently a skeleton crew has volunteered to hang around and try to finish up. Nobody knows if the network will put the show on the air again, or if it's over right now. I guess we'll see next Thursday night."

"Crazy business," Thorn said.

"Brutal business," said April.

She shifted in her seat, eyeing the door and her path of escape.

But Buddha wasn't finished.

"Do you know if the killer gets caught this season?"

"I have no idea. Why would that matter?"

"It might be helpful to know."

"I don't see how."

"My point, Ms. Moss. If I knew how these TV cops caught the killer, it might give me something to work with."

"It's TV. It's fake. It's all made up. You're not going to learn anything about good police work from watching that show."

"I know it's fake," she said. "But the killer doesn't seem to."

April touched a fingertip to the base of her wineglass and gave Buddha a searching look. Eyes wandering over the sheriff's face as if noticing for the first time the strange markings.

"Tattoos," Buddha said. "My father put them on when I was a toddler."

"My god."

"In case you were thinking that since I had all these tats on my face, I wasn't a professional. Someone who couldn't tell fake from real."

Thorn watched April register that. Two tough women sorting it out.

April studied Buddha for several seconds, and said, "Do you have anything else I can help you with?"

No longer patronizing this young woman from Oklahoma with the ridiculous haircut and the damaged face.

"Yes, ma'am. I've got a few more questions. Can I get you another glass of wine?"

"That won't be necessary."

"Well, okay, we're interested in any obituaries that might have appeared under your byline this past Monday. Were there any?"

"Why?"

"Just a long shot. Maybe our subject is on a schedule. Reads an obituary on Monday, acts on it a few days later."

April took a long breath.

"So did you have one Monday?"

April nodded.

"Who died?"

"Major league baseball player. Joe Camarillo. He played for the Boston Red Sox, hit the winning home run in the last game of the World Series a few years ago. He went to Gables High, so there's a local connection."

"Died young?"

"Heart attack. He was forty-seven."

"I don't suppose you have a copy of the obit."

"I don't carry them around with me, if that's what you're asking."

"But you keep files at work, right? Everything you've written."

"At home I have a complete file. I work from there most of the time."

Buddha leaned down and drew the electronic tablet from her purse, and went through the glass-tapping exercise.

"Now what?" April said.

"I think she's going online, looking up the obit of the baseball player. She's very computer savvy."

Thorn watched Buddha move through different screens, until she arrived at her destination and began to read.

April finished the last sip of her wine and waved at her waitress friend, and drew a squiggle in the air.

Buddha looked up from her electronic gizmo and took a breath.

"What is it?" Thorn said.

Buddha shook her head. Couldn't bring herself to say it.

"What?"

"A bat."

"With wings and sharp teeth?"

"A baseball bat," Buddha said.

"Jesus."

"But the paragraphs three and six, that's just articles and conjunctions. I don't know what we do with that."

"A goddamn baseball bat."

"Thorn," April said. "What are you all talking about?"

Before he could respond, April's phone rang. She dug it out of her purse, checked the caller ID.

"I have to take this. It's work."

Thorn pushed the red baskets back to the center of the table. He'd finished every scrap and there was a five-pound lump in his gut. His lips were sticky and were beginning to pucker from all the sodium. But he wasn't hungry anymore. He might never be hungry again.

April said hello, listened for a few seconds, then turned her eyes to the table. After a moment more, she scooted her chair back a half foot and turned her back on them.

"So we're staying in Miami tonight?"

"This time of day it's two hours of hell getting back to Key Largo."

"You need to use my phone?" Buddha asked Thorn.

"Why would I?"

"Call someone, tell them you're not coming home tonight."

"Nobody to call."

Buddha nodded.

"Me either."

April came to her feet, standing stiff, the phone pressed to her ear.

"I'll be right there," she said. "Ten minutes."

She snapped the phone shut, and Buddha stood up.

"What happened?" Buddha stepped closer.

April opened her mouth, then caught herself and shut it. Thorn would not have believed it possible, but April Moss's face was even whiter than it was a moment earlier.

She sidestepped Buddha and hurried for the exit, Buddha trailing, Thorn bringing up the rear.

A few feet before the door, Jeff, the guy with the shaved head and ratty jeans, stepped away from the bar and blocked their path.

"Is there a problem, Ms. Moss?"

With a cold, dry hand the lanky guy took hold of Thorn's forearm, a pincer grip. Thorn's hand tingled. The guy smiled at Thorn without malice, his body relaxed like one who'd handled much tougher badasses than Thorn.

"There's no problem, Jeff."

The man nodded respectfully and with the airy grace of a kung fu master ceasing combat, he released Thorn's arm and drew his hand away.

April slipped past and fled Poblanos with Thorn and Buddha trying to keep pace. She didn't say another word, just crossed the street, got into her blue Mini Cooper, and squealed away.

TWELVE

AT SEVEN THORN AND THE young sheriff had dinner at Perricone's restaurant, a rustic Italian bistro with lots of outdoor seating. A little pricey, but it was a short drive from their riverside bungalow at the Waterway Lodge, and Thorn had pleasant memories of the place. A few years back he and Rusty had eaten a celebratory meal there after a day at the Miami boat show. Rusty had been aglow with Christmas morning excitement after placing an order for a Hewes Redfisher—the first brand-new boat she'd ever bought.

It was on that same skiff, *Happy Daze II,* two weeks ago, that Rusty took her final voyage.

Thorn ordered a bowl of mixed greens. Oil and balsamic vinaigrette, doing penance for his lard intake. Buddha had a Caesar salad with the veal parmigiana, which she claimed several times was the best meal she'd ever tasted.

After fumbling his fork a couple of times, he switched to his left hand.

"I'm sorry," Buddha said. "Your fingers are blue."

"I'll live. But next time, try aiming an inch higher."

"Were you going to shoot me?"

"I was trying to get your attention."

"You know the rule. Never aim a gun unless you mean to fire."

"You were right, Buddha, I was wrong. I got what I deserved."

"I'm sorry. This time yesterday I didn't know you. I had a different idea in my head. Somebody a little gaga."

"Don't be so quick to revise that view."

Between courses she got out her electronic tablet and showed him the Monday obituary of Joe Camarillo, the baseball star from Miami. And she was right. The bat was in the ninth paragraph but the other crucial words were 'the' and 'of.' The closest nouns were "book" and "history" and "blue collar." If the killer was being guided to his victim by the third word in every third paragraph, neither Buddha or Thorn could guess how he would decide where to go and whom to kill.

"We must've read the code wrong. Or maybe it changes week to week."

She shook her head in frustration.

"It was too damn easy. I was worried about that."

"We'll find out tomorrow," he said. "When the victim turns up."

"That's cold, Thorn. Somebody's going to die. Some innocent person."

"First, we're not absolutely sure of that. And second, we've spent an hour noodling over this and don't have a clue. You could call Sheffield, give him a chance at cracking it. Have him hand it off to a cryptologist."

"I feel helpless," Buddha said. "Somebody's marked for death. Somebody's going to get bludgeoned with a baseball bat."

The waiter was standing there with the check.

"Bludgeoned with a baseball bat?" the young man said.

"We were joking," said Thorn.

"That's a relief. I thought you didn't like your dinner."

The young waiter wasn't smiling as he set the check down warily and backed away. Thorn raised his empty hands to show the kid he was unarmed.

Working on the front lines of commerce in Miami could be risky. The truce that kept chance encounters from erupting into bloodshed was fragile. You didn't joke about violence in public places, just as you didn't kid about bombs at airport security checkpoints. The new gun-friendly law was called Stand Your Ground. Florida's citizens had the state's permission to use deadly force against anyone they considered a threat to their safety. With so many people standing their ground, Miami had become a hair-trigger society. Determining which threats qualified as worthy of lethal response was the new survival skill. The rule was "Be nice or die." In fact, be very nice, or very quick on the draw.

By 10:15 they were back at the Waterway Lodge.

Their bungalow was a separate building set off a hundred paces from the main inn. It backed up to the river and had a small patio, tile roof, and Bahama shutters, and maybe twenty years earlier it had been charming. Now it was flaking paint, the shrubbery was withered, and broken lawn furniture and palm fronds lay at the bottom of the empty swimming pool.

The Miami River was no longer a real river, and hadn't been for over a century. It was nothing but a dredged trench with a few doglegs, but mainly it was carved straight as a ruler out of the limestone; the ancient overhanging oaks had been stripped away, the rocky rapids dynamited to help drain the Everglades, and to allow the big ships deeper penetration into the city. Its stagnant waters had a sour industrial smell, like solvents blended with kitchen garbage and engine oil. There'd been talk for years about cleaning the river, but such talk always seemed to die out for fear that disturbing the toxins that coated the bottom might send them downriver and wind up poisoning a chunk of Biscayne Bay.

Split into a duplex, their bungalow had a common wall separating the two bedrooms, but there was no connecting door. Buddha made absolutely sure of that when they were checking in. The innkeeper, an elderly gentleman, kept smirking at Thorn as though he knew the lack of an adjoining door wouldn't keep these lovebirds apart.

Their rooms were small and stuffed with marble-topped dressing tables and four-poster beds and lacy curtains with framed needlepoint on the walls. Not exactly Thorn's style, but Buddha seemed pleased.

She said she needed to write up her notes, edit her questions for tomorrow's interviews, and she was going to puzzle on the baseball player's obituary some more. Thorn had spotted a riverside bar a few blocks east and told her he was going to have a nightcap. He wanted to stretch his legs. They'd rendezvous at seven A.M., track down breakfast somewhere.

At the East Coast Fish House he took a table outside with a view of several Haitian freighters docked nearby. The rusty boats were stacked high with bicycles and mattresses, washing machines, bathtubs, and cargo containers that no doubt held an assortment of American castoffs.

A short voyage from Miami, all that second-hand junk would soon become somebody else's luxuries.

Inside the bar an overhead television was playing a Marlins game and the pool table was busy. There were a few suits and ties mingling with the dockhands and off-duty patrolmen and late-shift workers who just couldn't bear to drive home yet. The bar had a nautical theme. Hawsers and portholes and posters advertizing tropical cruises were mounted on the walls. The place reminded Thorn that there were, in fact, still vestiges of the old, funky Miami hanging on. Relics of that carefree tourist town that once survived off snow globes, toy alligators, and goofy wish-you-were-here postcards, a place he remembered fondly. Somehow a few spots like this bar had retained the screwy charm of a half-century earlier, before waves of refugees turned the city into an overheated international stew of factions and cultures and militant exiles, many of whom liked to claim credit for turning that sleepy town into the dynamic city Miami was today.

Thorn would gladly have the snow globes back.

It was after eleven when he finished his nightcap, and he was waiting to pay his bill at the register while the bartender served two matriarchs at the far end when a black man in a bus driver's uniform came huffing through the door.

"You see it?" he called down to the bartender.

"See what?"

"Where's the channel changer?"

"Where it always is," the bartender said, popping open two more beers.

The bus driver went halfway down the bar, leaned across and snatched the remote, and aimed it at the set.

April Moss was standing in front of a two-story coral rock house, looking grim but composed under harsh TV lights. A tall, agitated male reporter was jabbing a microphone inches from her lips.

"It's a police matter," April was saying. "You'll need to speak to them."

"Is it true the killer contacted you? You spoke to him directly?"

"No, it's not. He called the paper, not me. And that's all I'm saying at this time. No more questions."

"Sources tell us your obituaries in the *Herald* are provoking this madman to murder. How does that feel, being a killer's inspiration?"

April slowly turned her face to the man and gave him a withering glare.

Some of the bar patrons whooped at the reporter's chastened face.

"Bite his nuts off, April," one of the cops called out.

After April turned and walked away, the reporter repeated the high-lights of his interview, then tossed it back to the anchors.

"What's going on?" the bartender asked the bus driver.

"Some guy in a suit—you know, like Spider-Man only it's all black, that kind of suit, stretchy, all-over thing—he's running around murdering people. He says he's done four already and he's just getting warmed up."

A few of the drinkers inched closer to the bus driver.

"He reads the death notices in the paper, the ones that broad writes, and they tell him who to whack next. Fucker called the *Herald,* said the lady was the oracle of death, he was just following her commands."

"Oracle of death?" one of the cops said. "Aw, shit, here we go."

A couple of guys playing pool wanted the Marlins game back on.

"Somebody's ripping off a goddamn TV show," the bartender said. "Nottoli, that moron from sanitation, he's in here watching it every Thursday night. Same storyline, guy in a catsuit killing people, leaving obituaries behind. Stupid-ass show."

"You got a phone?" Thorn asked the bartender.

The guy pulled a handset from his back pocket and gave it to Thorn.

"Waterway Lodge, you know the number?"

"Fuck no, what am I, four-one-one?"

"Try the bulletin board," the bus driver said, and went back to the TV where the anchors were taking turns titillating each other with this horrifying turn of events.

The news ghouls hadn't yet assigned the murderer a nickname, but that was coming. At that moment there was probably a conference room full of brainy folks running through the possibilities.

Among the hundreds of business cards tacked to the bulletin board, Thorn finally found one for the inn. He punched in the number, got the leering desk clerk, and asked for Ms. Hilton's room.

Buddha picked up on the first ring.

"Turn on your TV. The eleven o'clock news."

"What is it?"

"Turn it on."

"There's no TV in my quaint and charming room. What's going on?"

"I'm not sure. A news crew was at April's house, interviewing her. The reporter said her obituaries were inspiring a killer."

"She spilled it," Buddha said. "She promised not to, but she spilled it."

"I don't think so. She looked blindsided. Sounds like the killer called the paper, and I bet that phone call she got at Poblanos was her boss calling her afterward."

"He called the paper?"

"Sounds that way. They know he wears a black suit. He claims he's killed four already and he's just getting started."

"Where are you?"

"That bar we passed on the river. Four blocks east."

"I'll get dressed and come over."

"Why?"

"So we can watch TV, talk it through."

Thorn watched the two anchors, finished with the boogey man story, yukking it up with the weather guy.

"There's nothing we can do tonight."

She was silent for a moment.

"Thorn?"

"Yeah."

"We set him off."

"What?"

"This isn't a coincidence. A few hours after we come to town and start asking questions, the guy pops up, changes the rules."

Thorn was silent for a moment, running it through.

He said, "You didn't mention the Zentai suit to Frank, or April, or anybody else."

"Just you."

"Which means nobody we talked to could've leaked that. Had to be the killer. The guy tells them he wears a black suit. Why's he do that?"

"He's feeling it."

"Feeling what?"

"Invincible."

The Marlins game was back on. They were down by five runs in the eighth. Losing in front of a couple of dozen fans in a luxurious new stadium.

"Okay, what does it mean, we show up, sniff around, a few hours later the guy breaks radio silence? What's the thought process?"

"I'm not a profiler, Thorn. I'm a small-town sheriff."

"Bullshit. You're more than that, Buddha. A lot more than that."

She was silent for several moments. A woman unfamiliar with praise.

"You still there?"

"The guy outs himself," she said. "To me that says he's ready for the limelight. But he wants it on his own terms. A control freak. Wants to manage the message."

"I'm coming back," he said. "Keep your door locked."

"Don't get all spooky, Thorn."

"If this character wants to manage the message, then you and me, we're a problem. We're wild cards. He knows about us. We lit his fuse. Keep your door locked. I'll be there in five."

You are carrying an aluminum baseball bat down a Miami street in the dark. Your body is out of body. You are walking on the street and you are floating above all this. It is eerie and wonderful and scary as shit.

You never liked aluminum bats. They're lighter, yes, move quicker through the air. But you dislike the noise they make when they smack a baseball, that hollow *boink*. They sound like something you'd hear inside a factory, rivets pounded into steel, some assembly line noise.

The old ones, the wood ones, impacting the leather ball, there was a satisfying thump, two real objects made from living things, clashing against each other. The sturdy wood crushing the hard leather sphere. Sending it flying.

Like you are flying now. Taking this risk. Thrust into action.

But it's okay. You're ready for a change. It's time. The killings were starting to feel ordinary. This is different, a wild, dangerous swing into the uncharted. You have no blueprint. You've not planned this step by step like the others, but thrown it together. It is the last-minuteness of it that thrills you. The spontaneity. Riffing, riding the wave of the hurtling moment. Going someplace, you don't know where. Feeling your way, relying on instinct.

You knew this day was coming. It was time for this phase. So it's okay. Today is as good as any day. Today, you have decided, is perfect.

You are holding the bat in one hand beside your leg, concealing it as you walk. You are a shadow in your black suit, in the suit that merges with the shadows. You feel tremors in your gut, stronger than any you felt before.

You see the inn where they are staying. Their red car parked outside a separate bungalow that stands beneath a giant oak. No streetlights here. Only dim lights from across the river, the freighters and the warehouses on the other bank. The tremor in your gut is taking root. You are bathed in sweat, the suit clinging to you, growing heavy.

You have been thinking of this moment for years. Planning it without ever picturing the specific way it would unfold, but priming yourself, waiting for the catalyst. Wondering if you would have the courage, the moral strength. And now you know. You are more than anyone imagines, more than you yourself thought possible.

At the bungalow there are two doors side by side. You are not sure which is hers, which is his. You stand a few feet away in a pool of darkness and choose the left. First one, then the other, that's all the plan you have.

Before you move, you listen for voices or the sound of footsteps, but there is only the incessant rumble of traffic on the adjacent streets and a radio blasting reggae on one of the freighters. The rank scent of the river in the air.

You step forward and the shudder is still with you. You wonder if it's possible to sustain this mad exhilaration, to nurture it, to endlessly ride this wave of dark rapture as if you have leapt from a cliff edge and will fall and fall but never reach the earth.

You knock on the left door. Five hard raps. Then five more.

"Thorn?" A woman's voice.

You do not speak. There are no peepholes in the doors. You stand out of view of the single window.

"Thorn, is that you?"

The door opens a few inches and her face appears in the crack.

Her face is covered with black lettering. Weird woman. No security chain. She squints at you in your black suit and tries to shut the door.

But you're quicker. You ram the tip of the aluminum bat through the opening and it thuds into flesh. Her face or throat.

You pry the door open, thump her in the chest, and then hit her flush in the face. She falls backward into the room, nose pouring blood, and you are inside.

You shut the door.

She backs away. She's wearing a robe that falls open. Naked beneath. A shapely woman, heavy breasts. While she's reeling, you rip her bathrobe off, pull it free of her arms. Now she's fully exposed, perfectly vulnerable.

She shoots a look toward her suitcase on a stand and you follow her glance and see the butt of her service revolver peeking out. You step between her and the luggage. She has no escape. You are bigger, stronger, armed with your primitive instrument.

"Who are you?" she says.

The two of you are doing a subtle dance. A step to the right, a half step left. She counters you, mirroring your moves as if she's your partner, your other half.

"You don't know me," you say.

You speak without thinking. A violation of your rules. Engaging with them. You've never done it before. But then this is the start of a new direction. Crossing a great divide, the beginning of the next act when new laws apply.

"I do know you," she says.

"No, you don't. No one does."

"You can stop doing this. It's not too late. You can stop."

You slash the bat at her, but she skips away.

You don't like being lectured to by this woman. It makes you feel childish, as though she's torn your suit away, left you as naked as she is.

You feint in and she tries a martial arts kick.

But the bat is already in motion and it cracks against her shin.

She buckles, stumbles backward, moans. She throws punches at the air. She's a trained fighter, but her training is futile against your blitz. You swing the bat, wade into a flurry of grunts and shrieks, push ahead with chopping blows and more chopping blows. Driving her backward, and backward again.

Your bat pings against bone and pings again. It's a disgusting noise. You wish you'd found a wooden bat. But no, there simply wasn't time to shop around.

THIRTEEN

THORN STARTED OFF AT A lope, trying to stay calm, telling himself this wasn't super-serious, just worrisome, somewhat alarming. But after trotting along the riverfront for a block, a tingle swept along his shoulders, a creepy sense of foreboding that someone was following him, a black presence, the boogeyman.

Too much beer, too little sleep.

He looked over his shoulder, saw nothing. But he kicked it up a notch, running now, stretching it out. Not a full sprint, but close. The tingle turned into chills as he pictured Buddha alone in that isolated building, apart from the inn, set a long block away from a nearby apartment complex. Not that anybody would come to her aid if she called out. Not that the cops were cruising that bleak quadrant of town. Center of the city, but as devoid of human presence as the middle of the Mojave.

Streetlights too dim. Shadows everywhere.

He rounded a corner and saw someone on the sidewalk coming toward him. All black, head to toe. Jesus, right there in the open, right there in front of him like an everyday thing.

Thorn got his legs driving, going to tackle the guy, lower his shoulder, level the asshole. Twenty yards, ten, the guy in black halted, seeing Thorn flying at him, stopped and waited like he wasn't all that worried, like maybe this happened all the time, forced him to draw his gun and bring down some charging beast on the city street. Thorn hadn't considered the guy being armed, but kept coming anyway, closing fast.

Fucker set his feet, turned sideways like a marksman at the range, raising both hands. Then Thorn was there, ten feet off, and saw the guy's face. A black man, African American, in dark trousers and a brown T-shirt. His fists up in a fighting stance.

Thorn swerved at the last second, the guy taking a swing, but missing.

"Sorry," Thorn gasped at him. "Sorry."

And got back up to speed, a full-out sprint, seeing the bungalow, the red car out front, the lights on in Buddha's side, door shut.

Everything appeared normal, but his gut wasn't buying it. He covered the last twenty yards in a flat-out dash.

Breathing fast, not quite gasping but close. He halted at the oak tree.

Light-headed, out of fucking shape, hands on his knees, bent over. He didn't want Buddha to see him like this, didn't want to rattle her with his own paranoia. He took a few seconds to get his breath then walked to the door and knocked.

No response.

He waited, knocked again, spoke her name. Said it a little louder. His chest was still thumping. Breath heaving too loud to hear clearly.

He tried the knob and it turned, and he knew that was wrong. Way wrong. With the door still shut, he crouched and set his shoulder against the wood midway for maximum leverage, and rammed forward, ducking as he came into the room, set to roll across the hardwood floor, to dodge a bullet or a fist, but there was nothing.

The room was empty.

Her small suitcase was on the folding stand. The lid open, everything packed neatly, clothes in folded squares, a plastic bag full of her toiletries. Her phone on the made bed, her electronic tablet lined up beside it. Her black ballistic nylon holster was wedged into a corner of the bag. The butt of the pistol visible. Otherwise the room was exactly as it had been when she'd first walked in and done a tour and pronounced herself pleased. A woman on the road for the first time in her life, staying in a room she considered swanky.

The bathroom door was shut and a slit of light showed at the bottom. He thought he heard water running but wasn't sure. Still breathing too hard to be certain.

She was drawing a bath, or brushing her teeth.

"Buddha?"

When she didn't answer, he stepped closer to the door, suppressing his breath, listening. It was water, then the water shut off.

"Your door was open. Buddha, it's me."

No answer. Something wrong.

He noted the hinges. The door opened outward, into the room.

He tried to flex his puffy right hand. He couldn't trust it to turn the knob and yank open the door. Which meant he'd have to stand to the left against the wall and backhand it with his working hand. Awkward as hell.

He called her name again and stepped closer. On the bed her cell phone began to play a tune. Paul McCartney on the piano, McCartney singing, "Hey Jude, don't make it bad. Take a sad song and make it better."

He reached out and knuckle-tapped lightly. Nothing.

McCartney continued to sing, continued to tickle the ivories.

Thorn was stepping to a safe position, to plant his back against the left side wall, when the door blew open and slammed his forehead, staggered him, froze him in place. Dazed, he watched the door close slightly, knowing he should be taking defensive action but unable to marshal his thoughts, watching the door slam open a second time even harder, cracking him in the forehead again, exploding a shower of fiery yellow pinpoints on the inside of his skull. He'd seen those starbursts before, knew what followed, the long slow drooping into darkness.

The two blows sent him tottering backward into the room and hunched him over, gasping, tasting the burn of acid in his throat, the fried cheese, the gristly chicken nuggets, all of it moving upward.

He coughed, cleared his throat, swallowed back the first hot squirt of vomit, then lifted his hands to shield himself from whatever attack was coming. Vision blurry, room tilting hard to the right like a ship riding slow-motion down the backside of a thirty-foot wave.

Backlit by the bathroom fluorescents, a black figure in a bodysuit held a purple baseball bat. Slender, long arms. He cocked the bat to his shoulder and took a step toward Thorn.

Still bent at the waist, Thorn got a sidelong look as the black figure took another step and set his feet. Going to send half-conscious Thorn sailing over the center field wall. Knock him the fuck right out of the park.

In the bathroom Buddha groaned, and the Zentai figure halted, held his bat steady, and turned his head. Thorn looked through a blue diamond light, felt the ship beneath his feet begin to sink.

Zentai man turned away and walked back to the bathroom, and Thorn watched through the open door as he raised the bat above his head like a woodsman about to split a piece of kindling.

Growling, Thorn lurched across the unsteady floor into the bright tiled room spattered with red, grabbed the Zentai creature's shoulder. But his crabbed right hand and bloated fingers slipped off the arm, as the bat swung down against the naked woman huddled in the white porcelain tub. Thorn rammed him backward against the sink, and the Zentai man clubbed Thorn in the shoulder, a half blow in that cramped space, but enough to stun his right arm, send splinters of pain into his neck and spine. Then Zentai used the butt end to spear Thorn in the gut and drive him backpedaling to the bathroom doorway.

"Hey!" a voice called from the other room.

The bat, aluminum and purple, swung twice more at the helpless shape in the tub. Finished with the woman, Zentai man took aim again on Thorn. Hitching up the bat on his shoulder, setting his hands on the narrow shaft, knuckles lined up nicely, bottom hand grazing the knob, a good, relaxed grip. Ready to send another bomb over the left field wall.

Arms cocked, black figure inching forward.

"Hey, what's going on in there?" Somewhere in the scramble of Thorn's memory he recalled the leering innkeeper, his creaky voice.

Thorn thrust his shoulder at the Zentai man but caught the flash of purple and tried to duck. Knowing he was late, his skull could never withstand the blow, this was it, the end of a long, torturous road, the same road everyone walked that ended at the same place. A flood of calm filled him. Some automatic chemical mechanism to ease the pain before a final flicker of sight. All that in the split second as the purple aluminum bat carved its arc through the air.

134

Halfway through the swing the bat struck the medicine cabinet, tearing it off the wall, and the aluminum club broke loose from the Zentai's grip, hit the tile floor, chiming and chiming as it bounced. Just luck. Just a small miscalculation saved him. Nothing he'd done.

The man shoved Thorn to the ground, stomped the side of his head against the tile, then vaulted over him and bolted from the room. Thorn managed another wild grab, snagged a patch of his stretchy legging, tearing a hole in the ankle. But the Zentai man pulled from Thorn's grasp and was gone.

He came to his knees, his palms against the sticky tile, the blood of Buddha. On all fours, he pulled himself to the tub, reached out and touched her arm, shook her, tried to rouse her from her agonizing slumber.

But she was dented, broken and gone. No pulse, no movement, no breath. She was back on the wheel of rebirth, if there was such a wheel, turning and turning again, taking her spirit into the next realm, the coming incarnation, the young sheriff from Oklahoma gone off to reap the karmic rewards of a life of endurance and decency in the face of unspeakable suffering.

Thorn picked up the baseball bat.

The room was tilting and a soft pounding grew in his ears like the synchronized footsteps of a vast army on the march, the rhythmic thump of thousands of feet thudding against the earth, accompanied by the low hum of chanting voices as waves of warriors approached the battlefield.

He seemed to be looking through a pinhole at the room before him, as he carried the baseball bat to the door and found himself suddenly outside, then found himself again a half block down the darkened street, sprinting with the bat after the phantom in black, toward another pinhole of light he could barely make out miles in the distance.

Next he found himself standing before a galvanized pole, heaving for breath, and he was cocking the bat onto his shoulder, taking aim at the pole, then he was hammering the bat against the steel, feeling the shock in his joints, the ache in his hands, but drawing the bat back to his shoulder again and ripping it forward and clanging metal against metal. Doing it again and again and again.

He was still at it, breathless, sweating, heart floundering, when the sirens shut down and the flashing lights surrounded him. Still drawing back the aluminum bat and slamming it into the immovable light pole, continuing to do it as the guns approached, as the voices commanded him to halt, to drop his weapon, Thorn taking another full swing, another bone-rattling crash, until this time the purple bat, spattered with Buddha's blood and dented and bent, finally cracked in half, the slender shaft staying in his hands while the barrel spun away and clattered across the street.

Then there were rough hands on his shoulders and he was jammed to his knees. His arms jerked behind him, wrists cuffed. Thrust forward, Thorn's face against the coarse city asphalt. On his lips the taste of blood and salt from his watering eyes, and in his throat the sour burn of rage.

FOURTEEN

FRANK SHEFFIELD AND THORN SAT side by side in wicker chairs on the bungalow's patio. Thirty feet before them the river sparkled with the reflection of shipboard lights. A breeze sifted in from the east, pushing away the stench of diesel oil and rotten vegetation. Inside the bungalow the crime scene technicians were at work. Photographs, scrapings, dusting the walls. Men and women in sterile suits taking rational measurements, methodical recordings. With their science and their finely calibrated instruments they would eventually explain the order of events, the size and shape of the instrument of death, a precise and orderly description of what took place. But none of it would approach the root cause, the breakdown of the civilized contract that allowed for such a thing. Nothing yet invented could quantify that.

Thorn's head had been wrapped in a small turban of gauze by Miami-Dade Fire Rescue paramedics. A lump had risen in the center of his forehead like an emerging third eye. His face was bruised, ribs tender. The paramedics had pronounced him fit for service. He might be groggy for a week or two. Recovery time depended on his general health and the thickness of his skull.

"Then he should do just fine," Sheffield had said.

Frank reached over and patted Thorn on the knee.

"Let me know when you're ready to begin."

Thorn shook his head, which he instantly realized was a mistake. His gray matter felt as loose inside his skull as Jell-O wobbling in a dish.

"You took a shot," Frank said. "Lucky it's only a concussion."

"Yeah, I'm some lucky guy."

"Your friend, the sheriff. Anybody to contact?"

"I don't know," he said. "I suppose Starkville has a mayor."

"I'll take care of it," Frank said.

"A baseball bat. A fucking bat."

"Bad as I've seen in a while," Frank said. "You start to think murder is murder, then something like this happens."

"Buddha was coming into her own. A smart, exceptional woman."

Thorn watched a man in a dinghy heading upstream in the dark. A German shepherd puppy sat in the bow, nose lifted into the air. To that dog, undiscriminating, at peace, all smells were good smells. Maybe Buddha had made her transmigration already, maybe that was her new state of being. A dog drinking in the night air. By Thorn's reckoning that would be progress from her human phase.

"You might be wondering why it's me, not the new girl, Mankowski. Well, she wasn't that interested. Something going on with Cuba has her all atwitter.

"And Miami PD, they'll be assisting. There's turmoil in the department, mayor trying to unseat the chief. Typical banana republic bullshit. So I'm taking the lead. Miami PD's okay with that. Nobody's fussing."

"Is this a serial?"

"At this point, my friend, I don't know what the hell it is. Maybe we'll wake up tomorrow, find out it's some kind of publicity gag for that TV show. It's all been a put-on."

Thorn stared at Sheffield. The man was lean and tanned, had shaggy brown hair with streaks of gray, and pouches beneath his eyes. Handsome still, but with major wear and tear. In his wrinkled khakis and blue Hawaiian shirt, he looked more like an aging surfer than an SAC.

Like most in his profession, he'd developed a Kevlar sensibility. You couldn't hold his bad jokes against him. Gallows humor was his bulletproof shield. Thorn shared the tendency, though he doubted he'd be making jokes of any kind for a good long while.

Without warning, Thorn's eyes burned and clouded. A bad time to succumb to a long-delayed wail of woe over Rusty. That loss now compounded by Michaela Stabler, and Buddha Hilton. Three more women with the misfortune to cross Thorn's path. Three who'd been living worthy, colorful, rich, strange, complicated, idealistic lives, struck down for no reason.

He held on, riding out the surge of anger and grief.

Frank patted him on the knee a second time.

"It's okay, man. You're still here, you're in one piece more or less, and I promise you, I'm going to get this fucktard. I'm going to be the ton of bricks that flattens his bones and grinds his guts to sausage."

Thorn shifted in the chair, let out the breath he'd been holding, guarding against a breakdown in front of Frank.

"And where am I while you're making sausage?"

"Where all law-abiding citizens are. Standing on the sidelines."

"Unacceptable."

"You think I'm going to let you tag along? Why would I do that?"

"Because you need me."

"When I'm ready for things to spin out of control, I'll give you a call. How's that?"

"He won't kill again till next Saturday," Thorn said. "But Monday he gets his marching orders."

"Do that again."

"Are we collaborating?"

"Riddle me this, Thorn. You want to sit in a room for a few days, stare at some blank walls? Because we got a nice holding cell up in North Miami where we put material witnesses that refuse to cooperate."

"You need me," Thorn said, "a lot more than I need you."

"Granted, you got a head start on this. But do I need you? Not really."

"I know how he selects his victims. How he locates them. How he chooses his weapon. This week he made an adjustment, picked a victim without the obituary's guidance. But the baseball bat, that was in the newspaper. Buddha and I knew a bat would be his murder weapon four or five hours ago."

Frank raked his fingers through his hair.

"Earlier today," Frank said, "you told me you had personal reasons for pursuing this asshole. I want to know what those are before we go any farther down this path."

"All right," Thorn said. "Rusty's obit in the *Herald* steered the killer to the Oklahoma victim. That victim was Rusty's aunt, someone she was very close to, and someone Buddha was close to as well. Personal, personal, personal."

"Six degrees of personal."

"And in the last half hour, it's gotten a hell of a lot more personal. I'm staying with this to the end, Frank, with or without you."

Sheffield glanced at Thorn, then looked back at the river.

"You're going to need a wardrobe upgrade. That outfit might be haute couture in the Keys, but it won't cut it in this town."

"I'll deal with it tomorrow."

Frank used both hands to scrub the weariness from his face.

"So give me something, Thorn. How does this guy choose the vics?"

Thorn took his time recounting the theory Buddha had developed. Monday obituaries led to Saturday murders. Three paragraphs down, three words in. Paragraphs three, six, and nine.

Frank sat back, chewed on that. Nodded.

"This fucking world," he said.

"Very crude code. But it fits the Oklahoma murder Buddha was working. And a baseball bat appeared in last Monday's obit, ninth paragraph, third word. If we look through previous Monday papers, my bet is, we find matches with other Saturday killings."

"I'll put somebody on that tonight." Frank's phone buzzed. He pulled it from his pants, checked the ID, and put it back. "So returning to the scene in Sheriff Hilton's room. How'd it go down?"

"Asshole was wearing a black suit, spandex or whatever the hell it is."

"Most likely it was Lycra."

"You've been reading up," Thorn said.

"Lycra bodysuits. They're called Zentai. Some kind of Japanese fetish. Those Japs, man, when it comes to sex, they're as depraved as the Germans."

Thorn was quiet, watching the rubber raft's wake slosh against the seawall and the hulls of the ships. Feeling his gut roll as the image appeared again—Buddha curled in the bathtub, broken, bloody.

"Okay, so you walk in on this guy. He's using that aluminum bat on Ms. Hilton. You witnessed that, the actual attack?"

Thorn described his entry into the room, told him about going to the bathroom door, about the door smashing him in the forehead. Twice.

"Thought the bat did that," Frank said. "It was the door?"

"If it'd been the bat, we wouldn't be having this talk."

"So you're smacked in the head, you're cross-eyed, but you still saw some of what happened, the guy in black finishing off Hilton."

Thorn nodded.

"Description of the perp?"

"Thin, strong. Like you said, I was out of it, the room was spinning. What about the innkeeper, you talk to him? He should've seen something."

"Zero help. He came running when he heard the commotion, got one foot into the room, glimpsed you stumbling around, and scurried the hell out of there to do his Braveheart call to nine-one-one."

"That's all I got, Frank, slim build, well developed."

"Height?"

"I don't know. It was a whirlwind."

"You're not forgetting anything?"

"I tore the suit. Somewhere around his right ankle."

"That could be helpful."

"That's all I can remember. If something else bobs up, you'll get it."

"Because if I got the sense this was your approach, a one-way street, well, that would be the end of my cooperation. We clear on that?"

Thorn shrugged, a vague affirmative.

"Now you," Thorn said.

Frank looked up at where the stars would be if the sky weren't polluted with Miami's extravagant light.

"Promise you'll stay with me on this."

"I do solemnly swear."

"It's not too late to fuck up and lose my pension."

"I swear to stay on the rails so Frank can have his government check."

Frank reached down, plucked a blade of grass and began to chew its tip, then flicked it away.

"Never saw an aluminum bat broken in half before."

"Cheap materials," Thorn said.

"It's not the materials. You beat the shit out of that bat. You destroyed it. The murder weapon, I might add. You demolished some crucial evidence. That's what I'm talking about, Thorn. That kind of behavior. I know you were crazed, but hey, man, you can't let shit like that happen. Those Miami cops were a hair trigger from taking you down."

"I'll try not to lose it again, Frank. What can I say?"

"Try hard, Thorn. Try very hard. This isn't the Keys. This isn't live and let live. You're in the war zone, baby. Everyone's on edge twenty-four seven. You hear me?"

Thorn nodded. He tried to look sincere. Frank sighed. Not buying it, but what could he do?

"So what do you have, Special Agent?"

"All right, okay. Number one, it goes without saying, but I'm saying it anyway, this guy is one brutal motherfucker, so he's enjoying his work. What that means is he's not stopping till we pull his plug."

Thorn waited in silence.

"Forensically, it's early. With the guy wearing a bodysuit, techs tell me it's unlikely we'll have hair, fingerprints, any DNA. They're looking for strands of Lycra from his suit, which could possibly lead somewhere, help identify the manufacturer, start to narrow down the point of purchase. There's a couple of retail outlets locally that sell these things. We'll hit them soon as we can, but my bet is this suit came from some online merchant. Lots of outlets internationally. If that's the case, it'll be very hard to trace the origin. But we'll run all that down. Maybe we'll get lucky and the guy bought the thing in Miami and some salesclerk remembers him. We'll see."

"Buddha thought the guy was half-assed about covering his tracks. He tore up a sales receipt for the murder weapon he used in Oklahoma and left it behind in a trash bin not far from the murder scene. That's one thing that led her to Miami. The weapon, a hand spear, was bought in a sporting goods store here in town."

"Good," Frank said. "I prefer half-assed criminals. Makes life easier."

"Unless the bread crumbs are on purpose."

"Why do you say that?"

"I don't know. Guy's smart half the time, dumb the rest. Seems fishy."

"Smart and dumb coexist," Frank said. "Not uncommon, some crook who's come up with an elegant scheme, except it's got a glaring error the doofus overlooked."

"Buddha suspected we were being played."

"You know where that sales receipt is?"

"In her purse or her luggage. She was a very organized lady."

"Then the ID techs will catalog it," he said. "We'll check it tomorrow, take a look-see at the sporting goods place.

"How it appears right now, our best hope with forensics are the bloody footprints. Size ten, maybe a little larger. Something funky about the tracks, but that's probably because of the stitching in the suit.

"I got a foot specialist I use, Henry Roediger, he does morphology studies on shoes and bare feet—our Cinderella analyst, we call him. Our if-the-shoe-fits guy. He can tell us if the killer's got hammertoe, a bunion deformity, give us the biomechanical foot type, the average gait. Before he's done with his casts and his lasers, he'll tell us what this fucker had for breakfast a week ago."

"Any sightings? Guy walking around town in a suit like that, people had to notice."

"On that score, we have an embarrassment of riches," Sheffield said. "Minute this hit the airwaves, the phone calls started. Already topping fifty. This time tomorrow we'll be in the multiple hundreds. Every part of town, Gables, Grove, Kendall, Overtown, Aventura. We got short, fat, tall, skinny, men, women, children. Blue suits, red suits, green. Dicks hanging out, tits showing. Men in black carrying bows and arrows."

"Jesus."

"The usual flakes. And lots of old folks looking out their windows thinking some guy in bike pants and a tight shirt is our killer. Happens every time there's something big. Add the crazies to the drunks and the pranksters, it'll be a never-ending gush of false alarms. Shit, after the Twin Towers went down, we had ten bomb scares an hour for two months."

"Passenger manifests," Thorn said. "Everything flying from Miami to Dallas/Fort Worth last weekend. How hard would that be?"

"Not hard to get, but I don't know what good it would do."

"The guy's name could be on that list. I don't care if it's five thousand names, that's a smaller group than what you've got now."

"Ever heard of false ID?"

"You looking to get out of work, Frank?"

"Don't start with me."

They fell into silence. Thorn considered the Atlanta pedestrian stop, a Saturday event. He could give Frank that, have him use his channels to run it down with Atlanta PD. He could give him the pinking shears, the ding in the blade, and he could tell him about his own name printed on the backside of the obituary Buddha found at Michaela Stabler's murder scene. But he didn't. He held on to that. Holding on was all he was up to at that moment. He just sat quietly, gazing out at the dark, gleaming river.

FIFTEEN

A FEW MINUTES LATER, FRANK stretched his arms and scooted his chair around so he was facing Thorn.

"Okay," he said. "I can hear your brain buzzing. Unburden yourself. You'll feel better."

For a second Thorn was tempted to blurt it out. But that second passed. Thorn trusted Frank more than he trusted most lawmen, but he had no faith in the bureaucracy Frank worked for. Information had a way of disappearing inside its formless structures and never giving back much return on the investment.

He decided to hand Sheffield just enough to keep the dialogue going, but reserve the small concrete leads he might be able to handle himself.

"Buddha had a theory," he said. "She thought the guy outed himself because he wants to run the show. When he found out the two of us were on his trail, that threatened his power to shape events. He was afraid of losing control of the message."

"Plausible. Ergo the attack on the sheriff. Which of course also suggests a high threat level on you."

"Bring it on."

"You packing, Thorn?"

"No."

"Good. Let's keep it that way."

"I got two questions. How'd the guy learn about us, and how'd he track us down to the Waterway Lodge?"

"Start with the second. Who knew you were staying in this dump?"

"Only one I mentioned it to was April Moss. I asked her about the place this afternoon. If it was still in business."

"So we find out who April talked to, who she might've spoken to. Then again, there's a chance the guy picked you up somewhere along the line, tailed you here, saw you check in. Today when you were driving around, you happen to notice if you were being followed?"

Thorn said no, he hadn't done that. He'd had no reason.

"So we interview Ms. Moss, see if she mentioned the delightful Waterway Lodge to anybody. If she didn't, then somebody had you in their sights earlier."

"If we were tailed, where'd it begin?"

"I don't know. Walk me through your day."

"Midmorning we drove up from Key Largo, got to the nursing home, the Floridian, a little after noon, hung around till April showed. Watched some of the TV show get made. It was midafternoon when we drove over to see you, three-thirty, around there, spent maybe half an hour, got to Poblanos a little before five. Maybe half an hour there, then we came here, checked in, got cleaned up, went to Perricone's. After the restaurant we returned here and split up. I went to the East Coast bar, Buddha stayed put."

"When you made this date to meet the Moss woman at Poblanos, there anybody listening in?"

"Her mother."

"So maybe the old lady lets it slip to whoever where you're meeting up with her daughter, and this whoever goes and hangs around Poblanos, picks you up there. Tags along, watches you take rooms here."

"Either way, April or her mother, it circles back to that TV show. One of those people."

"Maybe."

"It's the TV show."

"A possibility. But don't be in a hurry to hang this on somebody, Thorn. You fixate, that's how you make mistakes in the investigation biz."

Thorn wasn't going to argue the point. But Frank was wrong. One way or the other, this was about *Miami Ops.* Everything pointed back to it.

"When you and April were talking at the bar, how much did you reveal?"

"Buddha let a few things slip. The killer might be copycatting the show, and it looked like he was using April's obits for his blueprint."

"But before the barroom talk, she was in the dark about all that? She didn't know the nature of your investigation?"

"Why is that important?"

"Building a timeline. Who knew what and when they knew it."

"Well, before the bar, April didn't have any hint of what we were doing. All Buddha said at the nursing home was there was an urgent police matter she needed to discuss with her."

Thorn shook his head, blinked his eyes, trying to kick-start his brain.

"Look, we can finish this tomorrow when your head clears."

"Probably better."

"You want, I can put you in a room at the Silver Sands. Dig a mattress out of storage. I been having a bedbug issue, and the room might smell a little rank, but the rent's cheap."

Thorn shrugged. He wasn't sure what he wanted to do. He sure as hell wasn't staying on at the Waterway Lodge. He tried to think of his next move. Tried to get the logical synapses firing again, but the haze was clogging things.

He kept replaying his day with Buddha, running and rerunning the snippets of conversation, the way she'd showed up at his house in the dark, the bonfire, shooting the pistol from his hand, Thorn reading her backward tats in the mirror, the Four Noble Truths, the drive to Miami, sawblade, pinking shears, incest porn, Zentai, *Iklwa,* Buddha's face-off with April Moss. Something going on between those two women, some weird recognition. All those left-field questions about Thorn's long-ago date with April. Did Thorn take advantage? Did they use protection?

Frank said, "There's something I'm puzzled by."

"Yeah?"

"Homicide boys bagged all Sheriff Hilton's stuff, took it off to run through their magic machines. What I didn't see was her phone or that iPad she was playing with. You know what happened to those items?"

"Killer must've got them."

"Come on, you can do better than that."

Thorn watched a man on the upper deck of one of the freighters smoking a cigarette. When he was done, he flicked it into the river. It hit the gleaming surface and continued to glow orange for a moment more before winking out. Thorn was surprised the river didn't erupt in flames.

"Even killers need to call their moms."

"Hey, Thorn. A guy murders someone with a bat, assaults a witness, he's scared off, must know the cops are on the way. But before he flees he stops to select a few pieces of choice electronic hardware, then shoves them in the pocket of his Zentai suit? I don't think so."

Thorn kept his eyes on the river.

"Plus," Frank said. "Quick look at the bloody tracks tells me the guy was running out the door. A straight line from bathroom to the exit."

"I don't know, Frank."

"Maybe you were too groggy to recall. Before the paramedics got here, before the place was swarming with cops, is it possible you sleep-walked those items out to the rental car and stashed them?"

Thorn closed his eyes and opened them again. It was all still there.

"I could get a warrant, or just go crash the window and have a look."

"Go for it."

"So is this how it's going to play between us?"

Thorn waved away a night bug.

"Just a reminder, Thorn. My pension, man. I'll help you how I can, but I'm not going to give you carte blanche. There'll be no running rough-shod."

Thorn kept his eyes trained on the dark river as if something important might happen there at any second.

Headlights swept across the grounds, then shut off. A car door slammed. Frank looked over to see who it was. Thorn kept watching the river.

"Well, well," Frank said.

He heard the click of footsteps on the concrete walkway.

Frank stood up. Thorn kept staring at the thick brown syrup that was the Miami River. A grim blend of sludge and flushed bilges and toxic runoff.

"Good evening, Ms. Moss," Frank said.

April murmured a quiet hello.

"My name's Frank Sheffield, special agent in charge, Miami field office of the FBI. We've met once, though I doubt you remember."

"I know who you are. I covered some of your work."

Thorn kept his eyes on the river.

"I hope they were some of my honorable successes."

"A couple were. Nobody's a hundred percent."

"We were just talking about you. We had some questions."

"I heard about Sheriff Hilton," April said. "It's terrible."

Thorn was silent, looking out at the hard gleam of the river.

"You'll have to excuse him. He took a couple of raps to the skull."

"I'm here," Thorn said. "I'm listening."

"Thorn, I'm very sorry about your friend. It's dreadful."

"I only met her last night. I wouldn't call her a friend."

"He appreciates your condolences," Frank said.

"The reason I came," she said. "I wanted to see if you were planning to stay on in Miami. Until this thing gets resolved."

He thought about it for a moment and grunted.

"I believe that's a yes," Frank said.

"Do you have a place to stay?"

Thorn watched one of the freighters moving ghostly slow downriver. Heading back to Haiti with its haul. Silence was brimming up inside him.

"I told Thorn he could crash at my place on the Key. He'll have to sleep on the floor. Water's turned off, just one working toilet, but it's clean. Well, sort of clean."

"Is that what you want to do, Thorn? Stay with Agent Sheffield?"

Frank said, "If you've got a better idea, I'm sure he'll listen."

"Here's the thing," she said. "My mom and I live about ten minutes from here, a little way up the river. It's a neighborhood called Spring Garden."

"Oh, you're in Spring Garden?" Frank leaned forward. "Old area, shady streets, historic homes, one of the last gracious corners of town."

"It is," April said. "I have a garage apartment that's empty, it's private, has its own entrance. Queen-size bed, full bath. You could come and go, Thorn, be completely independent."

"Wow," Frank said. "You got an extra bunk?"

"It's yours, Thorn. A day or two, or as long as you need."

Thorn watched the motorized rubber raft come back down the river, the dog still in the bow, his nose in the air, ears flapping. All smells good smells.

As April Moss described her neighborhood and her house, her voice had warmed to the subject, and her tone, so different from the hard-edged one she'd used earlier at the bar, summoned a swirl of images he'd been trying to resurrect all afternoon.

Until just now he'd only managed to recall a couple of disjointed moments, but when he heard her natural rhythms of speech, it took him back to that night, and that distant stretch of time snapped into focus.

He saw again her intoxicated gaiety as they drove away from the Islamorada bar, heading back to his isolated house on the bayside, a talkative, drunken, silly girl singing some Margaritaville ditty. That's where the interlude had started to feel like a grave mistake, and he was about to swing around and return young April to her girlfriends who were staying at the local Holiday Inn.

Then came her sudden queasy surge, April leaning her head out the passenger window and letting go. Afterward asking Thorn to please take her somewhere she could lie down. Thorn drove on, got to his place, helped her up the stairs of his stilt house. He could still see her wobbling to his bathroom, hear her retch a second time, and afterward her shyness and discomfort.

The long night that followed, young April sleeping it off in Thorn's bed. Her snoring, her fluttering lips, her bursts of incoherent language. Then this anonymous girl waking at dawn, coming outside in one of Thorn's long T-shirts, onto the upstairs deck where he had spent the night in a lounge chair staring at Blackwater Sound. The coffee, the sunrise, her shaky quiet.

Then her slow unfolding as they talked in fits and starts, finally landing on the subject of her future plans, what she hoped to do, the life she imagined for herself, college, grad school, a job in the city, her plan to be a crusading newspaper reporter. Afterward, there was a contented silence, and finally he remembered her leaning close to him, an awkward kiss, a kiss of simple gratitude, Thorn believed, a reward for keeping his respectful distance the night before. For not taking advantage. Nothing more than that, a light, dry kiss followed by a shy, winsome smile.

After that they wandered back inside and circled each other for a while and smiled, and said whatever they said and circled some more, until another kiss happened, a different, more substantial one, and the two of them by mutual consent and with full knowledge melted into the open sheets, and then there was a long gentle morning, her pale skin against the white cotton, the leisurely kisses, her coltish moves, girlish giggles, the wild surprise of orgasm.

It was all still there, preserved at some substrata of memory, the golden sunlight, the last coolish breeze before summer set in, the blooms of jacaranda outside the window, light twirling and spitting through a wind chime of broken mirror fragments someone had made for him years before.

Though what happened between them was no more than skin brushing skin, only simple need and mutual pleasure seeking, still that morning together seemed to be a happy few hours for both of them. Ending at the motel door where she was staying with her girlfriends, no promises made, no plans to stay in touch, April reached up for a kiss that both of them knew was their last.

"Miami hailing Thorn," Frank said.

He looked at Sheffield, who said, "Hey, this good lady is offering you a place to stay. Sounds like a damn fine place."

"I'd like that," Thorn said.

A few minutes later, driving Buddha Hilton's rental, staying close to April's Mini Cooper, Thorn leaned over, popped the glove compartment, and drew out the sheriff's phone and the electronic tablet and her service revolver and the evidence bag with Rusty's obit. He set them on the passenger seat, where Buddha had sat all day as they toured the city.

April led him through an edge of Overtown, with its ratty public housing, busted-out streetlights, old wood houses missing windows and doors, vacant lots surrounded by razor wire, soup kitchens, halfway

houses, and the occasional corner groceries and barber shops forti-
fied by prison bars and rolldown shutters, then she cut south along the
river where the neighborhood improved by a few degrees, rolling past
the once-genteel homes of Miami pioneer families, some freshly reno-
vated, most untouched for a generation.

April pulled through the front gates of her place and rolled up to her
modest but tidy two-story coral house and parked and Thorn parked
beside her.

In the passenger seat Buddha's phone was blinking with a message.
A missed call, a waiting voice mail. Thorn fiddled with the device, trying to imitate the sliding motions he'd seen Buddha use earlier.

Finally the screen changed and revealed a small icon lit up in the corner. While April stood beside her car looking off at the dark sky, Thorn
touched a fingertip to the icon, then pressed the phone to his ear.

A good old boy introduced himself as Officer Ben Hardison of the
metro Atlanta police department. "But everybody calls me Big Ben, like
the clock," he said. "You can too."

He'd pulled that file Sheriff Hilton wanted, which he'd sent her as an
e-mail attachment, though there wasn't much to it. Just a pedestrian stop
and a brief questioning. No ID taken, no name, nothing. Didn't even
merit entering it in the record, but he did it, just out of habit.

However, there was something the sheriff might find some use for.

" 'Cause I wanted to help you out with your situation, I went and had
a look at the dashboard video of the night in question. Hadn't been de-
leted off the server. Subject's standing there in the headlights in that
crazy suit.

"I ordered the hood removed. Video's grainy, but you might find
somebody in your tech department could clean it up for you. From what
I can tell, it's a foxy young woman. Dark hair cut short. I've emailed you
a link to the video. Anything else you need, you get back to me, little lady,
you hear?"

ACT THREE

HUGE

SIXTEEN

"THIS IS HUGE," DEE DEE said. "Huger than huge."

It was Saturday morning, dawn. Sawyer and Dee Dee were in her tenth-floor condo on Brickell, lying naked on top of the open sheets. A small blue slice of Biscayne Bay was visible in the distance, but mostly her view consisted of three other tall white condo towers boxed in close.

As usual they had the weekend free. Gus wanted everybody to stay close, make themselves available for pressers. TV, radio, newsprint, do every interview offered. Be shocked, sympathetic to the victim, but mention *Miami Ops* at every opportunity. Thursday at ten. Thursday at ten on the Expo Channel.

Talking point: "The entire *Miami Ops* family is horrified and outraged at these gruesome murders that bear such a striking similarity to the events depicted on our show."

After the news broke, it turned into a crazy all-nighter. Most of the crew and cast converged on Gus's penthouse condo on the fifteenth floor of the same building where Dee Dee and Sawyer were shacked up.

With the cable news channels babbling in the background, Gus and Flynn and several members of the film crew talked, drank whiskey, and shook their heads and tried to figure out how this would impact their future.

For several hours in a row all the cable networks led with the story, a killer stalking the Miami streets. One of the wardrobe girls went online and checked the websites for all the national papers. Most had front-page headlines featuring the killer with a striking resemblance to a character from a TV show. The murderer was apparently following the blueprints he'd found in obituaries written for *The Miami Herald.*

Everybody's cell phones kept going off. A dozen calls from the west coast; Exposure Channel people; the geniuses at Clintron, the production company that put together the deal with Expo. Gus's agent—who also repped Dee Dee and Flynn—and Sawyer's agent, a young woman working out of New York, both called. Each pretending they were checking in to be sure their good friends on the *Miami Ops* team were safe. Yeah, right.

All the film execs and development people and lawyers and agents so concerned and courteous and worried, but all clearly faking, calling for other reasons entirely. Sharks on their best behavior, circling around the other topic, eager but unwilling to broach the obvious.

The closest anybody came to outright rejoicing was Murray Danson. On a conference call with Gus, Sawyer, Flynn, and Dee Dee, Danson said with his usual bland indifference, "This could help with ratings."

Gus laughed at him.

"Help?" he said. "This fucking nails it. Now get off my back, asshole. As of now, you're putting us back on payroll. Tonight either start churning out checks or we start shopping for another outlet. And I want to see a second season contract on my agent's desk Monday morning, you got that, Danson?"

"Did you hear me, Sawyer?" Dee Dee was saying.

"Yeah, this is huge. I heard you."

Dee Dee was spread-eagled on the sheets, a luscious white X against the black silk sheets, her wrists and ankles bound with pink rubber exercise bands whose other ends were attached to clips on the sideboards of the bed. It was a position she'd invented and named the Flytrap. An erotic cardio workout, missionary position on Benzedrine. Burn a few thousand calories while swapping some serious bodily fluids.

Freaky and mechanical, the way it worked: With Sawyer lying atop her, his cock inside, Dee Dee brought her extremities together, foot straining toward foot and hand toward hand until she was squeezing Sawyer's body tightly. Then as she exhaled, she relaxed and let the pink bands draw her limbs apart until she was spread again, and lay wide open, a moment or two, allowing hips to thrust against hips, groin to grind groin.

After an interval to catch her breath, she repeated the process, slowly closing her arms and legs around him, encircling him, clenching tight, tighter than tight, a crushing embrace, almost asphyxiating, then slowly letting go, one rep after another, picking up the pace, faster and faster, the two of them becoming a carnal exercise machine, Dee Dee pumping her hard body full of blood and contracting sphincters until both of them were gasping, and damned if Sawyer could believe it, but even though it was all so freaking weird and motorized, his climaxes went beyond anything he'd known.

Throughout it all Dee Dee cycled from vulnerable to dominant and back again. Creepy and exhilarating, she worked on Sawyer like a carnivorous flower, opening and closing around him, until she'd extracted a spurt of nectar.

All this was performed, as everything that took place on her bed was performed, with the curtains open and their activities in plain view of hundreds of adjacent condos.

Sawyer was a private guy, but since their first night together, Dee Dee had been coaxing him step by step out of his shell, into exhibitionist territory.

"They're watching," she said, that first morning as they lay exhausted. "Who?"

"I'd say about three dozen." She nodded at her picture window. Sawyer looked out at the nearby towers and saw the winks of light that he came to discover were the telltale signals of the binocular and telescope voyeurs.

Sawyer resisted, but Dee Dee wore him down, first with the shades open in the dark, then at dusk and dawn; now, after months of open-curtain sessions, they left them drawn back all the time and Sawyer had embraced the role, feeling a strange kinship with those horny snoops who lived vicariously through his hours with Dee Dee Dollimore. Even coming to accept her view of sex as performance art, something they did as much to satisfy their fan base as each other. Nothing was too hare-brained or extreme as long as it kept the audience enthralled.

Sawyer understood very well this was not the basis for a long-term relationship, but it was a wild turn-on while it lasted.

"What's huger than huge?" she asked.

She shrugged out of her elastic cuffs and rolled over to face him.

"Monstrous," Sawyer said.

Jacking herself up on an elbow, she squinted down at him. The sheets were damp. They'd kicked the quilt—the one Garvey had made for him before he headed off to Harvard full of ambition—to the floor. Around them Dee Dee's collection of rubber toys was scattered across the dresser and the carpet. Pinks and blacks and flesh colors, mostly jumbos. One of them, a long skinny probe with a bulging tip, was still buzzing on a bedside bookshelf.

"Are you being sarcastic again?"

"This is gruesome, Dee Dee," he said. "Over-the-top gruesome. Why do I have to explain that to you?"

"You're not happy? This isn't your wildest dream come true? The big come-from-behind finish. Don't you get it? This is the *New York* fucking *Times, Good Morning America,* CNN, the tabloid shows. We'll be making the rounds. The Nielsens will skyrocket."

"Guy on CNN called *Miami Ops* 'an obscure third-rate crime drama.' "

"Any hype is good hype."

"You can't be happy about this, Dee Dee."

"Why not?"

"It's heartless. People have died. This is brutal shit."

"You're such a prig. The studio cuts off funds, we're dead in the water, might as well be cancelled. Now this happens. Sure, it's sad people died. Sure, sure, okay, I get it. And believe me, my heart goes out to them, and I'm sending their loved ones my thoughts and prayers. Hey, I'm not some cold bitch. But Sawyer, this is going to push us into the big-time."

She prodded him in the ribs. Prodded him a second time.

Sawyer closed his eyes and ground his head into the pillow.

"God, you're incredible. Lightning strikes, this amazing thing happens, and you're glum. We're all going to be crazy famous. This is what

I've been working for, what you've been working for. We're on the big stage. The paparazzi are staking out your mom's house. I got plans for all that money that's going to start pouring in. Oh, I got big plans."

"Yeah, yeah. Our fifteen minutes have started."

"Fifteen minutes?"

Sawyer rolled onto his side. Dee Dee stared at him blankly. Was she putting him on? Could she not know the Warhol line? Lately he'd been finding out more and more she didn't know. Blank stretches in her education. Stuff that hadn't bothered him a month ago, stuff he'd ignored, so lost in the fever of lust.

"Yeah, okay," he said. "The eyeballs will be there this Thursday, sure, that's probably going to happen. The Expo Channel is going to light up like Christmas. We'll hit Danson's number, the studio will piss itself, yeah, yeah. But what about the weeks after that? After the ratings spike, then what? Is it going to take more murders to keep us going?"

"Look, once people start watching the show, see how good it is, they'll spread the word."

"Is it? Is it any good, Dee Dee?"

"What a party pooper. You're absolutely zero fun."

"This whole thing," he said. "It's sickening."

"If you weren't such a stud, I might have to dump you."

"I can't believe this. A woman got beaten to death with a baseball bat, everybody's popping champagne."

"I'm sorry for the poor girl, and for whoever else this maniac murdered. I'm sorry, I'm sorry, I'm sorry. Bad things happen. Bad people do bad things. There's a lot of terrible shit in the world. Okay? I get it. I truly do get it."

She trailed her fingers down his ribs, coasting past his navel. Sawyer was unresponsive, and as she reached his pubes he recoiled.

Dee Dee jerked her hand away.

"Hey, mister. Let me ask you something."

Sawyer cocked his head her way and took her in.

"You ever fail at anything? Anything at all? Your whole life?"

"Once or twice."

"Well, I've failed plenty," she said. "And I've butted up against some of the ugliest shit there is in this world, stuff I've never told you about and never will. And this show, this thing that's happening now, this is as close as I've ever come to making it. So okay, people died, well, that's too bad for them. But there's a lot of ways a person can die, okay, without actually dying."

She swiveled around and from the bedside table she nabbed the remains of the joint they'd shared last night. With a huffy sigh, she scratched the Bic into flame, lit the roach, and sucked in a lungful. She didn't offer a hit to Sawyer. Just drew the bright glowing weed down to her fingertips.

When she'd released everything from her lungs, she stabbed it out on the wooden tabletop. She rolled out of bed, crossed the room naked. In the nearby buildings Sawyer saw a dozen flashes, the voyeurs doing a quick refocus.

Sawyer lay back and looked at the light streaming in, at the clouds reshaping along the horizon. He knew the cop drill, and what was coming next.

While he listened to Dee Dee humming to herself in the dressing room, Sawyer considered his alibi. One that would be impossible to prove, and just as impossible to disprove.

Last night he left the sound stage at nine-thirty, a fact easily verified by several crew members. He called Dee Dee's cell to set up a dinner date, but all his calls went to voice mail. Odd, but not without precedent.

So he returned to her condo, where he'd been living for the last few months. Didn't ride upstairs, simply got his running shoes out of the trunk of his Honda, slipped into his shorts in the front seat, and went for a late-night jog in the muggy summer night. No security cams in the outside lot. Didn't swing by the front and wave to Maury, the bellman, just ran off into the darkness.

Out on Brickell Avenue he ran south for a while, kept on running across the Rickenbacker Causeway, energized by the ocean breeze, the city lights, the black sweep of the bay. He watched the twinkling yachts cruising back to port and stopped at the apex of the bridge to catch his breath, then looked down at the iridescent water. He watched other joggers pass, watched cars flash by.

He'd seen no one, spoken to no one. Had jogged on the causeway for an hour, then taken a cool-down walk along Windsurf Beach, and wound up sitting there in the sand debating what he should do now that the show seemed to be finished.

No way to prove any of that. They'd have to take his word. Or not.

When he returned to his car after his run, his cell was ringing, and it was then he got word about the Zentai killer calling the newspaper. He'd thrown on a shirt and pants and taken the elevator up to Gus Dollimore's penthouse and joined the others. That weird, restrained celebration.

Sawyer would have to defend this story, stay disciplined, keep it straight and simple and not let them find the smallest inconsistency. He scripted a line in his head, some righteous indignation:

"You think I copycatted my own show? You think I murdered a complete stranger for publicity? That's insane. I'm not that desperate, man. TV shows fail all the time, and new TV shows are born, and writers go on writing."

"Close the curtains," Dee Dee called from her dressing room.

"What?"

"I said shut the curtains, Sawyer. Shut them tight."

That was a first.

He rolled out of bed, padded to the edge of the window, and pulled the cord, no doubt sending dozens of devoted fans into shock.

"All right," Sawyer called.

"Now lie down, close your eyes."

Sawyer picked up Garvey's quilt, refolded it, set it on the shelf beside the bed. He switched off the skinny vibrator that had been humming for the last hour, and lay down on the bed.

"Your eyes closed?"

"They're closed."

Sawyer stretched out on the sheets, propped his head on a pillow, shut his eyes. Waited.

"Are your eyes shut?"

"Shut," he said.

He heard her slip into the room, heard her muffled breathing.

"Okay, you can look."

Sawyer opened his eyes and found Dee Dee standing before him in a black Zentai suit. The Lycra hugging her so tight it showed every ridge of muscle, the perfect swell of her breasts, her nipples taut, the neatly bar-bered Mohawk of pubic hair, the slabs of muscles in her thighs.

"Look what I found, honey."

Her hands were hidden behind her back.

"Not funny, Dee Dee."

She stood motionless at the foot of the bed, crouched forward like some jungle creature about to spring.

"So let's try it, big boy. Let's see what it's like. Huh?"

"Nothing doing," he said. "Take it off."

She inched down the side of the bed, slinking closer, her hands still hidden. Head lowered, rocking back and forth, an eerie cobra dance. Sawyer was growing mildly spooked.

"This isn't cool."

He shifted his legs, set his feet against the mattress, ready to dig in and thrust himself away. A chill rippled on his backside.

"Come on, goddamn it. Stop this shit."

She crept forward another foot. Sawyer outweighed her by at least forty pounds, but Dee Dee had a crushing grip in both hands, and her core strength was astounding. From hours of Pilates and free weights and gymnastic work on the horizontal bar, and those pink rubber straps, she was all sinew and gristle, a body as sturdy, limber, and powerful as a python's.

As she took another half step, Sawyer sat up, poised to hop sideways, make a break for the bathroom, when her left hand appeared from be-hind her.

Empty.

Then she took another step and her right hand flew out. In it she held a black square of material. Underhanded, she tossed it at him, and it fluttered open on his chest. A matching Zentai suit.

"Okay, bad boy. Let's you and me field-test this baby."

"Christ almighty."

"What? Did I scare you? You think I was coming for you like I did for Slattery?"

"You can't let anybody see you like that. It's incriminating as hell."

She eased down on the bed beside him and Sawyer felt a shiver pass through his gut. This black specter. Not Dee Dee, but her absence, her shadow half. Sawyer's heart was bumping. Her body shape was even more pronounced without the distraction of her features. Its crisp lines, its haughty sexuality, the aggressive tilt of pelvis, the vulnerable swan's neck and proud lift of chin. Absent her coquettish eyes, lush mouth, and sculptured cheekbones, the essence of Dee Dee was intensely primal, a woman stripped of her singularity, yet somehow more magnetic.

She stroked a Lycra hand across his bare thigh. Part silk, part rasp.

To his surprise, his cock had firmed. Racing blood, inflamed nerves.

"Hey, not to worry, Sawyer. I would never murder you, babe. I need those words you give me. I need you more than ever, now that I'll be a star."

She had a Lycra hand on his cock, starting a slow pump, when Sawyer's cell rang on the bedside table.

"Leave it."

Sawyer leaned over, checked the ID.

"It's Flynn."

"Leave it, sweetie. Dee Dee's got you in her grip."

He lay back and tried to give himself over to the strange sensation, that sleek material riding up and down his length.

The phone rang again. Sawyer turned his head.

"Now it's Gus," he said. "Something's going on."

Dee Dee released him and made a pouty huff.

Sawyer answered, listened, set the phone down.

"Okay, so what is it?"

"Get out of that suit right now."

"What?"

"FBI's in the lobby. We're assembling downstairs in five minutes."

SEVENTEEN

THORN WAS UP BEFORE THE sun that Saturday morning after laboring through a night of vivid, jerk-awake dreams whose particulars whisked away in the seconds it took him to walk into the bathroom, leaving behind only hazy after-images of Buddha Hilton and two young boys playing on a grassy lawn, tossing a ball back and forth and back and forth while Thorn watched from some hovering distance.

Where those dream images originated was clear enough. The walls of the garage apartment were covered with framed snapshots of the tow-headed twins, Flynn and Sawyer, shirtless at ten and eleven and twelve and thirteen in a variety of settings but almost always doing something outside and together: rowing boats, playing tug-of-war with a heavy rope, dressed in matching seersucker suits for Easter services, playing bocce ball and horseshoes, tossing a Frisbee, shooting arrows side by side at straw-filled targets, romping with a succession of large mutts.

There were also shots of them standing alongside various men. A swarthy Cuban gentleman figured prominently in several, a red-haired fellow with a freckled forehead showed up in almost as many, and there were other men who'd apparently held shorter tenures in the Moss household. As he browsed the images Thorn was struck by a repeating pattern. In all the shots that featured the Moss twins and their mother's apparent boyfriends, the brothers invariably stood at attention, stiff and awkward as if posing in a police lineup. Their postures and their matching forced smiles made it clear these male invaders into the Moss sanctuary never stood a chance.

Then there were the half-dozen prom night photos with an impressive collection of young ladies in ball gowns. Flynn preferred buxom, hot-blooded playmates with theatrical eyes and bold smiles and racy evening wear. Girls who appeared more fully ripened in both body and worldly experience than he.

Sawyer's dates were mostly dark-haired, understated, trim young women, often as tall as Sawyer or taller. April look-alikes with pale skin and long limbs and easy smiles.

The previous night when April showed Thorn the room, she seemed startled to find so many photographs hanging there. She apologized and acted ill at ease, telling Thorn she'd not been up there in several months, since the day Sawyer moved out to live on his own. It was he who'd decorated the room, framed and hung the snapshots, a sentimental kid, she said. A boy preoccupied with his past.

When she opened the closet door, they found it crowded with the boys' abandoned clothes. Mainly faded polo shirts and battered jeans and some dark suits and button-down dress shirts—Sawyer's corporate uniform, April explained, worn during his brief career as an attorney.

Thorn was welcome to any of the castoffs. She'd been too busy lately to cart them to Goodwill.

Now freshly showered, Thorn tried on a pair of blue jeans with ragged knees, and found them a perfect fit. He chose a dark green polo shirt with a crocodile on the breast, then checked himself out in the closet mirror, and shook his head. He looked closer to a preppie than he'd ever been. On his forehead, the lump had receded and was changing from blue to a moldy green. The swelling in his hand had also subsided and he could almost make a fist.

Out of curiosity he slipped on a pair of discarded boat shoes, the pricier version of the brand he'd lived in for most of his adult life. The shoes were maybe a half size larger than his usual fit, but felt a hell of lot more comfortable than the ones he'd been wearing the last few years.

Stashed beside a simple wood desk, he found a black nylon computer bag. Thorn emptied it of the yellow legal pads and documents and slender laptop computer, and refilled it with Buddha's electronic tablet, the evidence bag, and her service revolver. Only two rounds left in the cylinder. He tucked her phone in his pocket.

Last night after April left him, he'd smuggled the loot up to the apartment, and now he carried it all back down to the car and locked the black computer bag in the trunk.

The neighborhood was quiet. Boxley, the Doberman he'd been introduced to the night before, trotted over to see if Thorn had acquired any new crotch smells since their last encounter. After satisfying himself with the state of Thorn's privates, he wandered back to the front gate and lay down to stare out at a trio of gray squirrels that were chasing one another up and down the trunk of an oak tree.

Like many houses of its era, April's home was masonry vernacular, a blocky two-story with parapets and arcades and a shady porch on three sides. The garage apartment was a separate structure that echoed the main house. This was one of the dwellings built by second-generation settlers in Miami. Approaching a century old, they had been designed and constructed by laymen from plans probably drawn up at kitchen tables. Sturdy and rectangular, yet somehow graceful.

As Thorn was headed toward the kitchen door, Jeff, the guy from Poblanos, appeared, squirming out of a crawl space hatch in the concrete apron of the house. He pushed himself out the small trapdoor, then bent back to the opening and dragged out a white garbage bag. He shut the grillwork behind him and latched it.

He saw Thorn and walked over. No greeting.

He untied the red drawstring and gave Thorn a look. A half-dozen large wooden traps, each with a fat brown rat smashed in the spring-loaded guillotine.

"You get an early start," Thorn said.

"It's rat season," Jeff said.

"It's always rat season," said Thorn.

"Which makes this rat season."

He smiled and cinched the bag shut and carried it to a pedestrian gate, let himself out, and walked across the street to a dark green pickup truck with orange tiger stripes running down its sides. He slung the bag of rats into the bed, started the truck, and rolled slowly away.

The house was still, no lights upstairs or down. April had given Thorn a key in case he got up early and wanted coffee.

Coffee, however, was not what he had in mind. He let himself in and cut through the kitchen, then went down the hallway that split the house in half. Parlor, dining room, and a maid's room on one side, April's home office and a sewing room on the other. Three bedrooms and two baths upstairs, the one zone he hadn't yet seen. Last night April had confined the house tour to the downstairs only.

The walls were thick and solid with high ceilings and dark exposed beams. Ceiling fans were quietly at work in every room. The house had no air-conditioning, but the interior spaces were as cool as a spring-fed grotto. It had the solid, sound-absorbing feel Thorn had found in other Miami houses of its vintage. There were fewer and fewer of them remaining as the years went by and more citizens of the city grew so fabulously rich they could afford to level the historic homes and replace them with estates twice their size and half their elegance.

More family photos were mounted on the hallway walls. The boys at five or six with Garvey, their grandmother, who'd been a lively brunette with a pinup-girl body. A series of snapshots taken in Manhattan and on some Ivy League campus showed April in various flannel shirts and jeans, grunge but not grungy, a young mother, hand in hand with Flynn and Sawyer in Central Park and at the Statue of Liberty and the Empire State Building and inside what looked like an efficiency apartment. If April wasn't attending the boys, Garvey was.

Moving past the photos, Thorn heard someone stirring upstairs, a toilet flush, the creak of the pine floors. He picked up the pace, slipping down the hall and through the library with its floor-to-ceiling shelves covering one wall, chock-full with hardbacks, leather-bounds, high school yearbooks, a host of ancient paperbacks, and two different sets of encyclopedias.

He passed through the open door into the sewing room, where each of the walls was hung with a quilt. A red and yellow starburst on one, flowers and colorful vines and hummingbirds and vases of flowers on the others. An antique Singer sat between the two windows and a tall case stood close by, its every shelf piled high with folded fabric.

He started his search with the small sewing stand next to the Singer, going through the drawers from top to bottom. Pawing through bobbins and thread and packages of needles, thimbles, safety pins, buttons, and pincushions and cloth tape measure.

In another cabinet beside the shelves of fabric, he located a collection of scissors. There had to be at least twenty in various sizes. At the front of the second drawer was a pair of pinking shears.

He reached out, then caught himself in time and drew his hand away.

On a sewing machine table Thorn found a dark blue swatch of cloth the size of a handkerchief and used that to pick up the shears by the blade. He looked around for a piece of paper to cut, but found nothing suitable.

Footsteps sounded on the creaky stairway. For a second Thorn bobbled the pinking shears but caught them before they clattered onto the table. Using the blue cloth, he slipped them into the back pocket of his jeans and covered their exposed grips with the tail of his polo shirt.

He stepped into the library and was pretending to scan the titles on a high shelf when April appeared in the doorway.

She was wearing brown shin-length chinos and a simple white blouse with short sleeves. Leather sandals and a thin silver necklace. Her hair was loose, held off her face with two tortoiseshell clips. Thorn was no expert, but he didn't believe the flush in her cheeks was rouge.

"You a reader, Thorn?"

"I like a nautical adventure now and then. A good mystery."

"Not the girlie-girlie highbrow stuff?"

"In a pinch I'll read anything. Even highbrow."

"When the boys were young, I read to them every night because that's supposed to instill a love of books. But turns out Flynn is dyslexic, and Sawyer only read what was required in school. Now he'd rather write than read. So there's another myth down in flames."

"How does Flynn learn his parts?"

"Someone reads him the scripts aloud and he memorizes his lines. He memorizes everyone's lines. Has incredible recall."

"Compensation," Thorn said.

"Yeah, we're very big on compensating in the Moss household."

She waved a hand in front of her face to disown what she'd just said.

"I need my coffee."

Thorn seconded that.

He followed her to the kitchen and she made some strong Sumatran stuff whose aroma alone was enough to rev his heart.

She asked him what he liked for breakfast and he told her whatever she was having was fine. So it was scrambled eggs and Canadian bacon and whole wheat toast with apple butter, and a bowl of mixed fruit with shredded coconut.

"Haven't had ambrosia since I was ten years old."

While she made breakfast he stared out the back window into a wide lawn that ran down to the river.

She set a plate before him and took the chair opposite.

"How's your head feel?"

"Like there's two of them."

"Do you need a doctor? I have a good GP, he's a friend. I'm sure he could squeeze you in."

"It's Saturday."

"If it's bothering you, I could call him; I know he'd see you."

"Thanks. I should be okay as long as no one slams a door on my head."

Without appetite, he picked up his fork and started with the Canadian bacon, cutting one of the disks in half and folding it into this mouth. Chewy and perfect. He tried the eggs and they were better than scrambled eggs had a right to be. His taste buds seemed to be waking from a long sleep.

"I can't imagine what you endured last night. That whole thing. Witnessing what you did, the killer assaulting you, murdering your friend right in front of you. That's what you were talking about at the bar, isn't it? The baseball bat in my obituary of Joe Camarillo. You knew something like that was going to happen."

Thorn set his fork down.

"Yes, that's what we were talking about."

"Jesus God. Something I wrote caused that."

"It didn't cause it. It may have guided the asshole, but there's no reason to feel guilty, April. None of this is your fault."

"Oh, really? You wouldn't feel guilty if you were in my place?"

"You wrote an obituary. It's your job. You do it very well. Some guy comes along and finds a word here and a word there and takes those words and uses them to go kill somebody, that has nothing to do with you."

"I wish I could look at it that way."

April tasted another bite of her eggs, then set her fork down and pushed her plate away. She stared out the back window at the Siamese cat that was now sitting very still on the porch rail beneath an active birdfeeder.

"There's five satellite trucks parked down the street. All the networks, two cable news crews. Last night they parked right out front, but they were disturbing the neighbors, so I made a fuss until they moved down to a park on the corner. I'm going to have to face them again. There's no way to avoid it. Ben Silver, the publisher at the paper, called twice already to tell me to be less hostile on camera. He's thinking about our circulation. This could be a major coup. He's standing by the phone, waiting for another call from the killer. He wants to bond with the guy, get a dialogue going."

"Better him than you."

"Fortunately the Zentai Killer called them, not me. He doesn't seem to have any interest in me personally. Just what I write."

"Is that what they've named him? The Zentai Killer?"

She nodded.

"Pretty lame."

Thorn finished his breakfast in silence. April kept her focus on the Siamese. Sitting so still he might have been a plaster cat.

When he'd finished, he carried his plate to the sink and rinsed it.

She started to rise, but Thorn told her to sit still, he'd do this.

He scraped her leftovers into the trash, and washed her plate and silverware, then he scrubbed the pans and dried them and set them in the rack. When everything was put away, he came back to the table and sat across from her.

"You any good with cell phones?"

"Cell phones?"

"I have an e-mail with a video attached. I don't know how to open it."

He dug out Buddha's phone and slid it across the table to her.

"You don't know how to operate your phone?"

"It's the sheriff's."

She gave him an uncertain look, then dug into the phone, worked with the device for a while, and asked, "Who's the e-mail from?"

"A guy named Ben Hardison. He's a cop in Atlanta."

She went back to the phone, tapping and sliding her finger across the screen until she had it.

"Okay. You want me to run the video?"

He got up and stood behind her.

"Ready."

She tapped an icon and a video began to play. Headlights were shining on someone in a black Zentai suit standing on a sidewalk. The person was holding a small paper sack. One of the cop's beefy shoulders blocked part of the view. Even in the flare of the headlights the exact shape of the person's body was indistinct. Taller than average, thin, with wide shoulders and a narrow waist. But beyond that he could tell nothing for sure.

Then Hardison must have instructed the person to remove the hood.

Thorn squinted and leaned forward as the black mask came off. A hand came up in front of the face, blocking the glare of the car's headlights.

"Is that . . . ?" April said.

"Can you run it back, see that part again?"

April replayed the last few seconds, watching the Zentai person remove the hood a second time. Short hair, hard cheekbones. Heavily made-up eyes.

"Dee Dee Dollimore?" April said.

"One more time," Thorn said.

A third time they watched the hood come off and both bent close to the image. The grainy black-and-white picture was poorly focused. The woman held the hood in one hand and shielded her eyes with the other.

"No, that's not her. This face is fuller."

"You're sure?"

"I don't know. It's so blurry, she's wearing so much makeup. When was this taken? Where?"

"Three weeks ago, Atlanta."

"Why would Dee Dee be on the street in Atlanta in that suit?"

"I don't know," Thorn said. "But I'm damn well going to find out."

EIGHTEEN

THORN TOOK HIS SEAT ACROSS from April.

The ruddiness in her cheeks had crept down her throat and a faint gloss shone on her upper lip. A single bead of sweat sparkled at her hairline. The room temperature couldn't be more than seventy, so her high color wasn't caused by heat. At another time, in another circumstance Thorn might be idiot enough to take credit for April's flush. But not here, not now. There was something else overheating her, something well below the surface.

"Do you have a piece of old newsprint handy?"

"Newsprint?"

"I want to try an experiment."

April stood up and went into the pantry and returned with a sports page.

Using the blue swatch of cloth, he drew the pinking shears from his pocket and cut a circle around an article about the Marlins' latest lousy season.

"Where'd you get those?"

"Your sewing room."

"Why have you been sneaking around my house?"

He held the finished circle of newsprint up to the light, cocking it left and right. But no matter how he tilted the page, he could see no imperfections in the saw-blade edge. He opened the scissors and peered at the jagged blade. No dings anywhere. He set the pinking shears down, feeling a tingle of relief.

"Are these the only pinking shears in the house?"

"Now stop right there."

"I'll explain it to you later. I promise."

"Who the hell are you, Thorn?"

"Just a guy, trying to figure a few things out."

"But that's not true, is it? You're not just a guy. You're not some Key Largo beach bum who's wandered onto the scene."

"And where's that coming from?"

"How do you know a man like Frank Sheffield?"

"It's a long story. We go back a few years."

"You're some kind of freelance detective, aren't you?"

"Hardly."

"Yes, you are, Thorn. Maybe you don't even know you are, or you don't want to acknowledge it to yourself, I don't know. But I did some investigating of my own last night, went on the Web, made a few calls to my friends in the media and law enforcement. I have a lot of contacts in South Florida, Thorn. And your name produced some interesting responses. This isn't the first time you've been involved with violence and crime, is it?"

"What difference does it make?"

"I want to know who you are. Who I have staying in my house."

She took a sip of coffee. With her elbows on the table she held the mug in both hands and looked over the top of it at Thorn.

"Admit it. You're not some beach bum."

Thorn brushed a few crumbs off the edge of the table into his open hand, then got up and carried them to the sink and dusted them off. He came back and stood behind his chair, holding on to the top rail.

"Look, I'm an ordinary guy. Over the years I've had a bad string of luck. From time to time I've had to set a few things right. Help people put their lives back in balance. That's all. A couple of times, bad things happened in my vicinity. But whatever I've done, I've always had good intentions."

"And that's how you got to know the special agent in charge of the Miami field office of the FBI, from putting things back in balance?"

He shrugged.

"Is that good enough, April?"

"For now," she said, "I guess it'll have to do."

"So," he said, "are there any other pinking shears in the house?"

"It's possible. You'll have to ask Mother. That's her domain."

Thorn pulled the chair out and sat.

She took another sip of coffee and set the mug aside. Eyes straying to the window, where the birds were raining seeds and husks down on the Siamese who continued to watch from the rail. Ever patient, ever ready.

"And your other questions?"

Thorn asked her if she'd mentioned to anyone that he and Buddha were staying in the Waterway Lodge.

She thought about it for a few seconds and shook her head. Nobody.

"You're sure?"

"Absolutely. Now what else?"

"I need to look at your files," Thorn said. "Recent obituaries."

She rose and led him back down the hall and into her office. She sat in a wooden swivel chair, inched it up to an ancient rolltop.

"You want to go through all the obits? There's years of them."

"Mondays only. Go back a few weeks."

"How many weeks?"

"Try six. What date would that be?"

"Middle of June."

"Start there."

April pulled open the drawer on the right side of the rolltop, which was full of file folders. She thumbed through them and extracted a black one.

"My collected works."

She opened it on her desk and Thorn came up to her chair, looking over her shoulder as she paged through them. Then paged through them a second time, then turned a look of dismay on Thorn.

"Is this some kind of practical joke?"

"What?"

"When you were searching my house, did you tamper with these?"

"What's wrong?"

"Some are missing. From July, one from June."

"You're sure?"

Once more she worked through them slowly, double-checking the dates, going all the way to the end of the fat folder.

"Maybe you misfiled them."

"Everything I write goes in here. I'm obsessive about it. All in order."

"What's not there?"

"Four from July, one from June. Five in all."

"Including Rusty's?"

"Hers isn't here, that's right. What the hell is this?"

"Give me a minute. I'll be right back. And while I'm gone, think about who had access to this file in the last four or five weeks. Everybody, every single person who could've been in this room, opened that drawer, and taken something without your knowledge. Okay?"

He left her doing the grim calculations and walked out to the rental car, retrieved the evidence bag, locked the car again, and carried the Ziploc back inside.

She was sitting in an upholstered chair when he returned.

"Gus Dollimore," she said. "The boys, and Dee Dee. And Mother, of course. I'm not exactly a social butterfly. Mother and I don't have dinner parties. The boys stop by after work now and then, and Gus has been with them several times lately. He always travels alone, and Dee Dee usually tags along with Sawyer. They have a beer or a glass of wine alongside the river, hang around for a while, talk about the show, blow off steam. A few times they've stayed longer, cooked dinner, wandered around the house."

"So there's them. Then there's Jeff Matheson."

"The pest control guy."

She squinted at the wall, then blinked hard as if banishing a thought.

"That's right."

"I met him this morning coming out of a crawl space. He had a bag full of dead rats. Is that normal, him coming so early?"

"He works odd hours. Nothing like a normal schedule. For the last few months we've had a terrible rat problem, the place is just infested, and Jeff's been putting out traps and trying to seal all the entry points. Not an easy job in this rambling old house. Off and on since May he's had the run of the place.

"And there was a plumber for a few jobs, but I was with him most of the time he was working. Beyond that, no one."

"Jeff, the rat guy, you trust him?"

A look he couldn't read whisked across her face.

"Jeff's a good kid. He went to high school with the boys. He practically grew up in this house. He's down to earth, an animal nerd. Yes, I trust him completely."

"What's the name of his company?"

"Miami Humane Wildlife Removal."

"And what about the others during that time period? You're confident about them?"

"Do I trust my own boys? Would they go through my files, take something without asking? No way in hell."

"You're sure? Maybe doing research for the show, something like that?"

"They'd ask permission. I'm certain."

"Gus and Dee Dee? Have they ever come into this room?"

Her mouth was partly open, but she couldn't bring herself to speak.

"Why would someone steal obits from my files? They're in the paper. Anyone could buy a paper."

"Breadcrumbs," he said.

"And what's that mean?"

"Somebody's thought this through very carefully. I think they're trying to misdirect things."

April stared up at the bookshelves.

"Tell me something," Thorn said. "If you saw one of those missing obituaries, would you be able to say for sure it was from your files? Do you make marks on them? Date them, anything like that?"

She shook her head.

"Just cut them out and file them away."

Thorn opened the Ziploc bag and drew out Rusty's obituary and handed it to April.

She looked at it, touched the jagged saw-blade edge, then turned it over and saw his name in black ink.

The flush in her cheeks bloomed a deep crimson. With such a high-strung sympathetic nervous system, April Moss would never hack it as a liar.

"You wrote that?"

She swallowed and her eyes flicked around the room as if searching for a better answer than what she had.

"I did, yes," she said. "You were on my mind. I wrote your name. Yes, I'm guilty of that."

"It's okay," he said. "I understand."

"Do you, Thorn? Do you really?"

He sloughed off the question.

"How'd you decide to do Rusty's obit? Would you have done it if you and I had never met?"

"Maybe," she said.

She was staring down at Thorn's boat shoes.

"No, that's not true," she said. "I wrote about her because her story touched me. But the reason it jumped out of the pile was because of you and your connection to her. I was thinking about you, imagining your life down in the Keys, wondering how you were doing, how you were dealing with her loss. Of course I was remembering the night we had together, and the next day. Is that what you wanted to hear?"

"I wasn't angling for anything."

She drew herself up, planting her feet on the floor, her back straight, chin lifted. Holding her body with great care as if trying not to spill some precarious weight balanced on her shoulders.

"I was just curious," he said. "I thought it might've played a part. But that doesn't matter. It was very kind of you to write about her. You did a beautiful job. It was touching. A lot of Rusty's friends were pleased to see her life and accomplishments described with such clarity and feeling. Count me as one of those. So, thank you. Thank you very much."

April's eyes were full of things she wanted to say, but she held on to them and instead drew a long, slow breath like a diver about to go deep.

"Since we're being personal," he said, "I keep wondering what was going on between you and Buddha at the bar. That weird back-and-forth."

April closed her eyes and drew another careful breath.

"What is it?"

Gradually the tightness in April's face relaxed into a helpless smile. She looked up at a high place on the wall. Another look passed across her face, one that Thorn believed he recognized. A milder version of the expression Rusty had worn toward the end, when she was bracing herself and summoning strength. A woman bravely accepting the inevitable.

April said, "Sheriff Hilton was a very perceptive lady."

"About what?"

"I believe she had it all figured out. My dark secret."

"I'm not following you," Thorn said.

"When you showed up at the Floridian, Garvey saw it right away. She doesn't understand what the big deal is. Nothing is ever a big deal to Mother. She has no dark secrets. The woman is incapable of dark secrets. Everything that crosses her mind instantly comes tripping off her tongue. She's always been that way. Born without a censor."

"What are you trying to say?"

"I wish I could be more like Garvey. No filters, no worries about propriety, unconcerned what people think. But no, I'm not her. I've always tried very hard to guard my reputation, to please others, to behave in a proper manner. You, on the other hand, you seem to be cut from the same cloth as Garvey. No filters, not particularly concerned about anyone's opinion."

"You're trying to tell me something, but it's catching in your throat."

"See, that's what I mean. You're perceptive. Maybe not as much as your young friend, but for a man you're quite sensitive."

Thorn was quiet. Something had come loose inside April Moss; one stone in an ancient rock pile that had been securely balanced had been dislodged, and the delicate equilibrium disturbed. A landslide looming.

"What are we talking about, April?"

"We're talking about what your friend Buddha was saying to me, and what I was saying back. A woman's secret code."

"Okay."

"She saw what anybody might have seen if they were paying attention."

"And that was what?"

She rolled her bottom lip under her upper teeth and sucked it for a second, then swallowed the hardness in her throat, and looked into Thorn's eyes, making some last reckoning before she went on.

"What, April? What could anybody have seen?"

"The striking resemblance between you and Sawyer and Flynn, your sons."

At that moment there was utter silence in the house, like the quiet that comes after some crash of thunder has exploded in the sky, when every twittering bird goes still, when all the insects cease their chirring, the wind drops away to nothing, and the faint ticking of every clock halts in every room.

He heard the shush of his own blood in his ears, and then the slow restarting of the world, its mad scramble, its bric-a-brac, its jumble of books on shelves and papers and flowerpots and the rumbling of some appliance as it switched on again after a short sleep. Thorn looked around this pleasant room, seeing it with a sudden vividness as if he'd just been transported here from some faraway place. Startled to find himself with this woman, in this study, on this July morning with everything changed.

"You tell the bozo yet?"

Garvey was in the doorway, braced inside an aluminum walker, wearing gray slacks and a bright red T-shirt, with her dark hair braided in two pigtails.

"Hey, handsome stranger, you missed all the fun. Shitty diapers, fistfights in the living room, broken teeth, screaming nightmares, braces and the mumps and chicken pox. All that never-ending teenage angst. You missed the drama and the sulking, then you come sweeping in just in time for dessert. If you weren't such an irresistible dreamboat, I'd kick your sorry ass straight out the front door myself."

NINETEEN

THE GRANDFATHER CLOCK IN THE corner chimed nine times, then went back to counting off the seconds. Thorn stood near the front window of the study, looking out at Boxley, who was giving a thorough crotch sniff to Frank Sheffield. Sheffield patted the dog's head and tolerated the nosing with a faraway smile.

Frank pulled out his phone and tapped in a number.

"Sheffield's here," Thorn said.

"That's your reaction?" said Garvey. "Like no biggie, this happens every day? Get two brand-new sons, twins no less. Come on, say something, loverboy. My daughter and I have devoted the last twenty-five years to taking care of the results of your shenanigans with a schoolgirl, a teenager who hadn't even graduated twelfth grade. Which, if it isn't illegal, it should be. So come on, Don Juan, what the hell do you have to say for yourself?"

"Leave him alone, Mother. He's absorbing it."

The phone in Thorn's pocket began playing "Hey Jude." McCartney back at his piano.

Thorn drew it out and pressed the answer button.

Frank Sheffield said, "Tracked down Sheriff Hilton's cell number. Now we know you're a liar and a thief. How am I supposed to trust you?"

When Thorn didn't reply, Frank said, "I'm at the front door, could somebody let me in."

"Agent Sheffield is at the front door," Thorn said.

April stood up and walked toward the doorway, but Garvey hobbled into her path.

"I'll get it," Garvey said. "I'm no cripple."

When she was out of the room, April said, "Let me answer the two questions that you haven't asked yet. Yes, I'm absolutely sure you're the father. And no, the boys don't know. Unless somehow they've figured it out on their own the way Sheriff Hilton did. But I doubt it. They're so preoccupied with the Zentai Killer, and what all this means for their show. I don't think they've even noticed you yet."

"We need to talk, April."

"Yes, I suppose we do."

"I mean all of us. All of us together."

Frank knocked, gave the doorbell a quick buzz.

"You, the boys, and me. Can you arrange that? All of us sit down."

"Talk about what, Thorn? I don't know what that would be."

"Where we're going with this. What it means."

"What it means?"

"I don't know. Like the role I'll play in their lives."

"Good lord, Thorn. It's too late to be their father. The boys don't need a heart-to-heart from you about making something of themselves or whatever wisdom you think you can give them. They've been doing damn fine just the way they are, and so have I. So, okay, I've got no problem if you want to speak to them, get to know them a little, let them have a glimpse of who you are.

"But don't think you're going to be anybody's mentor. They're grown. They're who they are and you aren't going to change that with any talk. And just so you know, neither of them have ever expressed any interest whatsoever in tying flies or lying around in a hammock all day or dropping out of the ordinary world. So, if you feel compelled, then speak your piece, but please don't start thinking you're part of our family, Thorn. You're not. What happened between you and me was a biological mishap. Nothing more."

A moment later Sheffield came into the study, followed by Garvey.

He'd shaved his stubble and gotten his hair trimmed, and was dressed in black slacks and a white button-down business shirt with a blue linen sport coat that he was probably wearing only to cover his sidearm. He looked at Thorn, then at April.

"Did I just walk into a therapy session?"

"We were just finishing up," April said.

She stepped over to Thorn and patted him on the back. A buck-up gesture that roused Thorn from his daze. He blinked and looked at April, but something was jammed in his throat and he couldn't speak.

"Can I borrow your charming houseguest for a few hours? We have some errands."

"Take him," Garvey said. "Just don't let him loose around any school-girls."

Garvey wobbled past him inside her walker. A sour grimace puck-ered her lips as if she intended to spit in his face. But April put a hand on the old woman's shoulder and helped steer her toward the door.

Outside in the driveway, Frank led Thorn to his dark green Taurus. "Schoolgirls?"

Thorn shook his head. Still nothing to say.

He got in the passenger seat, shut the door, then immediately opened it and got out. He walked over to the red rental and retrieved the com-puter bag from the trunk, and returned to the Taurus. Frank started the engine.

"Let me guess," Frank said. "You also came across the sheriff's iPad?"

Thorn didn't reply. He looked out the windshield at the satellite trucks that had begun to roll up and gather along the sidewalk outside April's house. One of the blond female anchors climbing out of the CNN truck spotted Frank and jogged over to block his exit.

Frank put the Ford in neutral and gunned the engine at her good-naturedly, but the CNN woman didn't flinch. Her camera guy peeled off and stood directly in the car's path while the newswoman came to his window, bent down, and pointed her microphone at him.

Frank sighed and zipped his window down.

"Could you give us an update, Agent Sheffield, on the progress of your investigation?"

"Nope."

"Just now you were inside with April Moss. Could you describe her state of mind? Is she feeling remorseful?"

Thorn threw open his door and walked around the car, shouldering the cameraman out of the way. Other reporters and their attendants were flowing through the front gates, converging on the Taurus.

"What the hell kind of a question is that? She has no reason to feel remorseful or guilty or any of that. Where do you get this shit? She writes obituaries, for god's sake. She doesn't have the slightest shred of blame for any of this. Somebody should take that microphone and—"

"Hey, buddy," Frank called. "*Tranquilo.* Dial it back."

Unruffled, the blond pointed the microphone at Thorn and said, "Are you Ms. Moss's significant other, her boyfriend, her agent, what?"

"Please identify yourself, sir, for the record." A roly-poly reporter with a flushed face had wedged himself into the tight circle that was forming around the Taurus.

"Get in the car, buddy," Frank said. He was standing behind his open door, using it as a shield against the news people. "Get in the car now."

Frank said to the chubby reporter, "This gentleman is assisting with a federal investigation. If you continue to obstruct his activities or mine, you're going to spend some of your very precious time twiddling your private parts in an interview room. So if you want to keep your pretty faces on the air, get the hell out of our way."

"I'm Joe Sharpe with Fox News, investigative reporter, Agent Shef-field. I have every right to ask any question I want of a public servant like yourself. You can't threaten me or any of the rest of us. This isn't a police state. Not yet anyway."

"Investigative reporter," Frank said.

"That's right."

"I know your work, Joe."

The stout man nodded as if such recognition was to be expected.

"And I know you couldn't investigate your way out of a used barf bag. I'd be shocked if you could unearth a pubic hair in a Mexican whorehouse."

Some chuckles passed through the news crowd.

Thorn glanced back at the house and saw April staring out the study window. From that distance, Thorn couldn't read her face. She stood there for a few seconds until someone in the throng of news reporters caught sight of her and called out her name. April lowered the Venetian blinds and a second later they snapped shut.

Sheffield tooted his horn, then nosed through the camera crews and headed west through the city. The traffic was light, Frank driving smoothly, in no hurry. Thorn watching it all, but lost inside his head. Hearing a buzz growing in his ears, like his blood pressure kettle was about to whistle.

"In case you were wondering, we're going to Sports Craze, a big box store out in west Miami. The ID techs found the torn-up receipt in the sheriff's luggage like you said. Receipt for the spear used in the murder of Michaela Stabler shows it was purchased on July twenty-second, and just so happens that same store also sells purple aluminum baseball bats, one of which was bought with cash late yesterday.

"I made a date with the manager, Hilda Ramirez, who has been so kind as to pull security videos from the twenty-second and yesterday. The lady is all aquiver. Apparently she's a crime buff. Never met a real G-man before. So Frank Sheffield is going to make her week. That's a big deal to me. I haven't made a lady's week in quite a while.

"Hilda tells me the Sports Craze folks have their surveillance broken down by departments, got like thirty cams running in each store. Snooping the shit out of the employees and customers. She can separate out the baseball and softball department. Save everybody a ton of time."

"You a father, Frank?"

Frank looked over. Thorn's eyes were trained on a spot in the distance.

"Had a semi-stepson for a while, when I was living with Hannah Keller. We got close, the kid and me. His name is Randall, smart little boy, computer whiz, not too keen on playing catch, but I took him out on the water and he dug that. It's been nearly a year since Hannah and I split, so I don't see him anymore. Miss the little guy. Why do you ask?"

"And your own father, he play ball with you, take you fishing?"

"Some of that. He wasn't the most involved pop on the block, but sure, we played pitch. Took in some ball games. Can't say we ever fished."

Frank wheeled the Taurus out of traffic and into a Shell station. He drew up alongside the vacuum and air hose concession. He patted Thorn on the shoulder.

"What's wrong, man? You sound like day-old shit."

"My parents died in a car accident the day I was born. I was adopted by a cardiologist and his wife. More like grandparents than parents. The doc was a good, decent man, I respected him, but he was a busy guy. We didn't play ball. We didn't play anything. I spent a lot of my time alone. Not that I minded, but most of what I learned as a kid I learned on my own."

"Is this your concussion talking?"

"My head's fine, Frank. It's not my head."

A yellow Hummer pulled up to the Taurus's back bumper and honked at them to move along. A soccer mom with a cell phone at her ear. The Taurus was blocking the lady's shortcut through the gas station to an adjoining road. Frank didn't move. She honked again, holding it down for several seconds, and Frank drew his pistol from beneath his sport coat and held it out the window, aiming up at the sky, turning it to the left and right so the Hummer lady could admire its beautiful lines. A south Florida nonverbal communiqué. There was no more honking.

"How does someone who never had a father learn to be one? From reading books, watching dads on TV? How?"

"Most guys, it probably comes naturally. Or else they do a lousy job, there's a lot of that going around. Anyway, what the hell is this? At this late stage, you thinking of going into the father business?"

"I never missed being a dad," Thorn said. "Never thought about it one way or the other. It's always been a full-time job taking care of myself, all the crazy shit I've fallen into; it's been no kind of life to raise a kid around."

"If you'd had a kid," Frank said, "you probably wouldn't have been falling into so much crazy shit."

Thorn shrugged.

"Chicken or the egg," Frank said.

After a minute of silence, he pulled back into traffic. Thorn kept his thoughts to himself as they drove west along Tamiami Trail, then headed south for a while and finally pulled into the vast parking lot of Sports

Craze. Big as a Wal-Mart. Filled with everything a dad could ever want to buy his boy.

Thorn drifted along behind Frank as he moved through the maze of recreational equipment, working his way to the manager's office.

"I got it all set up," Hilda Ramirez said after Frank introduced himself. She was a middle-aged woman with harsh red hair, large gold loop earrings, and impossible breasts. She had on the same Adidas jogging suit that all her sales staff wore, but it didn't look like she'd ever sweated in it.

She led Frank and Thorn into a conference room next door to her office where there was a large flat-screen TV mounted on the wall.

"I copied the videos to a DVD so you could take it with you."

"Very thoughtful."

"Could you tell me what this is about?"

"No," Frank said.

"Not even a hint? Is it a murder, a robbery?"

"Let's see the video," Frank said.

"Not even a little bitty hint?"

"Not even."

"All right. This first one is the baseball bat. Bought at eight forty-eight in the evening on Thursday, July twenty-ninth, two days ago." Hilda aimed the remote at the screen and clicked it. "The subject enters the picture at two-seventeen."

She sounded like someone schooled in police procedure by cop shows.

The time counter in the upper right corner started at two minutes.

The camera must have been mounted on a pillar near the register, because its downward angle suggested it was only slightly above head high. A useful perspective on the hands in the cash drawer and faces of the subjects.

This camera was trained on a register where a hefty guy in a similar Adidas track suit to Hilda's was finishing up with a lady customer who was buying a T-shirt. A few seconds later a figure in a bulky trench coat and a black baseball cap tugged low on their head handed the clerk an aluminum baseball bat.

Thorn's stomach clenched.

"That's the bat you were interested in. A Rawlings Plasma, chromium-enhanced alloy. Its handle flex is stiffer than most multipiece bats."

Hilda smiled at them.

"A trench coat in July in Miami," Frank said. "That should've been sufficient cause to arrest the guy on the way in the door."

"Oh, well," Hilda said. "We get all kinds in here, but trench coats, no, not many of those."

"Guy was spiffed up for the video cam."

"Isn't there some kind of computer trick for you to see the perp's face?"

"Freeze it, please," Frank said.

Hilda stopped the video at 2:22.

Frank turned to her and said, "You think we've got some way to put a face on someone based on the back of their head?"

"I was just wondering."

"Not even Hollywood has that yet," Frank said.

"It was just a question."

"Let me have the remote."

Frank put out his hand and she gave it to him. Hilda shot Thorn a look, seeking his support. Thorn shrugged, and looked back at the screen.

Frank ran the video through the complete cash transaction until the person collected their change and tucked it into the coat pocket and turned toward the camera, ducking their head as they came around, the bill of the baseball cap dipping too quickly to see anything of their face.

Sheffield reran it a half-dozen times, pausing at intervals, freezing the image of the turning customer until he'd found a frame that displayed the face.

"Anybody we know, Thorn?"

Too blurry even to be sure if it was a man or a woman. Height, weight, body type, no way to tell.

Thorn shook his head.

"Is that clerk working today?"

"Javier went on a cruise to Nassau yesterday afternoon," Hilda said.

"Great."

"I called him on his cell before he disembarked because I knew you were coming. He remembered the baseball bat, but he couldn't say anything about the customer's face. Just the big coat. 'Kind of creepy' is how Javier put it. And a strange voice, like he had a bad cold. But I think it is more likely the subject was disguising his voice."

"Good job, Hilda."

She smiled and touched a shy hand to the front of her track suit, honored by the praise of an official G-man.

"That's all he said?"

"Well, no, he mentioned the customer asked for a different model of bat, but we don't carry that."

"He specified a particular bat?"

"He wanted wood, a Louisville Hitter."

"Slugger," Frank said.

"Yes, I misspoke," Hilda said. "Slugger. Louisville Slugger."

"Moving on to the spear."

This time the customer was in baggy cargo pants, black high tops, and a double extra-large sweatshirt with the hoodie up. Same size person, same head duck as they swung back to the store with their purchase. Bought on Thursday, one week earlier than the baseball bat. And once again the killer purchased the weapon a few minutes before the store's nine P.M. closing time.

"Go back to six fourteen," Thorn said.

"What?"

"Run it back to six minutes, fourteen seconds."

Frank did it, and at six fourteen the subject's eyes flicked upward as if checking for the camera.

"It's a woman," Hilda said.

"Or a guy with thick makeup and long eyelashes." Frank looked at Thorn. "How'd you see that? Six fourteen?"

"Hunting spooky fish in cloudy water."

Hilda took a deep breath and blew it out.

Frank stared at the screen, stepping forward for a closer look.

"I don't know. Maybe, maybe not. Do long eyelashes automatically make it a woman?"

"I should be quiet," Hilda said. "But in my opinion, yes, this is a woman. Definitely a female."

Frank cocked his head and stepped back, then took another step.

"Or somebody who wants us to think he's a woman," Thorn said.

"Now, I have a tech lady who can handle this. Strip out all the crap, get a better focus."

Hilda tugged on the zipper of her track suit jacket.

"Will you at least let me know if you catch this person?"

"Thanks for your help," Frank said. "And we'll take that DVD."

While Frank wrapped things up with Hilda, Thorn wandered back onto the main floor. He worked his way toward the wall of baseball bats and balls and gloves and uniforms.

Ten minutes later, Frank tapped him on the shoulder.

"Am I going to have to put a GPS chip on you?"

"I need to borrow some money, Frank. I'm low on cash."

"What do you need?"

Thorn turned to the young woman who'd been waiting on him. A girl in her twenties with matching gold studs in her ears and nose, and a purple stripe down the middle of her platinum hair.

"What was the amount, Julia?"

"Six hundred and seventy-eight dollars and thirty-nine cents."

"Jesus, Thorn. What the hell?"

Thorn held up a leather baseball glove.

"Wilson A2000, genuine American steerhide with a dual welting finger design."

"And Dri-Lex in the wrist lining," Julia said, "so your hand stays cool."

"A baseball glove?"

Frank was shaking his head.

"No," Thorn said. "Three baseball gloves. And two balls. An extra, in case one rolls into the river."

"You're nuts, Thorn."

"I'll pay you back. Interest if you want it."

Frank shook his head some more, then said something to himself, pulled out his wallet, and handed the clerk a credit card.

"You care to tell me what this is about?"

"Not really."

"You've gone totally and completely nuts."

"Yeah, it must be that."

Outside they scouted the perimeter of the store, Frank leading the way. As they walked, he explained that he'd had Hilda pull the exit door video for last night, and just before closing time the person in the trench coat walked out into the center of the parking lot, about where the two of them were standing right now, then he or she had taken a hard right turn and walked toward the main thoroughfare.

"So?"

"Didn't park in the parking lot. Knew we'd be checking the video. Probably parked a block or two away, someplace without security cameras. I'll put a guy on it tomorrow, have him canvas the neighborhood stores and see what they can pull up. But I'm betting it'll be nothing. This wasn't the guy's first trip to Sports Craze. He or she did their homework, knew the area, knew the camera layouts."

They walked back to the Taurus and Thorn settled the outfielders' gloves into the backseat and got in.

"Six fourteen," Thorn said.

"Yeah?"

"Why does this person go to all the trouble to stay out of view of the video cams in the parking lots but at six fourteen he looks up at the camera that he knows is there?"

"To give us a wink?"

"Maybe not a wink," Thorn said. "Maybe a head fake."

TWENTY

"STORY MUST BE LOSING STEAM," Frank said. "Down to three trucks. Just the cable guys still hanging around."

He passed the satellite vans and gave a wave to one of the pretty women sitting under an umbrella talking on her cell phone. As he pulled into April's driveway, he aimed a remote at the gate and it rolled open.

"She give you a key to the front door too?"

Frank said, "What's eating you, Thorn? You sound jealous."

Thorn was quiet as Frank parked beside April's Mini Cooper in the shade of an oak. Garvey came hobbling out of the house as if she'd been on watch for their return. She was using crutches now, the kind that attach to the arms. Making good time across the gravel drive, she was at Thorn's door when he stepped out.

"Is this what you're looking for?"

Garvey held up a pair of pinking shears.

Frank said, "I'm going to run this DVD to the lab, see what they can do. You keep your phone charged, okay? Don't wander off anywhere. I should be back in an hour, say by one o'clock. Two at the latest."

"I have something else for your lab guys."

Frank switched off the ignition, waiting while Thorn dug Buddha's phone from his pocket and worked his way through the screens until he located the video from the Atlanta traffic stop.

He got it running, and leaned into the car and handed it to Frank.

"A woman in a Zentai suit," Thorn said. "Three weeks ago in Atlanta. Buddha believed there was a connection to this case. The Atlanta cop e-mailed her the video."

"Man, you play by your own rules."

"I wasn't sure it was relevant. Now it looks like it might be."

"Anything else you been holding out on me?" Frank kept watching the video, then ran it back and watched it again.

"That look like the same woman in the sporting goods store?"

"Possible," Frank said. "Grainy as shit. Hand in front of her face, it's hard to see much."

"Like she was blinded by the light, or trying to hide from the camera." Frank ran it through again.

"Yeah?"

"How she's blocking the glare," Thorn said, "it looks weird."

"Well, you're our specialist in that department."

"The Atlanta cop should've made her lower her hand."

"Looks like he'd already decided this wasn't worth his time."

"Your techies can handle it."

"Any other instructions, Agent Thorn?"

"Check unsolved murders for Atlanta, night of July tenth."

Frank sighed.

"And I thought it was me running this investigation."

Frank took a few seconds to forward the e-mail to his own account, then handed the phone back. Thorn hauled the white Sports Craze bag out of the rear seat and carried it over to Garvey.

"Pinking shears. April said you were looking for another pair."

"I am, yes."

She extended them but Thorn raised his hand and halted her.

"There's probably enough fingerprints on those without adding mine."

He watched Frank pull out of the drive, the gate rolling closed behind him. Boxley came trotting over, nosed Thorn's crotch, got an update on Thorn's day so far, then trotted off toward the seawall that ran along the riverfront.

Thorn set the bag on the asphalt and dug out the sales receipt.

"My daughter's upstairs crying. Ever since you left she's been bawling like a lost puppy. Now don't ask me why. I don't see the point in crying over spilled sperm. But I'm just an old lady doped up on pain meds and waiting for the grim reaper. So what do I know?"

Thorn held out the sales receipt.

"Do me a favor, Garvey. Cut the edge of this."

"Oh, goody," Garvey said. "I heard you were some kind of private eye. Is that what you do, have people cut pieces of paper and figure out if they're guilty of murder?"

"Yes," he said. "That's what I do."

"Can you believe it? My daughter is the guiding star for a serial killer."

"Maybe at the moment she is. But we're going to put an end to that."

Thorn held the receipt steady as Garvey sliced the edge of the flimsy paper. Then he held the sawtooth pattern up to the sunlight. About two inches into the cut, he saw one tiny imperfection on the edge of a jag.

"Garvey, could you open the blades of the scissors so I can take a look."

"You're such a damned kook. You know that? Some kind of crackpot gumshoe. Like that Pink Panther fellow."

"Maybe I am. But a shade or two less pink."

"Ha," she said. "I like my gumshoes droll. The men in my life need a well-honed sense of humor if they're going to deal with a free spirit like me."

Holding herself steady with one hand, she opened the scissors with the other and extended them. Just as Buddha had predicted, there was a small ding about halfway up the blade, where someone had crunched down on a pin.

"Where did you find those?"

"Those what?"

"The pinking shears. Where did you find them?"

"In the parlor with Colonel Mustard, right next to the candlestick and the snow shovel."

Thorn smiled politely.

"Even a kook like you had to play Clue, right? When you were little. Or were you ever little?" Giving the question some Mae West hot sauce.

"I was little," Thorn said. "And I played Clue. But I don't remember any snow shovel."

"I was being creative. Don't you like that in a girl, creativity?"

"You're an amusing woman."

"Stop, stop. Turn down the charm before I swoon into your arms."

"Where were the pinking shears, Garvey?"

"Garage apartment," she said. "Where you're staying. In a dresser up there. April found them. I told her there was a second pair I kept in the sewing room in the same drawer where you found the first pair. So she wouldn't stop looking till we'd turned the house upside down. Doing your detective work for you, Mr. Panther."

"What do you think the scissors were doing in the garage apartment?"

"Beats me."

"You didn't put them there?"

"Never go up there. Stairs are too steep."

Garvey was watching cars crawl slowly by on North River Drive. People rubber-necking the coral house.

"Channel 7 put us on the news," she said. "Our address and names. Just right there on the television for the world to see. Live on this street, you don't need to go to the circus, the circus comes to you."

"Who has access to the apartment? Who's stayed there recently?"

"All these questions," Garvey said. "It's making me hungry. I'm getting out of this hot sun and going to have a sandwich. You want one? I make a mean peanut butter and jelly. You look like an extra-crunchy fellow to me."

"Thank you for noticing."

He picked up the sack full of beautifully stitched steerhide and followed Garvey back inside.

In the kitchen he asked her to put the pinking shears into a Ziploc bag. She flashed him a conspiratorial smile and made a small production of pinching the scissors with two fingers and slipping them into a plastic bag, then set the bag on the counter.

Thorn poured them both a glass of skim milk and sat at the kitchen table where he and April had eaten breakfast.

"Yesterday, at the Floridian, did you hear April mention the name of the bar downtown where she was going to meet the sheriff and me?"

"Poblanos," she said. "One of my favorites. Attracts all that rough trade. Now those boys know how to treat a lady."

"You mention to anyone that April and I were meeting there?"

"I might have."

She finished the two sandwiches and started cutting away the crust.

"You might have. But did you?"

"I don't keep track of everything I say. What fun would that be?"

Thorn got up and carried the two sandwiches to the table, then helped Garvey out of her crutches. She heaved a labored sigh as she settled into the kitchen chair.

"It would help me if you could remember, Garvey. Poblanos. Did you tell anyone after we left?"

"Just everyone who'd listen. My daughter was running off to meet a sandy-haired dreamboat at a bar."

"Who's everyone?"

"You want names?"

"Names would be helpful."

"I don't know their names. They're nurses, two nice nurses, though they barely speak a word of English between them. They thought you were cute, so I told them that you and my daughter were getting reacquainted at a bar downtown, and after you got a few drinks in you, *cuidado, mamacitas,* lock up your chicas."

She ate a few bites of her sandwich and set it down.

Thorn tasted his and waited for Garvey's exuberant mood to settle. She was an excitable woman, brimming with energy, an impish light in her eyes. He wasn't sure he could take anything she said with complete confidence. So far he'd not yet heard her slip into anything that resembled a tranquil tone.

Maybe it was Garvey's theatrical instincts that leapt a generation and fueled a love for drama in her grandsons. It sure hadn't come from Thorn. And April seemed as understated and shy of the spotlight as anyone he knew.

"Dee Dee, Sawyer, Gus, and Flynn. There's your list of suspects."

"Suspects?"

"All four of them wanted to know all about who you were. They saw how April was acting around you, then after you and the tattoo woman went off, they came over one by one and wanted to hear what I knew. So I told each of them the same thing; You two were old friends and you and the lady sheriff were investigating something dark and mysterious, and you were meeting April at Poblanos later on in the afternoon.

"And all four of them have been up in that garage apartment any number of times. Sawyer and Dee Dee go up there to tango. Flynn stays over some nights when he wants some home cooking. Gus, he just wanders around wherever he pleases. How'm I doing? Am I being helpful?"

"Very helpful, yes."

"Can you deputize me now?"

"I don't have the power to deputize."

"Posh," Garvey said. "Don't sell yourself short, big boy. I bet you could deputize just about any woman you wanted."

April cleared her throat. Standing in the kitchen doorway with a serious look.

"When you've finished lunch, Thorn, I'd like to speak with you."

He excused himself and followed April into the front room opposite the study. The parlor was full of golden light filtering through gauzy curtains that stirred in a midday breeze. Nothing in the room matched, a comfortable hodgepodge. Mission-style wooden dinner chairs. Two plush velvet chairs, a throw rug woven in a variety of earth tones. A china cabinet full of photos and carved knickknacks. On one wall hung a portrait of a beautiful woman of twenty or so in a black dress, smiling mysteriously off to the right as if someone in the portrait room had caught her fancy. It was Garvey as a young lady, the mischief already taking root in her features.

In a corner of the room was a flat-screen TV standing on an ornately carved table. The usual electronic accessories arrayed on the table beside it.

Thorn chose a wingback chair next to the coffee table.

April stood uncertainly in the doorway assembling her thoughts.

"I'll move out," Thorn said. "Find somewhere else to stay."

"That's not necessary."

She eased into an ancient leather chair beside a front window. The angle of sunlight split her face in half, putting one side in shadow, the other lit so harshly he could see the blue web of veins at her temple and a dusting of dark sideburn hair.

Thorn settled back in the chair. He could walk away from this. Get in Buddha's car and find a motel room. Work with Sheffield till they'd reeled in the Zentai Killer. Stay as long as that required and have nothing more to do with the Moss family.

"I asked the boys to come over and meet you. Flynn should be here in a half hour or so. Sawyer's out with Gus and Dee Dee on their yacht, cruising around the bay. He said he'd be over later, after supper."

"You told them about me."

"I told them a few things. Their father had appeared. A little about your background, how you live."

"And what do you want me to do, April?"

"What do you want to do?"

"I want to hide."

"So go. There's time. It's your call. If this feels wrong, just leave."

He sat and stared at the blank TV set.

"But if you do decide you want to wait and meet them, I think you should take a look at something first."

Thorn glanced at the parlor doorway. Ten steps. Five more to the front door. A quick sprint to the car.

"Look at what?"

"Are you staying?"

"Yes," he said. "I'm here, I'm staying."

"I don't want to prejudice you in any way. They're wonderful young men, both of them, and Jeff too. But given the situation, why you're here, the violence last night, I didn't want to hide this from you. I don't know if it's relevant, but I thought you should know, then decide if Agent Sheffield should see it too."

She picked up the remote and switched on the TV, then clicked past the cable news channel the set was tuned to and brought up a blank screen.

"It was the summer before their freshman year in high school. They were fourteen. There'd been problems in the house. Behavioral things. Acting out. Lots of screaming fights, moodiness, sulking, whole days when neither of them made more than a grunt. Refused to get out of bed and go to school. Sometimes it was Sawyer, sometimes it was Flynn. At first I thought it was just the adolescent hormone thing. And some of it was that, of course. But this was worse. This was scary. Depression, anger, screaming at me and Mother, calling us terrible names. Both of them taking turns.

"Then something violent happened. Something a long way beyond adolescent acting out. A judge was involved, the court system. As a part of the deal, the boys were legally bound to have a psychological evaluation.

"They met with a therapist separately for several months. Then they had one session together. The therapist was a friend of a friend, so I thought he'd be sympathetic and feed me progress reports. But he refused to tell me anything at all, not even a hint. Just kept telling me that they were moving forward. It was frustrating as hell. I pestered him, and he kept putting me off.

"After three months, he handed me this tape, a ten-minute film from their final session together. He decided I needed to know. Maybe it wasn't professionally ethical. He could have gotten in trouble with the judge. I don't know. And I'm not sure I should've watched it at all. It's colored my view of things, changed how I feel about my own flesh and blood. I stashed it away and I've never shown it to anyone, not even Mother. But since you're here, under these circumstances, and since the boys are suspects, I thought you should watch this."

Again Thorn measured the distance to the door and beyond. Thirty seconds and he'd be gone.

"They're not suspects," he said.

"Of course they are. Let's don't lie to each other, Thorn. Gus and Dee Dee and the boys, and even Jeff Matheson. They all had access to my files and to those scissors. I'm not stupid."

The TV set was flickering, stalled in a zone of static and gray light.

"And what would their motive be?"

"Those satellite trucks," she said. "Newspapers and TV commentators mentioning *Miami Ops*. This whole horrible thing has put them on the map. Their ratings are going to be through the roof."

"You think one of them could have beaten another human being to death to improve their TV ratings?"

199

April aimed the remote at the array of electronics.

"You really don't think one of your boys did this."

"Of course I don't. I just want everything on the table."

She got the video running and stood up, watched a few moments, then a phone rang somewhere in the house. It rang several times, then from the maid's room Garvey called that April was wanted.

She turned and marched from the parlor. Thorn sat and watched.

The therapist's office was nothing special. Diplomas on the wall, the usual bookshelves, stocked in an orderly way. A desk as anonymous as the rest of the décor. The man sitting behind the desk was bearded and had a ponytail and wore a red-and-white checked shirt.

The boys sat side by side, Flynn slouching in his chair, Sawyer erect, chin up. Sawyer in a pink button-down shirt, Flynn wearing a white one of the same type. Their hair parted neatly, their jeans pressed, their loafers shiny. If it weren't for the difference in their eyes, no way Thorn could tell them apart. But what he'd noted when he first saw their photographs had been true even ten years earlier. Flynn's eyes were tightened into a squint as though a blinding light were shining on his face, while Sawyer seemed so resolutely serene he might have been drowsing off.

The therapist was holding a wooden pencil in his hand and was drumming the point against an ink blotter. The three of them seemed to be locked in a silent standoff. A question asked but not yet answered. A pause that seemed to grow more unbreakable as it grew in length. A minute of silence was followed by another minute just as silent. Neither of the boys fidgeted. The only thing moving in the room was the pencil.

Finally Sawyer leaned forward in his chair as if stretching the muscles in his lower back. He hugged himself, then sat back and blew out a breath.

"I did not know what was going on," he said. "All right. I walked in and saw them, and didn't understand what I was seeing. So I freaked. Nothing more complicated than that."

The therapist pressed his palms together and rolled the pencil between them. Covering the hint of eagerness in his face with this nonchalant act.

"You didn't know this about Flynn. So when you realized it, you reacted strongly." The therapist continued to roll his pencil between his palms. He didn't seem to be questioning Sawyer's version of things, but to be restating his words for the record.

"You didn't just freak," Flynn said quietly. "You tried to kill him."

Sawyer leaned back in his chair, rocked his head back, and studied the ceiling. His Adam's apple bobbed.

"He's alive, isn't he?" Sawyer said, still staring upward. "I hit him, yeah. I hit him because I thought he was hurting you. It was disgusting. I pulled him off and I hit the fuck out of him."

"You hit him," the therapist said.

"You punched him and kept punching him. You broke his teeth, you broke his nose and his jaw. You would've killed him if I hadn't stopped you."

"We have different memories of the event."

"You were trying to kill him. That's not a memory. That's a fact."

"Whatever."

"Was it Jeff Matheson you were mad at, Sawyer?"

Sawyer looked at his nails.

"I wasn't mad at anyone. I was reacting to something that was wrong. I thought I was doing a good thing, I was rescuing my brother. Defending him against an attacker."

"Bullshit."

"You thought Flynn was in mortal danger?"

"Flynn was screaming like he was in pain, like he was being hurt."

"You're such a liar," Flynn said. "Such a fucking liar."

Sawyer turned his head slowly and examined his brother for a minute.

"You knew I was gay," Flynn said. "You knew it for years."

"No," Sawyer said. "I did not."

"Yes, you did. You damn well knew."

"Did you ever tell me you were gay? Did you ever tell anybody?"

"I didn't have to. You're my goddamn twin, you knew."

"You should've told me. We were always truthful with each other."

The therapist scratched some words on his yellow legal pad. He tugged on his graying mustache and said nothing. The ball was rolling. The long months of pushing it up the hill were over; now all he had to do was stand back and watch gravity take its course.

"Did you ever say the words? 'I am a homosexual. I love men.' Did you ever say those words, Flynn? One time, even once, out loud?"

"You knew. You damn well knew."

"And of all people. Matheson, that creep. Jesus Christ, Flynn. Jeff Matheson? I should have gone ahead and beaten him to death. That weasel. That shithead. Always hanging around, the way he looks at you."

Flynn stood up. He looked calmly at the therapist.

"Have you got enough? Will that make the judge happy?"

"We have more time in the hour."

"I'm done," Flynn said. "I've said all I'm going to say. Ever. If he goes to jail, he goes to jail. I'll bake him cookies."

He walked out, shut the door. A light step, the easy stride of an athlete.

Sawyer was washing his hands together, looking toward the window.

"I should've killed the asshole."

"If you had done that, your brother would still be who he is," the therapist said. "Nothing you can do will change him into someone else. There's nothing wrong with him. He doesn't have a sickness. His sexual orientation isn't wrong or immoral or any of that."

"He betrayed me," Sawyer said.

"I'm sorry," the therapist said. "How did he betray you?"

"We had a bond, a connection. He violated that. He deserted me."

"Every individual needs privacy at times," the therapist says. "Flynn had a secret. I'm sure he would have told you in due time. Your love for him and his love for you is very solid. It'll survive this strain."

"I don't care if it survives. He deserted me."

"Those are only words, Sawyer. He didn't desert you. He's changed. He's discovered a new part of himself. Now you need to adjust as well. All relationships grow and alter over time. It's natural and healthy. It's not always easy, but we must find a way to stay flexible and maintain the love and trust and faithfulness that underlie the bond."

"Enough of this shit," Sawyer said. "If Judge Parker wants anything else, then just tell him to fuck himself, lock me up, toss the key in the ocean. I'm not doing this anymore, not another minute. I'm out of here."

He walked from the room with the same light and certain step as his brother and shut the door crisply.

The therapist sat for a moment twiddling his pencil, then let go of a long sigh and looked up at the video camera. The screen went dark.

ACT FOUR

AT SEA

TWENTY-ONE

THORN SAT FOR A WHILE in the crushed velvet chair before the bright gray static, staring down at his own hands, still swollen from clubbing the baseball bat into the light pole. Another in a long string of similar episodes, Thorn going psycho, erupting in a volcanic fury. Like building that bonfire two days ago, Thorn in zombie mode, setting ablaze everything he owned, everything he cherished, everything he'd worked so hard to create.

Now his blood was circulating in Sawyer and Flynn. His volatile nature transmitted through the tangled web of genes and inherited traits.

What started in those innocent bedroom hours a quarter century before, a morning bathed in the quiet springtime sunlight, April Moss and Thorn tangled on the cotton sheets, their sweaty bodies cooled by breezes from Blackwater Sound; those few hours together had set in motion a long chain of events. Rusty's death nudging April to write an elegy of compassion for a woman she didn't know, an act that some unbalanced maniac used as a road map to murder a woman in Oklahoma, which propelled Buddha Hilton out of her quiet town and onto a jet plane, into a rental car, a journey that ended with her curled up in a cold bathtub in Miami, naked, suffering a gruesome end.

He stared at the gray fuzz on the screen. Opening and closing his swollen hands. He traced and retraced the chain, link by link, the long inevitable sequence. The moonlit night at the Islamorada bar, the pretty high school kid flirting, the giddy tequila shots, the drive back to his place, and on and on and on until it became this day in this room, a day haunted by the deaths of many and by the foretelling of more to come.

There was only one way to tell the story. Foolhardy, reckless Thorn had set this whole damn thing in motion, tipped the first domino, and a quarter of a century later they were still falling one by one by one.

He was still staring at the static on the screen when someone entered the room behind him, walked to his side, and reached around the edge of the chair to pry the remote from his hand. He aimed it at the television and switched the channel to the cable news.

April Moss was being interviewed once again outside the coral house.

Thorn turned his head and looked up at Flynn Moss holding the remote, studying the televised interview that was taking place just yards beyond the parlor window.

The blond CNN woman was asking April questions, and April was answering them quietly and with tense restraint.

"Ben Silver called Mom a few minutes ago, ordered her to get outside and face the cameras. She looks good on-screen, don't you think? Fleshes her out nicely. Direct sun pops the highlights in her hair, erases some of her pallor. Shows off the beautiful angles working in her face. But then you probably already noticed that."

Flynn walked over to a nearby chair and sat. He glanced at Thorn, shook his head, and grimaced or smiled. It was hard to tell. Then he turned back to the television. Flynn had on a simple white T-shirt, khaki shorts, and sandals. An outfit almost identical to the one Thorn had worn every day for most of his life.

The reporter asked April if she planned to write more obituaries. The question seemed to take her by surprise. She blinked and stuttered the beginning of a response and stopped.

"Ms. Moss," the reporter said. "Apparently your work is fueling these horrific murders. But the publisher of *The Miami Herald* tells us he has no intention of pulling you off your normal assignment. Will you go along with that? Will you write more obituaries even if by doing so you put more innocent people at risk?"

April stared straight ahead.

"It's my job," she said. "Unless they fire me, I'll keep writing."

"The killer called again. Did you know that?"

"I heard."

"He claims responsibility for five victims. On July third an elderly gentleman in Hialeah was his first. Then he's killed at one-week intervals afterward, cut the throat of a male nurse in Atlanta, shot a teenage boy in Fort Lauderdale, stabbed a female lawyer in Oklahoma, and the brutal beating of the sheriff last night. Do you have any comment on this string of horrors?"

April said she was sorry. Sorry for the families, for the victims. Very, very sorry.

"Do you know how the killer is selecting his targets?"

April said no, she had no idea.

"But he's using your obituaries as his road map. You have no clue what he's basing his actions on?"

"No idea."

"Have the police been exploring these avenues?"

"I wouldn't know what avenues they've explored."

Three other reporters had hustled over from their trucks to join the impromptu news conference and were half circled around her. The chunky guy elbowed to the front, jabbed his mike at April.

"Our Susquehanna overnight poll was just released. In our survey sixty-three percent of Americans believe you should be fired from your job."

"What?"

"Two-thirds of respondents said you should be let go."

April studied the man but said nothing.

"Do you think you should resign?"

"Why would I?"

"Because your writing has caused such gruesome results."

April inhaled through her nose, marshalling her restraint.

"I write obituaries. I celebrate the stories of people's lives. I believe I perform a service to the families of the deceased, and their friends, and to the public who otherwise might never have known these unique individuals."

"But you understand, don't you, why the families of the five victims look at this very differently. Whether you intended it or not, your writing has caused five deaths, innocent men and women. People consider you something of an accomplice."

"An accomplice?"

"That's what we're hearing."

"Go fuck yourself," April said quietly. "And when you've finished that, fuck your poll."

"Wow, she snuck that one by," Flynn said. "Good going, Mom. That should seal the deal."

"What deal?"

"Hey, we haven't been formally introduced. I'm Flynn Moss, your son."

He extended his hand.

Was this a smart-ass trick? Draw his hand away and wipe it through his hair? What the hell. Thorn reached out and the kid's hand was still there. Flynn with a powerful grip. Maybe squeezing harder and longer than would be considered polite.

When Flynn released his hand, Thorn said, "Seal what deal?"

"Haven't you been watching the news?"

"Not if I can avoid it."

"Well, it's the Saturday dead zone for the media jocks, but they're still going strong about the Zentai Killer, so that part's good. Only now it's exclusively about Mom and her obituaries. *Miami Ops* is out of their script."

Thorn shook his head, not getting the point.

"News people have trouble telling a story with more than one plotline. Either they're too dumb, or they think their audience is too dumb. But this story has two threads. This maniac is copying our show. And he's using Mom's obituaries to do it. How complicated is that? But no, that's not the story anymore. Now the simpletons have shrunk it down so it's only about the real-life obituaries. Make it stupid and easy, that's the motto.

"Looked for a minute like they were losing interest in the whole thing, backing away, then the killer calls, gives them names and dates, a little pep talk, and bing, they're pumped up again. The frenzy resumes, except it's all about whether Mom should quit. Her role in the thing. They made a choice: Where's the juiciest narrative, the rawest nerve?

"Surprise, surprise, they all arrived at the same answer. Doesn't matter if the killer is copycatting our show. Tell the obituary writer's story, go after her, drop the other thread. So that seals the deal. Whatever bump we were going to get in the ratings, it'll be gone by Thursday. The show's dead. It's over. Time to update the resume."

The front door opened and April stepped inside and settled her back against it. She was breathing deeply. Her eyes roved the foyer for a moment, then drifted to the parlor and settled on Thorn and Flynn.

"Come on in, Mom. Join the hootenanny."

"Not just now."

She pushed herself upright and headed for the stairway. She stopped and came to the room and looked at Thorn.

"Sawyer's not coming after all. He'll drop by later."

"Where'd he go?" Flynn asked.

"On the boat with Dee Dee and Gus. Said he wanted to take a deep breath. Which sounds like a good idea for all of us."

"Nice fuck-yous, Mom. Snuck in two of them. Good job."

April turned away and walked upstairs.

Flynn snapped off the TV and scooted his chair a half foot closer to Thorn. Leaned in and spoke in a conspiratorial whisper.

"So it's just us boys."

"The code," Thorn said. "The one the TV killer's using to pick his victims. How does it work in the show? What's his system?"

"Oh, yeah, yeah. I heard you were some kind of undercover dick or something."

Thorn let that slide.

"What's the key to the code?"

"So what's your story? You're what, like Tarzan? Live the jungle life in Key Largo, like hide up in the palm fronds and all that cool shit. Swing down on your vine and solve a caper every once in a while, then swing back up to your tree house. That how it is?"

"Exactly like that."

"So tell me, have you spread your seed to any other young girls? Do I have some half brothers or sisters I should meet?"

"We were talking about the code."

"*You* were talking about the code, Tarzan. I was talking about you, my old man, my papa, my paterfamilias, my liege."

"You're a smart young man."

"Am I impressing you, Dad? I very much want to impress you. Oh, yes. I want to earn your respect. So you can tell me how proud you are of me, and make me feel all worthy and noble and warm and gooey inside."

"We might get to that point sooner if you'd cut the shit."

"Oh, we're a smart guy, are we? Tarzan, the quipster. Flexing his muscles and trotting out one-liners. Man, you're a major cliché, Thorn. You're like right out of some fifties Bogart, Sydney Greenstreet flick."

"You do your own makeup on the show?"

That sat him back in his chair. He cocked his head and appraised Thorn with a flicker of wariness.

"I have a makeup girl like every actor on the show."

"But you can do it yourself if you have to?"

"What's this about, Tarzan?"

"It's about a young woman who was beaten to death last night with a baseball bat. You ever seen someone beaten to death?"

Flynn slid his gaze toward the TV set and was silent.

"Can you do your own makeup? Say the makeup artist doesn't show up one day and you have to impersonate someone special. Say it's a girl you're supposed to look like. Could you do that yourself? Make a latex mask like the one you were wearing the other day?"

"What is this?"

"This is a simple question. Father to son."

"Fuck the father shit, okay. Just leave that out of this."

"I can do that."

"Yeah, damn right I could do my own makeup. Give me twenty minutes, the right gels, powders, brushes, foundation."

"And the latex mask, the one you were wearing at the Floridian, did you make that?"

"Am I being accused of something? Because if I am, I want to hear it straight."

"Did you make that mask?"

"Are you asking me to incriminate myself?"

"Why do you say that?"

Flynn pinched his earlobe, rubbed it between thumb and first finger.

"I've done it a thousand times, made masks, worn eyelashes, mustaches, full beards. It's my trademark. I'm a mountebank. Know that word, Tarzan?"

"I do."

"Pick a star, Marilyn, Scarlett, Demi, Angelina. Ten minutes, I'm her."

"And Sawyer, is he capable of that?"

"Sawyer? Eyelashes? Can Sawyer do makeup, make a mask out of latex or gelatin?"

"Can he?"

Flynn moved his chair back to its original position. Settled into it and stared across the room at the portrait of young, mischievous Garvey.

"I wouldn't know what Sawyer's capable of."

"What about Jeff Matheson?"

"What about him?" The jauntiness evaporated from his voice.

"Would he be capable of applying makeup? Creating a mask."

"What kind of question is that?"

"As far as you know, does Jeff have any of those skills you have? To change his appearance. It's a simple question."

"I really don't know. We played around with shit like that when we were kids. Is that what you want to hear?"

"You got into your mother's makeup, you and Jeff?"

"A few times. We were kids. Got into trouble. Mom started locking her bedroom."

Out the front window Thorn saw the shadow of a bird arriving, then the ibis appeared, fluttering to a delicate landing, followed by another then the rest of the flock, touching down in the grass that bordered the drive. They began to hook their beaks into the dirt, strutting a few steps and working the soil.

For the moment all was quiet at the front gate. The reporters had returned to their trucks to monitor the airwaves for other stories, something darker than the Zentai Killer, something bigger, with a higher body count, a more appealing victim, or whatever it was they were always searching for, the fizzy next big thing to fill their bottomless appetites.

"The code," Thorn said. "What is it? How does the killer pick his victims in the show?"

"Man, you just keep coming."

"I do."

"There is no code. That's the twist."

"No code."

"It's an existential joke. There's nothing at the core. The killer leaves the obits behind at the crime scene to confuse the issue. Cuts the edges to make it seem like they're important. But there's no code. That's supposed to be next season's first big reveal. That is, when there was still going to *be* a next season. Cops and the Feds keep looking at the obits, studying them, trying to crack the secret, but there is no code. It's all a hoax. There is no God. No wizard behind the curtains."

"Nothing at the core."

"That's right, Tarzan. It's an elaborate con job."

"But why? What's the point?"

"Hey, it's a freaking TV show, man. There's supposed to be a point?"

Thorn looked over at Garvey's portrait, her earthy smile.

"So the killer's a psycho. Doing whatever he feels. It's all random."

"The killer is Dee Dee's twin sister, Valerie. That's revealed in the show coming up this Thursday. She's got all the twisted genes in the family. You even watch the show?"

"I've seen about thirty seconds."

"Maybe you should sit down and take a look so you'll know what the hell you're asking questions about."

"A twin sister is the killer."

"That's right."

"Bad twin versus good twin."

"Yeah."

"What's the issue between them?"

Flynn shook his head.

"Got me."

"Bad twin trying to create her own identity? Be free? That the idea?"

"Hey, that's beyond my pay grade, pal. Ask Sawyer, he writes the shit. I'm just a humble reciter of words. A player upon the stage, a mere mummer dancing to another's tune."

"How's that feel, your brother pulling your strings? Putting words in your mouth, turning you into whoever he wants."

"I'm an actor. I'm used to it."

"But this is your brother."

Flynn stared at him and didn't reply.

"What tune were you dancing to last night around eleven?"

Flynn stood up and marched over to the window and looked out.

" 'What tune were you dancing to last night around eleven?' " He parroted Thorn's tone and cadence precisely. "Where were you between the hours of eleven and twelve o'clock? Where indeed? Where was I? Let's see, was that me, Flynn Moss, sprinting down the Miami boulevards in a black Zentai suit carrying a baseball bat? Oh, no, oh, no. Did I just incriminate myself? Did I buy a one-way ticket to the rock pile, the slammer, the pokey?"

He pivoted back to Thorn and stabbed a finger at him.

"Listen up, Daddy-o, if you and I are going to work together, you're going to have to give me better material to come back on. Instead of this worn-out crap, right out of Cornball 101. It's stale, hombre, past its sell-by date."

"You always try this hard? Or does this bullshit come natural?"

Flynn raised his hands slowly and chopped the side of one into the palm of the other like a movie clacker.

"And cut."

"Hold on, tiger. We're just getting to know each other."

"We're done here," he said. *"Finito."*

His exit from the room had the same light-footed crispness Thorn had witnessed in the video when the therapist circled in too close to some painful truth.

TWENTY-TWO

SHEFFIELD SHOWED UP JUST AFTER two, knocking on the screen door. April and Garvey were in the maid's room. Thorn could hear them quarrelling as he let Frank into the house.

Thorn handed him the pinking shears in the plastic bag.

"These are the scissors the killer used to cut out the obituaries."

"And how the hell do you know that?"

Thorn explained about the ding in the blade, the corresponding notch in Rusty's obituary.

"Okay, that works," Sheffield said. "Sheriff Hilton was one smart lady."

"She was."

"The fucker called in, gave the paper names and dates."

"I saw it on TV," Thorn said.

"Doing our work for us."

"Cranking up the volume," Thorn said.

"My guys had that already, except for the teenage kid in Lauderdale. African American. Alvin Jaspers. Gangbanger, rap star wannabe. Murder weapon left behind. A .357 Colt. No prints. All of them jibe with the obituaries. Paragraphs three, six, nine, three words in."

"That the full update?"

"Oh, no. This morning I sent a couple of my junior G-men over for a little surprise visit to the Ocean Club where everybody's living, Sawyer and Flynn and Dee Dee and Gus, and they sat down and picked their brains for a few hours. They questioned some of the crew too just to keep our four primes from squirming too much. Got the whole skinny. 'Where were you last night?' 'Where were you last Thursday night,' you know, closing time at Sports Craze. Took prints for everybody."

"And?"

"Fill you in while we drive. We got to move, time's a-wasting."

"We need to talk to April first."

"About what?"

"Doing an obituary for Monday."

Frank looked back outside at the three news trucks parked on the street.

"What? Give the killer his next assignment?"

"That's the idea."

"Set a trap. Select a target, choose his weapon for him."

"It could work."

Frank shook his head.

"No way. He can't be that dumb. He'd know we were setting him up."

"Maybe not."

"He's copying the TV show, for christsakes, basing what he does on whatever system the show uses. He knows we know that. He'll see it coming a mile off."

Thorn flexed his right fist, then his left, the limberness coming back.

"There's no code in *Miami Ops,* Frank. The obits are just a red herring. TV cops studying the obits to figure out how they led to the victims, but that's all a ruse. The killer's playing with the cops, picking his victims at random. The obits aren't a blueprint to anything."

"Who told you that?"

"Flynn."

"But our guy has a code. Three down, three in."

"Yeah. He's using different rules."

"Rules he came up with on his own. Not from the show."

Frank kept staring out the window.

"And we know his code, but he doesn't know we know."

"If we have an edge, that's it."

Frank stooped forward and fluttered his arms like a swimmer loosening up on the blocks.

"I don't like it. Even if he fell for it, there's too many variables. We lead him somewhere, he makes our surveillance, gets spooked, he bolts. We never see him again. Or worse, he slips past, somebody dies, it's on us."

"It could work, Frank."

"No, thanks. I'm staying old school. Track the fuckhead down, catch him napping in his spider hole."

"Look," Thorn said, "there's not much time. It's got to be a Monday obituary. That's the one he acts on. If April's willing, she has to write the thing tomorrow. It's got to be real, a real person who died. The asshole could check that out. If he realized it's a fake, it falls apart. April has to tweak the writing, get the words we want in the slots we want them."

"No way. Not acceptable. Drop it."

"Hear me out, Frank. Say she does the obituary, it appears Monday. We know the guy's not going to act on it till Saturday. That gives us a week to catch him. We do the shoe-leather drill, get all the forensics back, you have fingerprints to work with, blow up the videos, the other things on your list. That's probably going to be enough right there. If somehow we can't nail the guy in a week, this gives us a fall-back plan.

"Get April to write it in a way that puts nobody at risk. Lure the asshole to the place of our choosing, nobody's there except us."

Frank walked into the parlor, looked around, buying a minute. Sunlight was glazing the wooden surfaces, putting a golden frost on the coffee table, the chairs, the bookcases. Sheffield prowled the room, his fingertips drifting across the back of the chair where Flynn had sat. Stopping for a moment to look at Garvey's portrait. That pretty lass with the naughty twinkle.

From ten feet away, Frank said, "Go see if she'll do it."

"It'll work, Frank."

"No, it won't. It'll turn into another giant clusterfuck. Like everything you touch, Thorn. It's your special gift."

"Better than no gift at all."

"All right, all right. Go talk to her."

Thorn walked into the dining room, calling out April's name. She appeared at the door of the maid's room, where Garvey was staying. He motioned for her to step close. Leave Garvey out of it.

At a bay window in the parlor, he explained his idea.

She listened without comment, staring out the window at the satellite trucks, at the flock of ibis, at Boxley lying in the shade. Thorn made his case as cleanly as possible. No emotion, no pressure. Write a real obit, but insert three words at the crucial spots; third, sixth, ninth paragraph, three words in. Where, who, and what weapon. When he was finished explaining, she shifted her eyes to his face, ten seconds becoming thirty, an awkward half minute. Then she turned away and walked back to Garvey's room and shut the door.

Frank was in the foyer, phone to his ear, when Thorn returned. He clicked off and tucked the phone inside his blue jacket.

"Well? What'd she say?"

Thorn pinched the front of his polo shirt and fluttered it to cool himself.

"She's going to think about it."

TWENTY-THREE

NINETY-TWO DEGREES AT TWO IN the afternoon. A sheer blue summer sky, glassy waters. In his white yachting trousers, white tunic, canvas slip-ons, and captain's hat with gold stars, Gus Dollimore was at the helm of *Pretty Boy,* a Hatteras GT he'd been leasing since *Miami Ops* premiered. Sixty-two feet, ninety thousand pounds, 1,900-horsepower twin diesels. A superindulgence. He'd used it in the last few months to entertain local celebrities, politicos, visiting studio guys, a couple of rock legends living on the beach, a pro tennis star, some Heat players, the new Dolphins QB. They'd partied, traded business cards. Gus never heard from them again.

You had to be delusional to think you'd catch anybody's attention in Miami with fancy cars and boats. Like whispering in a South Beach night club and expecting to be heard. Nobody in this town was impressed by anything. They'd seen better. Always something glitzier, bigger, faster, louder. But Gus kept trying, convinced this was a piece of the success puzzle. Glam it up.

Gus was hauling ass, taking them beyond the lighthouse at Boca Chita, twelve miles south of Key Biscayne, heading out to deep water. Up on plane, making forty knots with the full race diesels running smooth.

Midsummer party boats filled the bay, the sandbars jammed with boozed-up kids and loud music. But as they pushed farther into the open ocean, things thinned out. Only a handful of vessels scattered to their south and east.

Dee Dee was below in the salon, downing shots of Bacardi to keep her stomach calm—still jittery from the FBI grilling.

Gus drew back the throttle levers and the yacht settled to a gradual halt, its huge wake catching up, wallowing the ship for a few seconds.

"What're we doing, Gus?"

"It's Dee Dee," he said.

"What about her?"

Gus had dialed back the bluster. Talking so low, Sawyer had to step close, his shoulder brushing Dollimore's.

"You're going to have to grit your teeth on this. It'll be painful. More for you than me, but it's going to hurt us both."

Gus scanned the surrounding waters. A few go-fast boats ripping up the quiet sea a mile away, a trawler heading out, and two freighters a few miles away in the shipping lanes.

Gus nudged the throttles, got *Pretty Boy* idling forward.

"You don't look good, son. What're you, still spooked from going one on one with a federal agent?"

"Damn right I'm spooked."

"I can see why," Gus said. "You got some 'splaining to do, boy."

"What're you talking about?"

"Dallas, for starters. You give them your bullshit story, Danson stood you up?"

"I told them the truth. Danson made an appointment, didn't show."

"They ask you about Atlanta? Atlanta on the tenth. Weekend that guy got his throat sliced. An obit on the table beside him."

Sawyer stepped back.

"Oh, yeah, yeah," Gus said, "I remember now. I got it marked on my calendar. That was the weekend you were scouting locations on the Gulf Coast. I'm sure you got ways to verify you were in Sanibel."

"That was your doing, Gus. You sent me on that trip."

"Bullshit. Don't drag me into this. When they get around to asking, I got to give them the truth. You got a wild hair, thought we should shoot some locales outside Miami, break the pattern. I wasn't hot about it, but I suggested some places. You rejected mine, picked the west coast, decided

221

to do a spin through Sanibel or Marco Island, search out some fresh backdrops.

"Hey, I may not be Fellini, but I'm thorough as shit. I write it all down. Where everybody is, what they're doing. That's the show runner in me, pal. Got to keep track whether we're all rowing together or somebody's going off in some counterproductive direction.

"So it's all down in living color. I can PowerPoint it if I need to. Shoot it up on the screen. Every hour of every day, whether you're on the clock or off. I'm compulsive, what can I say? It's a disorder, but hey, if I didn't have such a raging goddamn case of OCD, keep such obsessive records of my cast and crew's comings and goings, I might be a suspect myself."

Gus's grimace softened into a half smile. A little lift of one eyebrow.

"Don't worry, Gus. I got credit card receipts for the hotel, gas, food. I was in Captiva, stayed at the 'Tween Waters Inn, two nights. I can prove it."

"Receipts? So what? Smart kid like you, you could check in to some motel, make a show, talk to the clerk so he remembers you, then sneak back to your car, drive to Atlanta. Avoid the whole airplane thing. How hard is that?"

"It didn't happen."

"Whatever you say, kid. Really, I'm hoping it's true. I'm sure as shit hoping I'm not up here on the flybridge rubbing elbows with the fucking Son of Sam."

Gus turned his eyes onto the blue-green sea stretching out toward the straight line of the horizon.

"This morning, that little meeting with the Feds, that was a warm-up drill. Minute the news vultures get a whiff, grab your cock and hold on. Like hey, what about those other killings around South Florida, they'd be a snap for a guy like you, wide-open schedule, coming and going whenever you feel. In forty minutes you could whip up to Fort Lauderdale, smack the teenager, hell, do it on the way home after work, who's going to know?

"Hialeah, same thing, a quickie, no sweat; and that sheriff in the motel along the Miami River, that's like a hop skip and a jump from the soundstage. Swing by there, take some batting practice. Home in time for the late news."

"Same for any of us, Gus. Flynn, you, Dee Dee. Hop skip jump."

"So where you claim you were last night, Sawyer, time of the murder? What'd you tell that nice lady agent?"

"I went for a jog out on the Rickenbacker."

"And she bought that?"

"She seemed to."

"Seemed to? Oh, man, you are so fucked."

"Where'd you claim you were, Gus?"

"Where I always am when I'm not working my ass off. Out on this baby. Blowing the television dust out of my lungs."

"You can't prove that any more than I can prove I was running the Rickenbacker."

"Beside the point, son. The actual issue is, you're about to go for a long swim in a cesspool of publicity. Maybe the Feds got evidence to hold you, take you downtown, maybe not. I'm not talking about any of that. Good chance you'll skate. Maybe they buy the Captiva receipts. But guys like Murray Danson, that's who you got to worry about."

"Danson?"

"Murray, the asswipes he works for, I know these people, I been around them all my life. Let me tell you how it works. Two strikes, you're done. You, my boy, got your first strike writing *Miami Ops,* which at this moment is dead last in its slot, a serious stinker. Throw in another strike, like even a hint of you being a suspect in a string of murders—shit, boy, you'll never blow your nose near a TV script again."

"And you?"

"Same for me. I got better alibis working than you, but as far as the Hollywood gang is concerned, unless the killer steps forward and takes credit, we're all going down. Guilty, not guilty, that's irrelevant."

"Where's Dee Dee in all this?"

Dollimore tapped the throttle levers, and *Pretty Boy* responded smoothly. Pinching the yin yang pendant he wore around his neck, Gus slid it back and forth along the chain and looked out at the Atlantic's blue dazzle.

"Dee Dee, I'm worried about that girl."

"Worried?"

"The way she's not around sometimes. Just up and goes off. Weekends especially."

"I see her on the weekends."

"You see her at night. At dinner at some restaurant."

"What're you driving at, Gus?"

"My girl, Dee Dee. She ever show you her hidey-hole?"

"Her what?"

"Her safe, her lockbox. Where it is, the floor, the wall, behind the bookcase, wherever the fuck she hid the thing."

"What're you asking me?"

"She has something stored away, son. Something that belongs to me. I want it back and she won't hand it over."

Sawyer asked him again what he was talking about.

"You know where her hidey-hole is or not?"

"I've never seen a safe."

"You've never seen a safe in her condo, nowhere else?"

"You should talk to her about this."

"I'm talking to you, hotshot. That's what we're doing. We're talking about some materials my daughter has in her possession."

"This is none of my business. I'm not getting into this."

"But son, you're already up to your fucking nose hairs in it. I'm trying to get you out of it."

"What's this have to do with the FBI?"

"It's all interconnected, my man. All one big web."

Gus scanned the waters, doing a slow circle in every direction. The closest boat was miles away.

"Let's come at this from another angle. You think Dee Dee is good at what she does? You think the girl can act?"

"She's okay. She's got the looks."

"Okay, sure, she's got a body, your basic, dime-a-dozen fox. But is there talent? Does she have acting ability, does she radiate? Aside from the fact that you're banging her three times a day, your dick is on fire, separating that out, in your objective opinion does she have talent?"

"I don't like the way you're talking."

"Sawyer, my boy, Dee Dee's killed the show. On her own, all by herself, she's taken us down. It's not your scripts, not Flynn, or the others.

It's Dee Dee. She murdered the shit out of that show. Reviewers say it, focus groups, the drill-down Nielsens. Single-handed, that daughter of mine has done us in."

Sawyer was silent. Trying to defend Dee Dee's acting ability was futile. Maybe the show's failure wasn't completely due to her, but some of it was, maybe more than some.

"You ever wonder why a man like me, a guy the last twenty years he's scratched his way up the sheer canyon walls of the entertainment business, why this guy would hire a woman so manifestly unsuited for the role she's holding? Do I strike you as a guy who willfully and purposefully shoots himself in the scrotum?"

"Yeah, okay. Dee Dee is a weak link. I grant you that."

"You think she got that starring part because I'm her old man? Some kind of nepotism bullshit? Am I a fucking softie?"

Sawyer didn't reply.

"Back when we started the show," Gus said, "I thought, Okay, maybe I could raise the level of her game. I actually thought I had that ability. But the girl's uncoachable. The girl's beyond my power to fix."

"I'm losing the thread, Gus."

"Dee Dee's got something precious of mine, which is the sole reason she is where she is today, and we're where we are. This material is in her hidey-hole. Until I have it in my hands, she's my albatross. She's everybody's albatross."

"She's blackmailing you."

"Blackmail, extortion, whatever name you want."

"What does she have on you?"

"Hell, we made some films. I'm not proud of it, but it was a long way back. I was young, stupid."

Sawyer drew a slow breath. Staring out to sea at the rippling silver light, the gulls circling over a school of bait fish, diving for them, squealing.

"Porn," Sawyer said. "You made porn."

"I was just getting started in the business. I had like a cheap Kodak XL55, a shaky tripod, used a white sheet to bounce the light. Primitive as shit. But I learned a lot. It laid the groundwork. My apprenticeship."

"You put Dee Dee in porn movies. How old was she?"

"Too young. Illegal. But contrary to what people say, girls that age, some of them can have a fully operational sexual side. Seven, eight. Dee Dee sure did. She was totally into it. Never cried, never protested. Hugging and kissing, had some cute little fake orgasms too. Once I showed her how it was done."

"You and her together."

"Some of that."

"You . . ."

Dollimore held up his hand.

"You want to rip my head off, shit down my throat. I understand that. What I did was disgusting and immoral. I agree, I agree a hundred percent. But you attack me, how's that going to play in front of the media, me with broken teeth, black eye, my jaw hanging loose?"

"You fucking asshole."

"What? You thought Dee Dee was a virgin? Like maybe she learned her moves in a nunnery? Come on, kid, we're all adults here. Men of the world.

"I told you this was going to hurt. I warned you. This isn't pleasant. But it's like right at the center of why we're where we are right now. It's the linchpin in this whole shitty mess you and me find ourselves in.

"Was I a lousy dad? Hell, yes. I tried to be gentle with her, but it was a dirty business, I admit it. We got busted, had our day in court, just like you had yours. Got a clean bill of health. Walked away, never did any more movies of that kind. Just the same way you walked away from your little brush."

"What brush?"

"Hey, sonny, we got no secrets, you and me. You may think we do, but no, you'd be wrong. Getting a court record expunged, that's like trying to wipe clean the memory on your hard drive. There's always traces. Back when I hired you, I had a look at your history. I like to know the story behind the story. Everybody's got a skeleton. I like to know about those skeletons, people who work for me, people I need to trust. I like to have the goods.

"You knocked that Matheson kid around, put him in the hospital, almost killed his ass. Young boy, beat him so bad he's never quite right afterward. What is he, like brain damaged or whatever? Jesus, something like that comes out at this stage of your career, you're majorly fucked. That's a third strike and like I said, in this business it only takes two."

"Who told you that? Jeff? Flynn? Who?"

"I got my ways of finding things out," Gus said.

"So you're threatening me? You'd give that to the press?"

"You sure you don't know about her hidey-hole? Nothing comes to mind, where these films might be stored away?"

"Screw you."

"Maybe she's been lying to me. I destroyed the master copies. I held on to a couple, don't ask me why, but I know where those are. Maybe the girl's lying. Maybe she doesn't have any movies after all. What do you think, Sawyer? You know her pretty good. Is she smart enough to lie?"

"If she says she has something, she probably has it."

"So you agree. She's not smart enough to lie."

"What is it you're asking me?"

" 'Cause see, if I go forward with what I'm thinking, there's one danger lying out there. Dee Dee says if any harm ever comes to her, the movies get FedExed to the cops. Along with a note. A dead man's switch. You know that old chestnut. I'm wondering if she set something like that up for real. You got a feel for that, Sawyer? You're there between her legs half of every day, you think she's capable of setting up a dead man's switch?"

Sawyer grabbed the front of Gus's white tunic and walked him backward to the chrome rail that surrounded the flybridge. Jammed him up against it, bent him back. Sawyer got his face up into Dollimore's. Bent him farther. The man was strong for his age, not an ounce of fat. He groaned, his spine grinding against the rail.

"I'm in a position to fuck you over," Gus said. "You're in a position to fuck me over. Mutually assured fucking. We can blow each other up, or we can dial it back."

"What do you want?"

"What I want is for you and me to do what's right. And if doing what's right gets the news cameras swinging back our way, so much the better."

Sawyer pressed him harder against the rail. Gus groaning.

"By doing what?"

"Do the right thing, hard as it may be."

"And what's that, Gus? What's the right thing?"

"Put this on Dee Dee. Where it belongs."

"You're shitting me."

"My own daughter, it pains me to say it, she's a monster."

Gus's feet were off the deck, and he was close to toppling backward over the rail. It was only Sawyer's hip pinning him in place. He could step aside and the old guy would sail away. That would be that. Gus knew it too, felt the physics of it. Looking into Sawyer's eyes without worry, a sly smile, as if he knew Sawyer could never go through with it. Or if he did, hey, what the fuck, it was as good a way to go as any.

"Dee Dee?"

"Forget it, kid. Never mind. Forget the whole thing. I got to piss. Let me go, you made your point. You're strong. You're moral. You love the girl, all that good shit. I get it. I'll go this alone. Now I truly got to piss."

"I don't believe you."

"You don't trust me, come below, hold my dick while I pee."

"What do you have on Dee Dee?"

"What do I have? Okay. You serious? You want to hear this?"

"What do you have?"

"Take the weekend you were in Dallas. Where's Dee Dee? I don't know. She evaporates. Didn't answer her cell two days straight, not in her condo. I asked Maury, the bell guy downstairs, if he'd seen her coming and going, he said right after you left, she cabbed it to the airport."

"You're lying."

"Check with Maury."

"I'll go ask her. She'll have an explanation."

"The weekend you were in Sanibel, same thing. No Dee Dee. This morning when the Feds were done with us, I start going over it in my head, I go out front, ask Maury if he saw her Saturday, the tenth, the Atlanta murder. Maury checks his book, and it's ditto. Cab to MIA. You're out of town, she flies off."

"There's got to be some reason."

"You keep me jammed up here much longer, I'm gonna wet both of us."

Sawyer dragged him off the rail and stepped back.

Gus winked at him as if it had all been in good fun. Dusted himself off, straightened his commodore's hat.

"And how she's been acting lately. Hitting the sauce, smoking a ton of pot. Things she's said, making hints, suggestions."

"What things?"

"The part you wrote for her, Valerie. How much she's learned from being inside a killer's head. How fucking liberating it is."

"Christ, that proves nothing."

"Hey, she's my daughter. You think I like saying this?"

"I'll talk to her."

"I think we got to give her up, son."

"I'll talk to her. Find out what's what."

"Honest truth, I was thinking it was the two of you pulling this off together. Like you took me seriously that day I asked what you were willing to do to keep the show going. Get your hands dirty, make a splash. I thought you took me literally. You and Dee Dee murdering all these people."

"Dee Dee has a Zentai suit."

It startled Sawyer, coming out impulsively. But Gus was unfazed.

"She was wearing it this morning," Sawyer said.

"Well, there you go."

"She had me close the blinds. She's never done that before."

"See what I'm saying. More you think about it, the evidence piles up."

"The way she's reacting to the murders," Sawyer said. "It's all wrong. She's excited. No empathy for the victims. How a sociopath acts."

"Is that conclusive?" Gus shrugged. "I don't know. How many people have Zentai suits? Well, I got to say, nobody I know. Before you wrote that into the script, I never heard of the things. So what do you think, Sawyer? What do we do? We put this out there, give it to the press, the Feds, what? I'm thinking if we sit on it, it'll come back to bite us. We're aiding and abetting."

"We talk to her first. We hear her out."

"I already did that, son. I told her what I just told you. I confronted her while you were busy with the lines, casting off, I said to her the stuff I just said to you. I asked her straight out if she'd done it."

"What'd she say?"

"What's she going to say? 'Yeah, okay, you got me'? Hell, no, she denied it. Now she's tipping the rum bottle down her throat, getting hammered 'cause she knows what a fucking hole she's dug for herself."

"You accused her of murder to her face?"

"I believe it to be true."

"No, Gus. This is impossible. She's not capable of it."

"Everything that girl knows, and I mean every single idea in her pretty head, she learned from TV or the movies. From watching them or being in them. Every damn thing. From that dead man's switch to killing people. Movies and TV, that's her education. That scene you wrote, her strangling Slattery, we shot that on a Thursday, two days later, killer strikes the first time. Old guy in Hialeah. Now is that a coincidence?"

"I don't know, Gus. I don't know what it is."

"See what I think it is, Sawyer, the girl knows if *Ops* goes down, she's finished. If her daddy doesn't work again, whatever's in her hidey-hole, it has no value.

"She'll never get another job in the business. Nobody in their right mind is going to hire that girl. So she sees the ratings tank, she's desperate. From where I stand, hey, if I'm done, I'm done. I won't be happy about it, but I got cash put away. I'll survive. But Dee Dee? No way. She knows this is the last gasp. That's what's pushed her over the edge.

"Then she gets her bright idea, how it would work. Where's she get it? Right out of Slattery's mouth. Make a big splash. Go national. All that shit you wrote."

Ninety degrees on a sunny day, and Sawyer felt a chill.

Gus turned to the controls and thumped the throttles hard, and the big cruiser lifted and began to slice easily through the still waters. He got them back on plane, then stepped away from the wheel.

"Take over, big shot. Got to point Percy to the pavement or my bladder's going to explode."

He took another step toward the ladder. But Sawyer simply stared at the wheel and stayed put.

"What're we going to do, Gus?"

"I know what I'm going to do. I just told you. Piss."

"Later, when we get back, what do we do?"

"We call those nice young federal agents, lay it out for them."

Sawyer scanned the waters around them. A single open fisherman a mile away, its outriggers up, trolling for mahi-mahi.

"Keep us on course. I'll be right back."

"Which way?"

"East is good," he said. "And keep a buffer between us and anybody else. Fucking boaters out here, half of them are drunk, the other half are so goddamn rich they don't care who they ram into."

Sawyer held them steady and watched Gus climb down the ladder to the aft deck. He tugged the throttles back a notch and took a deep breath of the ocean air. Squinted into the hard shimmer and pushed the yacht across the sweet blue waters.

He really did have to piss. Goddamn enlarged prostate. He should have the thing yanked out first chance he got.

Dee Dee was watching cartoons, SpongeBob SquarePants, fucking creature at the bottom of the sea, singing, wiggling around, doing an Elvis imitation. All these other fish creatures bouncing around in utter adoration.

She was sucking on the Bacardi, had it halfway done, some potato chips in a bowl on the table. Big dish of onion dip.

"You're going to lose your figure, girl, you keep eating like that."

"And what difference would it make?"

"True," Gus said, and ducked into the head and relieved himself.

She was still lying there when he returned, her plaid skirt up to her thighs, grease stains on her white shirt, shoes off, one sock gone. Hair a mess. Dee Dee in meltdown.

The last few years Gus had been watching her get stronger, all the exercise she did, and he suspected their sexual past had something to do with that. Girls got molested, some of them put on a ton of weight. Gus figured it was to put up a wall between them and any guy tried to touch them. A wall of blubber, and a good way to turn guys off. Never get screwed again. That was Gus's understanding of the situation.

Dee Dee's approach was different, build a wall of muscles. Get so goddamn hard no man, no matter how tough he was, would be able to wrestle her to the ground. Or if he did, she could clamp herself shut, keep any cock from getting in. Gus was thinking, Hey, even worse than that, letting the guy get inside, then snap the vice clamps; Jesus, it made his rectum tighten thinking about it.

"What you need is some fresh air, Dee, you'll feel better, nice breeze in your hair, some sun."

"I'm watching this."

"You're watching a fucking cartoon. That talking sponge would make anybody seasick."

"SpongeBob is cute, don't you think? It's a kids' show, so he's probably asexual. What do you think, Daddy? You think SpongeBob is sexually active? Does he have a male thingy?"

"Come on, Dee, let's get up."

She chugged some more rum, bubbled it right down. Which was fine by Gus, getting drunker, easier to handle, easier to get out the door before Mr. Eagle Scout got curious.

Gus changed his tactic, using the deep voice, the actor's voice he'd developed back in the day. It always worked magic with the women. A Barry White, cigarette-roughened golden voice, way deep in his throat.

"Come on outside, sweet stuff. I got something you need to see."

She turned her head, gave him a sideways glance. Set the bottle on the table. Gus, the snake charmer, working his magic.

"What do you think you're doing? Spit it out, old man."

Nope. Wrong. Charm taking a holiday.

He went over to her, stepping around the coffee table, checking out the windows to make sure Sawyer was doing as instructed, keeping them a long way off from other traffic. It looked clear out there. The boy cooperating. Gus wasn't sure if the kid knew what he was about to do and was giving his silent sanction. Didn't matter, really. But Gus was curious. Had he finally managed to convert the kid to Gus's world view? Take it by the throat, rattle it till it coughed up what you wanted.

He stood over Dee Dee and she stared up at him. Eyes red, lips having trouble holding any particular expression. What he didn't want, he didn't want to bruise her in any way.

The FBI were very good at reading bruises. All that forensic shit they had. The way they nailed bad guys these days, could tell exactly what happened, like a video replay, step by step, piece it together from abrasions and hair samples and all that techno shit that bored him silly when it was on TV. He'd tried to watch those shows, never managed to make it more than five minutes. Science fiction it seemed like, a bunch of blinking hardware. But still, it put the fear of God into him, made him picky how he handled this.

"Could you please stand up?"

"I know what you're doing."

"You're drunk, Dee Dee. You're seasick. You need fresh air. I'm trying to help you."

"You think I'm a killer. You think I killed all those people."

"I think we'll find you a really top attorney to make this all go away."

"Like you made the other thing go away."

"Yeah, like that. A good attorney, that's what you need. And some fresh air."

He extended a hand to help her stand.

"Leave me alone."

She chopped at his wrist. Not so drunk after all. It hurt like hell.

And just like that, his impulse control went out the fucking porthole.

He took her by the hair, short and black like his own, and yanked her to her feet and dragged her to the door and out onto the deck.

She fought him, slashing at his arms, but he batted the blows away, trying to be gentle, not leave any bruises. Then he muscled her to the gunwale. Not as strong as she looked. Ripped muscles, but when it came down to it, when it came to fighting for her life, they were gym rat muscles, machine muscles, or maybe sex muscles, but what they weren't was fight-till-the-death muscles. Not like Gus's. Do-or-die muscles. Now-or-never muscles.

He scanned the seas around them. Nobody anywhere. He backed her to the gunwale. He looked up to see if Sawyer had a view from up top. Maybe if the kid stepped to the back of the flybridge he could see, but not at the wheel.

Dee Dee was grabbing at the hand clenching her hair, shaking her head against his grip, the ugly horror in her eyes. It was a look Gus had never been able to extract from her before in front of the cameras. A real actress could do that easy, but not Dee Dee. He'd tried everything, coaxing her every way he knew how, but she'd never been able to contort her face into an authentic look of terror. Even though it was in her arsenal, he could see that now. Her throat constricted, trying to scream but unable.

He leaned back, got his feet set, then shouldered her over the side.

Didn't make a sound going over, landing on her back in the foam, a couple of sloppy strokes to keep her head up, trying to paddle out of the wake, big rolling wake back there, but the girl floundered. A Florida girl who didn't swim. Disgraceful.

Dee Dee had always been an indoor type. Not comfortable around the water, camping, hiking, all that shit. Which was probably Gus's fault, the way he'd raised her.

Gus watched her disappear into the Atlantic. Seeing her go down, he felt something shoot through his chest. A dark pang that was maybe a fraction of regret, a splash of anxiety, and a big dose of thrill.

An interesting concoction. Gus made a note of how that all felt swirled together so he could explain it later to the idiot actors he had to work with, explaining to them how it felt to be human.

TWENTY-FOUR

FRANK SHEFFIELD WAS DRIVING THE Taurus, Thorn navigating. It was midafternoon, hottest day of the summer so far. Humidity so thick you had to breathe twice to get one breath.

As they drove, Sheffield filled him in on the statements given this morning to Rivlin and Vasquez, the two junior agents he'd drafted into action. Dee Dee, Gus, Sawyer, and Flynn, a couple of hours with each establishing whereabouts on the dates in question—the murder dates, the Sports Craze purchase dates.

Dee Dee said she was home alone the night before, during the hours while Buddha was being murdered. No way to verify that, bellman was having a smoke, nobody saw her going up to her place. They'd have to check the security cams to see if they backed her up.

Otherwise, she had a fuzzy memory, didn't keep a calendar. Couldn't be sure where she was on the other dates, maybe the gym, maybe out on the boat, maybe eating dinner somewhere, or asleep in her apartment, or having sex. She did that a lot, she said, her and Sawyer going at it. The girl bragging about her libido. She had witnesses for the sex if they wanted any.

"Witnesses?"

"Her and Sawyer, they do it with the blinds open. Neighbors watch."

"She said that?"

"She did."

Thorn was silent, staring out his window.

"What?"

Thorn said, "It makes a certain fucked-up sense."

"Oh, does it?"

"A girl gets her sex ed in front of a camera, she might be a little confused what was for show, what was real."

Sheffield looked over at Thorn and shook his head at this sad world. He drove in silence for a while, then let out a sigh and got back to the highlights of the morning's interrogation.

Gus Dollimore arrived with three poster boards. One for each of the last three months. Big as bullfight placards. A square for every day of the week. Each filled in with elaborate details of the show's schedule, twenty-four seven. From the first day of principal photography through this morning. The actors, the upper-echelon crew, director of photography, first assistant director, cameraman. Everybody. Their schedules, their jobs, their performance, their comings and goings.

"Guy's seriously anal."

"Is it written in indelible ink?" Thorn asked.

Just the opposite. It was done with a Sharpie on easy-erase plastic.

"Best you can say is it tells us what Gus wants us to believe," Frank said. "Which is he spends a lot of time on his yacht. It's docked behind his condo. No dock master. He just walks out to the marina, cranks up, and goes."

"How convenient for him."

"Flynn spends his weekends cycling with a gang of bike freaks. They run from the Grove down to Key Largo and turn around and pedal back. Hundred miles, no sweat. The kid's got stamina, I got to say. Twenty people in his bike club can alibi him. That's like an every weekend thing. This one's the oddball of the bunch. Lives in a studio apartment over near the Biltmore in the Gables. Shuns the party scene, unlike the rest of these folks."

"He's an interesting kid," Thorn said. "And Sawyer, what's his story?"

Sawyer had flown to Dallas last weekend. Arriving Saturday morning around noon. That night Michaela Stabler was speared three times. Starkville, Oklahoma, it was a three-, four-hour drive away.

"That looks bad," Thorn said.

"Says it was for a meeting with some network guy from the west coast. The network guy stood him up. Whole trip was a waste. He flew back Monday early. Dee Dee picked him up at MIA. She corroborates that. Very selective memory. Remembered a traffic cop harassing her at the airport. Went on and on about that."

"And the Atlanta weekend?"

"Claims he was scouting locations for the show over in Sanibel. Two nights on the road. He's got receipts, can prove he was there. But hey, if he was trying to cover his ass, he could've registered, ducked out, driven straight through to Atlanta, slashed the nurse, returned in time to check out and drive back to Miami."

Traffic slowing around them. Thorn watched a motorcycle bomb past between lanes. A kid bent forward, nose to the handlebars, doing a hundred. Nobody in the cars around them gave the suicidal idiot a second look.

"What about the manifests?"

"All the airlines complied. We're waiting on a couple, but I'm routing them through Rivlin and Vasquez. They'll run everything into the mainframe, search for names of anyone on the cast and crew of *Miami Ops.*"

"And this guy we're going to see? The rat catcher? He on the list?"

"Him too. But, hey, no reason to fly under your real name. Coming up with false ID in South Florida, it's like buying a pound of bacon."

Fifteen minutes later they pulled into an industrial park two blocks south of the Opa-locka Airport. The place was full of businesses selling airplane parts, repair shops, import-export offices, storage depots, warehouses full of antique cars, and outfits that leased business jets. Bland storefronts doing big-time commerce.

"On the right, that shop in the back."

Miami Humane Wildlife Removal was stenciled over the door of a block building painted in an adobe brown. Out front was a green Ford pickup with orange tiger stripes running down the sides. Wire cages piled high in the bed of the truck, cables and nets.

Frank had called Matheson to schedule a meet, and the rat catcher was waiting for them in his office. Desktop bare, shelves empty as though he'd just moved in or was about to move out. The only sign of activity was a small laptop computer on a stand in one corner of the room, its screen saver running through a series of photographs of naked, big-breasted women.

On the walls he'd hung a few snapshots of his professional exploits, a series of color prints showing Jeff holding up an assortment of on-the-job creatures. The usual python pics. Monitor lizards, gators with their snouts duct-taped shut. Critters he'd no doubt removed from swimming pools and patios out in the western side of town in those sprawling neighborhoods chewing away at the Everglades. There was a feral pig, an indigo snake, a fox, several iguanas.

But the one Thorn was drawn to, the one he walked over to see before anyone said hello, was a black-and-white of Matheson standing in the middle of an empty warehouse circled by thousands and thousands of flying bats.

It looked as if he'd put the camera on a table and set the self-timer. The flash caught him in the midst of a thick swarm, bats zipping through his spread legs, dodging above and below his outstretched arms, skimming past his face, his ears. The membranes of their wings tickling inches from his nose. Must have been just after sunset because a few thousand more bats hadn't awakened yet and were still hanging behind him in the rafters of that big empty space.

In the photo Jeff wore some kind of protective suit, but he'd taken off his hood for the photo. Given the fact that he was ankle deep in guano and standing in the middle of a whirlwind of sharp-toothed blind mammals that had a fair likelihood of being rabid, the look on his face was eerily unruffled. Like a symphony conductor waiting tolerantly for his rambunctious orchestra to finish warming up before he lifted his baton.

"I got a tribe of rats living at my place on the Key," Frank said to Matheson. "They're fine, I got no objections to them. Make little beds out of grass and seaweed tucked in the corners of the attic, come and go, it's all cool. Only time I ever had a problem was a neighbor put out poison and all his rats came to my place to die. Crawled into the walls, under the floorboards, light fixtures, curled up and rotted. Smelled so bad I had to move out for two weeks, shut the place down for a month. I found a few carcasses, but there was no way to get rid of all of them.

"I called a guy like you, Jeff, a professional critter catcher. He wanted thirty-nine bucks a rat. Dead or alive. Thirty-nine bucks. I said no thanks and went and had a talk with my neighbor. Next time you put out rat poison, call me first, I told the guy. I'll stand guard at my ventilation grills, send them back so they can die at your place. A person should take responsibility for the things he kills. It's just common courtesy. Don't you agree?"

"Okay, I confess," Jeff said. He held out his hands for the cuffs. "I'm guilty, I did it. Just electrocute me now before I kill again."

"Oh, come on," said Frank, "that takes away all the fun. Give us a chance to prove it first."

"The Zentai Killer," Jeff said. "That's who I am, right?"

"If you say so." Frank moseyed around the office, taking a look at a few of the naked women, appearing and disappearing on the computer screen. Then coming over to stand by Thorn and look at the bat warehouse.

"None of them bumped you," Thorn said. "The bats, not even a nick?"

"Whatever you say, Officer," Jeff said. "I want to assist any way I can."

"Man, this is one tricky customer." Frank took his jacket off and hung it on the back of a chair. Letting Jeff get a look at his handgun, and sending the kid a message. Going to stay a while.

"You been taking rats out of the Moss house for months. Is that right?"

"Oh, stop the charade," Jeff said. "You're not here to talk about rats. I've still got three clients to see before my day is over. Some of us have to make an honest living. So let's do this. What've you got on me?"

The words were petulant, but the tone was utterly disengaged. Jeff had lowered his hands and was sitting erect in the chair, forearms on the desk, hands clasped. The poise of a man who made his living lulling dangerous creatures into dropping their guard.

While Frank was checking out some of the photos, Thorn took a turn.

"How're things working between you and Flynn Moss these days?"

Matheson's head ticked a quarter inch to the right as if he'd caught the faint scratch of claws inside his walls. A move so subtle that if Thorn hadn't been watching intently, he would have missed it. This guy had been doing his yoga and meditation and he'd found his still center a few inches below his navel. Or however the hell he managed to be so detached. But just a mention of Flynn's name made him twitch.

"Flynn Moss and I are old friends."

"Thorn?" Frank moved to his side, but Thorn went on.

"You a bike rider like Flynn?"

"I'm not part of that group. No, I'm not a bike rider."

"And you and Sawyer? How you two get along?"

Jeff was ready for that one and didn't flinch.

"I'm friendly with everyone in the Moss family—Garvey, April, Flynn, and Sawyer. All of them."

"You ever use prosthetic makeup? You know, a latex mask from a mold of your face."

"What the hell?" Frank put a hand on Thorn's arm and squeezed. "What're you doing?"

Matheson was chewing on something that hadn't been there before. Moving his jaws with his lips tight like maybe his mouth was filling with spit.

"You're their dad, aren't you?" Matheson was smiling as if he reveled in trading blows with complete strangers. "You're the father who never was."

Frank stepped away from Thorn and looked back and forth between him and Matheson.

"You notice the resemblance, or someone clue you in?"

"Those boys desperately needed a father growing up. They needed someone to show them how to be real men."

"Everybody needs a father," Thorn said.

"Now it's too late," Jeff said. "Sawyer and Flynn are set in stone."

Frank's cell phone jingled and he pulled it out, gave Thorn a look to shut the fuck up, and stepped over to a corner of the room to take the call.

"I'm a professional killer," Jeff said. "I've murdered more animals this month than you've seen in your entire life. An hour ago I was shaking duck eggs, destroying them before they were even hatched. Shaking them, not breaking them."

"Must be a kick," Thorn said.

"Condo full of geezers, gated community next to a golf course, the golf course ducks come over from the ponds and shit on the old folks' sidewalks and their cars, it drives them crazy, a big nuisance, so they called me.

"I located the nests and I shook twenty-nine eggs this morning. I could've smashed them, sure, but when the ducks come back, find the broken eggs, they just build another nest and lay more. But if you shake the eggs, scramble the yolks, and put them back in the nest like you found them, the ducks'll keep sitting on the damn things for another year and never realize anything's wrong. That's how stupid they are. Sitting on dead eggs."

Jeff was wearing a rumpled shirt and dirty cargo shorts. The office had a damp, underground smell like the burrow of a mole.

"We were talking about prosthetic makeup. Flynn tells me you two used to play with his mom's cosmetics?"

"He told you that?"

"Said she locked you out of her bedroom."

"You sit on dead eggs, don't you? You just sit and sit and sit, waiting for something to happen. Dumb as a duck. You think I'm going to answer a question like that? That's how dumb you are. You just keep waiting, keep sitting on that egg, see if I ever answer it."

"Maybe you just did."

"Okay, copper, time's up. You want to talk to me again, get a warrant. And bring backup. It'll take more than you two to handle me."

Frank clicked off the phone, nabbed his jacket off the chair, and took Thorn by the shirtsleeve and hauled him to the door.

Thorn shot Matheson a parting look, but the kid had sunk away into his boundless tranquility, arms resting on the desk, his imperturbable smile securely back in place.

Outside at the car, Frank put his coat on and looked at Thorn over the roof of the Taurus.

Behind Frank a great blue heron landed on the roof of an adjacent building and looked down at them. Four feet tall, six-foot wingspan. Great blues laid six or seven eggs per clutch; maybe half of them hatched. Not a bad ratio for a big bird living in the wild. The blue looked bereft up there, a long way from the watery plains where she hunted and made her home. Maybe she'd been living in somebody's artificial lake and made the mistake of shitting on their car and they'd called a guy like Matheson to come rattle her eggs. Just because the bird was majestic didn't give her a pass. Not around this town.

Frank followed Thorn's line of sight and the heron lifted off. Back to its search for a swath of green.

"Scratch one off our list," Frank said.

"Who? Matheson?"

"Miss Dollimore," he said. "A few miles east of Boca Chita, out in the Atlantic, the young lady went over the side of their yacht. Gus and Sawyer were up on the flybridge at the time, didn't notice. Claim they only realized she was missing when they were back at the marina. Some fisherman hauled her body out a half hour ago, called Marine Patrol."

"Jumped?"

"Jumped, fell, or pushed," Frank said. "Unless you can think of another way a thing like that might happen."

TWENTY-FIVE

BACK IN THE CAR, FRANK called Agent Rivlin, told her to start looking for a judge, get started on a search warrant. When he was finished with her, he was silent, waiting until the first red light to ask Thorn what the hell was going on back there at Matheson's office. That whole thing with fathers and sons.

Thorn settled back in his seat and gave Frank the short version of his one-day fling with April Moss, his newly discovered sons, Sawyer and Flynn. Frank listened without comment, not looking over as Thorn finished.

He drove for a few blocks in silence, then said, "Which explains the baseball gloves."

"I know it's pathetic," Thorn said.

"What was she, about twelve when this happened?"

"She was eighteen."

"You just made it under the wire."

"What can I say?"

"Try saying nothing for a while. How's that strike you?"

Then Frank launched into a thirty-minute lecture during the rest of the drive from Matheson's office to the Ocean Club on Brickell, where the Dollimores lived, a stern speech about everything Thorn had done wrong with Matheson, and how close Frank was to banishing him back to Key Largo, forbidding him to enter the Miami city limits ever again. Thorn had to admit, Sheffield had a point. His goddamn cannon had come loose again.

The only argument he might make on his own behalf, and he had the smarts not to try to make it, was that this was Thorn's tried-and-true interview method. Forget the curveball, the knuckler, the change-up; forget nuance and trickery. Thorn's approach: Surprise them with your best heat up the middle, test their reaction times. The absolute opposite of Frank's control game.

Frank's lecture worked. Thorn shut the hell up. Let the pro handle it. Frank took charge, spoke to the building manager, commandeered the tenth-floor rec room of the Ocean Club, three doors down from apartment 1047, the condo Dee Dee had been sharing with Sawyer. He spoke with the forensics team waiting outside Dee Dee's condo for the search warrant to arrive. Then he came into the rec room and took Sawyer's statement and took it again and then a couple of more times. All of it recorded on a little handheld silver jewel he produced from his jacket pocket.

From three o'clock to six, three hours straight, Thorn didn't say a word. He watched and listened to Frank Sheffield debriefing Sawyer Moss, and he spent some time rewinding the day in his head, but mainly he watched Frank work, watched and listened to Sawyer responding.

Sheffield patiently tried to trip up Sawyer Moss. Thorn's first real opportunity to meet this son was coming in this twisted moment. The kid wore a blue ventilated boating shirt and shorts and Sperry Top-Siders. Sunglasses hung from a cord around his neck. Face chapped from the afternoon's trip across the bay. Blond hair a mess.

Three hours. Same questions, different phrasing, different order, different pacing, Sawyer with the same answers, slight variations, a word here and there, being patient with Frank, as though he knew this drill, was trying his best to cooperate, do his civic duty. Patient, reasonable, seemed like a good kid.

Gus, the grieving father, was upstairs in his penthouse covering the same ground with Frank's team, Grace Rivlin and Robert Vasquez. They would compare stories later, see what fit, what didn't. A routine that Thorn guessed hadn't altered since the heyday of the inquisitions.

How anybody as relaxed and jocular as Frank could tolerate such plodding tedium was beyond Thorn. Sugarman was capable of it too. He'd seen Sugar plenty of times grind away at some doofus, playing Simon Says with him till, whoops, the doofus accidentally spilled the truth.

Going at it like some stubborn woodpecker tapping at the same spot for endless hours, probing for the weak fiber, working his way in, convinced there was something worth all his time and effort hiding back behind that hard shell.

Sawyer wasn't sure whether Dee Dee's fall overboard was a suicide or a fall. Frank didn't bring up the third alternative, just let Sawyer talk.

Dee Dee had seemed strange lately, but not particularly depressed. She'd been drinking heavily that afternoon, so it easily could've been an accident. Sawyer, the scriptwriter, came up with a scenario. She might've come out onto the deck for some fresh air, but instead of it making her feel better, she'd looked out at the rising and falling horizon, her seasickness had turned worse, and she'd puked over the side; had leaned out, lost her balance, and tumbled in.

She didn't swim, wouldn't even go into the wading pool at the condo. Maybe it happened like that, an accident. A slip. And if she'd called out for help, even right below them, twenty, thirty feet away, Gus and Sawyer wouldn't have heard her calls over the engine roar, the blast of wind, their own voices. And they were hauling ass most of the time, forty knots, they'd be a mile away in a minute or so, enough time for Dee Dee to slip below the surface.

The way Sawyer told it, the last time either of them saw Dee Dee alive was when Gus went below to relieve himself. According to Gus, she was watching TV, sucking on a bottle of rum, feeling queasy from the rolling seas and pouty like she got sometimes. Telling Gus he was making a big mistake, taking a cruise on a day when they should've been hanging at the condo waiting by the phones for the media schedulers to call about appearing on the morning shows.

Moody, testy, but not suicidal, Sawyer said. Though, yes, she had been behaving suspiciously in the last few weeks. And there were other things that made her father and her boyfriend start to worry she might be involved in these killings. Gus and Sawyer had talked it over and decided they had to share their concerns with the authorities. A hard decision they'd made out on the yacht.

What were those other suspicious things? Frank wanted to know. And then once he'd heard them, he wanted to hear them again, and then again.

For one, Dee Dee surprised Sawyer just that morning; before she came into the bedroom for more hanky-panky, she'd hollered for him to shut the blinds, something they never did. Never? Frank asked it blandly. As if he'd heard that one a hundred times, exhibitionists putting on a show for the voyeurs in adjacent condos. Never, Sawyer repeated, we never shut the blinds, then repeated it again as though he didn't quite believe it himself. Never.

When Sawyer had the blinds closed, Dee Dee strolled out in a black Zentai suit and hunched over in a threatening pose, hands behind her back as though she was hiding a gun or a baseball bat. It rattled the kid.

Thorn kept watching his son, listening for the squeaky giveaway in his voice, waiting for the telltale swallow, a lump of worry that wouldn't go down, some revealing sweat glistening on the upper lip, anything that would suggest Sawyer Moss was doing anything but telling the flat honest truth.

Thorn saw, heard, smelled nothing of that sort. From where he sat the young man seemed to be earnest, tender, and tough. Sawyer was shocked and pained by Dee Dee's drowning, but his reaction seemed proportional. Not trying too hard on anything. Not trying to convince, or overexplain. Getting a worried crinkle in his forehead when he recounted his growing misgivings about the girl he was shacking up with.

It wasn't just the Zentai suit. It started way before today.

How she'd been behaving for a while, beginning right after she learned *Miami Ops* was in danger of being cancelled. The very day, in fact, she found that out, she'd just finished doing a scene in which she'd strangled an old geezer in a hospital bed and left behind an obituary on his bedside table. Dee Dee was playing the part of the show's Zentai Killer. Two days after strangling Slattery, the real-life murders started with the death of the elderly gentleman in Hialeah.

Was there a connection? Sawyer didn't know. He couldn't believe it at first, but now he wasn't sure. Maybe Dee Dee was that desperate after all. Maybe he didn't know her as well as he thought. She was superobsessive about her career, about succeeding in the business.

He admitted he felt guilty about all of this because the Zentai storyline had all been his idea. He'd just stumbled across the Lycra suits somewhere while surfing the Web, he couldn't even recall where now, and decided to try to work them into the show. The suits were creepy and distinctive, and in retrospect he thought maybe it was one of the things that helped sell the series to the studio in the first place.

Sawyer apologized for going down that blind alley. He knew this wasn't about him. Not about him, but about what Dee Dee did, and maybe why she did it. Overcome with guilt, sensing the cops closing in, sensing that her own father and lover were starting to suspect.

Or hell, maybe she just fell overboard. Maybe it was that.

Going back to his growing mistrust of her, Sawyer described the previous night when the Zentai Killer called the *Herald,* and the Oklahoma sheriff was killed, how Dee Dee was nowhere to be found. Didn't answer her cell. Wasn't at the Merrick gym in the Gables, where she spent long hours on the machines; not at dinner, not with Gus, missed a date with Sawyer. Same thing when he was away in Dallas. She said she'd switched off her cell.

And there was that time when they were leaving the airport after the Dallas trip, and she told Sawyer she wanted him to write more murders into the scripts. She said she liked killing people. The more he went over these last few weeks, the more troubled he got.

Like the hours in the aftermath of Buddha's murder. Dee Dee was elated. Lit up by the prospect of major media attention. Ghoulishly overjoyed the show was going to be a hit. She knew exactly what she was going to do with all that cash. Not even a hint of empathy.

And then there were the weekends. She'd been disappearing lately, cell phone switched off. Sawyer had worried she might be fooling around with some guy, but then he started thinking about the killings, all of them taking place on the weekends.

It didn't sound like much to Thorn. Maybe a tad narcissistic and amoral on the girl's part, but he suspected it was more or less typical of show biz people, along with other terminally ambitious types whose career arc was their highest concern.

He listened and waited for something that would nail it down, prove beyond any doubt that Dee Dee was the killer. Wanting this to be the certifiable conclusion so he could escape and return to his island life and start rebuilding. Tie some new flies, start searching out the latest spots where the big daddy tarpons were hiding.

Listening to Frank and Sawyer going at it for hours, his mind wandered to that great blue heron on the roof of a shop in the industrial park. A bird out of its natural element. Looking forlorn and dead tired. Thorn identified with that big gawky bird, a kindred spirit, both of them displaced from their habitat.

Then it gut-punched him, made him groan. He was never going to be able to retreat completely to Key Largo. No complete separation from Miami ever again. He had two grown sons, and that blood connection with Sawyer and Flynn was never going away. Like it or not, he was bound to this rancorous city for as long as those two chose to live here.

How about Gus? Frank was asking Sawyer.

"What about him?" Sawyer sounding shifty for the first time.

"He and Dee Dee close? Like, do they have a happy, healthy, normal father-daughter thing going?" Frank was fiddling with his recorder, his eyes on the tiny machine in what looked like a gambit—trying to distract from the question's weight.

"I'm in no position to judge normal father-offspring relationships," Sawyer said.

Thorn leaned back in his chair, waiting for the kid to look over at him and acknowledge the zinger. He didn't. He kept his eyes on Sheffield, who kept his eyes on his little recording gizmo.

"Dee Dee ever mention anything weird going on between them? Tension, disagreements, problems of any kind?"

Sawyer worked his lips, then seemed to catch himself. Letting his mouth relax, giving Thorn a quick look to see if he was paying attention. Thorn sent him an encouraging smile.

"I guess they had issues like any parent and child," Sawyer said. "Nothing out of the normal range."

"Nothing out of the normal range." Frank looked up from the recorder.

"That's right."

"When you last saw Dee Dee, she was drinking rum, down in the salon, did she say anything to you? Indicate how she was feeling."

"She said her stomach was upset. She was feeling woozy."

Sawyer shifted in his chair. His butt probably hurting as much as Thorn's from sitting three hours solid.

"You need some coffee, a sandwich? I can order something up."

"No, nothing. I'm fine."

"So we're talking about Gus. Him and his daughter. You never sensed anything going on there that made you uncomfortable?"

Sawyer looked down, shook his head.

That was a lie, that silent head shake.

Thorn could see it so plainly he wanted to take the kid by the arm and give him a rattle to get him back on track, remind him that he was dealing with a professional interrogator who'd spent his life listening to dirtbags lie. If Thorn could spot it, Frank had spotted it for sure.

"So, okay," Frank said. "We're almost done."

Sawyer breathed in and out, keeping his face neutral, eyes on Frank. But Thorn could see his mother's sympathetic nervous system betraying him, the color stealing up his throat into his cheeks.

"So you never knew about Gus making skin flicks, him and Dee Dee in bed together."

Frank's own fastball down the middle worked its magic.

Sawyer's head sank, chin ducking to his chest.

"Gus ever tell you about those movies?"

"He did." Sawyer slowly raised his head.

"And after he told you, you kept on working with a scumbag like that? It didn't sour your romantic feelings for Ms. Dollimore?"

"He just told me this afternoon."

"Just today? While you were on the boat?"

"That's right."

"Before or after you realized Dee Dee was missing?"

"Before."

"What did he say exactly?"

Sawyer recounted Gus's confession. Dirty movies, the girl didn't protest. He'd started when she was seven years old.

"And when you heard that coming out of his mouth, you didn't pick him up and heave him overboard?"

"I came close," Sawyer said.

"Why's Gus pick today to confess something like that to the guy dating his daughter and writing his TV show? That strike you as weird timing?"

"Not really. Everybody's under so much stress, the show, the killer. I assumed he was unburdening himself. Taking some of the blame for how screwed up Dee Dee was. Like he was trying to understand what could've turned her into a killer."

"Yeah, maybe it was that," Frank said. "Gus taking blame."

"I'm not sure what you're driving at."

Frank took a minute, glancing around the room, letting the young man squirm. Then he turned back to Sawyer with a benevolent smile.

"Hearing your girlfriend got her sexual initiation from her daddy, sure, it's natural enough you'd be ready to throw the old man overboard. What I'm curious about is, how did it make you feel about Dee Dee? Normal reaction I'd guess would be shocked, disgusted. This is going to be hard to recover from. Not easy to get back in the saddle."

"Screw you."

"Sorry," Frank said. "Bad word choice. The question is, would you get over something like that, resume a normal, healthy relationship with her?"

"That's irrelevant and immaterial."

"So we're going to do some lawyer talk now?"

"Make your point."

"Okay, okay. How should I say this? All those suspicions you had, worrying maybe this woman you were involved with was not the sweet young thing you thought she was, let's put that together with the discovery that she'd been abused on film for years before you met her, all that coming together at once, it strikes me as a pretty combustible cocktail."

"Is there a question here?"

"Did you throw Dee Dee Dollimore overboard?"

Sawyer drew a breath, shifted in his chair, drew another breath.

"No, I did not. I absolutely did not."

Thorn studied the young man's profile. He wasn't flinching, was showing only pure indignation.

"So, let's say I believe you. But am I right about the other thing? Hearing about your girlfriend's ugly past, didn't that sort of turn you off?"

"Dee Dee was a victim. I'm sorry for what she suffered."

"Sure, sure, that's the right thing to say, Mr. Moss, but I want to know how you felt when you heard about this porn business. Did it revolt you, make you doubt Ms. Dollimore's past truthfulness? Did you start to question your own judgment?"

"Maybe some of that."

"You think that could've been Mr. Dollimore's intent?"

"I don't follow you. Why would it be?"

"Oh, now, come on, you write this television stuff, right? You know how nefarious and double-dealing people can be. That's your stock in trade. Thinking about it now, do you believe Dollimore might've been intentionally pushing your buttons, poisoning your feelings for his daughter, getting you worked up to provoke you into doing something you might not do otherwise?"

Sawyer rubbed one hand against the other as if he felt something sticky on his palms.

"I didn't throw Dee Dee over the side. I did not do it. How many ways can I say it?"

Frank said, "Is Mr. Dollimore more than a boss to you? Like maybe he's a father figure, something like that."

Sawyer looked up from his hands and eyed Frank, then Thorn.

"Now what are you implying?"

"I think you've got an idea what I'm implying. Like maybe when Gus went down to take a piss, he didn't take a piss at all, but he tossed his little girl over the side. Maybe telling you about your girlfriend's dirty movie past, that was a way to prep you, turn you against her. So when he comes back up and confesses he pitched Dee into the deep blue, you're softened up. That's what I'm wondering. Would you take a bullet for the guy? Would you go along with that, knowing what he'd just done?"

Sawyer stood up, staring at Thorn, then back at Frank.

"Let me get this straight. Now the story is, Gus drowned his daughter and he and I are colluding in some kind of cover-up?"

"Do I think you're in cahoots with Mr. Dollimore? At this point, I think anything's possible."

"Gus wouldn't do that."

"So bottom line, the story we're staying with is, Dee Dee comes outside, falls overboard while puking?"

Sawyer moved his lips but couldn't find anything to say.

"You know," Frank said. "We might be getting close to that magic moment, son, when it's time to hire yourself an expensive defense attorney."

Sawyer took his seat again.

"I'm talking to you voluntarily. I'm not hiding anything."

"Right," Frank said. "I appreciate that. The entire law enforcement community couldn't function without good citizens like yourself willing to share their knowledge openly and freely with folks like me. On behalf of—"

"Sorry to interrupt," Thorn said. "But could I ask a question?"

Frank puffed up his cheeks and blew out a lip-fluttering breath.

"What took you so long?"

"I know I don't have any special standing with you, Sawyer."

Sawyer looked over at him and said, "Well, you got that right."

"But maybe you could tell me one thing that's been bugging me."

Sawyer fixed his gaze on a tropical watercolor across the room.

"The Zentai Killer, the TV version, her name's Valerie?"

"Valerie Braun."

"What makes Valerie tick? Why's she doing what she's doing? Killing people, leaving the obits behind. Is it to get even with her twin sister? Because her twin is such a goody-goody big-time cop. Is that it, sibling rivalry that went out of control? Please don't tell me she was traumatized in her youth."

"Yeah," Frank said. "Like who isn't?"

"Sibling rivalry," Sawyer said. "That's a simplistic way to put it, but okay, that's close enough."

"I got to have things simple," Thorn said. "Otherwise, it's just *whoosh.*" He made a one-handed gesture, a projectile skimming over his skull.

"Is that all?" Frank asked Thorn.

"One more little thing, then I'm done."

"Oh, good."

"I saw the photographs on the wall of the garage apartment. When you and Flynn were kids, all the games you played. Archery, bocce ball. Kind of a unique assortment of sports. What I didn't see was anything with a ball and glove. So I was curious. You ever play catch with anybody? A glove, a baseball, throwing it back and forth? Hit some groundies to each other."

Sawyer combed a hand through his disheveled hair. It stayed disheveled.

"Never," Sawyer said. "Never played baseball. Never interested me."

"Well, it's not too late. Maybe you should give it a try sometime."

TWENTY-SIX

AGENT ALICE RIVLIN WAS WAITING by Frank's Taurus. When they arrived, she came around the front of the car with a sheaf of papers in her hand. Short, lithe, carrying herself with the proud and fluid stride of a young matador. Fierce but relaxed, glancing through the windshield at Thorn with something less than goodness in her heart.

Outside the driver's door she and Frank huddled for a moment. Rivlin passed him the papers. Frank studied them, they exchanged a few words, he nodded at the woman, gave her a pat on the shoulder, and they parted.

Walking away, Rivlin brushed at her blouse where Sheffield touched her.

Frank got behind the wheel and stretched around to set the papers on the seat behind him.

"She's sadly disappointed in me. That's what she said."

"Why?"

"Because I'm acting so goddamn unprofessionally."

"You are?"

"Carting you around. A citizen. Letting you sit in."

"Maybe I should speak to her, show her I'm harmless."

"Oh, yeah, that would go over big."

On the drive back to Spring Garden, Frank drifted off, started mumbling to himself, nothing specific Thorn could catch, though he recognized the tone. Taking both sides of some logical argument, the back and forth, presenting a thesis, tearing it down, brick by brick. Mumbling it all out as if Thorn were elsewhere.

On Dixie Highway Sheffield swung into a fast food drive-through, didn't ask what Thorn wanted, just ordered four fish sandwiches and fries and two Cokes, put his bag in the back and dumped Thorn's sack in his lap, and kept on driving.

Thorn watched the summer sky filling with honeyed dust, a fine powdery light that filtered through fronds and clusters of arecas and flooded the canopy of oaks and black olives with a mellow radiance. At that hour of the late afternoon, the sky was choosing and discarding pigments every minute, from a dusky wash of burnt rose smeared with plum sauce to wispy clouds with the smoky luminescence of a sheet of surf running up a white sand beach. Hawks and herons and egrets rode the high currents, taking their sweet time, luxuriating in the last moments of daylight.

Nothing the city fathers could ever build, nothing any developer could devise, no magical architecture, no wild aquatic designs, no sculptured neon or gleaming towers in the sky, no man-made extravagance could ever rival the simple interplay of tropical light and salt-laden maritime air that was freely provided every day. They might as well stop trying.

As Frank turned onto April's street and they saw the carnival of trucks parked from one end of the block to the other, Frank broke the spell.

"You buy any of that? Sawyer's version."

"I'd like to," Thorn said.

"I know you'd like to. That's the problem."

"What problem?"

"You're going to have to go home, Thorn, back to paradise. This isn't going to work, Sawyer and Flynn, this connection you have."

"I can still be objective."

"No, you can't, but it's more than that. There's the volatility issue. The chance you'll flip out and do something crazy just increased by a factor of ten. Plus, with you riding along, it'll jeopardize any legal action down the road. Halfway decent defense team gets hold of the fact the father of those two young men, a civilian, is mooching along with the agent in charge, man, no matter what kind of case I put together, that's a free pass for everybody."

"If either one of those boys is guilty of anything, that might be a problem. But they aren't."

"See, that's what I mean. You're biased. You're no help to me."

"Is this about Rivlin or me?"

"I think I got all the mileage I'm going to get out of you. You're done."

Frank pressed the gate opener and looked straight ahead while it rolled open. The newshounds were fast-walking down the sidewalk. Frank drove in and clicked the remote toward the gate and sent it rolling back the other way. Just in time to shut the news guys out.

"I can go places you can't," Thorn said.

"Like where?"

"Like deep into that house." He nodded at the Moss residence.

"I can manage without that."

"I've got an inside track, Frank. I'm a part of this family."

"And that's exactly why I'm cutting you loose."

"You know I'm going to keep going at this anyway. You should want me on a short leash, keep me close so I don't screw up your case."

Frank looked in his rearview mirror at the gathering throng.

"I'm going to have to do a presser, throw these idiots some bloody meat. I need to go back to the office and write this up while it's fresh."

Thorn was silent, watching Boxley walk to the crowd of journalists assembled at the gate. The dog nosed around the bars but showed no aggression. Nevertheless, a few of them took a step backward.

"Jesus H. Christ, I must be losing my freaking mind. Okay, okay. Tomorrow morning, I'll be here at nine."

Thorn opened the door, stepped out, leaned back in to say thanks.

Frank said, "But you get the least little tickle, any warning sign you're so much as about to sneeze, you call me first."

"That wasn't Dee Dee coming at me with a bat."

"Oh, yeah?"

"That was a man. That was somebody who'd hit more than a few baseballs in his life."

"You could tell that, could you?"

"Same way you can see from somebody throwing a ball one time if they've got a decent arm. This was a guy at home in the batter's box. The way he cocked it above his shoulder, the way he gripped it, how his knuckles lined up, how loose he held his wrists. I could see that."

"A guy trying to kill you, you noticed his batting stance?"

"It's why I asked Sawyer if he'd ever played the game. You heard him, baseball never interested him. And unless Dee Dee risked her manicure playing organized ball, it wasn't her. This was somebody with a practiced swing."

Frank considered it, staring out the windshield.

"Interesting," Frank said. "Eyewitness testimony is always interesting. Though rarely helpful."

"I was there, Frank, I know what I saw."

"You ever play ball, Thorn?"

"Freshman year high school, started shortstop."

"Somehow I can't picture you doing team sports."

"Little League, junior varsity. Then that one year in high school."

"You quit after that?"

"It got old."

"Now that sounds like you."

"Shortstop, batted clean-up. I used to have reflexes."

"Didn't we all."

Frank shot a thumb toward the backseat where the papers lay.

"Manifests of the Miami–Dallas flights on Saturday, the twenty-fourth, and Miami–Atlanta on the tenth. Got Sawyer Moss riding first class on a flight to Dallas out early on the twenty-fourth, returning Monday the twenty-sixth at eight A.M."

"Which he admitted to."

"No Dollimores on the manifests, which, as I say, proves nothing."

"It wasn't Dee Dee with the bat, Frank. That was a guy who'd taken a lot of rips at well-thrown balls."

"Okay, so tomorrow we dig into Ms. Dollimore's sports history. But Thorn, at this moment, our prime suspect is deceased. In second place, I've got Sawyer Moss, who also spent time in Dallas on that fateful weekend, and could've made the trip to Atlanta by car. Maybe those two teamed up, one goes here, the other goes there, confusing the issue.

"So hey, if you can't accept that hypothesis, then fine, go your own way. Otherwise, I'll see you at nine."

"You want to hear my hypothesis?"

"Not really."

"Somebody wants *Miami Ops* on the front page. So they invent this copycat killer to put the spotlight on the show. Only problem is, the crimes have to be discovered for the plan to work, and at the same time, the killer doesn't want to get caught.

"So he does dumb stuff like tearing up receipts for a murder weapon and leaving it behind near the crime scene, gets the cops on the trail. He gets impatient, time is running out on the show, his breadcrumbs aren't panning out fast enough, so he makes a phone call, gets the news people whipped up. The investigation begins but it's all a tease. Breadcrumbs here, breadcrumbs there, leading this way and that. This suspect and that suspect, while the killer's sitting back reaping the rewards."

"You ought to apply for a job, Thorn."

"The Bureau looking for more whiz kids?"

"I was thinking the TV show. A moonbeam like you'd fit right in."

Frank put the car in gear and Thorn watched him ease through the crowd of reporters, window rolled up, face forward. The gate rolled closed behind him. Boxley went back on patrol.

Thorn walked to the front door and knocked.

A few moments later, April opened it. The look on her face was rigid and vacant. Drained by the pressures of the news crews, exhausted by worry about her sons, and confused by this man on her doorstep, her feelings toward him, his intentions toward her, and probably a dozen other competing emotions Thorn couldn't guess.

"Could we talk?" Thorn said.

"Not tonight."

"What's wrong?"

"You mean aside from all this?" She waved at the mob on the street.

Thorn shifted the fast food bag to the other hand and stepped back.

April said, "I've started the obituary."

"Good, but we need to run it by Frank, check the location he wants to use. The name of the target, the weapon."

"I'll have it for you tomorrow. My deadline's six P.M. to make the Monday edition."

"First you have to consult with Frank. How he wants to set it up."

"I know how to do my job. I'll have it tomorrow."

She backed into the foyer and slowly closed the door.

Thorn climbed the stairs to his garage apartment. He unlocked the door and went in, set the paper sack of fish sandwiches and the Coke on the small dining table.

The overhead lights were on, the ceiling fan turning fast. He hadn't left it that way. He remembered clearly shutting everything off.

He scanned the room, stood still, listening. He made a careful circuit of the space, smelled something he couldn't identify, a gamy fragrance like damp feathers mingled with the sulfurous muck of a tidal flat.

Before he'd left that morning, out of a lifetime of habit, he'd made the bed and pulled the flowered quilt up and tucked its border underneath the pillows. Now, sitting like smooth polished stones on each of the two white pillows, was a single brown egg about double the size of what a chicken would lay. Two eggs.

The rat catcher's calling card.

He turned from the bed. The bathroom door was closed. Another goddamn bathroom door, only this one opened inward. He stepped closer to it and caught another odor, sweet and sickening, something well past its prime.

He was expecting a handful of dead rats strewn around the bathroom, but when he cracked open the door, a low growling snarl rushed through the opening and brushed his ankles as it loped across the room and halted before the closet door.

A raccoon, extra-large, with a thick, handsome coat, well fed and pissed, hunched up and bared its teeth at Thorn.

He edged to the entryway door while the raccoon grumbled louder with each step Thorn took. Some of them could be rabid, and cornered like this one, they could get aggressive, but Thorn had cleared more than one raccoon from his dwellings over the years. All they needed was a clear path to an exit and some small encouragement.

Thorn opened the door wide.

The raccoon stood its ground in front of the closet. Thorn looked around for a broom, something long enough to prod it into motion, steer it to the door. But the small closet where the cleaning stuff was stored was next to the clothes closet, blocked by the growling raccoon.

From inside the wardrobe closet came a gurgling moan and a forlorn cheep, then it came again, and the big raccoon swiveled and clawed wildly at the louvered door, scrabbling with both front paws.

From long nights camping in the Glades, Thorn recognized the noise. Baby coons gurgled like that when scuffling with one another in the mangrove branches, early tests of strength and balance, establishing the pecking order. Matheson had marooned those babies within hearing of the mother and turned her into a more ominous species of animal than what he'd thought—one ready to brawl.

Where she'd planted herself made it impossible for Thorn to reach the handle of the bifold door and swing it open. With her babies threatened, this raccoon would not hesitate to do battle with a creature a dozen times her size. Risk everything to free her young. She'd slash him, bite him, take a deep gouging grip on his leg if he came close.

Jeff Matheson had gone to a lot of trouble to organize this wildlife tableau. A small drama no doubt intended to illustrate the natural protective behavior of a parent for its offspring, to mock his own desertion of family. Never mind that Thorn didn't know he was the father of two sons until today. In Matheson's mind, and maybe in Sawyer's and Flynn's, he'd deliberately forsaken his fatherly duties for a life of childish self-indulgence.

Okay, he got it.

Thorn yanked the quilt off the bed and gathered it in his arms, found a grip on two edges, then bunched it against his chest. In a motion he'd used hundreds of times to catch schools of baitfish, he floated the quilt like a casting net over the mama raccoon. He waited to see how she'd respond, then he waded in and grabbed the struggling lump, held her tight, and carried her to the doorway. He set her down and let her struggle some more, then came back to the closet and flung open the louvered doors and liberated her two bleating cubs.

Back at the door, he whisked the quilt off the big raccoon, revealing her to her youngsters, who scampered over and jumped aboard, clinging to her heavy coat as she lumbered outside and down the stairs to the yard without a thank-you or a parting snarl.

He spent the next half hour combing the room for any other morality skits or wildlife booby traps Matheson might have left behind, but he found nothing more. No scorpions, no pythons, no bright blue poison dart frogs. He opened all the windows to flush out the funky odor.

The muggy air of early evening was being whisked off by the rising breeze from an approaching thunderstorm, a sudden ten-degree drop.

He remade the bed. Then he ate his two cold fish sandwiches at the dining table and skipped the fries. He'd already had his quota of grease for the month. He washed it down with a fizzless, iceless cola.

Out his western window he watched the leading edge of the squall, the first strobes of lightning flashing like a salvo of silver spears flung by the foot soldiers leading the charge. Next the crash and clank of war machinery that rocked the floorboards of the apartment and rattled the glassware, followed by the deep concussions of the heavy stuff, then the rain came in gusts so strong he finally had to shut the windows.

The thunderstorm raged for an hour. By then Thorn was lying down, sharing his bed tonight with two eggs that lay side by side on the other pillow. Maybe they were dead, maybe not. The only way to know for sure was to wait.

TWENTY-SEVEN

SUNDAY MORNING THORN WAS UP at seven. He showered, selected a fresh polo shirt. Another day, another alligator on the chest.

He paced around the apartment for an hour, looking out his window at the eastern windows of the house. April's bedroom. Shades drawn. No lights. Car gone.

At nine when Frank arrived, Thorn told him about April, that she'd started her obituary for Monday. They knocked at the front door but no one came. Frank called her phone and they could hear it ringing inside. No one answered, no voice mail.

"You got a key?"

Thorn dug it out. He knocked again. Still no answer.

"We'll set the trap at the Silver Sands," Frank said. "It's out of the way, I know it like the back of my hand. The beach access is a minor problem. Might have to call on Rivlin and Vasquez. But between the four of us, we can lock it down tight."

Thorn opened the front door and they stepped into the foyer. Thorn called out. Nothing. He walked down the hallway to the kitchen, Frank tagging along, looking at the family photos.

"For a weapon I was thinking about a knife. Easy to defend against. Low collateral possibilities. The guy's used a knife already, so unless he's got a problem with repeating himself, that should work."

"I thought our killer drowned yesterday."

"Maybe she did. But like you say, a backup plan can't hurt. And hey, those scissors, the pinking shears, or whatever. No matches with any of the prints we took from the TV show people."

"Matheson had access to those scissors. You need his prints too."

"I'll see what I can do."

In the kitchen Thorn found a note propped up on the kitchen table.

Garvey and I went to breakfast at La Lechonera. Back later.

Frank read it over his shoulder.

"She have a cell?"

"Yeah, but I don't have the number."

"I need to talk to her. She'll have to work this in. The Silver Sands, the knife. I'll have her use my name."

"She said her deadline is six this evening."

"We'll keep calling."

Henry Roediger, the forensic podiatrist, never worked on Sundays. He reminded Frank of that twice, and he shared it with Thorn another time. It wasn't that he was religious or anything of that sort—he was a man of science after all—but he believed every man and woman needed a day of rest, and Sunday was his. Always had been.

"We appreciate your making an exception in this case."

Dr. Roediger gave Frank a token smile.

Roediger was a handsome man, average height, thick head of salt-and-pepper hair, a heavy jaw, and cloudy blue eyes that seemed to be in the early stages of cataracts. His white lab coat covered a striped blue shirt and a red tie knotted precisely and pants with scrupulous creases. His shoes were black gunboats, maybe size fourteen. The feet of a man twice his size. Apparently Roediger's career path had been genetically predetermined.

He worked out of an office in a one-story medical plaza in the south Gables. The office, the examining room, and the laboratory were filled with disembodied feet. Plaster casts of feet; colored diagrams of feet with every ligament and tendon and bone and muscle named in Latin; plastic replicas of feet; cutaway models of feet that displayed the many strands of fibers, small bones, pads of fat, and fragile joints, so anatomically complex it was a wonder *Homo sapiens* had ever managed to lift themselves upright on such intricate devices, much less run and jump and pirouette.

Twenty-six bones, Roediger explained, fourteen in the toes, five slender bones in the instep, and seven more bones forming the back of the foot. It was both a structural base and a lever. Keeping us balanced and moving. Tendons, those inelastic cords attaching muscles to bones, kept the shape of the foot intact. The thirty-two muscles and tendons provided power, balance, and direction. The 109 ligaments that hinged the bones to the joints, fibrous cords, maintained the static shape of the foot. And the arch, the wondrous arch, that curved structure, that inspiration for the great cathedrals of the old world, one main arch along the inside of the foot and three small arches, the metatarsal across the foot's ball, the outer and short arch. And the toes, oh my, Roediger said, the miracle of the toes, gripping, clamping, propelling, balancing, a marvel of engineering.

"I can't tell you how many times I've heard this speech," Frank said to Thorn, "and it never gets old." He winked behind Roediger's back. "Now, doc, the feet in question, the ones from the murder scene. What've you got for us?"

"You're making fun of me, I know," the doctor said. "But if you don't have a clear overview of the foot, fully appreciate what you're seeing, how can you expect to make an informed determination about the particular foot in question?"

"I was hoping you'd make that informed determination for us, doc. It's really too late in life to get up to speed on something so complicated."

"Always in a rush, Sheffield, always hurrying and scurrying. When do you stop and actually apply yourself to something? Absorb new information? Acquire deep knowledge? If you don't slow down, let your brain waves ease a little, give yourself sufficient time to truly absorb information, you'll always be skimming, sir, just gliding across the surface."

"Skimming is going to have to suffice for now," Frank said. "What do you say, let's glide into the lab, take a look at the killer's foot."

In the lab Roediger brought up a footprint on his large computer monitor, a bloody track the killer had left behind at the Waterway Lodge. Thorn stepped back from the computer to keep himself from putting a fist through the glass.

The track was closer to a smudge than a footprint. Hardly any definition, barely more than a swipe of blood across the oak floor.

"That's it? That's the best you have?" Frank peered at the image.

"Well, there's a reason for that. The paramedics who were first on the scene and the patrol officers were less than professional in their methodology."

"They were in a hurry and tracked through the blood."

"To be fair," Roediger said, "there was no way to get to the bathroom where the victim's body was located without disturbing some of the tracks. But they did more than that. They disturbed all of them, all but this one."

"And this one's not so great."

"Not great, but intriguing."

"Let's get to the intriguing part."

Roediger bent to the keyboard and tapped in something. The image on the screen broke apart into five different colors, blues, greens, reds, yellows, and whites. The footprint came into slightly sharper focus, but only slightly.

"In the collection of pedal evidence we commonly use white adhesive lifters or white gelatin lifters. Personally, I'm fond of the electrostatic dust lifter, a device originally used in the examination of dubious documents to interpret indented writing. Forensic podiatrists like myself found the electrostatic dust lifter also to be highly useful for lifting dry-residue footwear impressions at crime scenes.

"Ordinarily I like to transfer the dust print to the dark-colored lifting film, then photograph it. The floor or other surfaces should be clean and the impression is usually made up of dry material like gravel dust or other airborne particulates.

"We've found with the electrostatic dust lifter that we have the same success rate on porous or nonporous surfaces. We even use the device for obtaining lifts from carpets. In this case, on his entrance into the crime scene room, the killer had not yet stepped into blood, so it was very likely he made dusty tracks across the wood floor."

Thorn was just barely holding his tongue. Already on probation with Sheffield, he knew it wasn't a good idea to strangle the forensic podiatrist right in front of him.

"Unfortunately, with the death of Sheriff Hilton, no such data was collected."

"It wasn't?" Sheffield said.

"No."

"Why not?"

"No one summoned me to the crime scene."

"You're shitting me."

"I don't shit people. It's not in my makeup."

"But the Miami PD, their ID techs must use the same equipment."

"Oh, no. Their gear is vastly inferior. They don't have my budget."

"So all this electrostatic mumbo jumbo, why waste our time with that?"

"I wanted to inform you for future pedal evidentiary matters."

"Christ on a crutch."

"So what's this image on the screen?" Thorn asked.

"A simple crime scene photograph, nothing more. I've run it through our processor to colorize the sections of the foot where it appears the most pressure is being applied. We can work with that. It's basic, but it's useful."

"Talk to us, doc."

"Once I've colorized the photograph, I rely on an algorithm I developed that interprets pressure patterns, and from that I can project weight distribution based on the flattening of the footprint, matching it against our database on shoe types and shapes. Thus, from the pressure patterns it's possible to extrapolate several facts. In this case, I can say for certain this individual was running when this print was made."

"Running," Frank said.

"That's correct."

"Not tiptoeing?" Frank said.

"And we can also fix the weight range somewhere between one hundred and forty pounds to one hundred and eighty."

"That's it? Nothing more specific than that?"

"Afraid not."

"Which keeps all our suspects on the board."

"Ordinarily I could be a great deal more clear-cut about height and weight and gait and build, even sex, but with this print, no. It's not just the photograph, it's the object itself. One-forty to one-eighty is the best I can do."

"What about the object?"

"That image you're looking at," Roediger said, "is neither a shoe print nor the print of a bare foot."

"Which leaves what?"

Roediger bent to his keyboard, killed the image of the foot, and flicked away to an Internet search page. He typed something in the box and the screen filled with images of a kind of footwear Thorn had never seen. It hugged the foot and surrounded each toe separately. It looked like a joke shoe, something for Halloween.

"Oh," Frank said. "A guy I know jogs in those." Seeing Thorn's blank look, he said, "New craze in running. Like going barefoot, only it protects the sole from glass and shit. It's got no support, which is supposed to make the foot stronger, take you back to your stone age self."

"Vibram FiveFingers shoe," Roediger said. "It's a crock of snake oil. Does more damage than good. It's a podiatrist's dream shoe."

"Fairly obvious why our perp needs one," Frank said, "running around barefoot, that's a problem, rip up his suit, hurt his feet, so he gets himself a pair of these FiveFingers jobs. But how does that change the forensics? A shoe like that, it should be more revealing. It's got a sole you can work with, plus it's a replica of his foot shape."

"All true. However, I use two distinct programs, two different biometric modalities, each with separate and unique protocols. One applies to ordinary shoes, hundreds of shoe types and sole patterns linked to brand-name products; the other program works with bare feet. I'm not set up to deal with this hybrid footwear. My coding would have to be completely rewritten to account for all the variables in this particular type of shoe. I simply can't provide real scientific analysis of such a shoe without doing further research and study."

"What, like hours or days?"

"Always in a hurry, Agent Sheffield. Always skimming."

"How long?"

"A month," Roediger said. "Maybe two. I need to . . ."

But Frank had turned away and was stalking out of the lab.

Thorn caught up with him in the parking lot, Frank on his cell.

"Well, fine, I get it, Rivlin. It's Sunday, you're having people over, how nice. Tell you what, just turn the burners on low for two minutes, get on your goddamn laptop, and look through the inventory online. Call me back either way. If it's there, if it's not there, I want to know. Yeah, Vibram FiveFingers." He spelled "Vibram," then hung up.

"She was having brunch with her future in-laws."

"What inventory?'

"Dee Dee's condo. My people took the place apart, made a list of the contents. Ms. Dollimore had fifteen different dildos, Rivlin remembered that much, but she couldn't recall if there were barefoot running shoes. We find those, there's blood traces, we're home free."

"Now what?"

"See my video guru. You think Roediger's a character, just wait."

On the way out Old Cutler Road, Thorn tried April's home number again and got no answer. It was close to eleven. Even a long breakfast should be done by now. Maybe they were grocery shopping, taking a Sunday drive. It was odd that Thorn hadn't seen or heard her leave this morning. He'd been up, windows open. Probably when he was showering. Yeah, he told himself. When he was showering.

Frank got out his cell, speed-dialed Agent Vasquez, had him pull up the cell number for April Moss. He held on while Vasquez worked on it, then spoke the number aloud for Thorn to dial.

No answer. No voice mail.

"That's odd," Frank said.

"Maybe she shut her phone off, all those news guys hounding her."

"Maybe it's that," Frank said.

Thorn said, yeah, it had to be that. But he had a feeling. He watched the road curving through the cloister of shade, giant oaks and banyans lining the historic two-lane, mansions on both sides, golden blazes of sunlight spattering the asphalt before them. Runners on the bike trail, walkers, strollers. Out early to beat the coming heat.

The premonition was taking root, becoming a bright twinge in his chest. Like the one he'd had two nights ago while running from the riverside bar back to the bungalow, fighting back the panic, telling himself it was all fine, Buddha wasn't in danger.

A bright ache in his chest just like that one. Only more so.

TWENTY-EIGHT

FOR YOU THIS IS HIGHLY unusual. It is daylight and you are wearing ordinary clothes, walking down an ordinary sidewalk, past newsmen gathered around their trucks. Men and women with television faces and television hair, talking in their television voices.

No one notices you. You might as well be wearing the black suit, stealing through the shadows, vaporous, intangible. That is your new power, the gift to go away, to stand unseen, to walk like dark through dark, like a vacant wind across a treeless plain.

You no longer require the suit. You have learned to disappear while standing in full view. An actor's trick, vanishing into your part. It is more beautiful and liberating than the suit. So natural, so effortless. Camouflaged by normalcy.

That thought gives you an electric tingle. You have doubled yourself. The two halves of you have fused into a being more powerful than either of their separate selves, as when two chemical compounds synthesize to form a new and infinitely more complex creation.

On the TV news you saw they had shifted locations, and simple curiosity drew you here. You halt at the edge of the crowd and watch a woman speaking into the cameras. Behind her are the white towers of the Ocean Club, and its sister condos. The news reporters abandoned the Moss residence in Spring Garden and set up their cameras here.

Their story has shifted again, this time from the obituary writer to the television show.

For which you are grateful.

You stand on the edge of the crowd in your cloak of normalcy and watch the woman speak into the cluster of microphones. She is short and thick with curly black hair; she gives her name, spelling it, then spelling it a second time. Lisa Mankowski, special agent in charge, Miami field office.

A change.

A new pursuer.

You watch her answering questions. After a minute listening, you decide the other one, Sheffield, would be more challenging. This woman does not worry you.

You drift back to the parking lot, back to your car. There is still more to do. When the obituary appears tomorrow, you will follow its directives as you have followed the others. You will plan, you will execute.

Then you will cease.

You will erase from your mind all that you have done and all that has been done to you, and you will ease back to live among them with this new invisibility; you will take love and give love, speak and be spoken to, you will do everything exactly as they do. Like the traveler who has completed a great journey to the highest peaks and most dangerous canyons on the planet, but has kept his exploits secret, so that when he returns there is no fanfare, and no one even notices he's been away.

Once they got past the front gate security and were driving down the central boulevard of the lavish neighborhood of Coral Seas, Sheffield started ticking off the names of the owners of the estates on either side of the road. Sprawling grounds with manor houses that grew larger and more ostentatious as they drove. Car dealers, pro athletes, hotshot lawyers, surgeons to the stars. Thorn was silent. If any of these people ever wanted to build a bonfire and simplify their lives, they'd have to hire a dozen workers just to empty their garages.

"You don't recognize a single one of those names, do you?"

"Are they big shots?"

"Sometimes I forget you live under a rock at the back of a cave."

"A cave at the bottom of the sea."

"You never come up for air? Watch a little TV, indulge in the pop culture. Not ever? Hum along to the song of the day."

"Been indulging all week," he said. "That should last me a while."

Frank pulled into a long drive and stopped at the second layer of security, a massive wrought-iron gate. He buzzed the call button and spoke his name. At the end of the lane behind a wall of fishtail palms, Thorn could make out an English Tudor castle with a dozen turrets and a tower with cannon emplacements and two spires.

The gate rolled open and Sheffield bumped over the brick drive.

"Lydia owns Zenon Security. You never heard of that either, I'm sure, because not many people have. That's how they like it. Started out as an alarm company. Now they supply private security contractors to the government."

"Mercenaries," Thorn said.

"Word of warning, Thorn. Don't use that word inside these gates. You'll never be seen again."

"How do you know these people?"

"Long story."

"Never mind."

"I dated Lydia Zhee in college, the Tallahassee years. We stayed in touch. She started off in computers, migrated to security. We see each other now and then, go for a sail. A drink, like that."

"Why all these independent contractors? There isn't a lab in Virginia where all the smart guys do this kind of work?"

"Oh, I must've forgotten to tell you."

Thorn waited, hearing a different tone in Frank's voice. Deflated.

"Mankowski paid me a call last night at the Silver Sands, rousted me from a good sleep. She's decided she needs to take charge of the investigation. I am hereby out of the loop. The whole Zentai Killer show became too juicy for her to ignore. The TV time, it's jet fuel for her career."

"You're going to let that happen?"

"She mentioned the magic words. My pension. If she knew what you and I have been up to, the lady could put a turd in my file that would never go away. I'd spend my golden years spit-shining urinals at the bus station."

"So you're done with this? You're walking away?"

"Does it look like I'm walking away? We're here, aren't we? We saw Roediger. I'm working the Vibram foot thing with Rivlin. Long as we stay below the radar, it'll be fine. Let Mankowski have all the TV time she wants. More power to her. We'll keep working the street."

Sheffield got out of the car and Thorn stayed put. He said he wanted to keep trying April's number. While Frank was inside the Tudor castle, Thorn alternated between her cell and her home. Hitting redial, redial. Running down Buddha's battery with repeated attempts. Nothing and more nothing.

Behind the Tudor house, he noticed a Bertram fifty-footer idling down the canal, somebody rich and famous heading out to sea to play. It seemed to take a lot of goodies to keep these people amused.

Thorn rang April's numbers again. No answer. It was close to three P.M. Three hours till her deadline.

He called her a few dozen times more before Frank came striding back to the car.

"Lydia says to tell you you're cute," he said, getting behind the wheel. He nodded at the limb of an oak tree. "Don't bother looking for it, but it's there, video cam so small, you could inhale one and not know it."

Thorn kept looking but saw only the tiny oak leaves and heavy branches.

"Lydia says if you'd like to go sailing some day, she's got a Speedo with your name on it."

"I'll keep it in mind."

"The lady was helpful."

Thorn waited.

"That Sports Craze video, she blew up that single frame where the perp is glancing at the camera, cleaned it up best she could, but it's no good. All she can say is it looks like eye shadow and lipstick, long lashes. Maybe a woman, or somebody trying hard to look like a woman."

"And Atlanta?"

"Now that's different. Image is actually much worse, so Lydia couldn't do anything with the face. That hand blocking the eyes, that was a crafty move. Nothing conclusive there."

Frank started the car and pulled through the horseshoe drive. The big steel exit gates swung open and Frank turned onto the main thoroughfare.

"And how is this helpful?"

"Well, she pulled up images of all five of our suspects; all the *Miami Ops* people have photo spreads, the usual publicity bullshit. She found Matheson's picture somewhere out in cyberspace. So she lines them up side by side, gets them all roughly in proportion to each other, and what do you know? We got five people, different ages, different sexes, they're all slender, roughly the same height and weight within ten, fifteen pounds of each other, and an inch or two, same slim hips. Dee Dee being fairly flat-chested, that's not a giveaway either. So you got five people who could be standing there in that skintight suit on that Atlanta street."

Thorn waited. Frank was having fun, milking this.

"You know, a guy like me, by this age in life, I've been with my share of women. Without trying, I've made a fairly extensive study of the female body, and yet, I learned some things today I never knew."

"Sorry I missed it."

"Differences between men and women, anatomical differences, like how a woman's tailbone tips more strongly toward the back and tapers toward its lower end more than a man's. And how men's hip sockets are closer together. Male hip sockets face forward and a woman's angle to the side. Makes childbirth easier, and sex of course. Women are open, men are closed, in an anatomical sense."

"You're sounding like Roediger."

"You don't think this is interesting?"

"Just get there, okay. I'm tired of all these shaggy dogs."

"Why?"

"I want to nail this asshole and be finished."

"You homesick?"

"Damn right I am."

"Yeah, yeah, I understand that. But Thorn, please tell me you're not one of those guys skips to the end of the story to find how it turns out.

No, man. You got to savor the baby steps along the way. Otherwise, where's the pleasure?"

"Women are open, men are closed."

"Exactly," Frank said. "As I said, with this person standing out on the street at night in a black skintight suit, far as Lydia is concerned, that's as good as having a straight shot of her face. The way Lydia looks at it, you want to know the subject's gender, first place you check is the ischium."

"The ischium."

"Yes, sir. It's all about the tilt of the pelvis, my man. The axis of a woman's pelvis tips toward the front of the ischium. A man's divides into more balanced halves. It affects how you stand, how you sit, move around. It's like an anatomical marker."

"This computer expert, I take it, she's more than that."

"Right you are. Her company, it's not just mercenaries. Lately they branched out into running the training for the fine folks who fly our military drones. These people are sitting in bunkers out in Colorado, ten thousand miles from the battlefield, got a joystick in their hands, deciding who to blow up, who to let go. It happens sometimes, after they sort out all the intel, their decision comes down to a piece of real-time video.

"And that's when sometimes they need to know the difference between a man and a woman. How they walk, how they stand, how they shift their weight. Apparently it's all got a signature. Though most of the people they're looking at are wearing robes and veils, not bodysuits. So, turns out, this was a piece of cake for Lydia, reading the ischium."

"And the punch line is?"

"Lydia's ninety percent certain the person on the street in Atlanta was a woman. A woman holding a paper sack that more than likely contained a butcher knife she was about to use in a violent manner on a male nurse who lived two blocks from where this incident took place."

"The ischium told her that?"

"Ischium is all I remember. There was more. But, shit, I'm losing my short-term memory. Five years ago, I could've repeated everything she said, word for word, now all that fancy jargon just drifted back into the general sludge." Frank tapped a finger to his skull.

"I know the feeling."

"So it was Dee Dee Dollimore on the street in Atlanta."

"I don't think so, Frank."

"Still stuck on the baseball bat, the knuckles lining up?"

"Why's this lady only ninety percent certain? What's the ten percent?"

"I don't know. Something about how the perp lifted her hand to cover her eyes, it had a masculine look to it. She had all the lingo. The science of it. But nine out of ten, it's Dee Dee."

"I should've gone inside with you."

"We can go back, Lydia wants to meet you."

"No, thanks."

As Sheffield pulled onto Old Cutler, heading north toward the Grove, his phone jingled.

It was Rivlin calling back.

"Let me guess," Frank said. "No Vibram FiveFingers on the inventory."

He listened to her answer, then said, "I'm getting another call, I got to drop you, Rivlin."

Frank shook his head, saying to Thorn, "No Vibram at the condo."

Thorn watched Frank read the caller ID, then press the button on his phone, his face hardening.

"Go ahead," he said.

He listened to the voice for the next mile, then another mile, saying nothing. They cruised through the Cocoplum Circle, headed up Ingram Highway into Coconut Grove, Frank still listening, his face growing harder.

As they entered the business district of the Grove, Frank said, "Yeah, I got it. I got it, okay." Then he paused and said, "Right now, Sunday afternoon? Can't wait till the morning?"

Sheffield listened a little longer, then clicked off and swerved into a parking space across from Commodore Plaza.

"We're done," he said. "You're on your own."

"Mankowski?"

"Sorry, Thorn. It's been a blast."

"You're walking away? Like that?"

"Like I said, I'm sorry. Rivlin blew the whistle. Called the boss, told her I was letting you ride shotgun. Mankowski's pissed. Well, more than pissed."

"And what about April and the next obituary? The trap?"

Frank sighed.

"I'll bring Mankowski up to speed, she can decide. But I doubt she'll want to ride that horse. Meanwhile, she's set up some kind of pissant teleconference with an assistant AG in Washington, so I can answer some questions, go on record, help them decide if they're going to cut off my head or just my nuts."

"When it happens, it happens quick."

"Not usually this quick," Frank said. "Don't worry about me. Can you get back to the Moss house okay?"

"I'll be fine."

"Sorry, Thorn. Really. This isn't how I wanted it to end. You tell Sugarman hello for me, okay?"

Thorn climbed out of the car and watched Sheffield drive off.

He dug out his phone to try April one more time, and saw the battery icon blinking red.

TWENTY-NINE

THORN HIKED FROM THE GROVE to Spring Garden in a little under three hours, getting lost a couple of times, and taking a detour to charge his phone battery in a Little Havana RadioShack, a service he bargained down to five dollars, which left him with a single buck for emergencies.

If he was going to make peace with Miami, it wasn't going to start today. It wasn't a city hospitable for walkers. He stopped counting the near misses, the sideswipes, the horns razzing him, the pedestrian traffic signals that lured him into the middle of an eight-lane thoroughfare, then left him sprinting for his life.

It was just before six when he entered April Moss's pedestrian gate. Wagging his stump, Boxley cantered over and plowed his snout into Thorn's crotch for the latest update. April's Mini Cooper was still gone.

Thorn stood in the driveway and drew the phone out and called again. This time she picked up her cell on the first ring.

"Everything okay? Where are you?"

"Turn around," she said.

The gate slid open behind him and April pulled into a space near the front veranda. Garvey threw open the passenger door and ordered someone to assist her immediately. Thorn hauled Garvey out of the passenger door and settled her into her arm crutches.

"Oh, the places we've gone and the places we've seen. Some of them so boring I'm about to turn green."

"You look beat, Thorn." April gave him a tired smile and patted his arm.

"I was starting to get anxious."

"Oh, he was getting anxious," Garvey said. "Call the wedding planner."

"I went to my office at the *Herald*," she said. "Turned off my cell. I needed some downtime to get the obit done."

"Oh, yes, it was downtime. I can't remember the last time I was this far down."

"Garvey spent the afternoon at the Floridian doing some long-overdue rehab on her knees."

"She dumped me off like a kid at daycare. That's a glimpse at the horrors ahead: First it's the nursing home, then they pick you up and deliver you to the front door of the mortuary and push you out. See you later, masturbator."

Garvey hobbled up the front steps, sloughing off April's helping hand.

"What am I going to do with you, Garvey?"

"Call me a male escort. Or maybe if Rambo isn't busy, he can massage some of my aching parts."

Thorn followed them inside, and Garvey tottered off to her encampment in the maid's room.

April headed silently to the kitchen.

She browsed the refrigerator shelves for a moment while Thorn took a seat at the kitchen table.

"I've got turkey and cheddar. I can make sandwiches."

Thorn said that would be fine. She offered him beer, wine, or water and Thorn took the Heineken. She poured herself a Chardonnay and set his open beer in front of him, then put together the sandwiches and took her seat across from him.

"You turned your obit in?"

"I did."

"Without talking to Frank?"

"I did it my way."

Thorn ate some of his sandwich, tried not to guzzle the beer.

"Can I see it?"

"I don't have a copy. You'll have to wait till tomorrow."

"Why'd you do that, April?"

"You don't understand, do you, Thorn? You're smart in so many ways. Like I said before, you're sensitive for a man. But you've got these blind spots."

"I'm not arguing that."

"Somebody has taken my writing, the one thing in my world, beside the boys and Mother, that gives me sustenance. And they've tainted it. They've turned my words into some perverse, violent poetry they use for their poisonous end. I feel like I've been robbed of one of my most precious possessions. The thing that gave me my identity, my purpose."

Thorn waited, watching her tuck a strand of hair behind her ear. She looked down at her untouched sandwich, shaking her head.

"So you went to work to reclaim some of that."

"Yes."

"And the idea I proposed, using this as a trap, you wanted no part of that."

April lifted her eyes and gave him a weary smile.

"You do try," she said. "I'll have to say that. You may not get it exactly right, but you try to understand."

Thorn got up and poured himself a glass of water, drank it down, and returned to the table. April reached out and took his right hand in hers and laced her fingers around his, squeezing hard. Then she drew her hand away and hid it in her lap. She lifted the hair from her neck and let it drop.

"I never really knew who you were. We had those few hours together, and then I was pregnant, and the boys came. And I never knew the person who fathered them. I knew your name, where you lived, a glimpse of your world, but I didn't know you. So there was something missing all these years, a sense of what our family was about."

"What did you tell the boys?"

"The truth. A one-night stand. A handsome stranger swept me off my feet. That's what we called you, 'the handsome stranger.' We'd tell stories about you, concoct wild tales of what you were doing, what dragons you were slaying, all the exotic places you'd seen. You were a game we played, an invention that kept us entertained. Long, elaborate stories. Garvey's role was to put you in mortal danger, some terrible monster coming for you, suspending you on a fraying rope over a burning pit, and the boys always found a solution, a magical power you had that allowed you to escape. It was fun. It was our private family game."

"So the other men, the suitors in the photos with the boys, they must have had a hard time competing with the handsome stranger."

She smiled.

"It was hopeless. No one could live up to the stories we invented. I didn't realize the consequences of it while it was happening. I just thought we were having fun and being creative, and I was giving the boys an emotional foundation, a father substitute. But what we were doing was making you into an impossible ideal. Nobody could compare to the handsome stranger. The others would stay around for a while, then every one of them figured it out sooner or later, that they were in competition with some supernatural rival they could never beat."

"You could have driven down to Key Largo and told me."

"You could have driven up to Miami and looked me up."

"Did you think I was going to do that? Did you expect that?"

She took a bite of her sandwich, looked off toward the window onto the back porch where the bird feeder hung.

"Sometimes, when the boys and I were making up stories about the handsome stranger, I'd feel a sense of longing. I'd feel hurt and abandoned and even angry sometimes that you never reappeared. It wouldn't have been hard to find me. My byline was always in the paper. But finally I gave up on that fantasy, or that illusion, or whatever it was. It seemed juvenile and self-destructive. It kept me stuck in that same emotional place, a high school kid mooning over some brief encounter.

"I don't know how old they were, the boys, maybe ten or eleven, but one day at breakfast, we were sitting right here where we're sitting now, and when Flynn started in with a handsome stranger story, I told him to stop. I'd never done that before. I'd always played along, been amused, enjoyed it in a silly way. But I told him to stop. And he must have heard something in my voice. Both of them must have heard it because we never did that again. Never after that day. Flynn just stopped the story and got back to his food and we never spoke of it again.

"I don't know if that was right or wrong. It probably hurt them. They probably felt a sense of loss about no longer having the handsome stranger to fantasize about. I don't know. But that's the last we spoke of you.

"Garvey came up with another idea. She started making up stories about the Marvelous Trio."

"Trio."

"She left herself out. Trying to keep the spotlight on us, mother and sons. The Marvelous Trio had magical powers too and Garvey put us in all kinds of awful situations, and the boys would play along, but it was never the same as the handsome stranger. Gradually, as the boys got older, the Marvelous Trio stories stopped and that whole storytelling thing drifted away."

Thorn picked up the sandwich and put it down again. He looked around the kitchen, imagining the family gathered here, the young boys telling tall tales about him, making him into a hero, building some extraordinary version of a man that no one could ever match. He put himself in that long-ago kitchen, filling the role that had been left open for him. A role so far away from the one he'd carved out for himself.

"You never let me know about the boys," Thorn said, "because you were angry and hurt. Was that some kind of revenge?"

She gave it a minute of thought, then said, "I don't know. Maybe a little. But mainly once the boys and Garvey and I had built our family, our habits, our traditions, I didn't want to risk all that by inviting somebody to the party who had so much power to disrupt it."

"But I showed up anyway. You summoned me. Maybe it wasn't conscious, but you wrote my name on that obituary."

"I had no way of knowing what would happen. I didn't summon you. I was thinking about you, yes. But I never imagined, or even hoped this would happen. You and me around the breakfast table."

They finished their meal in silence, worked side by side at the sink to clean up. When the dishes were put away and the dish towel folded, she turned to him, close enough to touch, but not so close she was offering herself.

"Anything else?" she said.

Thorn stepped closer and opened his arms and April hesitated only a second, then stepped into his embrace, turning her head and resting her cheek against his shoulder. The smell of her hair, the fit of her flesh against his was both familiar and completely new. He heard something like a high wind coursing around them. As though the entire structure were being buffeted by a gale, testing its strength, making every plank, every wall shiver against its force.

She drew away and moved back to the table, touching her cheek with the fingertips of her right hand as if testing the solidity of her own tissues.

"Who did these things, Thorn? Who is it?"

"Sheffield thinks it was Dee Dee. And when the horror of what she was doing overcame her, she killed herself."

"Is that what you think?"

"No. The person in the motel room with the baseball bat wasn't Dee Dee."

"She didn't do it," April said. "It definitely wasn't Dee Dee."

"You're sure?"

"I'm a hundred percent certain, yes."

"And how do you know?"

April heard Garvey coming down the hallway, the rubber tips of her crutches squeaking against the wood.

"You'll see. Tomorrow you'll see."

THE MIAMI HERALD

Monday, August 2

Daniela Diamond Dollimore, Actress with a Caring Heart

By April Moss

To her television fans Ms. Dollimore was a sex kitten with lethal skills, known by her stage name, Dee Dee, but to her many friends in local aid organizations she was Danni, a tireless worker and a young woman with a warm and caring heart.

On July 31, Danni Dollimore, 27, a familiar and welcoming face in the food banks and halfway houses of Miami's inner city, drowned in a boating accident just south of Key Biscayne. "We were all shocked and heartbroken over Danni's death. Her smile, her compassionate spirit were something special," said Flora Marcus, director of Prayer House, the food bank and halfway house where Danni volunteered long hours.

"Diamond loved Spring Garden, the historic neighborhood along the north banks of the Miami River," said Ruth Wertalka, a long-time aid worker who got to know Danni at Prayer House. "It's a pretty area. Her boyfriend lived there, and Danni started hanging out there. But one day when she was out exploring the area, she strayed into Overtown and she was just shocked to find that a few blocks from the charming district she knew and enjoyed is an impoverished and crime-ridden ghetto."

Pained by the hopelessness she saw in those first encounters in one of Miami's toughest neighborhoods, Danni started looking for a way to give whatever assistance she could. How exactly she settled on Prayer House is not known, but everyone who met her there was thankful it happened. "I don't want to lay it on too thick," said Wertalka, "but Danni had an eye-opening conversion when she first bumped into Overtown, and it stirred her up like nothing ever had. She'd spent all those years as an actress, but she said it never gave her any real pleasure or satisfaction. Overnight she found her greatest joy came from feeding the hungry and giving hope and cheer to the hopeless."

"All that TV foolishness, that prancing and primping, was just an act," said Flora Marcus. "She left that nonsense behind when she came down here to her secret world. No makeup, jewelry or skimpy skirts, just jeans, baggy T-shirt and a great big smile for all our disenfranchised clients. Nobody knew she was a TV star. She just worked the chow line and slung the mop like every-body else. Every Saturday, regular as clockwork, she arrived in a Yellow Cab because she didn't want nobody around here seeing her driving a fancy car. Last thing she wanted was to call attention to herself, just wanted to fit in with all the other volunteers." On many Saturday nights when others in her profession were partying all night at South Beach clubs, Danni Dollimore would find a vacant cot in an out-of-the-way corner, and spend the night at Prayer House so she could be up early and get back to work.

Starting in April of this year, when Danni's television chores increased, she found she could only steal away for a weekend now and then at Prayer House. According to Marcus, this change in schedule upset her, but Danni coped. "She'd get here at the crack of dawn, turn her cell phone off, and she'd stay till the very last minute when she had to get back to her high-flying life. Danni told us she felt like she'd finally found her purpose in the world. She had an infectious smile. People down here loved that girl. She had a beautiful soul."

Born in Miami Beach, Daniela Diamond Dollimore seemed destined for a show business career. Her father, Gusman Dollimore, directed short films and independent TV specials for years before he took charge of the *Miami Ops* police drama in which his daughter starred. Danni's mother, Betty Parsons, was also a professional actress whose credits include character roles in action films of the 70s. Ms. Parsons, now a Realtor living in Daytona Beach, discovered early that her daughter had a tender heart. "She didn't just bring home the usual stray dogs and cats, Danni found snakes and iguanas, and more than once she brought home injured possums. She'd take them into her bed, hide them under her covers and I'd hear her in there talking to them, try-ing to console these smelly creatures. She just hated to see anything suffer."

Home-schooled in both elementary and high school, Danni was a loner with limited exposure to other children. One of her rare friends from that time, Mitchell Masur, remembers her as a terribly shy girl. "She barely said a word when we saw each other on the sidewalk. She was a mumbler. But every once in a while I'd get a glimpse of the girl inside. Funny and kind of wild. Back then she had a pair of Rollerblades and the two of us would go out skat-ing for hours, Danni just flying along, never saying a word with a huge smile on her face."

"Like an ice pick in the heart," said Bertie Mae Fields, one of the regulars at Prayer House. "That's how I feel, losing Danni. Isn't no fairness in the world if a girl as good as that, with all those great years ahead of her, can just up and die for no good reason. When she wasn't working the food line or scrubbing pots and pans, she was trying to teach me to read. She'd bring me books every weekend. I loved that sweet young woman."

A private memorial service will take place at the Spring Garden private home of a friend on Monday evening, August 2. In lieu of flowers donations to Prayer House will be gladly accepted.

THIRTY

THORN FOUND THE MORNING PAPER on the front sidewalk and took it back to the porch, where he read it with Boxley sitting erect beside him. When he'd finished the obituary, Thorn stared out at the quiet street.

The sky was leaden and low and in the east the sunrise was muffled to a vague pink. The air smelled tense and electric from an incoming storm. Overhead in the lowering sky two parrots groused at each other as they made their morning rounds. The Siamese padded up the stairs, eased in beside Boxley, and rubbed its cheeks against the dog's forelegs.

Thorn folded the paper in half and read the obituary again. Boxley turned his head to the side and settled his muzzle on Thorn's left thigh. On the second pass, he found himself admiring April's quiet way of disappearing while she brought to life a woman she'd clearly misjudged. Smoothly moving from quote to quote, words of people who'd known her best, building a compact portrait of a wounded child who found a way to hide in public behind the pose of a brainless nymphet.

Thorn and the dog and cat were still standing guard on the porch when April came to the front door and stepped outside. She had on dark brown shorts and a simple cream top with her hair pinned up. Her eyes moved languidly to his, dulled by the sleep she'd apparently missed.

"Coffee?"

"In a minute." Thorn patted the rocker beside him, and after a moment's hesitation, April came out and sat down.

"You're angry at me."

"Not mad, no."

"Yesterday, Flora Marcus, the director of Prayer House, called my office at the paper and left a message. She saw on TV that Dee Dee drowned and wanted to be sure someone knew about her secret life, and that she got credit for her good works. I wouldn't have discovered any of that if Flora hadn't bothered."

"Spring Garden, April, ice pick."

She nodded.

"I thought the ice pick was clever," she said with a weary smile. "Much better than a 'bullet to the heart.'"

"You didn't make that up. She actually said those words?"

"I don't make things up."

Thorn shook his head.

"At the *Herald* yesterday, I went over all the other obituaries for the last five weeks. I wanted to see how it could possibly be true, third word, every third paragraph. It was uncanny, some kind of terrible coincidence that those kinds of words landed in those spots. Not every obituary I wrote during the time fit the formula, there were lots of them with words that wouldn't work, but the few he's acted on are pretty clear. Knife, gun, spear."

"Why'd you do it, April? You made yourself the target."

"What other choice was there?"

"Because you feel guilty? Because of what the news people said, that accomplice bullshit?"

"Do you want coffee? I know I do."

She rose and walked to the screen door, then stopped and stared off at the distance.

Thunder rumbled far out at sea where the rosy gray dawn was darkening as though whoever was in charge of such things had changed his mind about lighting up another day. Thorn watched as the first pink hint of sunrise disappeared into the thick clouds until only charcoals and dark blues churned along the horizon. Around them the air was growing still and heavy.

"Garvey ordered pancakes for breakfast. Can I make you some?"

"You two are going to have to move somewhere until this is over."

"She won't stand for that, and neither will I."

"It's too risky, April."

"Pancakes? Or eggs? Carbs or protein, what'll it be?"

After the silent breakfast was done, Thorn went back outside to the porch and fumbled with Buddha's phone until he located Sheffield's cell number in her directory.

Thorn left a message on his voice mail and a minute later, "Hey Jude" was vibrating in his hand.

"You read the paper?"

"I read it," Frank said. "What is she, crazy?"

"She feels responsible."

"Look, they put me on administrative leave," Frank said. "Pending the director's decision, I'm off the streets, locked out of my office; they took my weapon, and if I'm not mistaken I'm also under surveillance."

"They're watching you? Why?"

"It's Mankowski's doing. Humiliate me, show me who's boss."

"You were wrong about Dee Dee."

"I was."

"We could use you over here for the next few days."

Frank was silent.

"You there?"

"I told Mankowski about the newspaper thing, three down, three in. And just like I thought, she didn't buy it. I laid out the whole situation, the Vibram shoes, the pinking shears, showed her the transcripts from the interrogations, the security videos, the whole deal. She blew it off, all of it. She's starting from scratch, won't even look at my notes. Says everything I've done is tainted."

"I understand."

"But I'd say fuck 'em and be over there right now, except some guys arrived this morning and cranked up the bulldozers and a line of dump trucks just pulled in. Some kind of bullshit legal papers came in the mail, but I was so busy chasing around town I haven't opened an envelope in days.

"Seems I missed a court date, so the city gave themselves legal authority to demolish the motel and sent over ten badasses to do the dirty work. These hombres don't speak English and I've used up all the Spanish I know. So it's only because I'm standing here in front of the place with a shovel in my hands that the Silver Sands isn't a pile of rubble at the moment."

"Take care of your business, Frank. I can handle this."

"The fucker won't come till Saturday. By then I'll have this mess fixed, and I'll be there."

"If he stays on schedule, yeah. Saturday."

"You have reason to think otherwise?"

"He came after Buddha late Friday, so maybe he's not fussy about Saturday."

"I might be able to get over there later today if I can resolve this."

"It doesn't matter, Frank. Save your place."

"What about Sugarman? He'd back you up."

"He's hiking the Grand Canyon with his daughters. Won't be back till Sunday."

"You lied about packing heat, didn't you? You got Hilton's handgun."

"Only two rounds left. But, yeah, I got it."

"Well, if I were you I'd get in your car right now, and go stock up on ammunition."

"Good luck with the bulldozers."

Frank sighed.

"Good luck with the ice pick."

The rain blew through, leaving behind a sparkle in the grass and so much moisture in the air that every solid thing turned blurry.

Thorn went up to the apartment and showered and dressed. Today the alligator on his chest was orange, the shirt blue. He tucked Buddha's .38 into the waistband of his jeans, leaving his shirttail out, then retrieved the Sports Craze bag, dumped the contents on the bed, and chose one of the two baseballs.

He spent a while pitching the ball to Boxley. It took the dog three throws to grasp the concept of retrieving and giving it up to Thorn. But once he had the hang of it, he didn't want to stop.

Thorn stayed out in the wide lawn tossing the ball until he was drenched with sweat, but if anybody was watching, if anybody was considering using an ice pick on someone in this house, they should be aware they'd have to come through him and a Doberman first.

At noon April called out to tell him there were sandwiches and iced tea in the dining room if he cared to come inside.

He washed up in the guest bath in April's study, and was heading back to the foyer when his gaze ticked across the shelves of books. He halted and stared up at the high school yearbooks that were stored on the top shelf.

There were four of them from freshman to senior year. He started with the earliest and flipped through the pages until he found the group pictures of the sports teams. He didn't spot his two sons on the football team or the soccer team or the tennis team. And they weren't anywhere in the hardy gang of young men who played baseball that year.

He was about to set the book aside when he noticed a familiar face in the back row of the junior varsity baseball team, a gangly boy taller than his peers, with unkempt hair and a face peppered by acne. His uniform was baggy and his nose was a half size too large for his face. On his lips the remains of a snarl lingered, as if just before the camera clicked he'd been trading taunts with a teammate.

Below the photo, his name was listed among all the other fine young freshmen hopefuls: *Jeffrey Jay Matheson (right field).*

Thorn paged through the other yearbooks. In his sophomore year Matheson made the team again. Still stuck in right field. No sign of Flynn or Sawyer on any of the other teams. In his junior year Matheson disappeared from the varsity. But at the bottom of the page he appeared in a small photo, demoted to team manager.

Senior year, he disappeared from the team altogether.

"Your peanut butter sandwich is getting cold," Garvey said. "Better get in here, Mr. Extra Crunchy, before I have my way with it."

He followed Garvey to the dining room. The table was set, April sitting at the head.

"Jeff Matheson," Thorn said.

"Yes?"

"Do you know where he lives?"

"What's this about?"

"He played baseball in high school."

Garvey sat down and cut her sandwich in half with a knife and started in.

"Is that important? Playing baseball."

Thorn said yes, it was, he believed it might be very important.

"He's three doors down. A yellow house."

"Three doors down?"

"It's where he grew up, where he's always lived. That's how he knew the boys so well. He spent more time here than at his own house."

Thorn gave her a questioning look.

"No, it couldn't be," she said. "It couldn't be Jeff. He's a gentle spirit."

"Is he?"

"I've never heard him say a harsh or unkind word."

"He must've worked very hard to keep that side hidden from you."

"What do you mean?"

Thorn waved the question away.

"The video you showed me, at the shrink's office, is there still something between Flynn and him?"

"Flynn moved on long ago."

"Did Jeff?"

She studied the back of her ringless hand.

"I don't know," she said. "I never see him with anyone."

"Is the handsome stranger going to eat or just stand there and talk?"

"The handsome stranger," Thorn said, "is off on his next adventure."

"Praise the Lord," Garvey said. "It's about damn time."

THIRTY-ONE

THOUGH MATHESON'S HOUSE WAS SIMILAR in style to April's, it had been designed by a lesser architect and constructed by indifferent carpenters. Over the years the structure had been so badly neglected, it looked as if it had been abandoned for years. Its walls were pitted and tagged with graffiti, windowpanes were cracked and held in place with masking tape, and sagging furniture cluttered the front porch. An ancient washing machine was rusting peacefully in the side yard beside the overturned hull of a motorboat, while the front walkway was lined with crumbling stone pots that held the withered stalks of plants. Even in its prime, this house had been no beauty, but now with its foundation sinking, it slumped to one side like a man struggling with a pail of water.

Jeff's tiger-striped pickup was not in the driveway or inside the garage, which stood open and was too littered with lawn mowers and bicycles and broken furniture to hold one more piece of junk.

Thorn mounted the porch and rapped on the door.

The door didn't cave in but seemed to consider it. Nothing stirred.

He knocked again, stealing a look over his shoulder at the well-maintained houses across the street. No one was standing at any windows he could see. No one out in their nicely maintained yards. Driveways empty. Solid citizens starting a new workweek.

He edged around the porch to the western side of the house. Going along, he made a show of calling out hello. He gave a window a furtive tug but it was locked. He tried another with the same result.

At the back of the house, the yard that ran down to the river was barren, no grass, no foliage, only a single leafless tree with a rotting tire swing hanging from a branch on the end of a tattered rope. A wood object lay in the mud in the shade of the tree. Thorn left the porch, walked over, and picked up the handle of the broken bat. An ancient wooden Louisville Slugger, two-thirds of it missing.

He dropped it and headed back to the house and found the back door locked. Pressing his nose to the glass, he peered into a laundry room and the narrow hallway that seemed to lead to the heart of the house.

He dug Buddha's pistol from his waistband, held it by the barrel, and cracked the glass with the butt, then reached inside and unlocked the door to let himself in. He tucked the pistol back beneath his shirt.

Any single piece of evidence against Matheson was flimsy and merely circumstantial, but the list was impressively long. A member of the base-ball team; a broken bat in a field; the young man's abrasive, unhinged manner when Thorn and Frank spoke with him at his office; the kid actually confessing to the crimes, an act so outrageous no one took him seriously. And yet those were the first words that came to his lips. The fact that Matheson had been at Poblanos Friday afternoon and could have tailed Thorn and Buddha to the Waterway Lodge. He had easy access to the Moss home, which made it a cinch to lift the obituaries and trim their edges with the pinking shears. And for motive, there was Flynn.

The twisted desire to promote Flynn's career, and perhaps be rewarded with his renewed attention.

For the next half hour Thorn roamed the house, opening drawers and closets and cabinets, peering under furniture, lifting mattresses from the beds and searching beneath them, rifling through heaps of laundry that were in various states of decomposition. He didn't know what he was looking for, but whatever it was, he wasn't finding it.

He unearthed nothing but a dismal collection of possessions, the mini-mal toiletries and dreary wardrobe of a transient who'd crashed here for the night. And the corroding appliances and featureless furniture one might expect to find in a flophouse going broke.

He made another circle of the house, discovering a door or two he hadn't noticed before, doors that opened on bare shelves or empty spaces. He was doing his second tour of the upstairs when he saw the seam in the faded wallpaper. Printed in reds and greens on the wallpaper was a scene of the English countryside with men on horseback chasing after their foxhounds, a scene repeated and repeated across the wall of the landing, all that action and color obscuring the hairline joint.

Thorn found a dime in his pocket and used it to pry the flap of wood open. Maybe it had once been the storage cabinet for a fold-down ironing board, but Jeff Matheson had stripped the interior space clean and turned it into a shrine.

The centerpiece was a snapshot of Flynn and Jeff as eight- or nine-year-olds standing beside each other, arms over the other's shoulder, with a green field behind them. Flynn's blond hair was barely long enough to comb and part. Jeff's style matched Flynn's, but his dark hair was coarser and a cowlick swirled at the back. Circling that photograph like the rings of Saturn were photographs of Flynn as a boy and Flynn as a TV star and Flynn romping in the surf and Flynn running through tall grass. Some of the photos had been trimmed with scissors, editing out others, leaving Flynn disembodied from his surroundings. There were shots of an older and more stylish Flynn coming and going from the Moss home and from restaurants and nightclubs around Miami. Flynn and Flynn and Flynn. There were reviews of *Miami Ops* posted at the bottom, newspaper clippings, a paragraph from Kansas City, one from Arizona, another from L.A. Words underlined, words scratched out, the editorial corrections made in a tiny harebrained scrawl. The whole creation had been coated with some yellowish gelatin as if to give it an arty feel.

At the very top of the collage was a handwritten note on a square of white paper. In block letters it read, *We had fun, but it's over. Please leave me alone.* It was signed simply *Flynn.*

But Matheson had not left Flynn alone. He had hovered, he had watched, he had collected. And he had even ingratiated his way back into the Moss household by clearing their home of pests. He never left the neighborhood. Never moved on. He had stalled out as an adolescent. Held on to his first crush with a feverish devotion.

As Thorn stepped back to close the door, he saw the object fixed to the back of the flimsy door, just above Thorn's head. A lifelike human face. A mask of Flynn Moss, with his dark blue eyes, his straight nose, broad forehead, thin lips, and ruddy cheeks. Flynn at his current age. Thorn reached out and touched the rubbery flesh, as firm and cool as a slab of liver. What ceremonies Matheson performed with that mask, Thorn would not let himself imagine.

He was shutting the flap of wood, returning it to its perfect alignment, when the front door opened on squealing hinges and shut with a solid thump. Thorn smoothed the door of the shrine, then hustled to the landing at the head of the stairs and listened.

Either Matheson was light-footed as hell, or he was standing in place sniffing the air. It would come as no surprise to learn the kid possessed a sense of smell so acute that he detected Thorn's odor the second he stepped onto the front porch. Thorn had met the type before, trappers, hunters, trackers, men and women who'd spent so many years catching animals, they'd trained their neurons and learned levels of stealth and observation and a stillness of breath that to ordinary folks seemed paranormal. The tick of claws on wood, the brush of rat whiskers against a solid wall were clashing cymbals to them. All they needed was one stray molecule of sweat, a microdot of urine.

Thorn held his ground. He could see the head of the stairs, and down below he could make out the right edge of the front door.

The whisper of a shadow crossed a slit of sunlight beside the front door. The faint groan of floorboards. Matheson smelled him, or felt the barometric disturbance or saw the scuff marks in the dust on the stairs. Whatever subatomic clues were guiding him, they were working. He was coming up.

That's when Thorn saw the door flap. There was a small telltale warp at the bottom where he had failed to press the seam flat.

Thorn ducked back inside the bedroom. Maybe in some distant incarnation that room had been used for guests. But there was nothing welcoming about it now, with its tattered bedspread and bare walls and a single bulb in an ancient fixture. Thorn pressed his back against the wall beside the door and waited. If Jeff was being guided by smell, then the jig was up.

But when he reached the top of the stairs, instead of heading straight ahead into the room where Thorn was hiding, Jeff turned right, away from his shrine, and drifted into his bedroom.

Thorn waited.

He waited some more. Jeff was mumbling. Jeff was opening a squeaky cabinet door. Jeff was pissing like a stallion.

Thorn slipped out of the room, eased down the stairway, and hot-footed it out the door in twenty seconds. He headed for the sidewalk, then saw Jeff's truck and made a detour. He went to the far side of the Ford, so he could keep one eye on the house, then drew open the passenger door. The cab was littered with receipts and fast food containers and the hand tools of his trade. Wooden traps and a jar of peanut butter to bait them.

Thorn checked the glove compartment and found it packed with old parking tickets and speeding tickets and more receipts and small note-pads. He shut the door quietly and moved to the bed, which was piled high with metal cages in which the boy trapped possums, raccoons, and foxes. The putrid smell of death and shit and fright was overpowering. No amount of scrubbing would ever cleanse the bed liner of all the blood and fur and rank karma.

Near the tailgate, peeking out from under a white garbage bag that held the carcass of some small mammal, Thorn saw a patch of black material that shimmered like moonlight on still waters. He tugged it from beneath the weight of the dead animals and held it up.

A black Zentai suit. He examined it quickly until he found the three-inch rip in the right ankle.

The gash made by Thorn's right hand. At the time his fingers were still swollen and sore from Buddha's amazing marksmanship, yet somehow he'd managed to snag the guy's leg and slash a fist-sized hole. He lay the suit over the tailgate and shifted one of the larger cages. It was filled with straw and smelled like shrimp left in the sun. And there were the shoes, the goofy, Halloween shoes. Vibram FiveFingers. One scarlet blotch on the silver mesh.

A swell of heat rose through his chest, funneled upward, and expanded into his face. His throat constricted and he stared up at the house. An urge all too familiar to him throbbed in his gut. A blaze of rage. He raised his shirt and was starting to draw the .38 when he heard the scuff of feet behind him, and a heavy cord tightened around his throat.

He managed to swing partway around and see Jeff Matheson holding the end of the snare pole, a solid grip on the handle that tightened the loop.

Dog catchers controlled enraged pit bulls with the same simple device, and Jeff seemed to be handling his end of the pole with certainty and skill.

"You were fucking around in my house."

Thorn kicked at the black suit that lay on the ground between them, lifting it with a toe, then letting it drop. It was all the communication he could manage, other than a strangled grunt.

"That's not mine. Don't try to pin this on me, motherfucker."

With a ferocity that had been building for months as he watched Rusty lose her hold on life, and saw Buddha's lifeless body curled naked in the bathtub, Thorn took hold of the rope with both hands, wheeled and kicked, and flung himself at Matheson. He knocked Jeff backward a foot or two. Sent him to the ground.

But Matheson didn't lose his grip on the pole and wrenched Thorn down with him. The angle of the noose bit deep, and Thorn, choking, tasting blood, tore at the rope, got some slack, worked it up and over his chin.

Scrambling to his feet, Matheson wiggled the pole in a practiced way, undoing Thorn's work. He yanked Thorn to his feet, smiling as he tightened the loop around his airway, and Thorn's afternoon went black.

He was still standing, weak-kneed, when he came to seconds later, held in place by the snare pole. Wobbling, blurry-eyed.

One idea in his head. One faint notion. He drew Buddha's pistol and aimed.

"Bullshit," Jeff said. "Guys like you don't shoot guys like me."

He jerked the pull cord, and Thorn's world grayed out and the pistol sagged and loosened in his grip.

Jeff walked him backward toward the house, away from the empty street and any chance of help. He kept the pressure on the loop, Thorn wavering on the uncertain edge of consciousness.

"Guys like you, all squeaky clean and upright, you don't have the balls to mess with a mean motherfucker like me."

But Jeff was wrong. One-slug-through-the-thigh wrong. And one more through the knee.

THIRTY-TWO

"MATHESON CONFESSED. NOT DIVULGING ANY details yet, but he's come clean on the killings." Frank Sheffield held his cell phone to his ear, getting the update from Vasquez, then giving it to Thorn in short bursts. "Blood on the running shoes matches Hilton's type. They're expediting the DNA, but it'll be tonight before it comes back."

It was nearly seven in the evening; the dusky sky showed ripples of red and silver in the west. A fading light that gleamed on the river and powdered the palms with make-believe frost. Thorn and Sheffield were standing at the back of a small gathering of mourners who'd come to April's house to watch Danni Dollimore's ashes tossed into the Miami River.

Gus and Flynn and Sawyer stood up front along with April and Garvey. Behind them in the second tier were a couple of dozen others he didn't know, most of whom appeared to be either some of the homeless folks Danni had fed and bonded with or the workers at the shelters that served them. There might have been a couple of fans of her TV show in the group, but he couldn't be sure.

He assumed the young couple in the back who kept taking snapshots might be followers of the show. Both of them had slightly dumbfounded looks, as if they weren't sure whether they should pretend to be sad or just go ahead and gawk at these actual living, breathing TV stars.

"Says he drove to Atlanta to do the nurse. Took a flight to Oklahoma City under an assumed name to do Rusty's aunt."

Sheffield looked bedraggled and his breath was boozy. He'd told Thorn about holding off the bulldozers all morning until a few of his cop buddies answered his distress calls and came en masse to the Key with sirens and lights blazing to show solidarity with their old drinking buddy. The demolition guys turned tail, and the rest of the afternoon Frank kept the beer flowing, putting a little pizzazz back into the sweet old Silver Sands.

The party was still going on, so Frank was free for an hour or two.

"Matheson says he bumped into you and the sheriff at Poblanos and followed you back to your motel."

"How'd he know to do that?"

"What?" Frank was listening to more of Vasquez's report.

"How'd he know who we were or what we were doing there?"

"That'll come out. This guy's cooperating. Vasquez says he sounds cocky, all pumped up over his big day in the spotlight, spewing everything. I'm thinking when the sedation wears off, and he starts feeling those two rounds you put in him, he won't be so cocky."

While Vasquez talked some more in Frank's ear, Thorn patted him on the shoulder and nodded toward the ceremony, and Frank nodded that he understood—Thorn had obligations.

Frank drew the phone away, covered the mouthpiece, and said, "I'm supposed to keep you company until Mankowski arrives. Monitor your whereabouts."

"I already gave my statement to Miami PD."

"This is Mankowski's baby," Frank said. "She'll be here shortly and take you up to North Miami to get you on video. You okay with that? If it's a problem, I could always let you slip through my fingers."

Thorn looked off at the solemn ceremony, the shutterbugs moving in for a good profile shot of Flynn.

Frank said, "My advice, whatever it's worth, get the statement over with. It's a pain in the ass, it'll burn a couple of hours, but better now than later. More time Mankowski has to think about this, more questions she'll be throwing at you.

301

"And listen, Thorn. She's been barking about you breaking into the subject's house. So you might consider rearranging the order of events, like maybe you found the Zentai suit first, then you cracked the glass. That might go over better, sounds like you had some probable cause. Not that you need it, being a citizen, but still, breaking and entering like you did, from how Mankowski sees it, that sort of muddies the legal waters."

He left Frank getting more of the lowdown from Vasquez, and walked up to stand beside April for the last few testimonials about Danni Diamond Dollimore, the girl with the secret life.

He listened to a woman with sparse gray hair and eyes the color of weak tea recalling an afternoon not long ago when Danni was cleaning the hard-used toilets at the shelter.

"I came in because, you know, I had to take a leak, and Danni looks up with a scrub brush in her hand, and she's just beaming. I never saw anyone happier than that girl at that moment, down on her knees in front of a toilet.

"I asked her what it was that was making her smile, and she said, 'This is the first damn thing I've ever done in my life that makes any sense at all.'"

When the last speaker had their say, the benediction was given by a man in khaki slacks and a blue shirt, with the wrinkled face of a seventy-year-old and the lucid blue eyes of a child. He explained that he was a recovering alcoholic, sober since the day he was defrocked, but although he wasn't an official priest any longer, he'd been told that his religious incantations still worked pretty well.

Afterward April left Thorn to attend to the serving table where platters of food, a big glass bowl of pink punch, and an array of flickering candles were set up alongside the river.

Thorn was working his way through the crowd toward Sheffield when Flynn stepped in his path. He was wearing a tight black T-shirt that showed off his narrow waist and well-honed pecs. His jeans were faded and his loafers scuffed. There was a gold chain around his neck and two small diamond studs in each earlobe. He didn't wear a wristwatch or rings. His haircut was the kind that was always nicely styled even when the wind was tossing it around. The worldly squint and hard set of his jaw that Thorn had noticed in his publicity shot were less pronounced in person, as if perhaps for the purposes of that photograph he'd been coached by some PR guru to assume a hardass persona.

"So, Tarzan, you going to swing back up into your tree house now?"

"Is that what you want me to do?"

"Doesn't matter what I want. That's never had any effect before, why should it start now?"

"If you give me a chance, I can give you the same."

Flynn looked off at the river.

"I don't think we've got anything to say to each other."

"I don't know. We've kept each other nicely entertained so far."

"Something I learned a long time ago," Flynn said, eyes drifting around the group, "minute you lower your guard, the assholes are there waiting to stomp your face."

"Can't argue with that," said Thorn. "A lot of assholes in this world."

Flynn waved his hand in front of his face. Stop right there.

"No way, dude. No fucking way. You're not smooth-talking me into anything. Maybe there was a time I would've fallen for that let-me-be-your-daddy bullshit, but that time's long past."

"It's happened to me," Thorn said. "Somebody gave me a gift, birthday, Christmas, whatever. It's some weird gadget, I can't see the point. So I wind up tossing it. Next thing I know, a situation pops up, I realize that weird doohickey would've been very handy. And I'm standing there wondering which trash can I threw it in."

Flynn canted his head to one side, then the other, studying Thorn's face.

"You're not very bright, are you?"

"Now see, there's something we can agree on."

April was coming over, taking her time as if she didn't want to interrupt, but wanted to be nearby in case she needed to quell an argument.

"You ever play baseball, Flynn?"

Flynn squinted at him.

"You can't be serious."

"Not ever? Not even PE in high school?"

"Hey, man, it was nice talking to you. Have a good life."

"Is that a no?"

"That's a triple no, Daddy-o, with a latte on the side. No baseball.

Zero. Is that some huge disappointment to you, your son didn't play America's pastime?"

"Yeah, it's a fairly big deal," Thorn said. "I'm actually happy to hear it."

Back toward the house he saw Mankowski stalking across the yard, Rivlin at her shoulder, the two women coming straight for Thorn. April arrived beside him and asked who it was and Thorn told her it was Sheffield's replacement. April watched the heavyset woman plow through the departing mourners.

"Do you need a lawyer?"

"A lawyer, no," Thorn said. "But if I'm not back in a few hours, you might want to start working on my obituary."

THIRTY-THREE

YOU DRIVE ALONG NORTH RIVER Drive, scouting the area. Your kayak is strapped to the roof of your car. It makes you conspicuous, but this is unavoidable. No one else is on the road, no one walking on the sidewalks.

Darkness smothers the river. A faint gleam coats its surface; above is the cloudy sky, no moonlight. Ideal conditions. If you believed anything was real beyond your own imagining of it, then you would give credit for this perfect darkness to good fortune.

The darkness springs from your mind, the kayak is your invention, the river and its oily gleam is nothing but a projection of what you require right now, what you have spun out of nothing and placed before yourself.

It is only ten P.M. but on this Monday night, in this part of town, Spring Garden, people are locked away inside their houses watching TV, wasting their time in pointless sloth. This would be sad if you let yourself consider it, the shallow lives people lead, the dry tedium, the lack of purpose. But you don't.

This is one of your skills. To move ahead with single-minded focus. It is embedded in your DNA. You are able to disconnect from the things that trouble others. You can make yourself smile and laugh and construct every lie of normalcy, but you are not one of them. You never have been.

A fresh Zentai suit is on the seat beside you. Tonight you will wear it one last time. It is familiar and comfortable and you enjoy the impact it creates, the shock. The wild eyes, the shivering, the coldness in their bones.

As you drive through the neighborhood, you rewind the tape. Start with the ancient Cuban man in a bleak apartment in Hialeah, asleep in front of his loud TV, your hands at his throat, your fingers cutting his air, his pleading look, the rictus of suffocation, his bleating, his eyes drifting upward.

The Atlanta condo. A slim young man who opened his door with curiosity, a half smile as if he thought you were one of his friends playing a trick. That look vanished when you wiped the blade across his throat, once, twice, then a third time as he stumbled back into his orderly, cheaply furnished apartment.

And the teenage kid with earplugs listening to a rap beat that you could make out from ten feet away, the kid sitting at his laptop, absorbed in some game in which he was disintegrating gremlins. Believing he was in control, believing he was the master of his artificial world.

You tapped him on the shoulder because you wanted him to see you, see what was happening, have a chance—even a slender one—to defend himself, and you wanted the slugs to enter through the front, not for any particular reason, just because it seemed orderly and fair. But mostly you wanted him to know how wrong he'd been about everything.

And the woman in her bed in Oklahoma, how she'd tried to lawyer her way out of the inevitable. You can still feel the heft of the spear in your hand, the resistance of her flesh and muscle fibers. It required more exertion than you had anticipated.

And the young sheriff with the tattooed face and ragged hair, who fought you hand to hand but was unprepared and ill-equipped to fend off your onslaught. And her defender, the blond man who tried to wreck your moment. You regret not staying longer and dispatching him.

The one tonight will be your last, so you will be deliberate and observant, you will absorb every detail, no matter how chaotic the scene becomes, for you want to record this one. This is special. This is the capper. This must last for the rest of your days.

As you have done before, you follow the obituary, complying with its commands. This time you will bend the rules to fit your own needs. By doing so you will bring your journey to a satisfying conclusion, circling back in a graceful, symmetrical way to where it all began. You will restore harmony and order and equilibrium.

At a vacant lot, you park your car along the crumbling sidewalk, strip off your clothes, climb into the suit, and slip on your new footwear. You get out of the car and unstrap your black kayak from the roof rack and carry it above your head to the stone steps that lead down to the waterline. You slip your black kayak into the river. You climb into the narrow craft, organize yourself and your gear.

When you are done and ready to go, you draw the ice pick from its leather sheath and hold it up so it may shine in the darkness. Its weight is ideal. Its hardened steel point is needle sharp. Its metal spike is five inches long and its wooden handle conforms exactly to the shape of your hand.

An excellent tool. It will easily penetrate the flesh and muscle and bone, slip deep into the organs and puncture them. Vital fluids will leak, and though you are not an expert in human biology, you expect the death to be slow. You will accompany the dying through the final stages, staying until the very end when it is complete. You will watch and listen and remember.

You slide the ice pick back into its sheath, tuck it in the band of your suit, and pick up your paddle and slip it into the sleek water. You push it behind you, and your craft glides forward. You are under way. You are a black mirror held up to the black night, skimming across the dark perfect surface of the world. This world that without your efforts would not exist.

It was not quite midnight when Thorn made it back to Spring Garden and rolled through the open gates. He got out of Buddha's rental and waited, but Boxley didn't trot out of the shadows to greet him. The main house was dark, April's car parked where it usually was.

He took out Buddha's phone and tapped it until he came to April's cell number. One more tap and he could be sure that all was well. He looked up at the dark house but hesitated. Didn't want to wake her.

Didn't want to arouse alarm. He held the phone at his side and looked around at the dark drive and yard and the river behind the house.

For Mankowski the grilling had not gone well. She must have honed her interrogation approach on people who had terrible secrets to hide or something big to lose. But Thorn had neither. The woman had tried and tried to chip away at his story, chip and circle and fake and bully and backtrack, trying everything in her arsenal, but none of it had had any effect on Thorn.

He answered every question he knew the answer to, doing it succinctly and without hesitation. Anything he didn't know, he admitted and refused to speculate. He didn't give her any smart-ass answers, didn't try to sugarcoat anything. He confessed to breaking into Matheson's house because he had reason to believe the young man had been Buddha Hilton's attacker. What was that reason? The way the killer held the baseball bat. The knuckles, the loose wrists, the cock of his arms.

Knuckles?

Mankowski shook her head. It seemed to be the one bit of body language she allowed herself. She did it a lot. Thorn seemed to bring that out in certain people, that same head shake of disgust or disappointment or amazement. People were always shaking their heads at Thorn.

When she took a break to consult her notes, or sip coffee, he repeated to her the question he'd asked Frank. Why did Matheson bother to follow Thorn and Buddha to the Waterway Lodge after seeing them in Poblanos? It was a simple question, but a pivotal one. If they couldn't explain why he'd followed, then they couldn't fully believe Matheson was the Zentai Killer.

Despite the bodysuit found in his truck and the bloody shoes. Despite the altar he'd built to worship Flynn. And the latex replica of Flynn's face. Despite his presence on the high school baseball team. And the general creepiness of the guy. Despite his confession.

Thorn wanted to be sure, but he wasn't. Not yet.

He tapped April's cell number. After three rings she answered, groggy.

"I woke you."

"Are you all right?"

"I'm fine."

"Where are you?"

"In your driveway," he said. "I wanted to make sure you were okay."

She was quiet for a moment, then said, "Was it really Jeff?"

"That's how it seems."

"You're not sure."

"Let's sleep on it. Maybe it'll be more believable in the morning."

"You sound worried, Thorn."

"I'm glad you're okay."

"I'm fine."

"Is Boxley in there?"

"At the foot of my bed."

"Maybe I should sleep in the parlor tonight. Between Boxley and me, we should be able to handle whatever comes up."

"Then you don't think it was Jeff."

Thorn looked up at the window of her bedroom. Still dark.

"It probably was," Thorn said.

"I thought he confessed?"

"I'll feel better when he gives them something specific that only the killer could know."

The curtain moved aside in her bedroom. She looked out at him with the phone at her ear.

"You have your key, right?"

"Yeah, I'll let myself in. Go back to sleep. That couch in the parlor looks long enough for me."

She was silent.

"It's going to be all right," Thorn said. "I'll stay here as long as it makes sense. Nothing's going to happen tonight. Go back to bed. Get some rest."

She pressed her hand against the window glass like an inmate at the end of visiting hours saying farewell to a loved one. Thorn kept looking up at her until she lowered her hand and let the curtains fall back in place.

The darkness permeates you and you permeate it.

You are quiet, waiting. Everything is in order. Everything laid out. You have worked to put each beat in the correct position, so the music will rise and fall, will spin and leap, will shoot forward, then march in short steps, short hard claps of thunder. You have written the script, applying your intelligence and your heart, and your sense of the mythic needs of the story, and all your actors are behaving as you designed. Everything is happening as planned.

You wait in the darkness. The darkness waits in you.

THIRTY-FOUR

THORN STOOD OUT IN THE shadows listening to the distant highways hum. A screech owl trilled a block away. The clouds were dense, the air as thick and breathless as mud. A bat whisked overhead through the dark, its silent flicker invisible against the sky.

He headed up the stone stairs to the garage apartment, to wash up, put on a fresh alligator shirt for the long night ahead.

He unlocked the door and stepped into the darkness and patted the wall for the switch, flicked it, but nothing happened.

Retreating a step onto the porch, Thorn waited, worked to hear any foreign sound, catch the trace of an intruder. He held still for a full minute, waiting, listening, and hearing nothing.

Then remembered. The ceiling fan's light fixture had a two-foot pull cord. This morning he'd tugged it on his way out.

Thorn was losing it. Spooked by shadows.

He stepped back into the apartment and raised his hand high and swished it back and forth, feeling for the cord. The single streetlamp that lit the driveway and the front of the house left the garage apartment in total dark. As his eyes attuned to the gloom, his fingers ticked the cord and sent it swaying.

He waved his hand some more and brushed the cord again and

thought he had it, when across the room, on the queen-size bed, a blue screen lit up.

Cocked against a pillow, Buddha's electronic tablet was playing a video, the music set low, an eerie string quartet.

Thorn lowered his arm and took a half step forward. In the blue halo he saw the ball gloves, the two duck eggs, and a baseball spread out across the bedspread where he'd left them this morning.

On the tablet's screen was the TV scene Buddha showed him in Key Largo in their first few minutes together. A murder from *Miami Ops*. The Zentai Killer was moving up behind the black man who was working late in his office. The reflection of the killer appearing in the picture window for a split second before he slipped his wire over the businessman's head and strangled.

Thorn pivoted to his right and slung a fist into empty space.

Ducking into a crouch, he took a step backward. The video ended and a second later the light winked out and the room was black again.

In his own house, Thorn could sprint its length with eyes closed and never bump a wall or piece of furniture. He could locate any drawer and choose a spoon over a fork without fumbling. But this room, though cramped, was still foreign to him. The narrow hallway ended in a bathroom. The double closet doors where the baby raccoons had been trapped were two steps from the bed. A slim space ran between the other side of the bed and the wall. Behind him was the small dining table where he'd eaten his fish sandwiches beside a window that looked west.

To start the electronic tablet, the intruder had to be standing beside the bed. But which side? Thorn chose the right, the side nearest the bifold doors, and stepped forward into the darkness, his hands open, held chest high, ready to defend, punch, or wrestle. To his right he thought he heard the dry brush of fabric against fabric and cut in that direction.

But somehow the Zentai man slipped behind him and struck. At first it registered as no more than a hard tap on the meat of his right shoulder.

Thorn swung halfway around to face his foe. Who wasn't there.

By then the puncture wound was starting to buzz in his flesh, a hot patch of inflammation spreading across his right shoulder blade, numb and fiery at once, as if he'd been set upon by a gang of hornets.

He rotated the shoulder and felt the deadened joint, a sting flaring through his right arm, echoing in the elbow joint like a well-struck gong, vibrating in the wrist, dulling the sensation in his right hand.

To his right he saw the shape. The Zentai man, blacker than the darkness around him. A missing cutout of the night, and the quick glitter of metal in his hand. An ice pick. The weapon April had ordered up had arrived a few days early.

The Zentai man moved right, cornered by the bed on his right, the closet doors on his left, and Thorn in front of him. In Thorn's shoulder the ache was taking root, its deadening tentacles piercing the layers of flesh below.

Despite the pain, wading forward into battle was his first impulse. All the pent-up rage, the hurt, the loss had him leaning forward, ready to leap into the phantom's embrace. But for once, just this once, he caught himself.

With only the vaguest plan, he took an oblique angle, two steps to his left, hopped up on the bed, snatched one of the ball gloves, and slipped it on his left hand.

He bounced on the bed. His right arm flopping at his side as useless as a stocking filled with dust. He thought he saw the Zentai figure moving onto the open floor, and he bounced once more and launched himself at the black body.

His dead arm clipped the Zentai man, and Thorn was butted sideways into the closet doors. He twisted hard, kept his feet, and saw the glint of the ice pick coming, and tried to smother it with the glove.

It glanced off the heavy leather and nicked Thorn in the cheek. A second strike came quick, but Thorn blocked that too, then a third wild swing dug deep into the glove's webbing. His attacker breathing hard.

Thorn bulled the man backward toward the bed, got him off-balance, and kept churning his legs till he had the guy caught against his good shoulder, driving him back onto the mattress.

They landed together in a sprawl, the Zentai man pinned on his back, Thorn's chest pressed to his chest, his weight keeping the lighter man down. But with his right arm worthless he couldn't bear-hug him, couldn't pin him for long, and he felt the guy wriggling his ice pick arm, squirming it free. Felt it break loose and pull back.

Before he could jerk away, Thorn heard the crunch of the blade entering his flesh, then felt the nasty shock somewhere near the base of his spine. He grunted, slid backward, got his feet planted on the floor, and pushed himself into a forward somersault, rolling up and over the Zentai man, toward the narrow aisle on the far side of the bed.

He flattened against the wall, bobbed to his right, shed the glove, and found the bedside lamp and switched it on.

"You're doomed," the guy said.

Standing now, with the ice pick in his right hand, its prong bloody.

"Flynn?"

The Zentai man inched along the foot of the bed, trapping Thorn in the narrow aisle beside the bed.

"What I want to know," Thorn said, "is where'd you learn to hit a baseball, son?"

"Fuck you."

"Who taught you to hit like that?"

"You're crazy. A time like this, you want to talk sports."

"Is that you, Sawyer?"

"If you must know, one of my daddies taught me to hit."

He kept coming. Thorn's legs were pinned between the mattress and the wall. He tried to maneuver them in the tight space, to balance himself. Feeling the blood seeping down his legs, the throb in his shoulder, another in his lower back. More than a throb, but Thorn couldn't find the word.

"One of those men in the photographs taught you."

"Paulo," he said. "His name was Paulo. Like you, he thought every red-blooded American boy should play baseball. So each time he came to screw my mother, we boys had batting practice afterward. The smell of my mother's juices on his hands, on the balls. Wiffle balls. Softballs. Batting and batting and batting. That's where I learned my skills. Paulo Montenegro. Wrists loose, knuckles in a straight line. Paulo hung around, then lost interest. Like the other ones. My mother is impossible to love."

"So this is her fault? This person you are, the shit you've been doing, you blame April?"

"All she had to do was pick up the phone and call my father, let him know. We could have been a normal family."

He was six feet away. Thorn's only opening was back across the bed, but by the time he unpinned his legs from the cramped space and mounted the mattress, the kid would be on him.

"You're Sawyer."

"That's a name," he said. "That's just a name."

"You're my son. My flesh and blood."

He laughed at that.

"In case you haven't noticed, you're dying, old man. Your flesh and blood is leaking out inside you and it's spilling on the floor. You're seconds from passing out. And when your knees sag, that's it, handsome stranger. You're done. You've finished your last adventure."

"Why, Sawyer?"

"Always why," he said. "You're so fucking worried about why."

"To save the goddamn show? Is that all?"

"You don't get it."

"You're not Flynn," Thorn said. "You're the smart guy who puts words in everybody's mouths, moves them here and there. You sit all cozy with the script in your lap watching it unfold exactly like you made it up. God in his heaven."

"That's better," he said.

"Take the hood off, Sawyer. Show me your face."

"You're just passing through, Thorn. You don't get to call the shots."

"Just passing through."

"Like the rest of them. Here to score what you can. Then you move on to something better. Come and go. Come and go."

Thorn felt the blood filling his shoes. He saw a yellow flicker in the light as if someone was tapping into the power line upstream.

"Is that what happened to Paulo? He went away, or did you drive him away?"

"Paulo was an asshole."

"And the others, the other daddies?"

"They're in the river," he said. "Wired to concrete blocks."

Thorn couldn't tell if he was serious or not. It didn't have the weight of a confession. Just a bland statement of fact.

"You're lying."

"Every one of them."

"How many?"

"I haven't kept count."

"You got them before they could abandon you."

"Me and Flynn and Mother."

"I see."

"You don't see shit."

"They were warm-up, your own batting practice. Those men in the photos in the hallway. That's your trophy wall."

"Every kid needs a hobby, don't you think, Dad? I was never good with traditional sports."

"So you invented your own."

"Next season," he said. "That's the big reveal. Turns out the evil twin got her start whacking her mother's boyfriends. I think it'll be a hit. A few wrinkles to work out, got to get the tone right, but I have the feeling it's going to be a winner."

He tugged off his hood and Sawyer stood there smiling. A handsome boy, a young man with eyes so clear, jaw so rock solid, hair so thick and golden, he could have been a TV star himself. Though following someone else's script was probably beyond his abilities.

Thorn had been wrong about Sawyer Moss. It wasn't a tranquil smile he'd seen, it was the smug and pitiless grin of one who mastered every challenge so easily they had only disdain for the struggles of others.

"Buddha, the woman you beat to death, she had you right. A control freak."

"And that's bad, because?"

"You hid the suit in Matheson's truck. You knew he was a suspect, somebody would find it sooner or later."

"And true to form, Jeffy confessed," Sawyer said. "Thinking he was taking a bullet for Flynn. Or just trying to get Flynn's attention. Who knows about that shithead."

He came a half-step closer, shifted the ice pick to an underhand grip.

"You're sure you're not insane? A psychopath? It would be so disappointing if it turned out to be just that. Doing all this elaborate scheming and killing without any purpose. I'd like it better if it was about something shallow and silly like making the show a success."

"It will be a success. It's going to be huge."

"And then what?"

"Then I get back to work. Brass ring in hand, door wide open."

"And how long will that last before you lick your lips and start again? Once you've had a taste, it never goes away."

"Like you would know anything about it."

"I know more than I'd like to."

Sawyer's smile had turned sour.

"I don't need your psychobabble, Dad."

"What do you need, Sawyer? Anything at all? Or are you totally self-sufficient?"

"Goddamn right I am."

"Sitting alone in a room, making things up. Hour after hour, getting every word in place, the dialogue, the action, the story. Doesn't leave you much left over for the real stuff, does it? Kind of drift away into your perfect world."

"I know what's real, what's TV bullshit. If that's what you're implying."

His son stood watching him, waiting for him to die.

"What a loser you are," Sawyer said. "What a putz."

"Poor kid, your only role model was the handsome stranger. An imaginary hero. Thin air. Words around a breakfast table."

"Fuck you, Dad."

"It's not going to be so easy this time, kid. I'm not dying. You want me dead, you're going to have to come over here and stick me a few more times."

Behind Sawyer there was a light tap on the door and April leaned her head into the room. In shorty pajamas and flip-flops, her hair loose. The door shielding Sawyer from her view.

"You weren't in the parlor," she said. "I got worried."

"Leave," Thorn said. "Go now."

Sawyer stepped around the door and took her by the wrist and hauled her to the opposite side of the bed. April, staring at the ice pick, released a moan of anguish. Thorn took the moment to edge forward a step and another until Sawyer swung back his way.

"What is this?" April said. "What're you doing, Sawyer?"

"This is fucked," he said. "You shouldn't be here. You're not part of this."

"Not part of it? I'm your mother, Sawyer. Anything you've done, I'm part of it. Now put that down. Put it on the table and we can talk."

"Bullshit." Sawyer took a swipe at the air in Thorn's direction.

"We can fix this, Sawyer. Whatever you've done, we can manage it. There are ways."

Thorn's eyesight was smeared and spinning. He'd lost touch with his right arm and his legs felt unsteady; the light had begun to flutter like heat waves off a summer highway. But he was hatching something.

When he was sixteen, Thorn had broken his right arm in a fall on the dock. For weeks, burdened by a cast, he'd distracted himself by working on his left-handed delivery. By the time he shucked the cast, he could toss a baseball thirty feet and hit the trunk of a tree with some regularity. Not great, not ambidextrous by any means, but he believed those hours of practice were still lurking in the muscle tissues somewhere, down there with all the other fluid moves—the graceful, effortless jumps and dives and sprints and the lazy, innocent grapplings of naked flesh in dusky bedrooms on a hundred tropical nights, and one memorable spring morning with the woman who stood across the room just now, talking to her son, their son, trying to reason him back from the nightmare he'd dreamed up and dragged everyone into.

Thorn scooped up the baseball with his left hand and rocked back and flung it at the boy, his boy. It dinged him in the temple, a glancing blow, but enough to rattle loose the ice pick from his hand.

Coming around the foot of the bed, Thorn scooped up one of Matheson's eggs and flung that too, and flung the second. One of them hit the wall, the other struck the boy's face and smeared him with yolk. April screamed for them to stop, as Thorn kept coming, a race against his boy, a race to the ice pick that lay on the wooden floor halfway between them.

The boy going for the ice pick and Thorn going for the boy, his egg-smeared son. Thorn looped his one good arm around the young man's throat and pulled him upright. But not in time.

Sawyer had the ice pick in his hand with Thorn behind him tightening the grip on his throat. His left forearm pressed so hard against the boy's airway, he could hear the cartilage pop.

Sawyer stabbed the pick into the meat of Thorn's forearm. Someone screamed. Maybe Thorn. He used whatever leverage he had left to crank his arm tighter against his son's neck. To stop him but not kill him. Strangle him till he passed out. Just enough. Just exactly enough.

Sawyer straightened his arm and held the ice pick out, taking aim at Thorn's arm. Screaming for him to stop, April came rushing to block the blow, but arrived a half second late and her hand only bumped his, enough to alter its trajectory by a fraction, just enough to plant the ice pick up to the hilt in Sawyer's throat.

THIRTY-FIVE

ON THE FOLLOWING THURSDAY, THORN was out in his yard carrying boulders back to the seawall when he heard Paul McCartney playing the opening bars of "Hey Jude" somewhere inside the house. He'd forgotten he'd brought Buddha's phone back to Key Largo with him, and it took a few minutes to locate it under a pile of laundry.

"Can I come down?" April said.

"Of course."

"I need to ask you some questions about . . . I need to know what Sawyer said to you before I came into the room."

"I can tell you now if you want."

"No," she said. "I'm not ready yet. And I need to hear it face to face."

On the following Sunday afternoon April's Mini Cooper rolled down the crushed seashell drive and stopped at the edge of the lawn. She and Garvey got out and walked arm in arm to the seawall, where Thorn was again setting the boulders back in place against the next high tide.

"I'm sorry we're late," she said. "I got lost."

"So this is the handsome stranger's hideaway," Garvey said, gazing around the grounds, then settling on the house. "Not the manly lair I was picturing. Hell, there're Nantucket cottages that aren't this quaint."

Thorn rinsed the dirt off his hands in the cool waters of the lagoon and climbed up the bank to give them both a light hug.

April touched a finger to his bandaged arm.

"You're healing?"

"They tell me I'll live."

She stepped away and took another look at the surroundings. Facing the ocean when she said, "I invited Flynn to come, but he's not ready yet. He's still sorting things out."

"That door is always open."

She'd dressed in ankle-length khakis and a subdued tropical print shirt. Her face was thinner, not gaunt, but if she wasn't careful, it would be soon.

"What happened to your stilt house, the one on Blackwater Sound?"

"It burned down a few years ago."

"That's too bad. It was a wonderful place."

"It was," he said. "Made some good memories there."

"And you made some babies too," Garvey said.

He took Garvey's arm and guided them over to the Adirondack chairs he'd set up in the shade of a gumbo-limbo.

"I grew up here," he said. "Same as you, still living in the family homestead."

"Ocean view," April said. "Good breeze, what more could you want?"

She looked over at the remaining boulders. Thorn had whittled the pile down to a half dozen. The seawall was turning out to be a lot harder to reconstruct than it was to tear apart.

"*Miami Ops,* I suppose you didn't hear what happened?"

He shook his head.

"Even with all the publicity, it still bombed last Thursday. Got cancelled the next morning. Flynn doesn't mind. His agent found him some commercials to do until something better comes along."

"He's a talented kid. He'll make it."

He got them settled, took their orders, and brought back a tray of iced tea and some fresh shrimp with his own cocktail sauce.

"And he cooks too," Garvey said. "Be still my heart."

April gave Thorn a smile that was only halfway there.

"I got a call from Sheffield," Thorn said. "About them nailing Gus for Dee Dee's death. Says they've got him cold. That forensic magic they do."

"Killed his own child," Garvey said. "What kind of monster does that?"

April closed her eyes for a couple of seconds.

"I need to tinkle," Garvey said. "You got any clean toilets in this joint?"

"Second door on your left. It's spotless."

"Do you need help, Mother?"

"Do I need help? Hell, yes, but the help I need seems to be already taken."

She winked at Thorn and headed off.

When she'd disappeared inside the house, April said, "I came all this way, and now I don't want to hear what you have to say."

"We can do it later. Or skip it entirely and just move on."

"I killed my son, Thorn. How am I supposed to move on from that?"

She stared out at the empty blue distance, her mouth tight, cheeks ruddy with emotion. If Thorn could have spoken his mind, he'd have told her that the nudge of April's hand against Sawyer's, that slight redirection of the ice pick that cost the boy his life, was exactly the kind of ending that Sawyer would have devised. Spreading the blame around in a clever, cynical way. Giving his mother and Thorn a lasting stain of guilt.

"You were very brave," he said. "You saved my life."

"Did I? I don't think so."

"When you came in the room, I had maybe another minute left before I passed out. Then it would've been over."

She sighed, and held herself very still.

"Okay. Go on, what did he say? He blamed me, didn't he?"

"No," Thorn said. "The killings were about the show. All about publicity, about turning the show into a hit."

"You're lying, Thorn. I can tell you're lying."

He held her eyes, reached out and lay his hand on hers. It was the easiest lie he'd ever told.

"Look, April, you didn't cause it to happen, and nothing you can do will change anything about it. If there's a reason why shitty things happen, I haven't discovered it. But I do know one thing. Going over and over how something came to pass, what you might have done differently, going left instead of right, right instead of left, it's pointless. You can get lost in that maze and stay lost."

"You can do that? Just move on, let go of the past."

"I try. I work on it every day."

She looked out to sea, and after a moment she began to weep quietly and without embarrassment.

Thorn kept his hand on hers until she'd weathered the moment.

Sniffing, she gave his hand a squeeze, then bent forward and pulled a Kleenex from her purse and blew her nose.

"Some day," he said, "I'd like to get to know Flynn better."

"And Flynn would like to know you. He just hasn't realized it yet."

A snowy egret touched down on the wooden dock and bent forward to stare into the dark mirror of the lagoon.

"Listen," he said. "Before Garvey gets back . . ."

"Yes?"

"I wonder if you could do me a small favor."

She smiled. There was weariness in it and the ache of sadness, but there was courage too, and a sturdy resolve that balanced out the pain.

She kept on smiling.

"Name it," she said. "It's yours."

THE MIAMI HERALD
Monday, August 16
Buddha Hilton, in the Line of Duty
By April Moss

Buddha Hilton, elected sheriff of Starkville, Oklahoma, at the age of 19, died in the line of duty while playing a crucial role in ending the violent rampage of the man who came to be known as the Zentai Killer.

From an early age Ms. Hilton pledged herself to a life in law enforcement. Her dream was to repay in some measure the citizens of her small Oklahoma town for their generosity and love. It was those citizens who had once liberated Ms. Hilton from nightmarish captivity and it was they who helped give her a fresh start in life.

Held prisoner in a darkened room where she was tormented by her father throughout her early childhood, Buddha was rescued from her ghastly conditions by an alert social worker who spotted Buddha wandering about in distress in the front yard of her father's rented home.

"There wasn't a person in town who even knew that little girl existed till that day," said Millie Janks, the social services professional who came to Buddha's aid thirteen years ago. "People had suspicions about her daddy, but no one could have imagined the horrors that were going on inside those four walls."

The Starkville of Buddha Hilton's youth was a more robust town than it is today. Before the interstate highway was built linking Dallas with Oklahoma City, Starkville was directly on one of the main routes between those two cities, and the citizens of Starkville enjoyed all the economic benefits of the traffic flowing through their area. But the motels and restaurants and shops and service stations that flourished when Buddha Hilton was first starting school are mostly boarded up these days. Along with the dwindling population came shrinking resources, including police and fire rescue services.

"We couldn't afford to pay her nothing," said Starkville mayor, Wally Bryant. "I told her she'd be perfect on some big city police force. I encouraged her to send her resume for some jobs in the larger towns hereabouts, but she wouldn't hear of it. She was a Starkville girl through and through. She wanted to make sure nothing like what happened to her ever happened in this town again. Even if it meant living on next to nothing."

In her high school years, Buddha had been a star pitcher on the Starkville Wildcats, a girl's fast-pitch softball team. She was so talented she received scholarship offers from several colleges in the region, but turned them down because she wanted to live out her dream of keeping watch over her hometown.

One scout for the National Pro Fastpitch league was so impressed by Buddha, he offered her a contract on the spot. "She said no and no and no," recounted Jeremy Blattner. "The girl had a seventy-mile-per-hour riseball, she could toss a two-hundred-foot frozen rope and somehow, she had the soft hands and lightning reactions of an infielder. Gritty, gutsy and quick. She could've made some serious money."

But it was no and no and no to leaving Starkville. Her heart was there and her adoptive mother was there, and all her friends and neighbors were there, and even though some of the memories were bad, all her memories were there.

After graduating high school, with job opportunities scarce, Buddha spent a year in the stock room at a Wal-Mart superstore near the new interstate. "She absolutely hated that job," said Buck Todd, a friend of Buddha's from high school who worked alongside her at Wal-Mart and is now assistant manager of the store. "She wanted to be doing something meaningful with her time. She wanted to lend a hand to people."

From her one year of working retail, Buddha managed to put aside enough money to pay for the laser removal of some of the facial tattoos her father applied when she was a toddler. "Those tattoos," said Buck Todd, "they bothered her off and on, but when she tried to get some of them taken off, it bothered her even more. Not the pain, but something else."

"I would've done it for free," said Dr. Edward Molk of the Juniper Laser Clinic. "I told her that when she walked in here. 'I'm waiving my fee. No charge for anything.' As long as it took, I'd work for nothing. But no, sir, that wasn't how that gal worked. If she couldn't pay for it, she wouldn't have it."

Under her watchful eye, crime virtually disappeared in Starkville. But Buddha's positive impact on the area extended beyond her duties as sheriff. A regular at the local swimming hole where drunks and daredevils routinely climbed up the eighty-foot cliffside to plummet into the icy waters of Miller's Pond, Buddha several times saved the life of an intoxicated diver who didn't resurface after his jump.

"Johnny Joe is a big man," said Trixi Moffett, his wife of twenty-three years. "He'd make three of that girl. Plus he'd been drinking whiskey all afternoon that Saturday, and whiskey always sets him off." As often happens with drowning victims, Johnny Joe Moffett panicked when Buddha pulled him to the surface. He fought against her efforts and climbed atop her and held her under, but somehow Buddha Hilton still managed to overcome this bear of a man and haul Mr. Moffett safely to the rocky shoreline. "Johnny Joe didn't even thank that girl," said Judy Ethridge, who'd been swimming at Miller Pond that day and witnessed Buddha's bravery. "He just vomited a little and stomped off to his truck. But it didn't bother her none. Buddha was like that. I never met a single person like her who'd always go the extra mile for you, no matter what. She was just born a saint, I guess."

Like many of her fellow citizens in Starkville, Mayor Wally Bryant was shocked to learn that Sheriff Hilton had been overpowered by an assailant. "Buddha put her time in at the gym and there's not a man in this whole county who'd voluntarily step into a boxing ring with that girl."

Talk of Buddha's death in Trueblood's Café on the once-bustling main street of Starkville mostly centers on the mystery of her violent end. "The man that killed Buddha Hilton must've blindsided her," said Sally Mayfield, owner and chef at the diner. Mayor Bryant had another theory of what happened that night in a Miami motel. "If Buddha had a flaw, it was probably that she could be too trusting. She thought the best of people, despite all evidence to the contrary, some of which she'd experienced firsthand when she was just a child. But despite that awful childhood, she always saw the good in people, even when there wasn't much good to be seen."

Services were planned to honor Buddha Hilton at the Starkville Elks Club, but the turnout was so large that at the last minute the venue was changed to the Starkville High School football stadium. Hundreds attended and over sixty of her fellow citizens came up to the microphone on the makeshift stage to pay tribute to her memory.